Rave reviews for Christopher O'Brien's
The M...

W9-BSQ-543

"*The Mysterious Valley* reveals a ...orts not by the thrill of the chase or awe of the unknown, but by an uncommon and valuable thirst for understanding . . . *The Mysterious Valley* is easily one of the best original mass market paperbacks of its type available today. Don't miss it."

Dom Ciocca, Jr., Fate Magazine

"O'Brien has become what is now a familiar combination of researcher and experiencer, and he writes from both perspectives with intelligence, humor and a compassionate insight that is much needed in this often frightening territory of UFOs and their attendant phenomena."

Sean Casteel, UFO Magazine

"O'Brien has a fine mind, investigative talent, and inquisitive nature—a requirement for any serious paranormal researcher."

Bill Briggs, The Denver Post

"It's an easy read. It's exciting and it's weird. *The Mysterious Valley* offers the facts, as close as they can be established, without the clutter of the author's personal opinions. . . . The breathless reader is left to invent his or her own tangled theory, drawn from the bizarre and inexplicable facts or the wildest imagination."

Phaedra Greenwood, Taos News

"This book is a compelling read. . . . O'Brien is to be commended here . . . he is careful not to speculate too far beyond what the facts will support. When he does speculate, it is not about the incidents themselves, but about their greater meaning in the realms of everything from politics and science to sociology and metaphysics."

Anthony DellaFlora, The Albuquerque Journal

"An absolute must-read."

Spirit Magazine

St. Martin's Paperbacks Titles by Christopher O'Brien

The Mysterious Valley

Enter the Valley

ENTER THE VALLEY

CHRISTOPHER O'BRIEN

St. Martin's Paperbacks

Cover photograph of the Sangre de Cristo Mountains, taken from 39,000 feet, is available as a poster. Contact 7400 N. Overhill, Chicago, IL, 60631.

ENTER THE VALLEY
Copyright © 1999 by Christopher O'Brien.

Cover photograph by Dan Connor.
Map by Myrna Schrader.

ISBN: 0-312-96835-3

Printed in the United States of America

St. Martin's Paperbacks edition / February 1999

10 9 8 7 6 5 4 3 2

Acknowledgments

A controversial book of this type could not be written without the help and guidance of many people. I'd like to thank and acknowledge the following individuals and groups:

Isadora and Brisa Storey, for lovingly putting up with the strange hours and countless phone calls. David Perkins for crucial inspiration, editing, and literary humor. Jennifer Enderlin at St. Martin's Press for recognizing the potential. Marc Resnick at SMP for his enthusiasm and editorial expertise. Kizzen Laki and the Crestone Eagle for believing it can be done. Tom Adams and Gary Massey for their knowledge and Texas humor. Shari Adamiak, Nancy Talbott of BLT Research, Myrna Schrader, Dan Connor, Laurance, "Pat," Fritz Kleiner, Rocky, Barbara and William Howell, Bucky, Kailash, Don Richmond, Barry Monroe, "Tokio," and the members of Laffing Buddha for their infinite patience and talent. The San Luis Valley Skywatchers Network—my eyes and ears. A big thank-you to everyone who has supported my efforts and all the many witnesses who have courageously come forward, making the writing of *Enter the Valley* possible.

Many thanks also to Javier Sierra and *Año Cero* magazine for graciously granting permission to utilize Sierra's well-researched material and for use of his rare 1991 photograph of Sister Marie for this book (see photo section).

SUGGESTED RULES OF INVESTIGATION

1. Controversial subjects generate polarized responses.

2. Record or write down everything as soon as possible, no matter how inconsequential or insignificant it seems at the time.

3. Always credit your sources and respect requests for anonymity.

4. Always be ready for anything, anytime. Look for coincidences when investigating claims of the unusual. Often there may be a synchronistic element at work.

5. It is impossible to be too objective when scientifically investigating claims of the unusual.

6. Always assume a mundane explanation until proven extraordinary.

7. Appearances can be deceiving. There may be more happening than meets the eye.

8. If you publicize claims of the unusual, choose your words wisely, for your spin may have tremendous influence.

9. Media coverage of the unusual, because of its sensational nature, is often inaccurate and cannot be accepted as totally accurate by the investigator.

10. The human mind, when faced with the unknown, reverts to basic, primal symbols to rationalize its experience.

11. When investigating claims of the unusual, one cannot reach conclusions based on intuition alone.

12. There is a possibility that the (sub)culture itself may cocreate manifestations of unexplained, individually perceived phenomena.

13. We must be extremely careful not to perpetrate our own beliefs, suspicions, or actual experiences into the minds of those who want to have a "special" event happen in their lives. In other words, no leading questions.

Contents

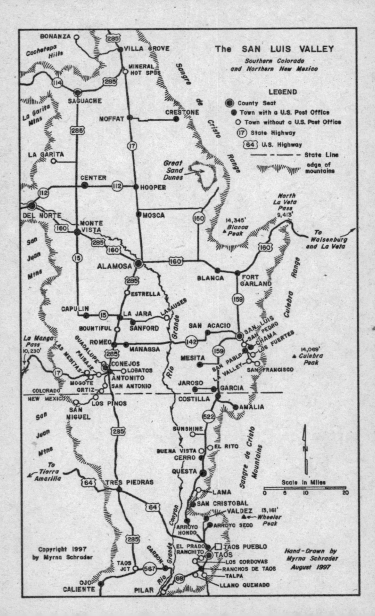

The SAN LUIS VALLEY

Southern Colorado
and Northern New Mexico

LEGEND

◉ County Seat
● Town with a U.S. Post Office
○ Town without a U.S. Post Office
⑰ State Highway
⟨64⟩ U.S. Highway
———— State Line
ⱳⱳⱳⱳ edge of mountains

Copyright 1997
by Myrna Schrader

Hand-Drawn by
Myrna Schrader
August 1997

FOREWORD

In his first book, *The Mysterious Valley*, Christopher O'Brien took us on a guided tour of "North America's virtual attic," the San Luis Valley of southern Colorado and northern New Mexico. And what an excellent adventure it was! Both spooky and exhilarating, *The Mysterious Valley* chronicled Chris's dogged efforts to document the seemingly endless varieties of weirdness in the sun-drenched and remote corner of paradise where he makes his home.

Due to its relative isolation, the San Luis Valley has offered Chris "a pristine investigative environment," a sort of "paranormal laboratory" where unexplained phenomena could be studied with a low signal-to-noise ratio.

Apparently, somebody left the barn door open. When Chris started his investigation in early 1993, he was immediately besieged by reports of virtually every modern manifestation of so-called paranormal phenomena: UFOs, alien abductions, Bigfoot, Devil encounters, strange creature sightings, phantom helicopters, Men In Black, and, of course, the ubiquitous animal mutilations. To make this strange brew even spicier, Chris was confronted with a continuing pattern of covert military activity.

It has been fascinating to watch Christopher O'Brien's journey of discovery over the last few years. In many ways, it parallels my own voyage through the murky and turbulent waters of unexplained phenomena research. Chris was drawn to Crestone in the San Luis Valley. I was drawn to the neighboring Huerfano Valley (the somewhat-Mysterious Valley, as I like to tease Chris). I arrived in 1970, fresh out of graduate school, with a desire to be a professional musician (like Chris) and an investigative journalist. It's been said that anything really worth knowing can't be taught. At any rate, nothing in my experience had prepared me for the Pandora's box of weirdness that I opened when I undertook an investigation into the wave of bizarre cattle mutilations sweeping the West in the mid-1970s.

Cattlemen were up in arms. Hundreds of animals were being found dead and strangely dissected. Chris prefers the term *unusual animal deaths*, but I'll stick with *mutilations,* the terminology of the media. The animals were not mutilated in the sense of being slashed and gashed. Cuts on the animals were frequently described as having been done with "surgical precision." In the so-called classic cases, the animals were reported to be drained of blood and missing some combination of ears, eyes, tongues, teeth, hearts, sex organs, udders, and portions of the lips or snouts. The rectums were described as "cored out." Almost invariably there were no signs of a struggle, no tracks, no clues. As Chris likes to say in his television interviews: "This may be the greatest unsolved serial crime spree of the twentieth century." Not only was the world stranger than I thought, it was stranger than I could imagine.

In *The Mysterious Valley*, we witnessed the birth and growing pains of a very fine investigator. Chris summarizes his progressive realizations in his often-quoted

Suggested Rules of Investigation. Researchers would do well to review them occasionally. Rule 5 reminds us: It is impossible to be too objective when scientifically investigating claims of the unusual. In his two books, Chris has meticulously and objectively documented his investigations and observations. The books are, among other things, classic pieces of cultural anthropology in the tradition of the field studies done by Claude Lévi-Strauss and Margaret Mead.

Referring to the beginning of his investigations, Chris says, "If I had known what I was getting into, my naive excitement would have undoubtedly been tempered with the realization that years of frustrating and unrewarding hard work lay ahead with no promise of any firm answers. I never dreamed I would solve these riddles, but I felt compelled to investigate the extent of these elusive events."

And investigate he did—with a vengeance. Taking the "microscopic approach," Chris feels that researchers must cover their geographic areas "like a soaked blanket." As physicist Peter Atkins has said, "Armchair brains can avoid unnecessary exercise by adopting easy explanations." No one can accuse Chris of being an armchair theorist or taking the easy way. Chronically underfunded, cold, tired, hungry, it doesn't matter. He manages to find time to pounce on each new report with boundless enthusiasm and tenacity. He advises investigators to work on their "bedside manner." Witnesses to bizarre events are frequently in agitated states of mind, and a great deal of compassion and patience is called for.

Chris could offer us all a lesson in effectiveness and time management. He is a family man, a craftsman, and musician. He is also a "gumshoe" detective, library researcher, and avid reader. Somehow he manages to find time to convey his findings to the public through his books, articles, newsletter, lectures, TV and radio programs, and cyberspace.

I heartily agree with Chris's hands-on approach to field investigations. It is only through direct contact with witnesses that we can begin to accumulate reliable data. Many of our colleagues (especially those in ufology) spend countless hours in paper chases. At best, they receive government documents with most of their contents blacked out "for national security reasons." At worst, they receive material of dubious authenticity (through backdoor channels) that seems designed to promote disinformation and muddy the waters. In short, we can't count on the government to provide the truth. We are lucky to find individual witnesses whose testimony is not excessively tainted by individual/cultural bias, media spin, or overactive imaginations.

In *Enter the Valley*, Chris explores the possibility that "the (sub)culture itself may cocreate manifestations of individually perceived phenomena." He surmises that individual perception of anomalous events is highly influenced by a complex equation of "bioregional" factors: racial and religious orientation, media dissemination of related events, individual expectations, and the need for some witnesses to have "special events" in their lives. With these factors in mind, Chris ponders: "I suspect that the perceptions of an experiencer of 'the unknown' are subtly shaded by his or her personal/regional mythos that ties him or her to a particular locale."

In *Enter the Valley*, Chris takes us even deeper into the "local mythos" of the seemingly serene San Luis Valley, searching for nothing less than "the origins of human perception." He pokes, probes, and prods the Valley to reveal its innermost buried secrets. Carefully combing the historical record, Chris presents us with a cast of some of the most colorful people the West has ever produced: the vision-inspired Espinozas (America's first serial killers?), the man-eating Alferd Packer, the bloody flagellating Penitente cult, Sister Marie de Jesus Agreda, the "bilocating" nun, the possessed treasure hunters, witches, ghostly apparitions, and many more. Did these characters somehow set the stage for the current outbreak of paranormal phenomena?

Early in this book, Chris states, "In my mind, UFOs and unusual animal deaths are inexorably linked to religion and belief." The UFO cult suicide (just do it!) at Rancho Sante Fe, California, reminds us all that a little belief is a dangerous thing. The other side of the coin is televangelist Pat Robertson, suggesting that UFO believers should be stoned to death. Consult Chris's first rule of investigation: Controversial subjects generate polarized responses.

Chris learns a valuable if unexpected lesson about the nature of belief with the "crystal skull" episode. In his first book, he described a mysterious glass skull that seemed to generate a rash of unexplained phenomena around it. The artifact was later found to have a prosaic explanation. Chris's conclusion: "Perhaps if enough people think something is magical, and focus their intent on it, then maybe a mundane object can actually become magical." Who knows what a large-scale focus of intent or "need to believe" is capable of?

Clearly, we are no longer dealing with fringe phenomena. Recent polls reveal that about half of all Americans believe "UFOs are real." Roughly one in three think "we've made contact with aliens." As any politician will tell you, these are not insignificant numbers. Through a barrage of movies, paranormal television shows, books, and commercials, the public has been inundated with images of space aliens. Extraterrestrials are used to sell cars, washers and dryers, film, beer, pizza, insurance, telephones, soft drinks, and cereal. Why? Where is this all coming from?

Techno-shaman Terence McKenna, incorporating the ideas of Jacques Vallee and Colin Wilson, has an interesting perspective: "The flying saucer is an object from the collective unconscious of the human race that appears in order to break the control of any set of ideas that are gaining dominance in their explanatory power at the expense of ethics." According to McKenna, UFOs (and presumably other related paranormal phenomena) are intended to "confound science, because science has begun to threaten the existence of the human species as well as the ecosystem of the planet." McKenna compares this "confounding" to the career of Christ, "in which Roman science and Roman militarism were unseated by a peculiar religion that no educated Roman could take seriously." The evidence presented in Christopher O'Brien's Mysterious Valley books may, at first glance, seem absurd and insignificant, but it is exactly the kind of confounding that brings down mighty empires.

In my research, I came to question whether we are dealing with something truly "other." I've had long-running debates with my colleagues about whether we are dealing with an "off-planet" intelligence or a "non-human" intelligence. Psychedelic argonaut Terence McKenna has tried to convince me that the "machine elves" he encountered under the influence of DMT were "truly other." I hold a minority viewpoint, but the jury is still out on this crucial question. From my own experience, I am inclined to think that these phenomena emanate in some fashion from our individual and/or collective psyches. If one accepts James Lovelock's scientific premise that the entire earth is a superorganism (The Gaia Hypothesis), is it not possible that Gaia itself plays some role in manufacturing these "emanations" for reasons not yet evident?

Early in his investigations, Chris noted, "The phenomenon seems to counter all attempts to analyze it, supplying data to both affirm and negate all possible explanations." It's almost as if the phenomenon has a built-in "ridicule, or giggle factor," which allows skeptics and the scientific community to dismiss it out of hand as pure nonsense. In the San Luis Valley, Bigfoot shows up in the midst of a UFO/mutilation flap, abductees describe their alien abductors as "dressed in gold lamé like Elvis," giant thunderbirds and prairie dragons appear, and, of course, there's that strange yellow antique helicopter that bedevils Chris.

Rereading Chris's books, I'm struck by the sheer *theatricality* of the reports. Chris and I frequently laugh ourselves to tears over the levels of absurdity that are sometimes reached. Humor is quite helpful in dealing with these matters, as Chris will tell you. We are both reminded of the Trickster. Both destroyer and creator, subhuman and superhuman, the Trickster is, as anthropologist Paul Radin says, "an outlet for the most unashamed and liberating satire of the onerous obligations of social order, religion and ritual." In the Philippines, the Trickster takes the form of a creature that flies around at night extracting the organs of its victims with its razor-sharp tongue. In several Native American versions, the Trickster eviscerates its human and animal victims. It is especially fond of coring out the rectum of animals.

In this book, Chris chronicles an encounter between a Hispanic hunter and a "leprechaun" in the woods. Although technically not Trickster figures, wee-people, elves, and fairies are notorious for their hijinks. A common story in the folklore of the British Isles describes being "elf-shot." The little people were said to discharge some sort of blast, or "green rush," which inflicted inward, invisible wounds on their human or animal victims. Humans thus afflicted became disoriented and exhibited strange behavior. Cattle, if they were "elf-shot" and died, had their "aerial and aethereal parts" removed for nourishment by the wee ones.

In *The Mysterious Valley,* Chris wonders aloud if we are possibly dealing with "something ancient and extremely illusive." In this book, he ponders whether an "outside influence" diabolically tricked the murderous Espinozas with a vision of the Virgin Mary that commanded them to rip out the hearts of six hundred gringos. "Is it the water or something?" Chris asks, "Or do residents of this region have a predisposition to unwittingly interact with some kind of demonic force, or presence?"

Chris pays homage to writer-researcher John Keel, who first proposed the concept of "ultraterrestrials." According to Keel, UFOs are not extraterrestrial but ultraterrestrial, a shape-shifting phenomenon from another order of existence. The ultraterrestrials are generally manipulative and hostile to humans and can manifest as aliens or any number of other paranormal entities. Keel concludes that "we are biochemical robots helplessly controlled by forces that can scramble our brains, destroy our memories and use us in any way they see fit. They have been doing it to us forever."

Chris sees other evidence that humans are being cynically manipulated by so-called paranormal phenomena. In this instance, it may be our government engaged in "mind conditioning" or "mythological engineering." It is a fact that the military has a strong presence in southern Colorado. What it is doing during its many covert maneuvers is difficult to determine. Chris asks if "some witnesses may be actually observing secret military craft that effectively *give the impression* of something otherwordly . . . maybe our government is trying to fool or condition us all."

Some researchers have speculated that, with the end of the Cold War, the military is subtly attempting to generate a new external threat (space alien invasion) to assure continued high-level funding. As researcher Jacques Vallee has stated: "The belief in extraterrestrials, like any other strong belief, is an attractive vehicle for some sort of mind-control and psychological warfare activities." Chris takes this a step beyond: "Is it too fantastic to suggest the possibility of the government's role going even further into the realm of societal or military control mechanisms to be engineered and administered through beef, a primary food source?" And to make things even gamier, a variation of mad cow disease has now mysteriously turned up in Colorado's mule-deer population. Hmmm.

Christopher O'Brien has admirably managed to avoid being swept away by the bewildering material he is uncovering. "Always assume a mundane explanation until proven extraordinary," he tells us. He loves to taunt his lecture audiences by telling them, "I'll win every debate on the paranormal, as long as I'm allowed to take the skeptical side." As one might imagine, the skeptics have a field day with the material in Chris's books. The most common criticism is that UFOs are misidentifications of natural phenomena or spring from the imaginations of the witnesses. In the same vein, animal mutilations are seen as misidentifications of routine predator damage to dead animals. The skeptics frequently refer to a paper published by sociologist

James Stewart, "Cattle Mutilations—An Episode of Collective Delusion." Stewart concludes that a wave of mutilations in South Dakota and Nebraska during the 1970s was "a classic case of mild mass-hysteria." Supposedly, ranchers had become stressed by economic pressures and were caught up in a "delusionary spiral." This caused the ranchers to interpret everyday occurrences "in a new and bizarre manner."

Other skeptics are more vociferous, thundering forth that the current widespread "irrational" belief in the paranormal is leading mankind into "the New Dark Ages." Paranormal researchers are condemned as quasi-fanatics using mutilations to bolster their UFO religious beliefs. Ironically, the mainstream UFO research community has largely shunned the mute phenomenon as being just "too weird." One national magazine called mutilation researchers "the bottom feeders of the paranormal." I might point out that the bottom is where the rich nutrients lie. Longtime mutilation researcher Tom Adams has compared the "purist" UFO community's attitude to "whistling past the graveyard." Meanwhile, the poor Western ranchers have been in a "delusionary spiral" for more than thirty years now.

Thanks to the evidence-gathering efforts of Chris and other field investigators, a substantial and growing body of evidence has now been accumulated. The position of the skeptics (most of whom have never bothered to examine the physical evidence) is becoming increasingly untenable. In a recently published report by biophysicist W. C. Levengood, "A Study of Bovine Excision Sites from 1993 to 1997," a curious pattern has begun to emerge. Levengood's studies note that "the vegetation in the immediate vicinity of an excised [mutilated] animal was significantly altered physiologically." Among other anomalies, Levengood found evidence of "energy with cell damaging, microwave characteristics." The apparent microwave energy, in some cases, damaged the plant mitochondria (altering plant respiration) and eventually killed the grass. Levengood is also puzzled by the unusually high concentrations of "microscopic beads of magnetite found at excision sites."

In a California mutilation case that he worked on with a professional animal pathologist, Levengood concluded that "very unusual energies were involved in the heating, compacting and dehydration of blood."

Levengood's findings seem to corroborate the work of Dr. John Altshuler, who has examined the blood, tissues, and organs of numerous "excised" animals. A doctor of pathology and hematology in Denver, Altshuler has confirmed, in more than thirty cases since 1989, that the animal tissue had been cut with high heat. "Cooked hemoglobin" was noted, indicating "high heat as in laser surgery . . . probably above three hundred degrees F." As Chris O'Brien likes to tell the skeptics, "If it's coyotes doing these things . . . , then it's coyotes with three-hundred-degree breath."

So where do we go from here in trying to solve the mysteries of the paranormal playground known as the San Luis Valley? Early in his investigations, Chris becomes keenly aware of the basic rule of anthropology: The mere presence of an observer alters the situation he or she is studying. He later comes to suspect that "it is conceivable that the expectations of the observer may actually be a causative factor in the way the event occurs." He refers to one of the basic tenets of quantum physics that "an observer may influence the outcome of an experiment or even create a particle."

The basic theory of quantum physics, the ultimate

weirdness, was worked out in the early 1900s. What the quantum physicists discovered is that there is no clear line between the observer and what is being observed. All matter is said to have no definite reality and to exist in an "indeterminate" state until it is observed or measured. Science is still trying to come to grips with the staggering implications of these findings. Physicists are understandably perturbed by the notion that consciousness literally creates "reality," making anything possible.

Physicist John Archibald Wheeler, one of the leading proponents of the quantum view, coined the term *participatory Universe* to describe the role of the observer in bringing the world into being. According to Wheeler, the mind's reality-making abilities can even transcend time and alter events that occurred in the past. Wheeler and most of his scientific colleagues, however, adamantly deny that the mind could play a role in the creation of paranormal or psychic phenomena.

The late theorist Michael Talbot, in his book *The Holographic Universe* and other works, is one of the few modern thinkers to explore the implications of quantum physics for understanding paranormal phenomena. He calls physicists "idiot savants" and "oddly schizoid when it comes to extrapolating or expanding beyond their immediate findings." In Talbot's "holographic Universe," separateness ceases to exist and the innermost processes of the psyche can spill over and become as much a part of the landscape as the flowers and the trees. Reality itself becomes little more than a mass shared dream."

Whitley Strieber, in his best-selling book *Communion*, states that encounters with UFOs and alien beings "may be our first true quantum discovery in the large-scale world: the very act of observing it may be creating it as a concrete actuality, with sense, definition and a consciousness of its own." Talbot gives a quantum twist to this idea: "UFO entities may very well be archetypes from the collective unconscious of the human race, but we may also be archetypes in their collective unconscious." Strieber refers to this process as "spinning each other together" in an act of cosmic communion.

World-class physicist David Bohm has said, "The inseparable interconnectedness of the whole Universe is the fundamental reality." In his book *Quantum Reality*, Nick Herbert calls quantum wholeness "a fundamentally new kind of togetherness . . . a true mingling of distant beings that reaches across the galaxy as forcefully as it reaches across the garden."

Just as ambiguity and uncertainty have now become essential ingredients of science, perhaps the wild improbabilities described in Chris's books will eventually become the elementary truths of the future. The paranormal will gradually become "normal." We of course prefer to think of our work on the fringe as protoscientific rather than pseudoscientific. Truthseekers are encouraged to withhold judgment long enough to see the real value of what Chris has accomplished. Great breakthroughs in understanding always involve giving up some great prejudice.

Niels Bohr, one of quantum theory's founding fathers, has said: "A great truth is one whose opposite is also true." Chris often reminds me that good science requires being suspicious of our own hypotheses. I build them up, and Chris gleefully helps me tear them down. Without the tremendous amount of raw data generated by Chris's fieldwork, we would all be diminished. For this, the research community and the public owe him a tremendous debt of gratitude.

Quantum physics has been described by its founders

as "nonrational" and "counterintuitive" (much like paranormal research). Without reason and intuition we are working with a strange toolbox indeed. As psychologist Abraham Maslow said, "If the only tool you have is a hammer, then you start treating everything as if it were a nail." If we are to resist this urge, we must kick this thing up a notch. "Paradox is not resolved by the same level of thinking that created it," says *Apollo* astronaut Edgar Mitchell in *The Way of the Explorer*.

Reading this book, I'm sure you will be inspired by Chris's courage and relentless "need to know" attitude. We don't really know *what* we are dealing with out in those forsaken cow pastures in the middle of the night. As we follow the course of his investigations, we see how his innate curiosity gradually overcomes his fears. As he will tell you, "I'm no hero, I'm just a naturally curious guy."

Perhaps that's the point of all this. Recent studies have shown that even an act as mildly challenging as doing a crossword puzzle daily causes the brain physically to grow. Capillaries in the brain extend their networks, and the density of connections between neurons increases. Maybe paranormal phenomena are a type of evolutionary imperative, or mechanism, that increases our survival odds by challenging and thus strengthening our brains. I dunno. It's just a thought. It has been shown that it's a use-it-or-lose-it situation. Brain cells that receive no stimulation and chemical messages to stay alive will eventually "commit suicide." Well-used synaptic connections generate electrical currents and encourage further development and sophistication in that part of the brain. So read this book and grow your mind.

Some reviewers have compared *The Mysterious Valley* to a "real-life *X-Files*." Chris Carter, the creator of the wildly popular television show, has said: "Science and technology have accelerated to a point where they may be beyond our ability to comprehend. We need mysteries, we need stories, we need something beyond the temporal." Well, Christopher O'Brien has some stories for you. Some of them are so riveting that they've been told and retold in these parts for more than one hundred years. Settle back for some masterful old-time Western storytelling and a breathtaking ride through the fun house. Let the confounding begin.

David Perkins
Gardner, Colorado

CHAPTER ONE
A VALLEY FULL OF SECRETS

Whether you're a hardened skeptic or a true believer, you have to admit that we live in a strange and mysterious world. There's little doubt that our reality inspires, awes, and even frightens the human species into addressing energies and events that we have not yet begun to define or explain. I personally *believe*, unquestionably, that something strange and wonderful is going on around us, and it probably always has been. "It" doesn't happen often, but invariably our mundane lives provide us with direct contact with these mysteries, sometimes so irrefutably that we're compelled, almost forced, to seek answers. Or hide our heads in the sand. Some of these events are as simple as thinking about a friend, and *ring*, he calls you on the phone, or as complex as the "alien abduction" scenario.

Human history is rife with examples of philosophical and scientific jump starts: Plato's *Republic*, Galileo's and Hubble's telescopes, Einstein's General Theory of Relativity, Bell's Theorem, etc. We may even have a genetic compulsion or predisposition to explore the farthest boundaries of our reality in an attempt to explain the last dwindling secrets hidden from the light of truth. This has always been so, and this propensity doesn't appear to be ending soon. The very fact that you are reading this book is an indication that you are intrigued by these subtle aspects of our so-called consensus reality. This book attempts to provide a different context for examining these last remaining scientific and sociological mysteries.

UFOs, abductions, unusual animal deaths, religious miracles, the motivations of serial killers, psychic powers, strange fantastical creatures, ghosts, undefined natural phenomena, treasure legends, folklore, secret government activity, indigenous people's myths, to name a few, are but a modest sampling of these sensational riddles puzzling the curious people worldwide. On the surface, these phenomena seem unique unto themselves, separated by time, circumstance, and distance.

Unbelievable as it may sound, the above sampling of phenomena are found in a single, well-defined geographic location. Welcome to the San Luis Valley in south-central Colorado/north-central New Mexico. There may be no other place with the variety and intensity of examples of "the unexplained" in all of North America. And it is all occurring above seven thousand feet at America's rooftop. One could literally call this wondrous place "the high ground."

Sacred sites exist, in one form or another, worldwide. The pyramids of Egypt, Central America, and China; the megalithic structures in the Peruvian Andes; Stonehenge; the sites of Fatima and Lourdes; the great temples, shrines, and monasteries of the East . . . The list is impressive and so are these sites, which have always been considered special and important locales. The perception of these specific locations as holy places often survives the downfall of one civilization and the rise of another. Most, if not all, of the great European cathedrals, for instance, were built on important pagan holy sites. Many are located where Druidic rituals and observances were conducted, in particular, sacred oak groves.

There is quite an impressive body of data that supports the idea that the ancients had special knowledge relating to earth energies and connecting "ley lines." Countless books have been written about the standing stones and megalithic sites in the British Isles—immense stones carefully placed at key locations by ancient and mysterious builders. But as these sites are scientifically investigated, an important point should be made. We must remember that these sites occur in areas that also feature specific local phenomena and a resulting cultural mythology. These phenomena may have a unique character that directly relates to the beliefs of the current and past inhabitants.

Parts of the world have their own peculiar myths and legends. The San Luis Valley in south-central Colorado and north-central New Mexico is considered a sacred site by many of its original residents. As you will see, along with the designation comes a bewildering kaleidoscope of paranormal phenomena.

Enter the Valley is a follow-up to my first book, *The Mysterious Valley (TMV)*. In *TMV,* I attempted objectively to scrutinize the amazing so-called UFO and cattle mutilation reports that I investigated from 1992 to the spring of 1995, along with presenting a detailed examination of the historical record of these occurrences. I attempted to give the reader as complete a feel for the region's activity as possible. I quickly realized that I could not possibly cover all of these events in one book.

Since the July 1995 completion of *TMV*, a fantastic array of high-strange, real-time events have occurred, some of historic significance. I cover and analyze these current cases fully.

Along with the periods of intense activity, I was rewarded with months of quiet time, when I received no reports for weeks on end. During these downtimes, I researched far back into this wondrous locale's history, myths, and legends. I am convinced that there are clues to be found and pondered in the dim past.

Needless to say, *TMV*'s documented history of unusual events in the world's largest alpine valley only hinted at the dazzling variety of anomalous phenomena reported here. As you will discover, there is even more mystery to wonder at. Up here at the high ground, we'll peer into the dark corners nestled inside North America's virtual attic. Along with the dozens of reports of current unexplained activity, *Enter the Valley* addresses many, but not all, of the additional mysteries I've found here.

Throughout the beginning sections of *The Mysterious Valley,* I listed a series of axioms or Suggested Rules of Investigation in the order in which I realized them. This list is important and is included in this book. I cannot overemphasize the importance of these rules. These axioms govern all aspects of my investigative efforts. *TMV* gave the reader a complete history of cattle mutilations and UFO sightings that have been reported here in the San Luis Valley and stretch back over thirty years. The amount of data I've managed to compile since 1992 is a testament to all the investigators and researchers who have forwarded me data.

Because I cover so much new territory in this book, I have been forced to concentrate on the more compelling UFO and unusual animal death (UAD) events that have occurred since the writing of *TMV*. I have included a complete Report Log to give a sense of the intensity and the variety of phenomena reported here in the San Luis Valley.

As in *The Mysterious Valley*, I've attempted to convey the process of discovery concerning the events and information in this book. In the majestic San Luis Valley, we are all on a journey of discovery and wonder. I can only hope my efforts inspire you to do the work where you live, for we *all* live in a strange and awe-inspiring world, and we need as many aware people as possible, documenting the weird and wonderful.

The fact that we all discover, or are exposed to, data in a sequential manner is important. Our brain is set up to accumulate linear data in a nonlinear fashion. A subtle, fluid dance of synchronicity weaves through our lives, interlocking the possibilities of choreographed awareness. Coincidences challenge us toward expansion. The perceived meaning *has* meaning, if we are sensitive enough to detect its flow.

CAN I GET A WITNESS?
JUNE 24, 1995

The beautiful high-mountain summer was in full swing. Outside the window, broadtail and rufus hummingbirds angrily buzzed each other, like little rocket-powered dive-bombers in the brilliant sunshine. Underneath their feeder, several of our little town's resident deer browsed quietly, always alert to any danger. And where was I, the amateur gumshoe? Stuck behind my computer with the overwhelming task of writing *The Mysterious Valley* looming over me. I'd never written a book before, and I was insecure concerning the monumental task I had agreed to complete. If you had asked me five years ago what I'd be doing in five years, "investigating enough weirdness to write a book" would not have been my answer.

With the help of Colorado–New Mexico journalist/theorist David Perkins, Paris, Texas, investigator Tom Adams, Linda Moulton Howe, Kalani and Katuiska Hanohano, Dr. Lynn Weldon at Adams State College, law enforcement officials, courageous experiencers, dogged researchers, and countless others, I had diligently accumulated several large boxes of research materials over the course of my then three-year investigation. I had completed the arduous task of organizing it, but the very act of writing it all down in a coherent fashion was daunting. However, I'm persistent. I'd been banging away, writing five to six pages per day.

That fresh, lovely morning, I had finished my coffee and decided to go to the post office to pick up the mail. I had only two months left to complete my manuscript, and to be honest, my self-confidence that morning wasn't very high.

After many months of investigating flap levels of unusual activity, the countless reports I had been fielding, sometimes several per day, had inexplicably ceased. The San Luis Valley had been "officially," and I might add blissfully, quiet for two whole months without a single report. Perfect timing. I was writing up a storm with no distractions.

I've always wondered about the downtimes with no reports. To me this is an indication of the absolute reality of perceptions of unexplained events. If folks here were reporting only misidentified, mundane occurrences, then why no reports? If this were truly the case, you would think that there would always be at least a trickle of reports, not a complete cessation of activity.

This fact alone has convinced me these waves of "unexplained" reports are real cause-and-effect events.

I darted into Crestone in my little Toyota truck. "Town" was in full swing, and I noticed cars from several different states parked in front of The Road Kill Café (now called The Kitchen Table) as I made the turn to head up the small hill to the post office. The following letter, one of hundreds I've received, awaited me in my mailbox:

Dear Christopher:

I have been interested in the phenomenon [sic] since I had read the newspaper reports about NORAD picking up an object on radar which reportedly crashed near Greenie Mountain.[1]

In April I attended your lecture on the Mysterious Valley during the convention in Colorado Springs. I subscribed to your newsletter as a result.

This past weekend (June 15–18), six of my friends and I camped out in the North Crestone Creek campground. All of us were anxious to view the night sky in hopes of seeing something out of the ordinary. Over the course of three evenings, we all saw a host of satellites, airplanes, and shooting stars.

On the evening of June 17, we all were watching the sky from the area just west of the bridge at the entrance of the North Crestone Creek campground. As you no doubt know, this area provides an excellent view of the Valley. At exactly 10:58 PM, just as we were ready to head back, all seven of us saw an aerial phenomenon, the like of which none of us had ever seen before in our lives. We were looking north, when a sizable, bright, yellowish-orange oval-shaped light appeared out of nowhere and blazed across the sky from west to east. It was traveling parallel with, but 35 to 40 degrees above the northern horizon. It was hurtling through the sky at a high rate of speed (faster than any commercial aircraft, but slower than a shooting star). It was silent, and had no "tail." We watched it for approximately 7–10 seconds (enough time for all of us to see it and make comments about it). It disappeared behind some cloud cover over the mountains.

Those present during the sighting were two criminal prosecuting attorneys, a computer programmer, two employees of the rape assistance and awareness organization, a realtor and a crime-victim advocate. All are from Denver, except the computer programmer, who is from San Francisco.

We were all fascinated and knew that we had seen something "mysterious." Our question is did anyone else report this same phenomenon to you? Can you rule out that it was a simple meteor? I am looking forward to the next issue of the Mysterious Valley [Report].

Sincerely,

Chris Ramsay

One of the seven witnesses, Dave Brase, is now working as a law enforcement officer. He confirmed details of the group's sighting by phone and remarked, "I've worked outdoors all my life, and I have never, ever seen anything remotely like it."

*   *   *

Before Chris Ramsay's letter, I had not received a report of an unusual aerial object in two months, and two more months went by without receiving another—not even a report of our "cheap fireworks." I always get reports of these perplexing objects during our many active UFO sighting periods. These dazzling orbs of bluish-white light that I've dubbed "cheap fireworks" are not mundane celestial objects. I have seen them below me in altitude with a completely uniform overcast sky. In 1993, one man called to report a very small one that he had just seen. He described the experience of seeing one of these enigmatic forms flash within ten feet of his location, like "watching Tinker Bell crashing." There had been no reports of cattle mutilations (or "mutes," as longtime cattle death researchers refer to them) during this four-month period, and I'm sure that here in the San Luis Valley, cows had died naturally and were scavenged, and meteors had flashed majestically through the thin mountain sky. But come on, folks, why wasn't at least one of these mundane events misidentified and reported as high-strange?

Where do the ships and meteors go when they're not flying around here? Or are they flying around but no one is reporting them? This very question has dogged ufologists for decades. It reminds me of the old question, "If a tree falls in the forest, and no one is there to hear it, does it make any noise?" If the group of seven skywatchers had left just a minute or two earlier, would that same object have soared across the sky? The object could have been a meteor, but then again it may have indeed been something unusual, something out of the ordinary. I received no other reports of this event.

*   *   *

I'm not complaining about those downtimes when no reports occur. It allows me the time to dig even deeper into the history of the wondrous Southwest. I have a curious, inquiring mind. What some find tedious, I find compelling—like rooting around in old newspaper archives or dusty library shelves. The research aspect of my investigative endeavors is a constant source of enjoyment, for you never know what you'll find with the simple turn of a page. My "microcosmic approach" dictates that the interested investigator-researcher must cover his defined geographic area like a soaked blanket. I am convinced that any particular location has unique indicators, in the form of unexplained phenomena, that may contribute to our further understanding of all paranormal phenomena. In my mind, UFOs and unusual animal deaths are inexorably linked to religion and belief; haunted houses and spook lights are related to subcultural interpretations found in local legends and myths; and secret military activity and underground bases are entwined in perception of identified flying objects as UFOs. This idea of linkage is ignored by mainstream ufology.

One area I concentrated on was researching some of the San Luis Valley's notable characters from the past. I was convinced, early on in my investigation, that this region had some fascinating historical characters, especially because they lived here. I wasn't wrong.

THE COLORADO CANNIBAL

In 1990, one of the first musical gigs I played out of Crestone was at Packer's, a tiny saloon in an old nineteenth-century building in "downtown" Saguache, population 584. The colorful collection of tipsy cowboys, farmers and exuberant locals enjoyed the energetic mix of country and rock. I wondered why Packer, whoever he was, had such a small venue. I was told by the owner that the bar was named after Alferd Packer, the nineteenth-century cannibal. I hadn't known that the county seat had a famous cannibal in its past. Then I remembered an article I'd read just after moving to Colorado that talked about Alferd Packer.

In 1874, a series of events occurred that became the stuff of Colorado legend. Few sagas have gripped the imaginations of Coloradans like that of Alferd Packer. To this day, more than a hundred years later, archaeologists, scholars, and the curious are unraveling more facts about this classic story.

Cannibalism is a taboo subject in Western culture. Few subjects elicit the response one has to the very thought of consuming human flesh. The enigmatic Packer story had other possible contemporary accounts. Rumors of cannibalism on Gunnison's ill-fated expedition in 1853 were never verified, but the lifesaving cannibalism by members of the tragic Donner-Reed wagon train in the Sierra Nevadas became headline news across America in 1847. These stirring accounts of human hardship and sacrifice differed from the circumstances of Mr. Packer's case. His particular nightmare has few parallels in American history.

November 17, 1873, was a blustery day in Salt Lake City, Utah, when a twenty-three-member group, hastily assembled by Robert McGrew and George Tracy, set out from Utah and headed southeast for the newly discovered Colorado gold fields. After arriving on the Western Slope of Colorado, the group was warned by knowledgeable miners and Ute Indians not to attempt the journey, and five members of the McGrew-Tracy party chose discretion as the better part of valor and decided to wait for early spring before tackling the unforgiving San Juans. McGrew, Taylor, and five members set out from Ute Chief Ouray's camp at the mouth of Dry Creek, two miles south of present-day Delta, Colorado, into the forbidding winter. It was unusually cold and snowy that year, and the Utes again warned the eager group not to attempt the journey to the gold fields. Nevertheless, the expedition set out and headed east toward the little settlement of Saguache, at the extreme northwest corner of our mysterious San Luis Valley. The remaining sixteen members stayed to wait out the unusually bitter winter season. The greenhorns should have known that the dead of winter was no time to start out on a gold-hunting expedition into the rugged San Juan Mountains of south-central Colorado.

Gold fever can motivate men to do foolhardy things. Having second thoughts about staying behind, four days later, Alferd Packer, one of the remaining prospectors, convinced five other miners that they should try to catch up with McGrew's party. They had been told they weren't getting paid until they arrived in Saguache, and with so many other prospectors due to arrive that spring, the two-month head start would be ideal. Packer was right; the lucrative, mineral-rich swath of strata that extends from the central New Mexico border north to Interstate 70, in the heart of one of America's most punishing high-mountain environments, would be inundated with eager prospectors that following spring. A miner's claim, his fortune or ruin, could be determined by just a few important feet.

Chief Ouray, who realized that his warning to the remaining miners had no effect, urged them to travel the long way to Saguache and follow the Gunnison

River instead of attempting the shorter, more dangerous route through the San Juans. Heeding the chief's advice, the men set out. Within a few days, the small six-man party, with enough provisions to last only a week, realized they did not have enough supplies to last during the longer but easier route. They made the fateful decision to try the shorter, mountainous route. They managed to become hopelessly lost.

I have lived up here at eight thousand feet for almost eight years now, and I can tell you, you ain't been in nasty, cold, high-mountain weather until you've seen one of Colorado's occasionally brutal winters. The winter of 1873–1874 was one of those years, and Packer's party floundered through impossibly deep snow drifts that left the men exhausted and barely able to move. On the eighth day, the six men shared their final meal, a handful of flour they mixed with snow. The desperate men used their last remaining matches to start a small, smoky fire. To say that the outlook was grim is an understatement.

The rest of the two-month saga is still shrouded in controversy. Packer, with a coffeepot of glowing coals and strips of blanket wrapped around his frozen feet, stumbled into the Los Pinos Indian Agency on April 15, 1874, and told agent Charles Adams a rather harrowing story, claiming he didn't remember how he had survived his ordeal and made it to the agency. After the food ran out, Packer, who was an epileptic, claimed that the others left him behind because he was slowing them down. That was the last time he saw them, he swore. The following day, Preston Nutter, one of the men who had stayed behind at Ouray's camp, rode up. He was surprised to see Packer all by himself. He also noticed that Packer had Reddy Miller's knife hanging from his belt. Miller had been one of the five who left with Packer. Packer claimed that Miller had left the knife sticking in a tree when he and the others had left him. If that was the case, Nutter asked Adams later, "Why did Packer have the knife in Miller's sheath?"

Packer hung around the agency until spring made its customary appearance. Packer bid Adams good-bye and resumed his journey toward Saguache. When none of his companions made it out of the mountains, a suspicious Saguache constable named Lauder organized a search party to go into the mountains and find out what happened to them. He conscripted a reluctant Packer to guide the search team. They headed toward the Los Pinos Agency where, accompanied by Indian Agent Adams, the group followed Packer as he unsuccessfully tried to retrace their ill-fated route. Lauder was convinced that Packer was lying and that he had murdered and robbed his companions. After finding nothing, the search party returned to Saguache. Lauder arrested Packer on suspicion of foul play and, pending further investigation, incarcerated him in a small cabin that served as Saguache's jail. He then set off with a larger search posse to locate the bodies. They didn't turn up a trace of the missing members.

Early the following June, a group of journalists from *Harper's Weekly* arrived to research, write, and paint pictures of the Colorado mountains for a series of articles. Renting a buggy, they departed Gunnison and headed along the South Fork into the mountains. Stopping for a picnic that fresh spring day, they began exploring a nearby grove of trees. What they discovered sparked a controversy that continues to this day.

One of the illustrators, John Randolph, sketched the grisly scene that showed corpses strewn about, missing substantial portions of flesh from their arms and legs. Two bodies were missing all the flesh from their rib cages. The aghast reporters related the discovery to a nearby farmer, who immediately contacted Lauder, who led a posse to the remote mountain scene. After a careful examination of the "crime scene" on what became known as "Cannibal Plateau," the sickened men buried the bodies, and Lauder and Adams angrily headed back to confront a wretched Packer.

Upon the posse's return, news of the grisly find swept through Saguache like prairie fire. An ugly mob was beginning to form when Lauder went to the makeshift jail to attempt to get Packer's confession. Both he and Packer knew frontier justice could be swift and final. Lauder was able to convince Packer to tell the whole story, before the mob became judge and executioner.

Packer claimed he had left camp to forage for food and insisted that one of the starving men, Shannon Bell, had become crazed and killed their three companions while Packer was absent. "Bell had a big campfire goin' and the first thing I saw was Reddy Miller lyin' face down in the snow. Swann, Noon and Humphreys was wrapped in their blankets inside our windbreak, and Shannon Bell was kneelin' by the fire roastin' a big piece of meat."[2]

Packer pleaded to Lauder that Bell had killed all four of his lost companions and that Bell had tried to kill him when he returned to the camp: ". . . he [Bell] seized his hatchet and rushed on me. I dropped to my knees to escape the blow, pulled the trigger of my rifle and killed him with a single shot that went sideways through his body."[3]

Packer admitted that he finished roasting the meat and ate the ghastly meal Bell had been cooking. For several days he slowly ate enough cooked human flesh to restore his strength before setting out to hike out of the mountains with a backpack filled with human steaks. "I put some raw flesh in a sack, took Reddy Miller's knife and all the money from the dead men's pockets. I knew it wasn't right to rob the bodies, but somehow it seemed to give me hope. It kept me goin' because I knew that if I didn't give up, I would spend that money on food, on crackers and tins of sardines, cheese and bread."[4]

The following morning, Packer escaped the ramshackle jail. A controversy ensued, with some of the townspeople claiming that Lauder had freed his prisoner. Revisionist historians have suggested that the long incarceration had proved too costly, and that Packer had been freed because it was too expensive to feed and maintain him. Some say that Otto Mears, the town's notable landowner, may have pitied Packer and helped him escape. The two women curators at the Saguache Museum were shocked at this suggestion when I asked them about Mears's possible involvement. In any event, Packer was free. Like many others running from his past, he changed his name and moved to a new area where no one knew him.

One of the original twenty-one-member McGrew party of 1873, Frenchy Cabezon, ran a traveling peddling business visiting towns in the Rockies. In 1883 he happened to be in Wagonmound, Montana, when he spotted Packer exiting a local store. He immediately contacted the local sheriff, who arrested Packer on the spot. He was shipped back to Denver and then to Lake City to stand trial. And what a trial it was! Interest generated by the sensational case extended nationwide. This was, without question, the most sensational crime in the young state's history and one of Colorado's most riveting trials ever.

During the initial trial, "the Colorado Cannibal" inexplicably changed his story again. He now claimed that Israel Swann, one of the six men, had been "sacrificed," and the remaining men roasted select parts of Swann to ward off inevitable starvation. Then, several days later, Packer claimed, Shannon Bell smashed Reddy Miller's skull with a hatchet, and the remaining men butchered, roasted, and ate him. He further claimed that the maniacal Bell went on to dispatch Hutchinson and Noon in the same fashion. Packer claimed that he was terrified that Bell would eventually attack him. He remained on guard until finally Bell attacked. "He rushed me swinging his rifle. I parried the blow, and the rifle was broken by striking a tree. I then hit Bell with a hatchet until he was dead. I no longer had any fear of death except by starvation. I cut the body of my companion, ate as much as I could, and packed away considerable amount for further use, then I resumed my tramp, the sole survivor of a party of six."[5]

The jury and the vocal courtroom spectators didn't buy it. He was quickly found guilty of all five murders and sentenced to hang. The judge, on sentencing Packer, thundered, "Packer, you so-and-so, you have eaten half the Democrats in Hinsdale County . . . You are to hang until you are dead, dead, dead . . . Whether your murderous hand was guided by the misty light of the moon, or the flickering blaze of a campfire, you only can tell. No eye saw the bloody deed performed. No ear save your own caught the groans of your dying victims . . . To the sickening details of your crime I will not refer. Silence is kindness. I do not say things to harrow your soul for I know you have drunk the cup of bitterness to its very dregs."[6]

Packer was reincarcerated in an imposing escape-proof steel cage, and the moody prisoner attracted reporters from across America to interview "the

Man-eating Maniac" for the enjoyment of eager audiences spellbound by the lurid case.

In a modern-sounding twist, four days before Packer's scheduled execution, Packer's two attorneys managed to obtain a stay of execution on a technicality. It seems that Colorado had no death penalty provision for a capital crime committed before Colorado became a state; therefore, Packer could not be executed for his pre-statehood crimes. He was transferred to the Gunnison County jail where he became the object of many curiosity seekers who traveled to the town to gawk at the infamous "cannibal" as he languished in his cell.

Finally in August 1883, the second Packer trial commenced, and Packer was again found guilty. He was sentenced to forty years in the Canon City penitentiary.

Twenty-eight years after he stumbled out of the harsh San Juan Mountains, a sympathetic *Denver Post* journalist, Polly Pry, began a crusade to petition the governor for a pardon. The governor granted Packer a full pardon on January 10, 1901, and amid the public uproar, a *Denver Post* editor was shot by an enraged citizen in retaliation for his championing Packer's cause.

Packer, in a thank-you letter to Polly, stated, "Oh God, if I could have died in the mountains, I would have been spared twenty-eight years of misery. I have never closed my eyes in sleep since without that ghastly vision of the smoldering campfire, the dead companions and the lofty pines drooping with their weight of snow, as if keeping a sorrowful death-watch. But, those who have never been without their three meals a day do not know how to pity me."[7]

Alferd Packer, a broken man, died of a stroke six years later in Littleton, Colorado. Interest in the case has never waned. In 1989, a George Washington University professor named James Starr was intrigued by the fact that Packer had been convicted on purely circumstantial evidence. Starr had the bodies of the five victims exhumed and found that the men had been murdered. But recently, new tests have determined that Packer may indeed have told the truth during his first trial. He may have killed Bell in self-defense. The final chapter to this fascinating story may never be closed, but one thing is certain: Alferd Packer became a tragic and reluctant Colorado legend.

You may be asking yourself, What in the world does a cannibal have to do with the mysterious San Luis Valley? Sometimes men blinded by greed and the lust for gold are compromised into acts far beyond the norm. Other men have had far stranger motivations.

CHAPTER TWO
MOTHER MARY MADE ME DO IT

The label of a serial killer was unheard of in 1863. Few documented cases of note can be called serial killings until London, England's, infamous Jack the Ripper and the seven women he murdered in 1888.

Two books I discovered in June 1995 deserve a hearty mention. Jack Kutz's *Mysteries and Miracles of Colorado* and *Mysteries and Miracles of New Mexico* are both filled with wonderful, little-known accounts from the mysterious Rocky Mountain region of Colorado and New Mexico. The following story is the saga of an unforgettable San Luis Valley trio. They are characters from anyone's worst nightmare.

I was introduced to 1863 Conejos County serial killer, Felipe Espinoza, in *Mysteries and Miracles of Colorado*. The following account has few, if any, parallels in the history of the Southwest.

Little known to most people, Felipe Nerio Espinoza should, I feel, be awarded the title "America's most enigmatic serial killer." He was born in Veracruz, Mexico, in the late 1830s to parents of average means. In 1846, when Espinoza was still a boy, the Mexican-American War commenced. In March 1847, General

Winfield Scott was ordered to lead the United States Army, by sea, and capture the vital seaport of Veracruz. During the ensuing three-week siege, a massive American naval bombardment rained thirteen hundred shells down on the city and, in many instances, took out whole residential neighborhoods. Prior to the furious bombardment, young Felipe Espinoza was sent away from his home by his family, probably for safety's sake. When he returned to his grandparents' home he was horrified to discover that his entire family had been killed by a shell blast that had completely taken out their small house in the barrio. He was forced to identify the bodies of his parents, his grandparents, and his brother and sister, as they lay mangled on the floor in the convent of Santo Domingo with scores of other civilian casualties. Felipe was overcome with grief, and the young, frightened boy of twelve or thirteen went north to the U.S. Territory of New Mexico to live with his only surviving relatives—two cousins, Vivian and Julian. The terror he experienced over his family's untimely death never left him. "He never recovered from his grief. Almost nightly he tossed and turned in his bed reliving in frightening dreams the horror of lifting blood-stained sheets from the broken bodies of his loved ones."[1]

Little is known concerning Felipe's teenage years, but as he grew he evidently became more and more disillusioned with his unfortunate life. Chafing under oppressive poverty, the cousins finally rebelled, and in 1855—led by Felipe—they struck out on their own and became successful horse thieves. Stealing horses and mules from white ranchers in northern New Mexico, they brought them north and sold them to miners in the upstart mining camps in southern Colorado. Felipe had a lifelong, deep hatred for gringos, as he called the

Americans that poured into the mountainous region. After two years or so, the Espinozas moved their base of operations to Conejos County, in the San Luis Valley, and began selling stolen beef to the mining camps. Espinoza was haunted by the death of his family and held the Anglo-Americans directly responsible for his torment. The local Conejos Catholic priest told of hearing from Felipe the details of a strange vision after a particularly vivid nightmare. "The Virgin Mary had come to him and commanded him to kill 100 Americans for each of his [six] slain relatives. He wished to kneel at the altar and make a vow to do so. . . ."[2]

The horrified padre had absolutely refused his request and tried in vain to convince him that he was mistaken about the apparition. He later told Conejos County Sheriff Harding how he had tried to dissuade Espinoza: "I tried to explain to him that it could not have been the Virgin Mary who came to him in his dream. It was the devil, tricking him. But he would not listen. Or perhaps he could not listen. If you had seen the unholy gleam in his eyes, you would understand. He went away, and I have not seen him since."[3]

In May 1863, the unprecedented carnage began. The first victim was found between Parkdale and Cotopaxi, just east of Salida, along the windy fifty-mile route that follows the course of the Arkansas River down to Canon City. A young male had been shot between the eyes and his heart removed from his chest. The second victim was found a few days later. "Judge" William Bruce was discovered shot between the eyes and was also missing his heart, which had evidently been removed from his chest with an ax. A cursory examination of the crime scene revealed that three perpetrators were involved. Posses were hastily formed and dispatched, but before the month ended, another victim, Henry Hawkins, was discovered on the banks of Fountain Creek in the same grisly condition.

The next central Colorado victims were two young cowboys, Nelson Shoup and Tom Brinkley. Shoup was killed instantly during the ambush, about seventy miles north of the first killings. Wounded in the initial volley, Brinkley had managed to crawl away and tried to hide himself between some rocks. His luck quickly ran out. The Espinozas found him; Felipe shot him point-blank between the eyes and commenced his divinely inspired ax work.

Figuring they had found an ideal ambush location on the road to Leadville, the cousins waited for their next victim. George Carter never knew what hit him as he became corpse number five. Before the murderers could dispose of his body, a teamster named Henry Metcalf happened along and narrowly avoided a furious torrent of bullets. He was the first person to escape the Espinozas' diabolical ambushes and gave authorities their first description of the three marauders with their soot-blackened faces.

The trio of evil-doers lurked over the Upper Arkansas River Valley just over Poncha Pass from the San Luis Valley, in a canyon still renowned for its beauty. The sparse population of Fremont County recoiled and a panic gripped the entire region during that 1863 summer of fear. Miners, cowboys, and travelers ventured out only in heavily armed groups, and many volunteered to be deputized as the manhunt moved into high gear. But the elusive Espinozas managed to stay one step ahead of their many pursuers. By August, more than twenty men had been bushwhacked, and their hearts had been hacked out in the same horrific manner. Area residents had no choice but to take the law into their own hands, and at least one account of a mistaken killing can be attributed to revenge-minded posses who were hell-bent on annihilating the sordid threesome. The Espinozas finally " 'fessed up" in a letter written by Felipe in August. Territory of Colorado Governor John Evans received the following letter, but he never knew who, or what, he was dealing with.

We have cut the hearts out of twenty-six American dogs so far but we are willing to forgo further slaughter if you will grant me and my followers full pardons and permit us to retain 5000 acres we now claim in Conejos County with the free use of all adjacent grazing lands and that you will appoint me and any of my followers whom I designate as captains in the Colorado Volunteers. For these things we will desist from further molestation of your subjects. I will give you until the end of September to do these things and if it is not done, 574 more gringos will die. Among them will be yourself.

[signed] Felipe Nerio Espinoza.[4]

Governor Evans, quite taken aback, immediately sent a cable to Conejos County Sheriff Harding, who started an official territorial investigation into the killings. Evans announced that the Territory of Colorado was posting a dead-or-alive reward of $2,500 for Felipe Espinoza. The territory needed help, and there was one man who could get the job done. After the twenty-eighth victim had been discovered, an exasperated Colonel S. B. Tappan, commander of the Colorado Volunteers, dispatched Lieutenant Harold Baldwin to enlist the famous scout, Thomas Tobin.

TOM TOBIN, MOUNTAIN MAN

I found the following biographical information in a magazine article from the 1940s.

> Thomas Tate Tobin was born in 1823 at St. Louis, Missouri. His father was Irish, his mother, Nova Scotian. He came West in 1837, living for some years at trading posts. He settled on the Trinchea near Fort Garland in 1858, and spent the remainder of his life there when not on the trail. Tobin gained his great reputation as a trail man by his uncanny ability to detect and follow "sign." Those who had seen him trailing told me that he always took the most likely starting point, swung round and round in ever widening circles until he "cut sign," then clung to his "sign" until his quarry was overtaken. This technique in trailing Tobin probably learned from the Indians. . . . Those who had seen him on the trail told me that he often went on all fours with his face close to the ground, following "sign," that was imperceptible to less acute eyes. He "could track a grasshopper through sagebrush." . . . [Tobin was] asked if he knew Kit Carson [Colorado's most famous scout and mountain man]: "I et many a beaver tail with him."[5]

The $2,500 reward had motivated dozens of amateur manhunters to go out and blanket the south-central Colorado mountains in an attempt to track down the Espinozas, but Tappan knew he needed a true professional to get the job done. Tobin had been a scout for the Colorado Volunteers for several years before retiring to his farm on the Trincherea, near Fort Garland. He was considered the best manhunter in Colorado.

After Tobin's long conversation with Lieutenant Baldwin they set out to track the desperados, and rode to South Park to meet Colonel Tappan in Fairplay, Colorado. Tappan immediately offered the help of his whole volunteer corps, which Tobin politely declined. He asked for six well-provisioned, experienced soldiers, and a Mexican boy to take care of his horse, who accompanied him and Lieutenant Baldwin as they set off to hunt down the Espinozas.

The men immediately headed toward the latest crime scene on the South Platte. Tobin was able to pick up the trail without much trouble. They rode upstream and began the arduous task of following the careful killers' tracks. For three days the posse slowly followed the Espinozas' trail, pausing every so often when the prints became harder to locate. Finally, Tobin silently signaled for the men to stop near La Veta Pass.

I'll let Thomas Tobin himself finish the story:

. . . I watched carefully and soon located their camp. I told the soldiers not to speak. I raised my hand to squat down and cock their guns but not to fire unless I told them to. I took a step or two in front and saw the head of one of the assassins. At this time I stepped on a stick and broke it; he heard it crack, he looked and saw me, he jumped and grabbed his gun. Before he turned around fairly I fired and hit him in the side; he bellowed like a bull and cried out, "Jesus favor me," and cried to his companion, "Escape, I am killed." I gave a whoop and sung out, "Yell, boys, I've got him, so if there are any more of them they will make their appearance." I tipped my powder horn in my rifle, dropped a bullet from my mouth into the muzzle of my gun while I was capping it. A fellow came out of the ravine, running to an undergrowth of quaking aspen. I sung out, "Shoot boys." The three fired and missed him. I drew my gun up and fired at the first sight and broke his back above his hips. I sent the Mexican boy off on a run to tell Baldwin what had happened. The four soldiers who were with Baldwin came to where I was. Espinoza had started to crawl away. He did not go very far. He braced himself up against some fallen trees, with a pistol in hand waving it over his face, using a word in Mexican that means *base brutes.* I had run down to where he was; I spoke to him and asked him if he knew me. I told him who I was; his reply was *"base brutes."* A soldier went to lay his hand on him. I said look out, he will shoot you. He fired but missed the soldier. I then caught him by the hair, drew his head back over a fallen tree and cut it off. I sent the Mexican boy to cut off the head of the other fellow; he cut it off and brought it to me. . . . I put their heads in a sack and camped on the Sangre de Cristo that night. . . . I rolled up in front of the commanding officers-quarters and called for Col. Tappan. I rolled the assassin's heads out of the sack at Col. Tappan's feet. I said, "Here Col., I have accomplished what you wished. This head is Espinoza's. This other is his companion's, there is no mistake, for we have this diary and letters and papers to show they are the assassin's."[6]

Jack Kutz asserts that the governor reneged on the $2,500 reward, claiming to Tobin that "the Territory had no money available" to back up the reward. (Other sources claim that Tobin was eventually paid $500.) But, noticing that Tobin was wearing an old tattered coat, Evans offered to buy him a new coat, so he'd look good for the photographers covering the conclusion of the territory's most sensational manhunt.

Evidently Felipe Espinoza's head was kept in a jar of alcohol at Fort Garland and was finally sold to a traveling carnival. Imagine growing up in the 1870–1880s and seeing that sideshow face in a jar in some penny arcade, glaring out into oblivion. No one knows what finally became of the head of Felipe Nerio Espinoza.

I couldn't help but wonder, after reading several riveting accounts, why I hadn't heard of the Espinozas' "reign of terror" before. Tabloid mass murderers have always captured the American imagination. I admit, they've captured mine. Jeffrey Dahmer, Wayne Gacy, Ed Gein, David Berkowitz and his demonic voices: These societal aberrations have periodically and unquestionably stunned and affected our culture. I went ahead and checked the record to ascertain Felipe Espinoza's impact in nineteenth-century media in an effort to place his deviant actions into a broader cultural context. This search revealed that his story is not generally known, even in Colorado.

One can't help but wonder why Felipe's cousins allowed themselves to get involved. There is no evidence to suggest they had shared their cousin's "vision," so why did they embrace his pathology and embark on such an ill-conceived quest? Did they really think they could extort the territory for the lush Conejos ranchlands Felipe coveted? And what about Felipe's vision? Did he really believe the Blessed Virgin Mary had commanded him to exact such retribution on so many unsuspecting "gringos"? Could he have misinterpreted the message? Or, more realistically, was the message delusional? In a more sinister vein, did an outside influence diabolically design the visitation to trick the psychologically fragile Espinoza into enacting his reign of terror? Even the pious local padre had a sense that Felipe was being manipulated and tried to argue with him concerning the reality of his proclaimed "vision."

The Conejos area, where Espinoza lived, contains many interesting legends and stories pertaining to the supernatural and extraordinary. In *TMV*,[7] I noted several rare legendary appearances of Old Scratch, the devil, who it is said visits north-central New Mexico and south-central Colorado and, as I've learned, other rural areas of the great southwestern United States. There is a local perception that the Conejos towns of Sanford, Antonito, and Manassa may have hosted alleged appearances of this "devil" at dances and/or social events. It is interesting to note that I've never been able to find an actual witness to Old Scratch's urbane antics, but I've interviewed many people who claim solemnly that they "knew someone who was there."

Is there a connection between Felipe's vision of the Mother Mary and these local Conejos County devil legends? Let's face it, it's difficult not to leap to the conclusion that Felipe's "vision" was demonic in nature. What well-meaning, benevolent spirit like the Virgin Mary would demand such retribution? Appearances by the historically angelic Mother of Christ have usually been just a bit more benevolent and light-hearted in nature. Children have channeled as a result of her visits; the sun has zigzagged and spiraled playfully for thousands at her arrival; and fresh-water springs have joyfully emerged and bubbled forth at her behest. To my knowledge, no one has ever been instructed by Our Lady to slaughter six hundred innocent "gringos."

THE OTHER EXTREME

However, Mother Mary apparently instructed other emissaries around the magical southwestern United States. I was alerted to our next historical personage by international UFO investigator Antonio Huneeus, who visited my home in June 1997. He told me about an investigator friend in Spain, Javier Sierra, who had researched a rather enigmatic figure from fifteenth-century Spain who may have astrally traveled to the San Luis Valley. Consider the following:

Sister Marie de Jesus Agreda was born April 2, 1602, in Agreda, Spain. Christened Maria Fernandez Coronel, she donned the blue habit and took her vows as a nun in the Franciscan order, and in 1627 she became abbess of the Agreda Franciscan monastery until her death in 1665. Everyone agreed on Sister Marie's piety and devotion to her faith, but there was controversy over her book, *The Mystical City of God*, a life of the Virgin Mary supposedly based on divine revelations.

In 1620, teenage Sister Marie began having unnerving visions, or raptures. Cloistered in the convent, she would meditate for hours, sometimes all day, and return and tell her fellow sisters wondrous stories of her more than five hundred spiritual travels to a faraway land, meeting savages and telling them of the Word of Christ. She experienced many episodes of rapturous meditation and bilocation, and word began to spread of the young nun in the convent. Finally, convinced of the reality of her experiences, she wrote a book describing, in great detail, her missionary work bringing the Word of Christ to the savages of the New World.

In early fifteenth-century Spain, this was not a prudent claim to make. The Inquisition quickly put to death untold thousands found "guilty" of witchcraft and dealings with demonic forces. Before long, the Inquisition took a pointed interest in the good Sister of Agreda, and she found herself at the center of a dangerous, whirling controversy. She insisted to the father inquisitor that she was indeed bilocating and doing God's work, but to no avail. A very public trial ensued with the full brunt of the powerful Church bearing down on the poor nun.

During the height of her trial, a newly returned expedition of conquistadors and friars arrived in Spain with a wondrous tale. It seems that the Spanish explorers, while in the unexplored region north of Mexico, had encountered numerous Native American tribes in what are now New Mexico, Arizona, and Texas who had already been converted to Christianity and somehow knew of Jesus Christ the Savior. Even more fantastic were the Indians' claims of being visited by a white-skinned "Blue Lady" who appeared to many, drifting in a blue haze while she preached the word of the Lord in their native languages. She helped them to build crosses and places of worship and even handed out rosaries and religious objects.

From 1620 to approximately 1631 the Spanish nun flew from Spain to the North American State of New Mexico on more than 500 occasions. Thus it was established in the open case of the Holy Inquisition against the nun in 1635, in which it was affirmed further that no one in the convent noticed her absence during those flights. On occasion they would happen twice during the same day . . . How then can we explain a woman of scarcely eighteen years of age that could bi-locate to New Mexico, and while there, she would dedicate herself to distribute among the natives rosaries and other liturgical objects as she instructed them about the truth of the Christian faith . . . Her trips occurred shortly before the diocese of Mexico decided to send evangelizers [north] towards those unexplored territories. Her visits made their efforts considerably easier.[8]

These first Spanish explorers to the Southwest were amazed by the natives' knowledge of Christianity and were baffled by the rosaries they were shown and by their earnest descriptions of the "Blue Lady" who had come from afar and preached to them. "Finally, when the first Franciscans, led by Friar Benvenedes, arrived [at the Isleta Pueblo] they discovered a singular spectacle. Thousands of Indians approached the Franciscans and asked earnestly for baptism."[9]

Benvenedes wrote later of the Spaniards' efforts to ascertain how the Indians had knowledge of Christianity: "When those Indians were asked to tell us what was the reason for which, with so much affection, they asked for baptism and religious indoctrination, they answered that a woman had come and preached to each one of them in their own tongue."[10]

The rapid Spanish conquest and control of the area in the fifteenth and sixteenth centuries may have partially been due to Sister Marie's solo missionary efforts on behalf of a bewildered Catholic Church. "Only in New Mexico did the Franciscans baptize more than 50,000 people in record time and rapidly install twenty-five missions and minister to more than ninety towns. The Indians remembered with special veneration the Blue Lady, the one whom they gave this name due to her blue mantle of celestial tones she wore on her back."[11]

During the mid–sixteen hundreds, the celebrated bilocating nun from Agreda garnered national notoriety. King Philip of Spain may have enlisted her help in foreign affairs, and it is firmly documented that the king carried on a lifelong correspondence with her. It is surmised by some that Sister Marie may have even bilocated to foreign courts on covert foreign policy missions on behalf of Spain.

Now one would think that this story alone is compelling, but the unbelievable saga of our talented nun does not end there. Even in death, Sister Marie defies the rationalists and supplies nonbelievers and the faithful with evidence of her fantastic talents. In a secluded crypt on the grounds of the convent we find what proves to be the latest dramatic chapter to her incredible story.

Sister Marie de Jesus Agreda's body, it turns out, is incorruptible. Like a small number of deceased mystics and Catholic saints, the nun's body refuses naturally to decay, even after more than three hundred years. The flush of her cheeks and her lifelike features still baffle the Catholic Church and modern science. During an opening of her casket in 1909, a cursory scientific examination was performed on the pristine body in peaceful repose, astounding the scientists and doctors who were allowed to perform the examination.

In 1989, a Spanish physician named Andreas Medina participated in another examination of Sister Marie as she lay in the convent of the Conceptionist nuns, the same monastery where she had lived in the 1600s. Dr. Medina told investigative journalist Javier Sierra in 1991: "What most surprised me about that case is that when we compared the state of the body, as it was described in the medical report from 1909, with how it appeared in 1989, we realized it had absolutely not deteriorated at all in the last eighty years."[12] Complete photographic and scientific evidence was obtained by investigators before the respectful closing of her glass-lidded casket. She is beatified by the Catholic Church and may someday become a saint in the Catholic tradition.

Although the Blue Lady is said to have visited the Rio Grande River Valley as far north as the pueblos around Sante Fé, New Mexico, less than a hundred miles from the San Luis Valley, I can find no direct evidence that Sister Marie ever bilocated here. But I would not be surprised if she did. I feel that her compelling story may provide all of us with important clues pertaining to the understanding of unusual religious/belief-based phenomena.

MODERN MOUNTAIN MAN

I suspect that a certain percentage of any group of people are bound to act abnormally when faced with the unknown. Does one's perceptions of the local environment somehow affect how he or she responds to elements of reality not normally experienced? Can unusual circumstances, combined with a traditional local history of "the unusual" drive certain people to do things they normally might not even contemplate? I pondered these questions and looked for more examples of little-known social aberrations in the historical record. Meanwhile, back here in the late twentieth century, unusual events in the San Luis Valley began to escalate. Out of the church library, gumshoe, and back into the field!

Here is the story of an interesting character from the present day. Even with impressive documentation and physical evidence, I don't quite know what to think of the following events. Running from Colorado into New Mexico, for more than 220 miles, the rugged Sangre de Cristo Mountains, the longest continuous mountain range in the United States, border the eastern side of the San Luis Valley. I have traveled the mountainous region stretching from Alaska to Mexico, and the Sangres are truly one of North America's most breathtaking scenic wonders. Ten peaks soar to more than fourteen thousand feet in altitude and scrape the Colorado Plateau sky. A perfect natural barrier, the imposing rock wall soars over a dozen high-altitude lakes found nestled in vales located between the mountains. Most of the San Luis Valley's population is located in the center of the Valley, and I'm blessed to be able to look out my window and see four "14'ers" less than three miles away.

In a high, remote area in the northern Sangres and the Rio Grande National Forest and Wilderness area, a small trailer sits in a clearing surrounded by the quiet piñon forest. There are no houses, stores, or residents, just miles of dense forest in the area. The trailer belongs to Larry Williams (not his real name), a mountain man who prefers solitude over the company of people.

A mutual friend called me about Williams and told me I should contact him because he claimed that some very unusual events were occurring at his property. "Almost nightly" during June and July 1995, Larry noticed strange lights buzzing low over the forest that clings to the steep eastern side of the Sangres. He couldn't help but wonder what the lights could be. During several days in late July, he noticed increased military helicopter activity over his high-mountain property. He began to notice odd things around his place. A stream that flowed down from the mountains through his land inexplicably raised and lowered its water level for no apparent reason. Then something happened that he was really not expecting.

Williams arrived home from town August 15 at 8:45 P.M. and noticed a bright light off to the north. Checking to make sure he had his camera with him, he sat in his truck and carefully watched the light. It appeared either to get brighter or head south toward his location. The man took a series of sixteen still photos that show the light as it apparently flew toward him. The final photo was taken shooting straight up at an "enormous boomerang craft" as it hovered above him. Then, quite inexplicably, he found himself looking out over a dark, quiet Wet Mountain Valley.

He checked his watch and was startled to find that thirty-five minutes had elapsed since he last remembered checking the time right when the boomerang craft began to approach. Confused, he got out of his truck and looked around with a flashlight. He was amazed to find his truck sitting "six inches away from its tracks," like something had moved his truck up and over a half-foot. He was startled to find that whatever it was had moved his trailer "six inches off its foundation" and picked up his bulldozer and set it down "six inches from where its tracks ended!" Fresh branches, up to sixty feet off the ground, appeared to have been sheared off nearby trees.

This was the last straw. A couple of days earlier, he had discovered a number of animal skeletons scattered around his property. He could not venture a guess concerning why so many unexplained animal carcasses littered his land. "I've found elk, deer, fox, raccoon, and a lot of cattle skeletons have been found. They're just laying around. Nothing touched 'em and tore 'em up. . . . I've seen at least fifteen to twenty cattle carcasses and skeletons alone since last year. I don't know who they belonged to." Coincidentally, a rancher directly over the Sangres in the San Luis Valley has reportedly lost several dozen cattle without a trace since 1992.

Williams told me, "I've been waking up at exactly 2:00 A.M. and seeing lights pretty near every night since June. . . . We've found little tiny four-toed tracks walking around the perimeter of my place. I've seen some pretty odd things in my life, but nothing like I'm seeing in those Sangre de Cristos." Much to his dismay, he couldn't help but notice that he now had "a thumb-sized wart" after his thirty-five minutes of missing time. It required medical attention.

The same evening, at 10:00 P.M., a family of four was returning to Blanca, Colorado, after watching a movie in Alamosa with a family friend. This is about forty minutes after Williams claimed he was returned. As the family headed east on State Highway 160, about five miles out of Alamosa, a large bright light caught their attention. Surrounding the brilliant light were "lots of helicopters" traveling along with the single light in a northeast direction. They pulled over to the side of the highway and got out. The huge light never varied in intensity, and at one point the adults got so excited that two little boys in the backseat became very scared and started to cry. One of the excited witnesses, guitar player George Oringdulph, called me the following day to make a report. "It was huge, whatever it was, and it was pretty strange the way all those other blinking lights seemed to be flying with it."

On August 16, the day after Williams's close-proximity sighting, ten or twelve choppers were "buzzing all over his place." His trailer had also been broken

into and all his photographic equipment rifled through.
"Thank God I had my camera with me. Whoever they
were, I'm positive they were looking for those pictures
I took the night before!"

Williams reported the strange events to the local
sheriff, who conducted a brief investigation. Williams
was frustrated. "I showed 'em how my truck, trailer,
and bulldozer had been moved, but what could they
do?!" He is very protective of his property and his privacy and was not pleased when he found large boot
tracks and cigarette butts at the edge of the clearing
where his trailer sat. He was also perturbed when a
large mirror outside his trailer was repeatedly moved
from its secure position. Someone was snooping
around his place, and with all the other weird events,
Willliams was starting to get pretty paranoid about the
whole situation. I called the local sheriff and found that
investigating officers were skeptical of these alleged
high-strange events, but did acknowledge to me that
they had received reports of unidentified lights in the
same vicinity.

Williams also mentioned to me that images of a
"large post" kept appearing on freshly developed rolls
of film. He could not identify the location of these photos and doesn't recall taking the pictures. If something
like this happens only once, not a big deal. But after a
fourth time, one *really* starts to wonder. Williams was
not amused.

Members of two investigative organizations visited
Williams, and according to the witness, "Someone
used my name publicly even after being asked not to."
This incensed him to the point where he was absolutely
unwilling to talk about his experiences with investigators or the press. "I don't care if you weren't the one
who used my name . . . you can all *go to hell*!" he told

me angrily during our last conversation. It was hard not to remember Suggested Rule of Investigation 3: Always credit your sources and respect requests for anonymity.

Like other residents scattered sporadically in this sparsely populated corner of south-central Colorado, Williams has heard stories of troops on maneuvers, seen many helicopters, and heard stories of black-uniformed soldiers chasing people off of Methodist Mountain to the northwest. Sitting innocently on the top of Methodist are two groups of high-tech-looking antenna arrays. Several obviously are cellular phone towers and microwave relays, but there are other arrays nestled on the ridge. Rumors of chopper activity in the area had reached me several times over the past couple of years, but I had not actively investigated this forgotten, little-traveled region, where the reports originated.

One night in 1993, during a visit with a scientist who had worked for a major defense contractor for a number of years on classified military projects, I was told of an odd sight he and his family had witnessed sporadically since their move to the area in 1991.

"I've only noticed it late at night during wintertime. I look out at the mountains, and I see this small light just sitting there, way above tree line. It's not always there, but when it is, it's plainly visible. I've pointed it out to my wife, and we can't figure out what it could possibly be." We were sitting in his office located on the second floor of his new home at the base of the Northern Sangres.

"Where exactly do you see it?" I asked, hoping to get a more precise idea of its location.

"Just right up there." He pointed casually out the window at the Sangres rearing their majestic tops into the sky. I looked and obtained an accurate fix on the exact spot, filing the information away for later use in my attempt to identify the location(s) of alleged underground base(s) said to exist in the Valley.

That following summer, I was talking with a frequent visitor to the Valley who loves to visit the "clothing optional" Valley View Hot Springs, located south of the scientist's home. He told me a rather interesting story of a conversation he overheard while soaking in one of the several natural pools that adorn the foothills, east of Villa Grove. It seems our nature buff was told by "a local" that ten to twelve miles north of the Hot Springs, above the tree line, a secret underground base exists inside the Sangres; its main purpose is to send out fighter planes to "chase UFOs." Normally, when I hear such sci-fi-sounding information, I don't pay much attention, but this particular claim intrigued me. "Where exactly did he say the base entrance was?" I asked him. The visitor replied that he had asked, but the view from the pool did not afford a sight line up the range. He did say the man was "emphatic" about his claim. The "local" claimed that on several occasions he personally had seen jets flying out of the mountain.

This rang a major bell. It was the same approximate location of the scientist's sighting of an infrequent light, above the tree line. It seriously reminded me of a rancher named Harry King who claimed to see little jets flying *into* Middle Creek Hill, about thirty miles south in the Blanca Massif, back in the 1960s. Harry King was the brother of Nellie Lewis, owner of Snippy the Horse, considered the first publicized animal "mutilation."[13] I had heard continual rumors of "underground bases" during the eight years I'd lived here, so I figured maybe there was something to this latest "rumored" information. For instance, Tom Clancy mentions a facility in his book *Clear and Present Danger*, which features a scene with a helicopter flying to a secret base. Located where? In the Sangre de Cristo Mountains in southern Colorado.

Other strange sightings began to occur in the northern Sangres. On August 25, 1995, at dusk, a local electric company owner reported triangular-shaped objects over Methodist Mountain. The witness claimed that the objects were red and blue in color and that "there was a field of energy around them." The following morning, on August 26, a triangular-shaped object was seen from the Salida sales barn, a mile east of town. That night, at 10:20 P.M., campers on Silver Creek, near Poncha Pass, witnessed a red and green streak of light moving north just west of the Continental Divide, again, near Poncha Pass. The two witnesses were interviewed by Colorado MUFON. That same night, at 10:30 P.M., a very large white globe with red, green, and blue colored lights was seen hovering over Poncha Pass and reported by a former naval officer. The object was viewed from the McCoy trailer park in Salida.

The following morning, August 27, at 8:30 A.M., the beginning of a flurry of sightings began innocently outside of Grand Junction, Colorado, 150 miles north of the San Luis Valley. Two men, one a disc jockey from a popular local country-and-western radio station, were out for their usual Sunday morning jog in the Colorado Monument. As they rounded a bend in the trail, they were startled to see a large pencil-shaped craft darting low near the mountain range. As it darted about, it expelled two smaller objects, and all three flew at fantastic speed, and then there was a "flash," and they disappeared *into* the mountain without a sound. The DJ was so taken with his sighting he broadcast the details to his Grand Junction radio audience, requesting that anyone else who had witnessed the objects call the station.

That same morning, in the Collegiate Mountains just northwest of Salida, a Jeep full of tourists reported a cigar-shaped object similar in description to the object seen by the DJ and his friend.

I had a speaking engagement in Denver that weekend and missed all the excitement. The events of August 27 would become regional headline news the following Monday morning. It seemed we had another intense "flap" of UFO activity going on.

CHAPTER THREE

UFOS OVER SALIDA

Photographic evidence of the many unidentified flying objects reported in southern Colorado is, at best, extremely rare, and daytime footage is especially hard to come by. As I mentioned in *The Mysterious Valley*, until now, the only footage I was aware of, from a south-central Colorado sighting, was taken in the late summer of 1948. In 1993, Paris, Texas, researcher Tom Adams sent me a small article from a San Francisco newspaper that told of a Center, Colorado, resident named Grant Edwards, Sr., and his eight-millimeter UFO film he was screening to local San Luis Valley civic groups. I called Saguache County commissioner Keith Edwards, who lived in Center. He said yes, his dad was the same Grant Edwards, and he had been the one who filmed the objects. At the time, the possibility that this footage could be the earliest civilian film of UFOs never entered my mind. I redoubled my efforts to find out more about this obscure 1948 film. I knew I really had to do some digging to find out more, and I looked for clues wherever I could find them.

I called Keith back, and he referred me to Marianne Jones-Brown, a Crestone resident and Valley native who, Edwards claimed, had seen the film many times and was quite taken by it. She was right here in Crestone? Great, a local call. She remembered the film as if she had seen it recently.

"Grant brought it over to our house right after he filmed them [UFOs], and my dad and I saw it four or five times in a row, right there in our living room."

"When was this, do you remember?"

"Well, yes. It was in the late summer of 1948. When was that crash in Roswell, New Mexico?"

"July '47."

"It was the next summer, in August 1948." Finally, corroboration of that small, insignificant newspaper article.

"How old were you at the time?" I asked.

"I was ten, or so . . . in fourth or fifth grade."

"Well, what did you think? What was on the film? Keith told me it was daylight footage of a couple of round spheres hanging over the Forbes Trinchera."

"Oh, no, he filmed them down by the [New Mexico] border on the Conejos River, west of Antonito. And it wasn't two objects, it was five!"

"Really? Five!"

"Yes, he had just bought a new camera, it was brand-new. He'd just loaded it for the first time when his wife looked up and saw them and pointed them out. He shot the whole roll. It seemed like twenty minutes."

"I think those little eight-millimeter film rolls were only about two and a half to three minutes long." I have one of those obsolete cameras.

"It sure seemed a lot longer than that. I couldn't believe it. The UFOs would come down right over the trees and hover, then go off real fast, then the others would come down. They even flew in formation, with two together in front and the other three behind. At one point they hovered and turned on end like Frisbees. The film was as clear as could be! He did a good job of filming them. When they hovered low over the trees, you could even see his wife and daughter standing in the foreground watching them."

"You mean there were shots of the objects with people in the shot?"

"Yes, when they were low over the trees. I've watched all of the films they show on TV, and nothing compares with Grant's film. It was the best footage I've ever seen! I was really mad when I heard they took it." This piqued my curiosity.

"Who took it? You mean the film?"

"Yes, I remember hearing that the government sent two men, and they confiscated it. I think they may have been FBI or something. Two men just showed up at his house one day and took it. I guess they didn't like him showing it at the Chamber of Commerce or something."

"How long after he shot the film did they show up?"

"Oh, I don't know, maybe six months after."

Marianne sounded animated. Her recall seemed superb, and it was obvious that seeing the Edwards film at a young age had made a lasting impression on her.

She noted, "I've been fascinated with UFOs ever since. Too bad you didn't talk with my dad. He died three years ago. He was really into it and knew a lot about the sightings around the Valley. I bet there's some old farmers around who could tell you some stories. Back before they had the circles [center-pivot sprinklers], they irrigated by hand, and the farmers would spend hours at night just sitting in their trucks. And what would they do? Why, they looked up at the sky."

I asked her, "As a Valley native who grew up here, you must have heard a lot of stories about UFOs people see around here. What do you make of these events? I mean, what do you think, or who do you think is flying them?"

"Well, when Grant Edwards came over and showed us his film, I just knew what he filmed was not of this earth." She added wistfully, "I just wish you could have talked with my dad. He didn't talk about it [UFOs] unless he knew the person believed him. Then he'd talk about it. I think most folks around here are like that. Back when I was a kid, you just didn't talk about them because people would think you were a kook or something."

She added, "I've seen a few objects around the Valley. One night in 1965, when my husband and two friends were coming back from Valley View Hot Springs, we were on Highway 17, north of town [Alamosa], when we saw a real bright light over La Garita. It would come up and stay in one spot, then go straight down real fast. We pulled over and watched it for at least twenty minutes. A couple I know were at the Sky-Hi Drive-In [in Alamosa], and they saw it too."

Marianne was on a roll. She continued with another incident. "Back right after we got married, in '57, we were driving in the canyon over Poncha Pass when the whole canyon lit up. Something flew over. My husband is a civilian worker for the Air Force and is familiar with most of the aircraft they fly today. What we saw that night sure wasn't what the Air Force was flying in 1957. He was real impressed with this incident because he knew it wasn't one of ours." Later when I talked to him, Mr. Brown did not offer any further speculation.

I thanked Marianne and reviewed my notes. I racked my brain trying to remember the earliest civilian UFO footage I could recall. I was sure that the earliest films were from the early 1950s. If that was the case, the government confiscated what may have been the first corroborated and publicly acknowledged multiple-object UFO footage ever taken by an amateur film-maker. Where? Why, right here in the mysterious San Luis Valley, of course!

AUGUST 27, 1995, 9:25 A.M.

The sound of hammering roofers and gunshots at a rifle range fills the bright August morning. The nearby Arkansas River flows serenely in the morning sunshine as a pair of workers busily put the finishing touches on a gutter that adorns a brand-new house just northwest of Salida, Colorado. A cacophony of gunshots punctuates the hammering as members of a gun club practice skeet shooting just down a short, steep hill from the house. The Edwards family lives in the large, tastefully designed and decorated house located several blocks from the Fairview cemetery, and owner, Tim Edwards (no relation to Grant), forty-two, prepares to go outside and check on the carpenters' progress. Tim is an unassuming, successful local restaurant owner and outdoor enthusiast. A big-screen TV and a quality stereo set-up adorn the living room. The father and daughter head for the kitchen door. The etched-glass kitchen cabinets reflect the bright, slanting morning sun as a puppy yaps in the yard.

Tim's blonde, bright, and inquisitive six-year-old daughter Brandy walks out the back door into the lovely late-summer morning. It's Sunday, August 27, 1995, at 9:25 A.M. On the surface, just another lovely, typical Colorado high-mountain morning. Brandy looks up. . . .

Meanwhile, at that same moment, my partner, Isadora, and I are pulling into the parking lot of Boulder's

Broker Inn. I've been invited by the Denver-based Sophia Institute to speak at an inaugural conference that Sophia founder Jack Steinhauser has organized. Experiencer-author Leah Haley and her ufologist-author husband Marc Davenport greet us as we arrive. The two-day affair is in its second day, and I am the first speaker this morning. Marc has formulated an intriguing theory that UFOs are somehow time travelers appearing in our space-time continuum. We have a good, enthusiastic turnout, and I am impressed by the attendees' breadth of knowledge related to UFOs. I also appreciate seeing true pioneers like Marc and Leah again. Little do we know of the real-time drama unfolding one hundred miles south of us. . . .

Tim Edwards promises Brandy that they can go hiking today if the weather is nice, so naturally the first thing little Brandy does upon going outside is look up to see if it's going to rain. She immediately notices something dancing high in the air. She smiles. "Daddy, there's something up in the sky!" Tim, busy checking on the carpenters' progress, initially pays her no mind. She repeats her observation. Edwards, legally blind in his left eye, obediently looks up in the direction Brandy is pointing. The new gutter blocks out the disk of the sun, and the sun's corona blazes out into the brilliant sky. Movement near the sun catches his attention. What he sees high in the sky forever changes his life.

Edwards stands there for several seconds, dumbfounded, watching a sight the likes of which few have ever seen before. A bright object is darting playfully to the northeast of the sun. Are his eyes playing tricks on him? He watches for a couple of minutes in amazement, then runs inside and frantically starts making phone calls to anyone he can think of. Wasting precious time, he finally runs and gets his video camera and manages to shoot six and a half minutes of video-tape, over the next hour and fifteen minutes, of an enormous cigar-shaped object silently hovering and darting high in the sky to the northeast.

The audio portion of the tape records these comments among the initial witnesses: Tim, Brandy, and Tim's father, George Edwards.

Brandy asks, "Daddy, can spaceships grow bigger like that? Can they?"

Tim answers, "Uh-huh."

"It could?"

"Uh-huh," Tim answers again, obviously concentrating on following the darting object with the video camera. You can hear him breathing and understandably not paying full attention to his little girl. A small plane noisily flies low over their heads amid the *pop-pop* of some skeet shooters' guns.

Brandy is more insistent and comments rhetorically, "If a spaceship can grow bigger like that . . . then it *is* a spaceship!"

Tim asks her to go get the binoculars. He is joined by his father, George, and the two men watch for several seconds in silence while Tim films. Then Tim's dad chimes in, "Oh my God . . . Geez it stops like that . . . man, it's erratic!"

Tim agrees. "It's erratic as hell . . . it ain't no kind of aircraft, I'll tell you that."

"Ahh-h no," George agrees, and Tim turns off the videotape, concluding the first of nine different shot sequences.

The tape comes back on with Tim's father noting, "[If] you keep looking at it and you can see, like a . . . a ball going around it—I mean, way off around it, you know . . . like it's shooting things off it." Something appears to be flying out of the object.

Tim observes, "Well, the more you look at it . . . it's just amazing! Where's your spotting scope at, Dad? In the fifth wheel?"

"I don't think you'll get it on that spotting scope."

"You might be able to—it's stationary a lot."

Brandy, who has returned, observes, "Gosh, it's looking orange. There's something orange going around it." Several more seconds go by with the skeet shooters obliviously firing away, and Brandy, in the background, continues an unintelligible dialogue with no one in particular. The three are joined by Tim's oldest daughter, fifteen-year-old Laray, who is also spellbound by the enigmatic object high in the sky.

"I'm going to get under the edge of the house so the sun's not in our eyes." Tim moves the camera. He inadvertently discovers the resulting technique he will use for hundreds of subsequent hours of "solar corona" filming, a technique of videotaping into the sun's corona, using his gutter to block out the sun. The object darts impossibly around the sky with the roof edge providing a perfect point of reference in the foreground for analysts to study and ponder later.

"It's going all over the sky," Tim's dad says.

Tim observes, "There ain't no little airplane that goes five miles in two seconds."

"I know it, that's what I mean," George answers emphatically.

"It's moving more than five miles. It moved over to that part of the sky . . . it probably moved a hundred miles in the matter of a second or two!" Tim sounds genuinely amazed and baffled. Then something unexpected happens.

The elder Edwards is awestruck, "What are those up there now? Do you see that now? See the big one? See it going? Did *ya see it?!*"

"I can't see it with this," Tim responds while looking through the camera's tiny viewfinder. Another plane flies low over the house. Several more seconds go by with Brandy asking indecipherable questions, then the footage ends.

As soon as Edwards is convinced that the object is real and not a trick of light or a conventional aircraft, he calls his restaurant, the local radio station, the sheriff, the National UFO Reporting Center in Seattle, Channel Four News in Denver, and *Salida Mountain Mail* editor Chris Hunt. Hunt is instantly interested and immediately goes to the scene.

Hunt told me later, "Edwards thinks the object was extremely high up in the sky because routine airline traffic appeared to fly under it." He actually thinks it could have been even higher. Edwards said, "It could have been twenty or thirty or one hundred miles up for all we know."

Edwards has consistently told everyone, "It was kind of eerie . . . I know it wasn't from this world. I know I sound crazy, but I really believe it was from another world." Evidently, Edwards was not initially frightened by the unusual craft. "I was really excited just to get to see it. . . . I don't think there was any reason to be scared. Actually, I wish it had landed. If it had landed, it would have covered the whole town of Salida; it was that big."

Tim noted, "The object's north and south movements could be described as darting, but east to west, the craft appeared to step, or walk across the sky—almost like it was projecting itself to the next frame and location." He also claims that with his binoculars he and his father could make out two distinct rows of individual light panels on the object.

Hunt, who watched the footage within minutes after it was shot, commented, "At one point the camera zooms in, and you can actually see red and green lights sequencing around the rim of the craft."

Later, while watching the footage, I couldn't help but wonder what the heck the enigmatic object was! It looks unlike anything one would expect to see flying around conventional airspace. I could clearly see the object's two rows of sequencing lights. Both adult witnesses noticed that the object, at times, appeared to be boomerang or V-shaped.

Alerted by Edwards, portions of the footage were sent to news stations and immediately broadcast on several Front Range Colorado TV stations. The full footage was provided to Channel Three in Denver when they visited the Edwardses the following day. Within a month, I was interviewed by the Paramount TV program *Sightings*, *CBS News*, *Extra*, and *Inside Edition* about Tim's footage and the many sightings of unusual objects that have been reported here in southern Colorado.

Eventually, more than twenty-three witnesses came forward and related seeing a mysterious darting craft. A couple traveling over Cochetopa Pass, about thirty-five miles southwest of Salida, saw what they later told the Saguache County sheriff's department was a "bright cigarette-shaped object," and another couple traveling over Poncha Pass reported a "cigar-shaped" craft the following day, Monday, August 28, 1995. Seven witnesses reported a similar object to the Colorado University Astronomy Department, and an employee at the Crestone/Baca Grande Los Cumbres Golf Course later reported to me that he had witnessed a "cigar-shaped object hovering between Kit Carson Peak and Mount Adams"—just east of Crestone—at 4:00 P.M. on

August 27. He didn't immediately report it, because, "When it left, it disappeared right into the mountain! I didn't think anyone would believe me, so I didn't tell anyone. Then I read about that guy in Salida filming something the same day that sounds like exactly what I saw. So I figured I should tell you."

From no activity to a blizzard of reports scattered across all of central Colorado. My vacation was over; I had a lot of work to do. I found out about Edwards's sighting the following day, but something told me to hold my enthusiastic self back and carefully watch how the information was disseminated. I had worked tirelessly for two and a half years trying to prove to myself that something very strange and wonderful was going on here in the San Luis Valley, and just two towns away was validation of a lot of hard work. I decided not to call Tim, just to sit back and watch the drama unfold. And drama indeed unfolded. Michael Curta, Colorado state director of MUFON, stated for television cameras what I've proposed for quite a while. "Could it be otherworldly technology? Yes, it could. Could it be military aircraft? Yes, it could. Could it be some unexplained weather phenomenon? That's also possible. There's an awful lot of strange things that occur in the mysterious valley of Colorado, and this is racking up to be one of them."

The sighting immediately became sensational regional and national news. Phone calls and requests for interviews and tapes poured into the Edwards household, overwhelming the unprepared family. Tim immediately tried to find professional video labs and analysts to examine the footage. Of course, with all the media publicity he unleashed, every UFO investigative group in the state immediately descended upon him and his family. The Mutual UFO Network, the UFO

Institute, the Fund for UFO Research, the Denver UFO Society, the Sophia Institute; you name 'em, they showed up. I kept a low-key but close eye on developments, and, unbeknownst to Edwards, I combed the southern Colorado countryside for additional witnesses to corroborate his sighting.

Since that fateful Sunday in August, I have become quite friendly with Tim and his family and was stunned by the incredible amount of energy that Tim has devoted to getting attention for his video. Edwards started networking with investigators all over the world, trying to "get the word out" about UFOs in general and his footage in particular.

An article by Arlene Shovald in the *Mountain Mail*, September 7, 1995, dealt exclusively with the UFO sighting's effect on Tim.

UFO Sighting Changes Edwards' Life

. . . Since he video-taped an object in the sky that morning, he has been in demand by newspapers, radio, and television sources and the demands are taking time from his business, the Patio Pancake restaurant on U.S. 50.

Edwards isn't sure he likes the idea of being a celebrity, but he doesn't have much of a choice. Copies of Edwards' original video were aired on Channels 7, 4 and 9 in Denver, which includes the ABC, CBS and NBC Networks. . . . Edwards remains a bit uncomfortable with the whole thing, stating he is putting his whole family's credibility and reputation on the line with his report of the sighting, but fortunately, he has the video to back up his statements along with information from the National UFO Observatory [*sic*] in Seattle which was flooded with calls from Montana and Pennsylvania from people who had seen the same thing he'd seen.

Another article in the *Mail* celebrated the seventy-eighth anniversary of another curious Salida sighting. Arlene Shovald did an excellent job researching and came up with compelling stories, one of which occurred the same week as Edwards's sighting.

Edwards' UFO Sighting Not Salida's First

. . . The Salida *Record* of September 7, 1917, tells of Salida residents seeing mysterious "vehicles of the air" flying about the night sky during the previous week. Nearly every night some kind of light was observed in various positions in the "blue depths." The lights were described as very far away. They would disappear for an instant, only to reappear stronger that ever, and then vanish. Among those observing the strange phenomenon were some of the pillars of Salida society. . . . Rev. Oakley examined the object with a telescope one night and could discern what appeared to be a wheel. . . . While the wheel seemed to revolve, vari-colored lights appeared. Without the telescope, the light appeared to be about the size of a croquet ball as compared with the stars. . . . What the objects were remained a question. According to the article, it was surely not an "aeroplane" because an aeroplane does not have a wheel, which revolves slowly. The same might be said of a dirigible balloon. And besides, there was no known aviation field in Colorado. . . . The article concluded, "is it then some genius who has discovered some new principle of flight, and is trying out his invention? It's your guess. What is it?"

Twenty years earlier, in 1896–1897, strange floating craft were seen across the United States. I had never heard of any sightings of these enigmatic "airships" in Colorado until Arlene sent along this curious three-line article from the April 30, 1897, *Buena Vista Republican*: "The mysterious air ship about what so much has been heard lately seem to have passed over BV and made it's appearance at GJ [Grand Junction]. If anyone here saw it, they have not the hardihood to make the fact known."

As various paranormal television programs have pointed out, the word *salida* means "gateway" in Spanish. Tim White, the host of the TV program *Sightings*, stated the following before broadcasting Edwards's Salida footage the following November, "It takes a lot to impress the *Sightings* investigative team, and what you're about to see is among the most intriguing footage we've ever broadcast."

Since his famous tape was shot, Edwards has become a local clearinghouse for reporting UFO sightings in the upper Arkansas River Valley. When sightings are occurring, calls pour in from all over the region, and Tim has managed to interview quite a number of witnesses about their experiences.

The synchronistic connection between the only two known daylight UFO films from south-central Colorado is undeniable. The fact that the filmmakers shared the name Edwards is compelling, and so is the time proximity: late August, when both the 1948 and 1995 films were taken. I am convinced that these connections are important, but I don't know how or why. I am working on it.

*   *   *

The Salida UFO sightings, over the course of the next six months, became sensational front-page news in the *Mountain Mail* with more than ten stories published about the area's many ongoing UFO reports. According to Edwards, "Dozens of people in Colorado and other states looked my name up and called to talk about sightings they witnessed through the fall. I only wish I had documented some of them better."

Intriguing peripheral events began to unfold around the Edwards property. He started to notice strange brand-new sedans with "government plates" lurking around his home, and during episodes of the area's sightings, he videotaped many military-style choppers buzzing overhead.

During two days of UFO activity in September, eagles showed up and wheeled on thermal currents over his house, while UFOs cavorted high above them in the sky. Edwards felt intuitively that this synchronicity was an important sign: "I have said since day one, the main craft was sending a message to the world; it was aware of our presence and *wanted* to be filmed. It [Edwards's sighting] was science and history at the top of the technological ladder; a two-thousand-year history was transpiring, and it was very important for the world to know the truth. It was almost as if it [the main craft] was showing us where to look in the sky for our subsequent filming. The bald eagles are a key part of the spiritualism and message conveyed through our sightings."

Three days after the first sighting he noted in his diary: "Smoke-alarm goes off in the master bedroom. Throughout the fall of 1995, our smoke alarms in numerous rooms went off independently of each other, even though they're all wired together." On September 15, 1995, he wrote in his diary: "I'm still trying to get myself calmed down. Still couldn't eat or sleep. I have lost 25 pounds." The strain of the pressure prompted him to think later, "I feared for my family's safety at first. We didn't have the luxury of a long-term conditioning process." The arrival of the unmarked sedans and choppers during subsequent sighting periods didn't alleviate the feelings of fear either.

Although I had decided initially not to attach my name publicly to the Salida sightings, I did quietly begin a process of investigation of the primary witness. According to several people who knew Tim, he had become obsessed with his sighting experience. Owning and operating a successful restaurant is time-consuming, hard work, yet Tim still found time to immerse himself into the politicized, kaleidoscopic world of ufology. Tim's innocent exuberance and riveting videotape were immediately embraced by several well-known researchers including Whitley Strieber.

Edwards started feeling something harder to explain: feelings of destiny, the compulsion of some kind of purpose. He felt he'd been chosen to see and videotape the "main craft." At first he had tried to attribute these feelings to the excitement of the event itself, but this didn't explain the rising obsession with UFOs and the unexplained. One might expect the effects of any experience gradually to fade, but in Tim's case, the experience increased and reverberated around inside of him, seeking a way out.

Tim continued to lose weight and spent countless sleepless nights, tossing and squirming in bed, not knowing what to do with himself. He had a checkup with his family doctor, but nothing lessened the underlying imperative to find out as much as he could about UFOs and why he was "chosen" to view them.

It was in this period that I met Tim. During the sec-

ond week of September, I did some serious checking
around for additional witnesses, and after talking with
Saguache County Sheriff Al King, I had learned of the
Cochetopa and Poncha Pass reports. Then, in the middle of a rousing round of golf with a couple of duffer
buddies, a Los Cumbre Golf Club worker walked over
while we were on the fourth tee box and casually mentioned the object that he had watched disappear into
Kit Carson Peak. This unsolicited report from a fifth witness left no doubt in my mind: It was time to give Tim
Edwards a call.

I went ahead and called Tim. He seemed to know
who I was. He was puzzled, even a bit miffed, as to
why it had taken me so long to contact him. I listened
carefully as he described his sighting and the subsequent ufological media circus that had erupted around
him. I told him that this was exactly why I hadn't contacted him. I wanted to observe the process of dissemination he'd set in motion, from as objective a
perspective as possible. Since I hadn't found out about
the case before the press ran with the story, I opted not
to get publicly involved right away.

He was very excited while describing the whirlwind
events to me. Even though he had become an instant
celebrity, I didn't get the sense that his excitement was
at all ego-motivated, or that he had dollar signs in his
eyes. He seemed genuine and matter-of-fact, but he
was convinced *he* had been chosen to tell the world.
"I'm one hundred percent convinced this is a craft from
another world. . . . There's no doubt in my mind. . . .
The time has come. *They* are here." Edwards feels that
he was personally allowed to videotape his sighting by
the pilots of the craft. It was now his duty to spread the
word far and wide. And spread it he did.

At last count, Tim has given away dozens of videotape copies of his footage and TV news shows covering the event, press releases, newspaper and magazine articles, and video analysis reports. He has been interviewed on countless media programs: trips back east to syndicated TV talk shows and a speaking engagement and a video showing at the International UFO Congress in Mesquite, Nevada. Even the king of tabloid TV, *Inside Edition*, produced a show on his experience.

He told me he had hired an entertainment agent to handle all the media inquiries concerning his remarkable footage. The agent, Michael Tanner, was also involved with a video analysis firm, Village Labs, in Tempe, Arizona, founded by video analyst Jim Dilletosso. Both men were very excited about the footage. According to a Tanner press release, Dilletosso is "a recognized authority on film and video image analysis technologies and their applications to purported UFO evidence."

I found out that Tim and his wife, Cheryl, were getting ready to drive to Arizona and hand deliver the master tape of his footage to Village Labs the following week. Edwards was very concerned about sending the tape and was extremely hesitant about conventional mail delivery services. To ease his fears, he had opted for hand delivery.

Michael Tanner released the following information in a press release dated September 19, 1996.

The Village Labs of Tempe, Arizona has just completed today its preliminary analysis on the extraordinary UFO videotape recently recorded by Tim Edwards of a large object in the skies over Salida, Colorado. Jim Dilletosso, the president-founder of Village Labs who is personally conducting what is planned to be an exhaustive analysis of the unique video footage, has concluded thus far that, ". . . it is certainly not lens flare, a reflection of some kind or any type of 'over the shoulder' optic aberration . . . it is definitely a very large, solid and three-dimensional, possibly cylindrical, object at high altitude. We don't know how large it is as yet, but the object clearly is emitting brilliant white and colored lights, is demonstrating unusually rapid, darting movements in the sky, and we have confirmed on the tape the presence of smaller objects coming from it which confirms the witnesses' visual accounts." . . . Further testing of the Edwards UFO footage at the Village Labs will include in-depth thermal and motion studies, image enhancement and enlargement as well as computer graphics simulations of the UFO event based on the spectrum of data collected and the results of analysis.

After he performed further video analysis, Dilletosso was interviewed by UPN's television show *Paranormal Borderline*, where he stated:

When analyzing video, we have to take this low-resolution image, transfer it to the computer, and begin to study whatever we can. First thing, remove the noise—take out the video noise; take out the lines, and then look for data. . . . We believe that the object is about a half-a-mile long, about [2,000] to 3,000 feet long and about 75,000 feet in the air. What does that compare to? 75,000 feet, fifteen miles. Fifteen miles in the air. Half-a-mile long, two Sears Towers stacked end-to-end. A huge object! This analysis reveals to us that there are definitely structures to the light. The data seems to support the concept that these are moving lights—moving with the pattern—moving with some intention—they move one direction, move back the other direction and the brightness of the lights tends to support what the witnesses said. . . . The fact that in 1917, and 1995, in Salida, Colorado, two people viewed . . . eighty years apart . . . the same thing. I think that's a remarkable coincidence. What if the method of transportation for these large objects to come to our planet involved, a coordinate, with very specific physical properties? Polarity, resonance, magnetism, and they lock on to it, and that's where they arrive. There could be some interstellar homing-beacon— either purposefully, or naturally located high in the Rocky Mountains.

Dilletosso told Channel Four News in Denver: "At a technical and visual level, I believe this to be a real object—not a mistake—a large object a great distance from the camera because it has the optical characteristics of a large object, and most importantly, it fits identical criteria of objects like this that have been seen all over the world. . . . I think this is a very large craft, piloted by people from another world, visiting earth."

Dilletosso was referring to film shot in Krasnodar, Russia, in 1990, the footage captured in San Francisco by John Bro, and videographer Tom King's Phoenix film of objects that appear similar to the craft witnessed over Salida.

Chip Peterson, an aerospace engineer specializing in computer enhancement and stabilization, was contacted by *Sightings* and asked to take a look at Edwards's video. He was interviewed for a segment on the Salida footage and came to a more cautious conclusion: "When you look at moving video, what you're actually seeing is thirty frames-per-second flipping on the screen very quickly, and that's what we've got right here. What you're seeing is the edge of each frame I had to stabilize by hand in the center of the screen." Peterson pointed to the object on the screen, which shows a completely stabilized gutter edge and the impressively darting craft that appears to move great distances effortlessly in the blink of an eye. "After you stabilize the image, you can see the motion much more clearly. Based on what I know of atmospheric flight, it doesn't look like any conventional aircraft." It sure doesn't. Once the wobbly, handheld movement is factored out of the image, the object's movements look virtually impossible to perform based on our understanding of conventional propulsion and inertia.

Another analyst was enlisted to scrutinize the footage for the television news-magazine *Inside Edition*. John Deturo is a video analyst working at the United States Military Academy in West Point, New York, who has actively debunked supposed UFO footage. Deturo was also convinced that the image on the video was a real, three-dimensional object flying at an extremely high altitude.

I coincidentally received a report the same day as Edwards's sighting, August 27, 1995, of "fifteen military planes flying in formation" low over the town of Blanca, Colorado. The day after the Edwards sighting, I received an interesting report of an "underground boom" called in by June Walkley, an Alamosa resident, who was convinced that the deep sound was not a sonic boom.

Since his initial sighting, Tim Edwards claims he has captured "thousands" of small, fleeting aerial objects flitting in the sky over Salida. In just one thirty-second clip, Edwards has taped literally hundreds of these anomalies zipping merrily about. Local skeptics have scoffed at the claim, saying he's just filming cottonwood particles and insects floating in the air, but this investigator is not thoroughly convinced of this explanation. Sure, during daytime skywatch sessions I've noticed some particulate matter floating by, but what about the spheres Edwards videoed that hover, reverse course, dash away, *against the wind?* Or the ones that break into several objects, then re-form? Or the larger spheres that climb high in the sky and disappear behind high-altitude clouds?

A week later, September 3, 1995, at 11:00 A.M., one of my former skeptics[1] reported seeing a silver disk while driving south on State Highway 17 into Alamosa. Much to his surprise, on his return trip two and one half hours later, he saw a "silver pencil-shaped object" high in the sky to the west. He called and rather sheepishly reported his two sightings.

Monday, September 25, 1995, proved to be an exciting day around the Edwards household. Tim's mother, Jean, saw them first. Tim told me, "She looked up in the sky and observed a tiny silver object near the sun." Tim immediately called the Chaffee County sheriff's office, and Officer Chester Price drove out to the house. Jean Edwards had been alerted by her husband to go outside and look up in the sky for anything unusual because the local FM radio station KVRH transmitter had inexplicably shut down. As Price arrived at the Edwards house, he noticed that a small group had gathered in the yard and were watching several objects dart around in the sky near the sun.

Price later was interviewed by KVRH and was quoted elsewhere as describing the objects as "bright and shiny silver objects traveling from north to south around the sun." He estimated that he witnessed up to ten objects. KVRH received four other calls reporting the objects. The *Mountain Mail* article the following day mentioned that the transmitter went off at 9:00 A.M. and came back on at about 9:45 A.M., and the station had no idea why it went down. When Edwards called the radio station to report the sighting, several curious station employees went outside to have a look. Joann Gleason and Pidge Cribari observed something shiny moving quickly across the sky. The radio tower just happens to be right next to the Cellular One tower on Methodist Mountain. The *Mail* called Cellular One manager Nedra Swope to see if anything unusual happened to their tower. "Swope said their signal went out at about 1:00 P.M. and was still out at 4:45 P.M."

Tim managed to get *three hours* of taped footage of the unknown objects cavorting around the sun. In the foreground, distracting insects, ragweed, and cottonwood fluff flit by the camera, but sure enough, way in the background, high in the sky, you can plainly see the silver objects traveling high above the clouds. There is no bit of fluff or insect that can be visible so far from the camera.

The time proximity of the objects' apparent arrival and the inexplicable crash of the radio tower is highly suggestive of a connection. Were the objects truly responsible for the shutdowns, or was it just another "coincidence"? One witness, while watching the mesmerizing objects in the sky, told bystanders that he was reluctant to leave the Edwards house because he might get into a wreck while driving because he'd be so busy looking up at the sky!

It would be quite an understatement to say that Tim was surprised that he was able to witness and videotape even more objects after his celebrated sighting on August 27. He told the *Mail*, "To see similar objects a second time was more than I ever expected." It would not be the last time he and his family would witness unusual aerial objects.

Tim summed up the impact of his experiences during an interview on my *Mysterious Valley Report* National Public Radio show on KRZA-FM and in an interview with D'Arcy Fallon, a reporter for the *Colorado Gazette-Telegraph*.

Back during the first sighting when we got the binoculars on the main craft, I had a very overwhelming feeling come over me. It was aware of our presence and wanted to be filmed and photographed. It was sending a message to the world, and it was very important for the world to know the truth. I think this goes all the way back into history. You've got your sun gods and apparitions by the sun; weird things have happened by the sun throughout history, and it's interesting that the main craft was also up by the rays of the sun, flying around for an hour and fifteen minutes, and then a month later, all the other solar corona activity begins. . . .

The first two months after my filming was a very emotional time for me. I didn't understand anything about ufology, and the whole thing was a kind of a spiritual awakening for me. People that have had major sightings, close encounters, abductions, this and that, don't have the luxury of a long-term conditioning process; they're conditioned in a matter of seconds. One second, you've never even thought about the subject [UFOs] the next second, there's the knowledge of higher things, the knowledge that reality is much more than we ever imagined. They put some feelings in me I've never had before. When I was looking through the binoculars at the main craft, I got, like, an electric impulse though my body. . . . Now, I'm convinced we're not alone. Not since Jesus was here has something so major come down. Most people are terrified that something could be out there.[2]

Edwards thinks there's a purpose behind these sightings. "The UFOs are buzzing the earth because they're concerned about its inhabitants, much like humans are curious about whales and dolphins." And how should we respond? "Brotherhood, universal love, and get rid of the nuclear stuff."

Tim admits that he's undergone an undeniable life change. "Since August 1995, all my free time is spent researching and trying to get the truth out to the public, and since I've become so involved, I've lost my privacy, but I've gained a lot of good people, the new friends I've met." He adds, "I guess I needed a hobby, or something. I've put a lot of money out of my pocket into this, and I'll continue to try and get my story out and make more people aware that there's a lot more things going on in the world. Most of us don't have a clue what's really going on out there."

Salida's reluctantly famous videographer-witness thinks networking is the key. "The Internet is the best thing that's ever happened to ufology. When there's a sighting in Japan, for instance, we can hear about it in a matter of a few seconds. This information can't be covered up anymore. . . . The people in the Salida area—the majority of them—take this subject matter real seriously, and my belief is that something very profound is happening. . . . Cosmic awareness is going to help put the world in a better direction."

The Tim Edwards saga continues. His hours of raw video footage await a patient expert with the time to wade through the tapes. Much of his subsequent footage is inundated with airborne debris; however, there are strange objects present in much of the additional footage. Several other visual oddities can be seen in some of his later footage from the spring of 1996. Beautiful sheets of spiderweblike material waft hypnotically through the frame in several shots. These sheets of material have no known origin, to my knowledge, nor do the bizarre segmented shapes, and my personal favorite, the Rocky Mountain flying fish. In two sequences, the viewer is treated to an undulating fish shape that wiggles quickly through the frame, above the house against the sky and clouds. Tim freeze-framed the image on the second-generation tape he gave me, and the unmistakable image of a fish is a big hit at my various speaking engagements. I suggest to audiences that the best way to catch one of these rare Rocky Mountain flying fish is to use a sky-blue Rapalla lure. That usually gets a chuckle or two.

Jose Escamilla, from Midway, New Mexico (just up the road from Roswell), captured the imagination of ufologists in March of 1994, when he announced that he, his wife Karen, and his sister Becky had been filming strange "rods" and other shapes and craft flying over their home. Some of the tape they've shot reminds me of the later Edwards solar footage. Peculiar, almost alive, the aerial creatures seem to dance and dart around the screen, and as far as I know, no one has adequately explained what these images are. Tim's tapes contain many of these perplexing images.

*   *   *

Could we be seeing simple video camera focus·distortion of airborne debris? Are they as-yet unidentified atmospheric life forms? Could they be astral or spirit creatures? Until now, no "expert" has even ventured a guess that can be proved. There are many mysteries whirling around us that we have yet to define, let alone comprehend, and as is usually the case, the assistance of genuine experts could be a great help.

As the chill fall air oozed into the high-mountain valleys in late September 1995, I felt a tension in the air. Something seemed ready to bust loose. I redoubled my efforts to keep informed and up to speed, and as I found out, I didn't have to wait long.

CHAPTER FOUR
WE KEEP OUR EYES TO THE SKY

Because of the close geographical connection between the San Luis Valley and four bioregions that surround the valley (the Upper Arkansas River Valley, the Espanola Valley/north-central New Mexico hill country, the Upper Rio Grande River Valley, and the Huerfano), I decided early on in my investigation to examine the Greater San Luis Valley region closely and identify any elements that tie these neighboring areas together.

Just over La Veta Pass, directly east of the middle of the San Luis Valley, is the Huerfano (Spanish for "orphan"). This beautiful diamond-shaped county is truly an undiscovered southern Colorado gem. The Huerfano extends from the eastern side of the Blanca Massif and the Great Sand Dune area, southeast down the eastern side of the Sangres almost to the New Mexico border, where it jogs straight east out onto the Front Range—past Walsenburg and then north to Colorado City.

Little-known, even to many Coloradans, the Huerfano is steeped in traditional mystery. One of the earliest Spanish treasure legends in all of Colorado is centered around West Spanish Peak (13,626 feet) and East Spanish Peak (12,683 feet), two ancient volcanoes

sitting side-by-side, apart from the Sangres, guarding
the southern Colorado Front Range landscape like two
giant sentinels. I examine these wondrous treasure legends later on in this book.

With a population of just over six thousand, most of the
northwestern Huerfano happens to lie underneath the
shadow of one of America's extensive military (flight)
operations areas.

FLYBOYS WITH TOYS

The end of the Cold War with the former Soviet Union
finds our Air Force flyboys with billions of dollars'
worth of aeronautical toys and no defined enemy to use
them against. We've spent many billions of dollars on
hardware, and our pilots need to train, but who (or
what) are we training our pilots to do battle with? Use
'em or lose 'em seems to be the rationale. Either we
give our fighter pilots flight time, or we lose them to the
airlines. With thousands of sorties costing millions of
dollars, the Air Force is conducting business as usual in
the skies over the Huerfano. So are the multinational
arms developers who supply the toys. The F-22 has
now officially joined our arsenal of state-of-the-art aerial weapons systems as our most advanced "conventional" fighter plane.

There are legitimate arguments against so much aerial activity. Accidents do happen, and during a seven-
day period in September 1997, six United States
military aircraft crashed, including an F-117A stealth
fighter, which narrowly missed taking out spectators at
an air show in Virginia. Except for air show appearances and other exhibition flying, our flyboys scream

around in designated flight areas where training and simulated aerial war games are conducted.

As mentioned in *TMV*,[1] the La Veta Military Operations Area (MOA) covers the low-level airspace over parts of Huerfano, Custer, Saguache, Alamosa, Costilla, Chaffee, and Pueblo counties. Air Force and National Guard flight operations are conducted here almost daily.

For reasons not clearly stated, the government wants to expand our country's MOAs. Why? According to the Huerfano Valley Citizen's Alliance, a group dedicated to stopping expansion of the MOA:

> The Colorado Airspace Initiative (CAI) is the tip of the iceberg in an alarming trend—the military's insatiable appetite for new land to disrupt for practical maneuvers. The Military already controls an estimated 50% of the airspace in the U.S., and owns many millions of acres. The proposed CAI is only one of multiple initiatives for Military Operations Areas in the United States. . . . Huerfano County has already served as an aerial playground for the military since the late 1970's, when the La Veta MOA was approved. According to Air National Guard figures, the current utilization of the La Veta MOA is 2,929 sorties (individual jet missions) per year. Under the New Colorado Airspace Initiative proposal, not only will the number of sorties be increased to at least 3,120 per year, but the majority of these missions will be authorized to fly as low as 100 feet above the ground. An F-111 or F-16 flight directly overhead at 600 miles per hour is a bone-rattling, and brain-numbing experience. . . . The National Guard's rationalization for the proposed change is that modern warfare techniques require pilots to be

skilled in low-altitude, radar-evasive techniques. In addition to the low-altitude training, the new proposal will allow for every variety of air combat training, including "dog-fights," involving two to eight aircraft. The National Guard also anticipates releasing approximately 10,000 flares yearly as part of these maneuvers. Supposedly, the flares will "largely disintegrate" before they hit the ground. The plan calls for revised military training routes (MTR). These training routes are meant to be "aerial highways" for low-altitude flights at high speeds. The are *five major proposed air corridors*—all converge at a point near Gardner—then proceed north over Greenhorn Mountain to the Airburst Range near Ft. Carson where the pilots "complete their weapons delivery mission." This means that *Huerfano County will be the most heavily impacted area* under the new plan.[2] [Emphasis in the original]

This expansion does not make sense. The United States is not planning to go to war with any other country. Our Air Force is considered the very best and faces no perceived challenges anywhere on the planet. Why greatly increase the military operations flight area here in the Huerfano?

The following was published by the Open Space Alliance, a coalition of regional citizens' groups opposing expansion of the La Veta MOA. "The Air National Guard's (ANG) proposal, which started as the Red Eye Complex and evolved into the Colorado Airspace Initiative, revamps more military airspace in Colorado and Kansas than any other ANG project in the country." That means southern Coloradans are among the most impacted by these proposed expansions.

Backpacker Magazine stated in its April 1994 issue,

"There will also be no restrictions on the future use of Colorado's airspace by other branches of the military, leaving the skies permanently vulnerable."

Not only are "other branches of the military" interested in Colorado airspace, a new development, pointed out in an advertisement published by the Custer County Action Association, now concerns many area residents. "The people of Germany wouldn't tolerate low-altitude military overflights. Their property values, personal safety and quiet country-sides were all being destroyed. In peacetime. So the Luftwaffe had to leave. Guess where they went? Right here. The German Air Force will be flying out of New Mexico and over our mountains, valleys and national wilderness areas as part of the 'Colorado Airspace Initiative.' . . . They've sold our skies."

Amazing. The Front Range of Colorado reaps the rewards of an annual influx of billions of dollars, and the citizens of the SLV and the Huerfano, who gain nothing, have to tolerate the many ear-splitting overflights, some of them even conducted by foreign air forces!

Another article, published in the *Crestone Eagle* in May 1997 and written by OSA advocate Pat Richmond, addresses the probability that *unconventional*, secret aircraft are being flown here.

[The April 5–11, 1996, edition of] the Denver Business Journal (DBJ) has revealed in a cover to cover exposé that Pentagon "black" dollars are being channeled into Colorado's Front Range communities. Labeled the "hottest news story of the year," the journal's investigation and analysis of "Colorado's Stealth Economy" identified companies and agencies within Colorado that serve as a "spy-hub" for the nation. Economic analyst Henry Dubroff wrote, "make no mistake about it. The most important city in Colorado is Washington D.C." . . . While the DJB report may seem like hot news to some, residents on both sides of the Sangres know there have been unusual aircraft in our airspace for quite some time. Sightings of Stealth bombers or F-117s or black helicopters repeatedly have been brought to the attention of COANG's Brig. Gen. Mason C. Whitney. He seemed to know nothing about military operations by "secret aircraft" yet the DJB article makes it clear that the Colorado Air National Guard not only coordinates secret flights but also serves as landlord for the Pentagon's spy hub.

Without a doubt, the military is conducting undisclosed flights and aerial maneuvers in and around Colorado. With the second-largest source of state income being utilized and spent by the intelligence agencies and military in Colorado, you would think they would concentrate their activities in the remotest areas of the state. That may mean here in the San Luis Valley and possibly elsewhere in the state.

Pat Richmond wrote a follow-up article in the February 1997 *Crestone Eagle*, which pointed out the possibility that many of our nocturnal anomalous light sightings are very terrestrial in nature. Richmond also uncovered information concerning military air and ground operations conducted in the Rio Grande National Forest:

Open Space Alliance has discovered the existence of an Inter-Agency Agreement between the Department of Defense and the Rocky Mountain Regional Office of the National Forest Service [Department of

Agriculture] that could explain "strange lights" and other puzzling "phenomena" that periodically appear in the night skies of the San Luis Valley and surrounding areas. Contrary to media coverage promoting speculation about UFOs, some residents in the SLV, including retired military personnel familiar with Pentagon activities and procedures, have long believed that most night sky "sightings" are connected to military operations such as experimental testing of prototype craft, routine training maneuvers, or special aircraft used to provide coordinates for tracking and/or retrieving missiles launched from Ft. Wingate or White Sands. . . . "Is there an agreement between the military and the Forest Service that would allow night training activities within the Rio Grande National Forest?" Ron Jablonski—Rio Grande National Forest public relations officer . . . decided that he could not allow Richmond to see the document because it was "just a Draft. . . ." Jablonski stated the agreement between the military and the forest service would permit small groups such as the Green Berets to engage in special forces training within the forest. He emphasized that any activities involving helicopters or other aircraft over Wilderness Areas would have to go the National Environmental Protection Agency process and would require approval all the way to the top—the Regional Forest Supervisor. . . . Although Jablonski denied knowing the specifics of a finalized document, he referred to training activities being limited to times outside hunting season. He also offered the comment that trainees would not use laser weapons, but lasers might be used for locating or targeting either aircraft or ground personnel.

I find it ironic that similar assertions in *The Mysterious Valley* suggesting that a high percentage of the San Luis Valley's so-called nocturnal UFO sightings may be due to secret military activity have not been acknowledged by the media and opponents of the MOA. It's tough investigating in the realm of the sensational unknown; people assume you are "a UFO crazy" running around claiming "the Martians have landed." My hunch publicly has always been that the government is utilizing the San Luis Valley high ground for "secret" projects.

It would stand to reason that certain cutting-edge military technologies may be so fantastic in appearance that witnesses might think they were seeing something "otherworldly." This potential for misperception could also be used by the operators of these exotic technologies to examine their secret toys' impact on unsuspecting witnesses. Why not trot out new technology in a remote region and gauge the resulting perceptions as they filter into culture through the media? The military would want to know: What was reported? By whom? How was it perceived? How do the media and law enforcement view the claims? Do they publicize them? Do they put a spin on them? This rationale explaining some (but not all) of our UFO sightings may have more than passing relevance.

One underlying probability always needs to be considered. Something else has apparently been flying around here for hundreds, perhaps thousands of years, and no matter how hard the skeptic in me might try, the above hypothetical government-military scenario *cannot* explain away all our sightings.

We do know that the military has conducted operations here in the past. An ex-employee of the Rio Grande National Forest told me in 1993 that the military conducted secret maneuvers during the late fall, in the inaccessible Upper Sand Creek Lake region of the Sangres, back in the early 1980s. He was asked to "clean up" their mess strewn around the fragile environment after the troops departed. He saddled up and headed out with a pack horse and barely escaped disaster when an early blizzard bludgeoned the mountains. He was "lucky to make it out."

Other accounts tell of the "C.I.A. training Tibetan nationals" up on the Blanca Massif back in the mid-1960s, and an ex–county undersheriff mentioned to me that "Aryan groups" were known to train in remote, inaccessible areas in the Sangres.

My incidental sighting on January 23, 1995, of what appeared to be three military planes flying side by side, traveling west, and flashing synchronized strobe lights sequentially down the leading edge of all three aircraft may be tied to these "secret" nighttime operations. The reports I have fielded of helicopters or other craft shining intense spotlights at civilian cars on the ground in an unusually provocative and aggressive manner may also be tied to these maneuvers.

There's no question that our military "boys with toys" are utilizing this region's airspace as extensively and efficiently as possible, and it's even available to other countries, at a price, regardless of what our local civilian population thinks.

When examining all the elements that may be at work and play here, one must keep in mind we are dealing with a highly complex scenario. This potential for misidentification tempers my reaction to all "anomalous light" reports from the eastern side of the Sangres over the La Veta MOA and, for that matter, all of southern Colorado and northern New Mexico.

THE HUERFANO

Many reports of the sublime and unexplained from this forgotten corner of Colorado would've been lost to the murky seas of time had it not been for the dogged efforts of resident journalist-theorist David Perkins, a twenty-three-year veteran investigator of the cattle mutilation and UFO phenomena. "Izzy Zane," as he's known to his many friends, has lived and explored the Huerfano since 1970. One of the original independent "mute" investigators from the mid-1970s, Izzy has wrestled toe to toe for years with a formidable opponent: the tar baby called "the cattle mutilation phenomenon." In my estimation, Izzy has applied the most original thinking concerning the true nature of this much-ignored, high-strange phenomenon, which I cover in a later chapter. Many of his stickiest, most perplexing cases have occurred right where he lives, in the heart of Colorado's Huerfano. One puzzling series of Huerfano events best illustrates the complexity inherent in the UFO reports from this forgotten region of south-central Colorado.

The third week in September 1995, I received a call from resident Barbara Adkins. A woman with a lifelong interest in the paranormal, in 1993 she had heard through the local grapevine about my investigative work and has subsequently supplied me with leads concerning periodic Huerfano County sightings. She called with a sense of urgency, which I picked up right away. She said, "I'm here with someone who really needs to talk with you." A friend of Barbara's named Jeannie Shaw got on the phone.

FRIDAY, SEPTEMBER 22, 1995, 8:45 P.M.

The Navajo Estates subdivision sits on a small ridge east
of Silver Mountain, in the middle of Huerfano County,
with a commanding view of the long, sloping plain that
stretches toward Walsenburg.

Resident Jeannie Shaw, her fifty-two-year-old sister
Loni Smith, and Jeannie's two grown children in their
twenties are finishing up dinner. It's a beautiful evening
in the Colorado mountains. The few clouds in the sky
to the west drift majestically over the nearby Sangre de
Cristos, which are silhouetted in a lean alpine glow.
Almost imperceptibly, Jeannie begins to feel a "deep,
low humming sound" over the house, which sits on a
ridge east of La Veta Pass. After several seconds, her
sister Loni, who is visiting, looks toward the window.
She turns, and the sisters look at each other in quizzical
silence. Someone asks rhetorically, "What *is* that
sound?" The sound seems to be growing louder and
appears to be headed from the east, right in their direction. Jeannie's two kids bolt from the dinner table and
head to the window as dogs in the subdivision begin to
howl and bark. Now joined by the two sisters, together
the four of them peer out into the darkening sky. The
vibration grows steadily louder, and they can feel the
sound reverberating inside them more than they can
actually hear it. Then, outside the window, movement.
They can't believe their eyes! A huge lumbering craft
is rumbling slowly past their location at treetop level
"sixty to seventy feet" above their gaping mouths. The
four incredulous witnesses rush out onto the porch,
which affords them a picturesque view of their new
skyborne neighbor, the "hundred-*yard*-wide rectangle"

flying east over the Shaws' vibrating house.

Almost instinctively Robert, Jeannie's son, dashes down the porch stairs. He stops momentarily and before better judgment sets in runs down the arroyo stretching down the hill, attempting to keep up with, and get a better look at, the underside of the "monstrous" craft. Loni begins waving her arms theatrically from the porch, shouting at the slowly departing ship, "Here we are, here we are!" In horror, a very serious Jeannie punches her in the arm and tells her, "Shut up, . . . or they'll beam us up!"

Over the next eight to twelve minutes, the witnesses watch the craft fly slowly east, then loop around to the west where it disappears behind a ridge. A bright white light then rises over the ridge, flares, and blinks out. In a few short moments, eight to ten blinking lights appear over the ridge and begin flying in a crisscrossing pattern over the area.

"My legs buckled; I screamed. It was in our faces . . . I just couldn't believe it," said Jeannie Shaw later. "There were yellow and white lights oscillating around the front, which was rounded, and my son ran down the driveway underneath the object and kept up with it . . . that's how slow it was flying." She added, "As it moved away from us, we could see red lights on the rear. They looked just like giant Cadillac taillights." Loni added, "I never thought about UFOs before, but I'll tell you, we keep our eyes to the sky now."

Shaw estimated the object sighting at about eight to twelve, maybe as long as fifteen minutes before they lost sight of it. "We were so amazed, we really didn't time how long we watched it."

After an immediate call from Shaw, a neighbor corroborated their observations. Something mighty strange was going on. Shaw called the Huerfano County sheriff's office. According to Shaw, a bored-sounding deputy fielded her excited call. She was told, rather bluntly, that the officers on duty had also heard the low, rumbling sound (it had apparently rattled the sheriff's office windows) but not to worry about it. It was only "a helicopter." A bit perturbed, Shaw also contacted the *Huerfano World* newspaper and was told the paper had called the Walsenburg, Colorado, police department about the excited reports and was told "it was *two* helicopters." Shaw has a very hard time believing this explanation. "This thing looked like *the* mother ship," she told me. "How could they say it was only a helicopter?"

If this is a simple, mundane example of what our military is testing over civilian areas of the country, I don't wonder at all why the Cold War is over. If we have technology that can propel a three-hundred-foot rectangle at single-digit speeds, it's no wonder the Soviet Union and the Eastern Bloc countries opted out of the superpower game and are now playing catch-up—wrestling with establishing free-market economies instead of investing in trillion-dollar defense budgets.

The Shaws were apparently not the only area residents who witnessed the large bargelike craft lumbering over the verdant Huerfano. Jeannie rattled off the names and numbers of other witnesses who saw the strange, giant rectangle. One woman who lives about two miles away from Shaw, told reporter D'Arcy Fallon of the *Colorado Gazette-Telegraph* that she was just getting ready for bed when she heard a low humming noise and figured it was a helicopter. But the sound persisted, and her dogs were going wild. She looked out the window and gasped. Like Shaw, her knees buckled. "It was huge. I saw it going over the trees. It

was a shock to see something that big. I thought, holy
s__t, what is that?"

Shaw (and this investigator) have located even more
area residents who saw and/or heard the giant craft that
moonless Friday night, and in the process we found out
about other recent sightings in the La Veta, Colorado,
area.

HUERFANO CATTLE EXPERIMENTS

After almost an eight-month lull in cattle mutilations
reports, our mystery perpetrators may have returned to
the Huerfano and the greater San Luis Valley. But did
they ever leave? Our intrepid Huerfano investigator David Perkins related to me the following report, and we
both wondered if these were just the tip of the iceberg.

On Tuesday, September 26, 1995, Gardner, Colorado, rancher Larry Chacon found his old horse Whiskey dead with a six-inch-diameter perfect circle rectum
coring; half the tongue had been removed with a clean
diagonal slice; the upper eye was "sucked out"; and
the hair and hide were "blackened and stiff" as if heat
had been applied. As per usual, no additional tracks,
footprints, signs of predators, or a struggle were noted.

The Huerfano County sheriff's office investigated the
report, which occurred about fifteen miles north of
where the hundred-yard rectangle was seen by Huerfano residents earlier on September 22. Incidentally,
the horse was found in the same area where *San Luis
Valley Publishing* reporter Barry Tobin and I happened
to find an unclaimed dead and cut-up horse in March
1995.

Chacon had been renting grazing pasture from an
old "hermit" who had told him of strange activities on

the remote ranchland on the eastern slopes of the Sangre de Cristos. The old man told investigator David Perkins he had also "seen ships in the sky" over the ranch
and even claimed that one had landed near his cabin
a couple of years ago. He said "two bearded human-
looking" beings had appeared from the craft and
"floated" toward his cabin, shining a very bright spotlight. The man claimed that when they pointed the light
at his cabin, "the light went through the wall." Holding
a gun, he said he was blinded and paralyzed as the light
illuminated the inside of his cabin. The hermit noted
that the two beings were "not from around here."

To the northeast, during this same end of September
time period, Douglas County officials are investigating
a two-year livestock-killing spree on the Mike and
Kandy Toll ranch. The Tolls claim that thirty sheep and
a bull calf have been killed on their Franktown, Colorado, champion sheep spread. "The animals have been
brutalized, led astray, and possibly poisoned."

According to a *Denver Post* article, Douglas County
Sergeant Attila Denes said, "The Tolls hadn't reported
the incidents in the past because they had hoped they
would just go away, but it looks like she had several
incidents this week that made her think it over. A
seventy-pound lamb that drowned Wednesday would
have had to be lifted and placed in the three-foot tank
with its head held down in only 3 1/2 inches of water."

A neighbor claims to have found all her turkeys
locked in a hot enclosure with no food or water. She
said, "I hope it's not people just killing for the sheer
meanness of it." Good point. Why on earth were these
animals killed?

I bring up these recent Colorado stories to illustrate
the probable involvement of vandals in some cases in-

volving the mysterious killing of animals. I wonder where human culpability ends and nonhuman culpability begins.

In these unrelated Douglas County cases, law enforcement (and the ranchers) suspect someone in the rapidly growing suburban community around the Tolls' ranch. But I'm getting ahead of myself. I'll theorize about these mysterious animal deaths later on in the book.

GOOD MORNING!

The third weekend in September 1995, my rock band Laffing Buddha and I were wrapping up recording lead guitar tracks over an all-day, ten-hour session lasting late into Sunday night. We were able to book an eight-hour session the next day, Monday, and we were staying at guitarist Chris Medina's Uncle Frank's house, about five miles south of the studio. A veteran Denver firefighter, Uncle Frank has given us a standing invitation for the band to stay at his house whenever we're in town. So that night we finished recording and headed back to his house to recharge for the next day's session.

Uncle Frank Archuleta lives in a rambling ranch-style house with a guest bedroom at one end of the house, a spare bedroom used for storage at the other end of the house, and a master bedroom in the basement. Three of us make the trip, Frank's nephew Chris Medina, guitarist George Oringdulph, and me. As producer, I make every recording and mixing session. After settling in and joking around a bit, we bid Uncle Frank good night and arrange ourselves unceremoniously on the floor in the guest bedroom: me on the futon in my mummy bag, George at the end of the futon in his sleeping bag, and Chris to my right, in front of the bedroom door. He completely blocks the door in his sleeping bag as we drowsily watch a trashy movie on a big-screen TV at the foot of the futon and crack the usual cynical jokes. I suggest that we change the channel, and we begin to watch a "live" performance clip of a Texas alternative band named the Toadies. They thrash away on a local access show, as I quickly fade into slumber after the intense day of recording. The last thing I recall is Chris asking George, "How can a band like *that* get a record deal?"

The next thing I know, I wake up shivering. I blink and look around in the predawn light hesitantly glowing in the window, confused as to why I am out of my mummy bag and lying on a bare mattress. Where am I? I get up and immediately fall off the bed and stumble on some packing boxes. I am very confused. I fell asleep on a futon located on the floor. I awake a foot and a half off the ground. I gingerly tiptoe my way out of the storage bedroom, around boxes, file cabinets, weight sets, and bicycles, and head out into the hall. I woke up in the wrong room! What the hell is going on? I shake the remaining vestiges of sleep out of my befuddled head and trudge down the hall back to the guest bedroom. Now, fully awake, I try to enter, but Chris is snoring, and his prone form is blocking the door. I give the door a couple of knocks, and Chris has to get up to let me in. My mummy bag is lying undisturbed on the futon, and Chris is asking me, "Why are you banging on the door so early?" I feel an itching behind my left ear and start to scratch it, when I notice a large, rather painful bump. I mumble some kind of excuse to Chris, apologize for waking him up so early, and head into the bathroom to look behind my ear. In the mirror, I can barely see the hard, red bump and peel off a small scab just behind my ear. It's a dried clot of blood about the size of the head of a pin. Was it a bug bite? I head back to the guys, who are both starting to wake up. "Chris, do you remember me getting up and leaving the room last night?"

"No, I never had to move all night that I can remember."

"George, how about you?"

"I don't remember anyone leaving, I slept like a log," he answers.

"Then how did I end up down the hall in the storage room?" What was wrong with this picture? Chris would've had to move in order to let me out, even to hit the bathroom. He was completely blocking the door all night.

"Guys, this is really weird. Are you sure that both of you don't remember me leaving the room?"

Chris sleepily looks at me with his customary dirt-eating grin and says, "Maybe you were abducted or something . . ." He laughs.

That's exactly what was running through my mind, but I tell myself not to jump to any conclusions.

I run the whole late-evening scenario through my brain a second time. We'd all been pretty tired and I maybe remember the movie and a song or two from the Toadies, but how did I manage to exit the room without disturbing my two band mates? Now that I think about it, I don't remember having to get up at all during the night to go to the bathroom or get a drink of water, which is very unusual. I usually wake up a lot at night, especially when I'm not at home. The tight-fitting mummy bag, lying on the futon, is still zipped all the way up, which makes it very difficult to get out of. In the morning, I usually end up twisted around in the

tight-fitting bondage bag. I admit I'm convinced something strange transpired that night, but we have an important session all day, and I refuse to make a big deal
out of the experience. I can't stand it when I lose my
focus. But I do casually quiz both George and Chris
later that day during a break in recording. Neither of
them remembers one of us getting up, and we laugh
the episode off.

It's three weeks later and we're back in Denver. Laffing
Buddha was pumped. We had two ten-hour sessions
back-to-back, October 18 and 19, at Time Capsule. It's
"mix-dòwn" time, when the results of all the hard work
are realized in sonic form.

The mixes are starting to click, and I looked forward
to celebrating that night with Littleton resident Shari
Adamiak, associate director of the Center for the Study
of Extraterrestrial Intelligences (CSETI). Shari and I have
become good friends since our initial Crestone meeting
in the late summer of 1993. Soon after, Shari told Dr.
Steven Greer, director of CSETI, about the San Luis
Valley, and together with Shari, Dr. Greer attended a
miniconference in 1993 and conducted the first of several CSETI training intensives in Crestone in 1994.[3]
Both are very taken by our magical Valley and visit
often. Shari had dropped by the studio a couple of times
over the course of the three-month recording sessions
and seemed to like the band and our tunes. I looked
forward to playing a cassette of our newly mastered
songs on her nice home stereo.

During our visit to her tasteful top-floor apartment
with its panoramic view, Shari introduces me to the
Internet and shows me several paranormal-related sites.
I had my first international chat with a friend of Shari's
in Australia and an "experiencer" in Canada. At one

point, I mentioned the strange circumstances of the band's previous Denver trip, three weeks prior, and showed her the still-visible hard lump. She noticed that there was still swelling. I joked that a spider bite usually doesn't last three weeks. She didn't know what to make of the incident either and offered no theories.

The slight swelling lasted two months. The bump slowly reduced in size and ended up becoming a small, hard scar behind my ear. It's still there.

One incident that occurred while I was very young still puzzles me after all these years. It was around 1964 and Ann, one of my older sisters, had just moved out of the house, and I had just moved to her upstairs bedroom with my brother. We shared a built-in bunk bed on the south wall, with a four-by-five-foot window on the eastern side of the room that overlooked the back-yard. I had the top bunk. I remember waking one night to an intermittent rattling noise. I opened my eyes and immediately noticed a fluorescent light green glow faintly bathing the ceiling from a light source that seemed to be coming from outside, toward the front of the house. Looking for the source of the rattling noises, I was amazed to see the two drawers in the bed stand next to the bottom bunk floating in and out of the drawer openings. For some reason, this didn't seem strange to me. It was exciting! The green-colored glow seemed to be coming from the downstairs windows in the living room, which had magnificent sixteen-foot-high picture windows.

I tiptoed down the upstairs hallway and down the four steps into the front door entrance hall, then peered out toward the front of the house. I will never forget this image. To the southwest, there was a uniform overcast sky as far as I could see, about ten to twelve miles. The Seattle skyline was bathed in its customary incandescent glow, when I noticed that clouds about halfway across the lake were pulsing the weird green color. Suddenly, like magic, first one, then two perfect discs emerged from the cloud layer and began to head directly toward the water, curving to the east, directly in my direction. Disturbed clouds even trailed after as they broke through the cloud layer and headed down toward the water. I remember being transfixed . . . then nothing! The experience stands alone, out of context, in my childhood. I don't even remember much of what happened around that particular time period in my life as a first grader at Medina Elementary.

I told my brother about this "dream" experience in Boston in 1988, and the hair stood up on his arms as I described the green saucer shapes bursting down through the clouds and heading across the lake. He broke out in a visible shiver and said, "Of course, that was *you*!" I asked him what he meant. He told me that he had the exact same dream as a kid, but he thought he was watching himself, looking out the window. "I thought it was me standing there. Remember we had those blue and white striped pajamas when we were little? That was *you*!" I still don't know what to make of this apparent shared "dream" experience. This particular lucid dream, if that's what it was, is etched deeply in my memory.

Brendan and I have talked at length about several other shared dreams and experiences we didn't know we both had as kids. These "magical" childhood experiences may be examples of what author Colin Wilson called in an *Atlantis Rising* magazine interview "a kind of three dimensional consciousness, contrasting with the ordinary two-dimensional humdrum consciousness." We seem to de-evolve out of this three-dimensional consciousness as we grow and inevitably acquire layer upon layer of experience. He suspects that this fresh, childlike three-dimensional perception of reality may be an important key to understanding our vast potential as sentient beings.

Wilson's interviewer stated: "Wilson believes that we are on the threshold of a time when we will be able to find the kind of balance between modern rational thought and the ancient intuitive knowledge that will enable us 'to become masters of peak experience.' " Wilson intuits that this imprinted innocence may even be a clue to help us understand legendary megalithic cultures that lived tens of thousands of years ago in harmony with themselves and their environment until entropy and/or a cataclysm destroyed their "golden age."

I cannot simply discount several of my "magical," unexplainable childhood experiences. They have provided my existence with an undeniable context upon which to bounce all subsequent experience. But as I become older, and I hope wiser, I feel compelled not to read anything into these experiences that could adversely affect my so-called philosophic objectivity. I could, like many people, convince myself that these events never happened, but that's not how, as an individual, I perceive and react to my own "layers of experience." We can all only dance according to our individual perception of the song.

September 21, 1979, New Paltz, New York. College town, New York State. Brendan and I and two girlfriends head north from the Big Apple to visit several friends at the State University at New Paltz and to attend a Gentle Giant concert. Since the mid-1970s, English art-rock had fascinated me. Bands like Genesis, Pink Floyd, Yes, and Emerson, Lake and Palmer constantly graced my turntable. Gentle Giant, one of the more "out there" bands even by progressive standards, was one of my favorites. What other group could go from a heavy-metal band to an a cappella group to a chamber ensemble in one song? Then switch instruments with each other for the next song?

What a show! The crowd was mesmerized by the band's kaleidoscopic performance and a bit puzzled by the drummer's questionable stand-up comic routine, featuring non sequitur hemorrhoid jokes. The show ended with a rousing finale, and our group of six friends, ranging in age from eighteen to twenty-two, headed rambunctiously down the hill to skywatch in the center of the New Paltz athletic field, before carpooling to a party outside of town.

It was nice to get out of the city, breathe the fresh air, and really see the sky. I lay down on my back with my hands behind my head and basked in the starlight, picking out constellations and planets.

Suddenly I noticed five orange points of light, straight overhead, that seemed to drift in the sky pretending to be stars. They were definitely 1+ magnitude in brightness and about the size of a planet. I watched for several seconds to make sure my eyes weren't playing tricks on me. Sure enough, they were moving. As soon as I realized this, they stopped, then dimmed slightly. They were hiding. I felt sure that for some reason they had responded to my awareness of them.

I casually mentioned them to my friends, who initially paid no attention. They were too busy horsing around. Finally, my brother Brendan looked up long enough to see what I was describing, and the rest of the group began to watch.

The lights just milled around for several minutes with no discernible pattern to their movement. Brendan suggested that we communicate with them. At first, everyone laughed, but I was able to convince the group to lie on the field while Brendan traced out geometric shapes out of our line of sight behind us. We watched the objects closely. First, Brendan traced out a square. I stood in the middle to verify. Sure enough, the lights quickly arranged themselves into a square. I gave a running monologue. "Yep, now the one on the right is moving closer to the one on the left, while Mr. Lower left is heading toward Mrs. Lower right. . . ." You get the picture.

Next, Brendan traced out a circle. The objects obliged us and formed a circle high in the sky. I was watching, when someone asked rhetorically, "I wonder why they don't come closer." Brendan exclaimed, "Look!" The objects appeared to rush downward toward us. They became larger and brighter. Someone said something like, "No, not that close," and they slowly appeared to gain altitude. This brought out oohs and aahs from everyone. Brendan quickly traced out a triangle. Again, unbelievably, the lights responded in kind. It seemed almost unreal the way we were obviously communicating with lights in the sky. I suggested, jokingly, that he try "three wavy lines," a play on the parapsychology test card.

We stayed for a while longer watching the objects drift around, and like typical kids, I'm embarrassed to say, *we got bored and went to the party!* I reminded everyone the following day about our experience, and no one thought it had been a big deal. "Ya, that was kinda cool man, playing with the UFOs. . . ."

CHAPTER FIVE

CHASING COWS IN UFO CENTRAL

In *The Mysterious Valley*, I attempted to convey to the reader the on-the-ground intensity of our waves of UFO-type phenomena and unusual cattle deaths and the resulting effect these events have on the many witnesses and ranchers. When things are really popping around here, I'm run ragged trying to keep up with all the interviews, phone calls, site visits, and subsequent investigative work. I'm sorry to say that without working at it full time during intense periods of activity, there's just no way for one investigator to keep up in the San Luis Valley. There are countless reports and cases sliding off into the ghostly realm of undocumented history. I try not to think about all the cases that go by without proper attention.

The fall of 1995 found the greater San Luis Valley experiencing twenty "UFO" reports that included silvery objects, full-moon-size green orbs, swarms of small blinking lights, pencil-shaped craft, along with the usual variety of fireballs and streaking nighttime phenomena. As the Report Log in Chapter Twelve shows, many of these UFO reports occurred on the night animals were supposedly mutilated. There were five unusual animal death cases investigated during this time period, all with a regional correlation to attendant UFO and in one case military helicopter sightings.

One fall 1995 UAD deserves mention. I investigated this covered-up case that probably occurred on Sunday, October 8.

The following day, October 9, I received a call from a Blanca, Colorado, skywatcher who told me of a fresh case that may have been discovered the previous morning. As I rearranged my schedule for the day and then headed out the door for the two-hundred-mile round-trip drive, I hoped that this call was legitimate. I've been burned on more than a few.

The amazing distances locals must travel here every day are mind-boggling to most folks from outside of the Valley. Sixty miles to the nearest hospital, supermarket, movie theater etc., is the norm in many locales, and a two-hour drive to investigate a report is just part of the territory. The call came in, and I responded. Evidently, the rancher had discovered a cow "missing her rear end and bag" on his ranch the morning of the ninth and thought it had been killed Sunday night. I learned of the case from the rancher's sister the following day and she arranged for us to go to the ranch that afternoon. I made the two-hour drive with my brother Brendan and a friend of ours.

The fall colors of the aspen groves blazed up the mountain's sides like wide swaths of brilliant golden patchwork as we headed around the huge Blanca Massif. The air had a bite to it, and it was obvious that winter's chill embrace was lurking around the frigid mountaintops, waiting for the opportunity to cover the low-lying areas with a furry blanket of frost.

Upon arriving at the remote, idyllic ranch, it quickly became apparent that the rancher was a no-show. His sister introduced us to his wife, who claimed she hadn't gone out to see the animal since her first look at it that morning. I noticed a large, beautiful horse limping badly in a small pasture across the driveway. I asked the sturdy Hispanic woman what had happened to the animal. She told me they weren't sure what was wrong, but it happened the same night the cow had been killed. The corral area where the cow was supposedly found was empty. No sign of a carcass. We found large tire tracks indicating that a tractor had been used in the area recently. We decided to cover the front part of the ranch and look for a bone pile while waiting for the rancher to show up. The rancher inexplicably ducked our meeting. He never showed.

His wife was puzzled by his absence, claiming, "If he told you he'd be here, he should be here." We easily found where the animal had lain, less than one hundred feet from the house, and we found the drag marks and tractor tracks, but no dead cow. She described the condition of the vanished cow but claimed she didn't know who had moved it or what had happened to it. Another mystery.

I found out that evening, when I called the rancher, that he claimed the government had told him to bury it. He was told "it was an environmental hazard." According to the rather brusque Hispanic man, the officials had told him to keep the animal's death quiet. He had reluctantly admitted the animal's discovery and mumbled an excuse for not showing up for our meeting. He had told me during our initial conversation, "We found her right behind the corral, just a few feet away from the house. My dogs never even barked." I could tell he was nervous even talking with me about his dead cow.

It's interesting to note that it's a common practice in the San Luis Valley to leave your dead livestock on a bone pile or simply right where it dies. Carcasses from the 2 to 3 percent of all grazing animals that routinely die every year can be found lying in repose in the vast pastures of the San Luis Valley. It can literally take years for some carcasses finally to melt into the ground.

This is a perfect example of how authorities' secretive way of dealing with mutes illustrates the fear and uncertainty that are pervasive in many North American rural ranching communities where these types of unusual animal death cases occur routinely. I have found that authorities, while in office, can be extremely reluctant even to acknowledge the existence of these reports. In my experience I found the former sheriff was next to impossible to work with, unlike many sheriff's departments in the San Luis Valley that welcome any assistance they can get. This south central part of the Valley is a world unto itself. And does it have a history!

The quiet little ranch where this October 8 case allegedly occurred lay near the Taylor Ranch. Several ranches away to the east were rancher neighbors Clarence and Dale Vigil. The Vigils lost two cows to the cattle hackers, one in April 1993 and another in December 1993. Both cases were covered extensively in *The Mysterious Valley*. The small, isolated Chama Canyon area, in my estimation, is the epicenter of the entire cattle mutilation phenomenon. I can find nowhere else that rivals the ferocity with which this picturesque little region suffered, during two wild and woolly months in the fall of 1975. As many as one hundred head of cattle may have been "mutilated," shot or stolen. These cases may reflect the injection of the human element in the 1970s, a fact that has been ignored by all but a few investigators.

Evidence of possible Taylor Ranch involvement has never fully been made public, but ex–Costilla County sheriffs Ernest Sandoval and Pete Espinoza are on the record, claiming that at least some of the helicopter crews responsible for many of the mutilations were "taking off and landing at the Taylor Ranch." This is the first time (to my knowledge) that *any* law enforcement officials, anywhere, have publicly stated names of any suspected parties they feel were involved in a portion of the mysterious mutilation of thousands of cattle across North America and elsewhere.

When *The Mysterious Valley* was published in September 1996, I confess that I felt rather proud that I happened to be the first investigator to get law enforcement officials to go on the record with an actual name to associate with any of these thousands of puzzling cases. Espinoza and Sandoval's insistence was compelling, and the fact that they allowed me to quote them convinced me they weren't out to slag John Taylor's name. They were serious and felt they had acquired enough circumstantial evidence to feel confident in pointing their accuser's finger at him. I am surprised that with the publication of *TMV,* hardly anyone commented about this on the record naming of our first suspect in the history of the cattle mutilation phenomenon. No reviews or articles about *TMV* mention this fact. Nor do they acknowledge the revelation that the first "wave" of animal deaths in the early fall of 1975 featured mutilated cattle *that had been shot.*[1] Other interesting events occurred all through the fall into winter 1996.

LET'S THROW ROCKS AT IT

A couple of weeks later, my band Laffing Buddha had finally finished its first album at Time Capsule Studio in Denver. It had been a long, time-consuming, expensive, and tedious process, and now it was time to relax and celebrate. We couldn't wait to get back and play the tape for the two bandmates who didn't make that final trip.

As we were headed west over La Veta Pass, returning from our final mix-down session, that October 19, 1995, at 6:00 P.M., I was sitting in the front passenger seat looking to the northwest when I noticed seven blinking lights in close proximity to one another, ten or so miles to the north. I pointed this out to Lyman and George and told them it was highly unusual to see so many lights within five degrees of one another—even over the La Veta MOA. I commented that "we should keep our eyes open; something may be going on."

Two or three minutes later, bass player Lyman asked me quietly, "What is *that?*" He pointed to a small, orange-red dot moving quickly across the sky. It was traveling very fast and seemed fairly low—about three thousand to four thousand feet above the winding road headed west down La Veta Pass. An eighth blinking light hung tantalizingly low over Blanca Peak.

Lyman was excited by his sighting of something unusual in the sky. "I never see anything . . . you guys are always seeing something, and I miss out. All right! I finally got to see one!"

We watched the unusual, unblinking orange-red light disappear over the eastern horizon. These orange globes baffle me. They seem fairly small, yet they move with purpose, and I was sure something was going on. We all kept an extra vigilant watch the remaining forty-five minutes into Alamosa where the band is headquartered. As we pulled up to our rehearsal space, Chris Medina, one of our guitarists who hadn't made the trip to Denver with us, excitedly came running out.

A scant hour earlier, just before our "sighting," Chris and his cousin Roy had been returning from Capulin, Colorado, about twenty-five miles south of Alamosa, where Chris and his world-famous weaver grandmother, Eppy Archuleta, have a large wool carding and spinning mill.

As they headed east toward Highway 285, they both noticed four bright, glowing lights against the western side of Saddleback Mountain, just a couple of miles east of Sanford, about fifteen miles from their vantage point. This center of the valley region, north of the Colorado border, is a jumbled mass of brooding volcanic hills, "some of them . . . capped by remnants of flat-lying lava flows. Here turquoise is mined, a product of hydrothermal alteration of copper minerals in the volcanic rock."[2] This mineral composition gives the Brownie Hills, as they're collectively known locally, their ruddy brown complexion. This grouping of hills, including the Piñon Hills and the South Piñon Hills, known collectively as the San Luis Hills, is a barren, dry, no-man's-land, with very few houses or roads.

Having explored the area extensively, and knowing the locale well, Chris and Roy knew there was no light source anywhere close to the area, so naturally they hotfooted it over to investigate. They quickly located a four-wheel-drive trail, just east of town, and were able to wind up Saddleback Mountain to "within a quarter-mile" of the lights. The dark mass of the volcanic mesa loomed in the twilight, and the pulsing, large, bright array of lights stabbed beams into the surrounding hillside. They were the first ones on the scene.

"It looked like a football stadium, or like some big ships had landed," Chris excitedly told us. "I was pretty scared. I have no idea what it could have been—there's nothing up there." Chris's younger cousin Roy was feeling brave. "Roy wanted me to drive closer so he could throw a rock at it to see if we could hear it hit metal." Chris said the light sources were several hundred yards apart, roughly in a square pattern, and all four were blinking sequentially with one another! Several other witnesses saw the lights, which were visible for miles.

Chris noted, "There was something really weird about them, and I wasn't about to find out what was going on. You always think you'll be brave and walk right up to the mothership, until you're standing right there up close and personal. I wasn't about to get any closer. I was fine right where I was!"

Chris finally convinced Roy that they should leave, and they drove back down the hill toward town. On the way, a line of cars streamed up to the area to investigate. No reports were filed with authorities, and the "sighting" did not make the papers. Later I learned that a nearby mountain, where the local high school had outlined a big S out of whitewashed rocks, had hosted a homecoming bonfire the prior weekend, but this did not explain the strange sequencing lights Chris and Roy observed the following week.

THE CLOUD SHIPS

Winter arrived like a lamb, and the area experienced a rather mild winter. This season finds most folks indoors, so naturally the number of reports tends to drop. But during this mild winter, one report deserves mention.

Since Salida, Colorado, resident Tim Edwards's riveting footage of an enigmatic pencil-shaped object on August 27, 1995, numerous anomalous objects have been sighted by greater San Luis Valley residents. One sighting on Tuesday, January 25, 1996, at 4:30 P.M., was partially videotaped by one of the witnesses, Center resident James Armijo. With all those camcorders around it's inevitable that more quality footage will be obtained. *Courier* editor Mark Hunter and I visited with Armijo and his wife in Center on February 7, 1996.

Armijo, a gregarious man of thirty-one, told us that he had been at his cousin's house, six miles north of Alamosa. While standing in the yard, he noticed a bright silvery object "floating" low over Greenie Mountain to the west. He alerted his cousin Soccoro Guitierez, and they watched for about thirty minutes. Armijo claims he then remembered he had his new video camera in his truck. He ran and grabbed it and immediately focused on the object that seemed to be disappearing just over the mountains. Much to his surprise, he noticed two more objects hovering five to ten degrees above the mountains just to the south and north. He focused on the northern object and then zoomed in on the object to the south, which appeared disk shaped.

Armijo seemed matter-of-fact while watching the unusual objects hovering on his twenty-five-inch TV set. "I was born and raised here, and I've seen them all my life." He added, "If you really look at it, when I zoom in, you can see it's spinning!" After pulling the camera back to show both objects, he zooms in on the third object. The footage ends with another shot of both objects. "This is nothin', bud. You wait and see what I get. I always look to the sky."

Rewinding the footage, I scrutinize the close-up image of the second object. It is translucent and roughly disk shaped and has the appearance of spinning and/ or rippling. It reminded me of several Ed Walters photos from Gulf Breeze, Florida. There is an almost holographic sense to their appearance, like they're not completely solid objects. The wide-angle shots show glowing objects, but up close, they become translucent looking and ill defined.

Armijo is convinced that he will capture additional objects with his new video camera. He went on to describe two other sightings he and his wife had had in the prior two weeks that he had been unable to videotape. Now he takes his camera everywhere. What does his wife think of the sightings? "I don't want to believe, but I have to. I've seen them too!"

Earlier on the same day that Armijo's video was shot, I was heading south on Highway 17 into Alamosa. The sky was partly cloudy with a thin, multitiered layer of impressive lenticulated clouds hugging the tops of the Sangres. Often during similar weather conditions, disk-shaped clouds hover over this huge valley like fleets of arriving ships. January 25, 1996, at 10:30 A.M., was no exception. My brother Brendan commented on the array of "saucer clouds" in the sky that morning.

As we approached Hooper, I looked east across the valley toward the Great Sand Dunes. A perfect disk-shaped cloud appeared to be forming above the dune field eighteen miles away. I immediately brought Brendan's attention to it, and we marveled at how quickly it was building.

After watching five or so minutes we were side-tracked by conversation for a minute or two, before I glanced over toward the dunes to check on our rapidly forming cloud ship. The five-mile-long cloud had vanished without a trace! All the other nearby clouds hung innocently in the sky, unchanged, and were still right where we had last seen them, but the really striking one had vanished. We were convinced that we had witnessed something peculiar. I made note of it at home, but something struck me about the unusual sighting. As is my usual custom, I immediately sought a mundane explanation for the "saucer" cloud. Could the famous disappearing Medano Creek have had something to do with the rapid formation? Medano Creek, which disappears into the southern edge of the dune field, must pump a lot of moisture into the air when the hot ultraviolet rays of the sun heat the sand of the dune field. I wondered, could the cloud have been moisture rising up from the warm, creek-soaked sand into the frigid January air, where it condensed, forming the cloud? If this event had occurred in the spring or fall, I would have conveniently jumped to this conclusion. But the cold, sub-twenty-degree morning may not have been conducive for this effect. The event is still puzzling and in my mind remains unexplained.

Six hours later James Armijo shot his video. I sent Armijo's footage (certified, priority mail) to be analyzed by the TV program *Sightings*. I also sent along a second "viewing tape" I had taken of several of our recent mute cases. Much to *Sightings'* and my surprise, the package never arrived. I had been sending tapes back and forth to the program for almost three years, and this was the first time anything like this had happened. When I asked our postmaster, Monte Collins, if I could start a trace on the package, he had a hard time even finding a form. Certified mail doesn't normally disappear. According to *Sightings* producer David Green, a package did arrive a month later, with only the viewing tape inside. No trace of Armijo's master tape. I must say, this made me angry. Since 1993, twenty-four photographs, three cameras, and now a videotape had disappeared without a trace. When people ask me, "Do you think someone is keeping tabs on you?" I just smile.

I address what I call "local mythos" extensively in

The Mysterious Valley.[3] I contend that this area of research and investigation should be an integral part of *all* paranormal investigators' efforts. I suspect that the perceptions of experiencers of "the unknown" are probably subtly shaded by their personal-regional mythological bias that ties them to their particular locale.

The reason I bring this up is simple. In the San Luis Valley, I am occasionally reminded by residents that, "If there are disk-shaped clouds around, there are ships around." I can't remember how many times I've heard this. I have noticed over the course of my investigation that disk-shaped clouds do sometimes occur in close time proximity to sightings. Jacques Vallee and Aime Michel mentioned the French cloud ships of the 1950s in this context, but I've not heard of this phenomenon (and/or perception) recently. There are many types of craft reported in the San Luis Valley, but a new kind of report began to surface.

WHAT ARE THOSE THINGS?

Chances are the increasing number of reports I receive of huge craft blocking out the stars over the greater San Luis Valley are of terrestrial origin. They may belong to us, for they are often reported flying in the La Veta MOA. From time to time, usually during midfall, large triangle-shaped objects are occasionally reported in south-central Colorado. Typically, the report mentions "hypnotic" lighting displays, and the craft is usually reported as flying along in a leisurely manner.

Recently, an even newer type of report has surfaced. During the past two and a half years, reports have been logged describing "darker than dark" triangle-shaped shadows "blocking out the stars" as they sail slowly over. Most reports are from skywatchers, not motorists or casual observers.

Granted, some clouds at night can assume almost any perceived shape, but several of these reports have come from very credible witnesses who, you would think, are not prone to misidentification. These large craft invariably instill wonder in the witnesses who observe them, and the reports are often accompanied by awed descriptions of "the mothership."

I wonder if these innocent witnesses may actually be observing secret military craft that effectively *give the impression* of something otherwordly. Could our military be utilizing such fantastically advanced aeronautic technologies? Several recent sightings of these craft feature estimated airspeeds as low as the single digits! Now correct me if I'm wrong, but wouldn't you need a gravitational-based propulsion system to enable you to fly such a large craft (some have been estimated as being at least two miles in length)? And if you are trying to keep this technology secret, why light it up like a Christmas tree and send it sailing over populated areas? It's obvious to me that this is by design, and maybe our government is trying to fool or condition us all.

However, if these are ships from "off-planet," it is inconceivable to me that an ET mothership would fly so brazenly around one of the most strategically sensitive areas of North America and not be challenged by defensive-minded pilots. Or maybe those reports we saw in the San Luis Valley in the spring of 1993, concerning "dogfights" between UFO-type lights and conventional-looking fixed-wing aircraft, were our military standing tall and trying to chase off unwelcome ET spacecraft from the high ground here in the Rockies. This following report was experienced up close and personal, and if it belongs to us, I know why the Cold War is over.

THE OJO ENCOUNTER

February 16, 1996, at 10:05 P.M., Nick Archuleta, his wife Lorraine, and the couple's two-year-old daughter were driving north on State Highway 285, two or three miles south of Ojo Caliente, New Mexico. They were on their way to Capulin, Colorado, to attend Nick's brother Tobias's wedding. Nick, who was driving, needed to make "a pit stop." Climbing outside and walking around their pickup truck, Nick commenced to relieve himself. All of a sudden, while looking down at the ground, he noticed his shadow. Knowing there was no moon out that night, he immediately looked up to see what was causing the light.

Much to his amazement, "a huge ship" hovered "less than fifty feet overhead" with "a circle of fifty to seventy-five lights blinking in a clockwise pattern." He felt or heard a low vibrating sound, like a rumble. He yelled for his wife to look, which turned out to be a bad idea. She immediately "started screaming and getting all hysterical." Evidently, Nick was pretty calm about the sighting, but he was amazed. "It covered the whole sky, it was so big and close. I couldn't stop looking at it and get back in the truck." Then, without any sound, "it went straight up, maybe a mile, or so, until it was the size of a quarter." Then to the witnesses' consternation, "it zoomed at the speed of light back down," and again hovered fifty feet over them. Then it flew out about a quarter mile or so out over the small valley (which runs parallel to Highway 285) and leisurely started to head north.

Archuleta was excited. "I got back into the truck and went after it." He took off in the truck and continued heading north on 285. After driving about four or five miles, with his wife looking up and out the passenger window to report on the craft's progress, they caught up to it. Again, it hovered directly over their truck. "My wife threatened to divorce me if I stopped, but I really wanted to get another good look at it, so I stopped anyway." Nick climbed out, and the object "turned off the lights." They watched in wonder as it majestically headed east out over the mesa and out of sight.

The Archuletas estimated that the event lasted more than twenty minutes, and they heard a "low vibration" that they associated with the craft. They continued on their way, and it took them the rest of the trip to calm down after the close encounter.

I talked with another witness who lived twenty miles away to the west, and she claimed that several area residents had seen the craft, off to the east in the distance that same night.

Later that spring, the day Timothy Leary died, another mysterious cattle death and fiendish disfigurement was reported west of Saguache. For some reason I haven't figured out yet, I suspect that somehow psychedelics and psychoactive substances are synchronistically tied to the cattle mutilation phenomenon. For example, where do hallucinogenic pysilocybin mushrooms grow in nature? In cow pies.

THEY'RE BOTH LUMBERJACKS AND THEY'RE OKAY

May 13, 1996, at 8:00 A.M., two loggers were headed up the Cannero Pass Road, which turns to the south eight miles west of Saguache. As they traveled up the dirt road after making the turn, they noticed a cow lying near the road. One of the loggers (who has been avidly following my UAD investigation) blurted out, "That's a mute!"

They stopped and climbed over the fence to investigate, immediately noticing that the rest of the herd seemed "trapped in the corner of the pasture" and appeared to be agitated. "There were about thirty to forty head, maybe twenty cows with calves, milling around mooing like the dead one was blocking their path. . . . There's a stream that runs through the pasture with only about twenty-five feet between the fence line and the stream. The dead one was in the path, and they wouldn't go around it."

The other logger took up the story. "I started to walk over to the dead one, and the biggest cow in the herd charged over and stopped about twenty feet away and let out a moooo. . . . You know how a herd moves like water, one goes and they all start to go? Well, when that cow mooed, a mama and a baby ran past the dead cow. I mooed, and me and that cow kept mooing until the rest of 'em made it past. . . . I used to ride bulls, and it was pretty weird the way they were acting. I don't know, it was almost like us being there gave them courage to go around it [the dead cow]."

The two loggers described the mute as missing its rear end: "It was definitely cut in a circle," and "its udder and an upside eye and ear were gone. . . . There were what looked like strap burns behind the front legs. . . . We luckily had a camera with us and took a bunch of good pictures."

"Did you get any good close-ups of the incisions?" I asked.

"Yes. The jaw cut went up around the eye, and a

stain that discolored the ground spread out from its face. We didn't see it when we were there, but you can see it in the pictures." They had visited a one-hour photo shop and had the film developed. "It was *really* fresh. We could see that a little blood was still uncoagulated and oozing. It looked like it happened maybe two or three hours before, around dawn."

They quickly scoured the scene for clues. "There were no tracks or footprints that we could see. No bear or cat did that. We didn't spend much time because we had to get to work." Their untrained eyes revealed no additional clues. No drops of blood, cigarette butts, or clues to what or who did the unfortunate animal in were found. "When we came back about four hours later to cut samples and check around again, it was gone! Somebody must have hauled it away; there was no sign of it." The two loggers were convinced that their discovery was no accident. "I couldn't help but think that this was done for *us* to find. Like somebody knew *we* would be on *that* road *that* morning!"

The rancher wouldn't tell me where the cow ended up, and I could tell it would take quite a bit of hounding to get anywhere with him. If they bury it, in their mind, it goes away. Permanently.

The area where the animal was found was within five miles of Hoagland Hill where the cops were supposedly chasing "lights" on the night of May 4, 1996 and it's the western end of the area that had the first cases in the SLV back in the fall wave of 1975.

During the late summer and early fall of 1996, *Taos News* reporter Phaedra Greenwood and longtime *Spirit Magazine* reporter-investigator David Perkins covered a half a dozen mutilation reports from the Taos, New

Mexico, region of the southern San Luis Valley. Both Phaedra and David have done their homework.

WE NEED MORE HARD SCIENTISTS

While researching one of several articles concerning an ongoing "mutilation" wave, Greenwood contacted Dale Spall, an analytical chemist at the Life Sciences Division in the Los Alamos National Laboratories. Spall, who had conducted testing of animal mutilations to look for evidence of carcinogens and radiation back in 1978, at the behest of the infamous Rommel Investigation, is very interested in the phenomenon. He told Greenwood:

> "We looked at the liver, the spleen, did gross observation and a number of other studies. The problem with cattle mutilations is that a lot of information tends to be anecdotal in nature. There is a certain natural death rate among cattle [2 percent]." He said he thought most cattle mutilations were natural deaths and scavengers. "There is a distinct possibility some people are playing copy cat," he said. "Cattle mutilations follow a 15–20 years cycle," he added. "They've been reported in England, Brazil, Argentina, Venezuela." [Also in Puerto Rico, Canada, Ireland, Australia, Canary Islands, and probably other countries as well.]
>
> Spall said he experimented with one of his own animals; when he slaughtered it, he also did a mimic mutilation. "I cored the anus, took out the sexual organs, cut off an ear, cut out the tongue." He said he did the whole thing in about half an hour with a skinning knife. "If you leave it lying out for about six

hours, it does the same thing. The edges of the wound curl and stretch as they dry and look like precision laser cuts," he said. He admitted he had never seen the "cookie cutter" kind of edges mentioned by pathologists. He also said he had never heard of a mutilation that took place in the winter and thought this was because ranchers kept a closer eye on their cows in the winter. . . . He said he enjoyed his volunteer research and had actually brought a whole cow into the lab to do an autopsy which included an analysis of urine, blood and tissue. He also scanned the animal for radiation and took bacteriological samples. Unfortunately, all his reports disappeared from the lab, he said, and nobody knows where they are. "The deeper you get into it, the more mysterious it gets," he said.

What Spall didn't mention to Greenwood is that, on a whim, he had pulled the files out and left them on his desk one afternoon in 1994. He went to lunch, and when he returned, the files had disappeared!

I had spoken with Spall about cattle mutilations back during the so-called New Mexico Wave of 1993–1994, and Spall had related the mysterious disappearance of the 1978–1979 mutilation files from his desk. "I have no idea why someone would have just taken them."

DRAFT HORSES DON'T JUMP
AUGUST 6, 1996, ESTRELLA, COLORADO

Not all "unusual animal deaths" involve bloodless incisions and missing soft-tissue organs. This report comes from an August 7, 1996, *Valley Courier* article written by former editor Greg Johnson: "A large Morgan draft horse was found wedged in the fork of a large tree in Estrella [Colorado], about seven miles south of Alamosa near Highway 285, apparently dead from suffocation. . . . Gary Haddock, land use administrator for Alamosa County, said the horse . . . may have eaten some loco weed, or may have been trying to jump through the fork of the tree for some unknown reason, but fell short. . . . Haddock said he is treating the incident as a freak accident, and that he didn't know what would motivate a [twelve-hundred- to fourteen-hundred-pound] horse to jump in a tree."

Reading this strange account, and looking at the photograph of the huge horse with all four feet off the ground, I scanned my research for a similar event. I found one from Arizona.

Tom Dongo has been investigating reports of the unusual around Sedona, Arizona, for more than twelve years. He has seen many unusual events and described a particular incident involving terrified horses.

During an eight-month period at the end of the summer 1994, I was investigating a number of reports from a ranch outside of Sedona. Several Bigfoot sightings occurred around this time, and the owner of the ranch told me of an ordeal involving one of their horses. Well, I went and saw the spot where this happened, and it was pretty strange.

The rancher told me that one of his horses became wedged between two large branches on a good-sized tree near the house. It had evidently been trying to escape from something and became wedged while on a dead run. It was so stuck they had to cut the two branches to get it out. Fortunately, it lived. . . .

Just prior to the horse getting stuck, we had a near
encounter with a Bigfoot. It was dark, and we were
staking out the property. We heard something grunt
real loud on the other side of the apple orchard opposite the house. It wasn't a lion or a bear. Well,
when it grunted, six horses in a nearby corral went
wild. They were racing around and literally screaming. The next morning we found Bigfoot tracks near
where we had heard the grunt, and they had a thirty-
five- to forty-inch spread between strides! Whenever
the Bigfoot was around, their horses were literally
terrified.[4]

Now, I'm not suggesting that the draft horse was being chased by a Bigfoot, but in light of the time proximity with mutilations to the south, I wonder what
could have terrified the animal enough to prompt it to
jump off the ground into the crotch of a tree.

Unusual cattle death cases began to arrive with a
new wrinkle. This following case featured a new twist.

LANDING TRACES?

United Parcel Service driver David Jaramillo and his
family were spending quality time relaxing up at their
Osier Park cabin, Sunday, September 22, 1995, directly
west-southwest from Antonito, Colorado, just above the
New Mexico border, when they discovered a mutilated
cow near their cabin. The animal, lying on its left side,
was missing its udder, rear end, and tongue. A large
circular portion around the right ear was missing, and
the tip of the animal's tail appeared to have been
skinned. About one hundred feet away from the carcass, much to Jaramillo's surprise, he found three cir-

cles, four feet in diameter flattening the lush meadow grass. The circles were about twelve feet apart and arrayed in a triangle pattern. Around each circle were three four-inch holes, also in a triangle configuration, punched into the ground. In the middle of the large triangle, Jaramillo's brother found long tail hairs that appeared to be from the unfortunate cow.

Jaramillo happened to have his video camera with him and documented the entire scene. He tracked me down the following day while delivering in Crestone and told me of his find. We watched his videotape, and I cringed at the sight of one of Dave's relatives standing in the middle of one of the twelve-foot circles—perfect physical evidence now rendered not-so-perfect.

The animal had no brand or ear tag, and Jaramillo was unable to ascertain who owned it. His remote cabin was occasionally visited by the locals' herds that meander around La Magna Pass area during the summer and early fall, before they're herded together and taken down to winter pastures. As (bad) luck would have it, an early fall snowstorm that very night made the site inaccessible to me, much to my annoyance. Yet another chance to try and conduct "good science" was thwarted by this remote, high-mountain environment.

Jaramillo's footage was broadcast in a *Strange Universe* segment later that fall.

Approximately the same week, a rancher later reported to Undersheriff Brian Norton at the Rio Grande sheriff's office that he had discovered a mutilated cow in the center of a thirty-foot swirled circle in the grass. The area was only fifteen to twenty miles north of the Jaramillo site. The rancher's horse would evidently not approach the grass circle, and on examination, the rancher reported to Norton that there was a fine dusting of something similar to "baby powder" on the carcass and on the swirled circle. To my knowledge, there were no UFO sightings associated with this unofficial mute report. However, while they were examining the carcass, a "military helicopter" flew low over the site, obviously watching the rancher. The chopper swooped in, then left at treetop level.

Unfortunately, the rancher reported the case some time later, hence no exact date, but the late September time frame is interesting in light of the Jaramillo find. Norton told me of the report early the following spring.

THE BBC IN THE WILD, WILD WEST

The winter of 1996–1997 passed by with barely a whimper. The mild weather and record snowfalls relieved 1996's dry conditions, and the region's ski areas profited handsomely. The spring arrived, and the cattle death cases began in earnest, first just north of Taos, then in the heart of the San Luis Valley.

It was early in the morning when the rancher discovered his prized breeding cow dead in the pasture, about five hundred yards from the front door of his ranch house. He couldn't believe the animal's condition: left eye carved out and the left mandible neatly "sliced off." He muttered as he realized her young calf would probably die as a result of losing its mother.

The rancher had been hearing about area mutilations, and had watched a videotape taken by a neighbor of another strangely slain cow, less than a mile from his spread, in southern Alamosa County. He had not been convinced by the video that the animal had been killed and mutilated. He told his neighbor that it very well may have been done by a cat. Of course he couldn't explain the lack of any tracks or indication of a struggle, which are usually present after a predator kill. He blew it off, not thinking that in a few days he too would lose a cow under mysterious circumstances. He was getting angrier by the minute. So he placed a call to the sheriff's office to report the unusual livestock death.

The investigating deputy, sensing something very strange about the crime scene and the animal's demise, tried to obtain my number from Richard Gottlieb at the Narrow Gauge Bookstore in Alamosa. Richard immediately called me and told me of the deputy's call. A fresh one, less than eight hours old! I set up a rendezvous at the crime scene with the deputy sheriff and rushed down with a musician friend, Barry Monroe, and we examined the scene in the diminishing light. To my amateur eye, it looked like "the real thing," a true high-strange case, but I remembered that appearances can be deceiving. I made arrangements to return the following morning. The temperature would be just above thirty-five degrees, and the animal carcass would stay in pristine condition overnight.

Meanwhile, two weeks prior, your media magnet San Luis Valley investigator had finished a television shoot with England's British Broadcasting Corporation (Louis Theroux's "Weird Weekends") with an extracted promise to let the BBC know if we had any "fresh cases." The day they were finishing their shoot in Arizona, I called with the grim news. They rushed back to the San Luis Valley to film the investigation.

Louis Theroux, the correspondent, begins the questioning as we drive the several miles south toward the site. "So what's the story, Chris?"

"I received an interesting call yesterday. It seems the sheriff's office received a couple of reports, over the last four days, of cattle mutilations. The investigating deputy asked me to come down and check one of the cases out."

"Have you already been to see it?"

"Yes. I wouldn't have called you out, Louis, unless I suspected a report worthy of gathering forensic samples and conducting an investigation."

"What kind of animal is it?"

"It's a four-year-old cow with a calf about three and a half months old. It was part of a large herd of about one hundred and ten animals. Fifty-five cows and their calves. The rancher came out yesterday at five in the morning and found it 'mutilated.' Its mandible's been excised, and an eye was carved out."

"Is it the real deal?"

"Based on my amateur eye, it definitely looks bizarre. Strange."

"Has it got a name?"

"I don't know, Louis. I just call them all 'Bessie.' "

A fierce wind rips across the bleak pasture as we arrive, cameras and tools in hand. We approach the tarp-covered animal and pull off the tarp. We look down at the carcass, and I comment, "*That* is not natural!"

"Chris, how come the eye socket is bubbling?" Louis asks.

"Well, Louis, it's pressure from the fluids in the body going to the lowest point. You'll have a certain amount of activity until all the blood coagulates. The fact that the blood isn't coagulated is interesting."

Louis's cavalier demeanor rapidly fades. He stares at the carcass with a rather grim look on his face as I walk back to get my tool bag and gloves. Louis asks, "You're putting gloves on so you don't get gunk on your hands?"

"Several cases in the last two years have had people getting their hands really burned after touching one of these."

"No!" Louis wrinkles his nose as the wind changes. "It smells a bit . . ."

"Louis, you wanted to help? Here, put this tape measure as close to the head as you dare. That's right, right on the nose."

"On the nose? Do you want me to actually tuck it in the mouth?"

I begin the process of measuring out ten-foot, twenty-five-foot, and fifty-foot marks for gathering soil and plant samples.

Louis, the glib reporter, has lost a bit of his light-heartedness. "How does this figure as far as mutilations go, or mutes, as you call them? How does this rate? Is this an extreme one, an average one . . . ?"

"I'd say it's average for this part of the San Luis Valley. Over the last three years, we've had a number of intact rear ends."

"Rectums?"

"The rectum hasn't been cored. Farther south, in New Mexico, in all their recent cases, the rear end has been taken. I don't know if that's a trend, but this is a fairly typical average case."

Louis is getting back his English-style humor, "Maybe rectums aren't a hot commodity any-more. . . ."

"Yeah, right, Louis, maybe now it's lip and eye stew. Instead of udder-rectum soufflé. So, Louis, what do you think, now that you've seen one?"

"Well-l-l, it's pretty repulsive seeing the eye socket bubbling like that!"

We take the rest of the tarp off, revealing the intact

rear end. Louis starts to cough and retch. "Its rectum . . . is . . . bubbling!"

I start laughing and pat him on the back. "I know. It's tough, Louis, but you can handle it."

"Is that normal? Why is it bubbling?"

"Well, it's natural. The animal had probably eaten a lot. When it died, the vegetable matter all fermented and created gas. So what you're seeing is the process of that gas bulging out and bloating the animal."

"But why is it bubbling out of that little hole right there?"

"There is so much pressure that it split the animal's soft tissue."

Louis tells Simon, the cameraman, "Get in close on that bubbling rectum."

"Ohh, man! *You* get the close-up!" Simon is not having fun.

Louis looks down at the animal's missing mandible flesh and comments, "Well, at least it died with a smile on its face."

I start to videotape downwind. "Oooo-wee, geez Louise. That's the problem with these things . . ."

"What's the problem?"

"The problem is the smell downwind. You just don't want to get downwind."

The rancher arrives at the scene. Sternly, he climbs out of his truck, accompanied by his son and a couple of their ranch dogs.

Louis asks, "Chris, what are the characteristics of this animal carcass that mark it as a possible mutilation and make it mysterious?"

"Well, first of all, the cut around the jaw and snout area is peculiar. The cut obviously starts here and goes around in this direction. And then the eye was carved out. It wasn't plucked out, like from a bird. The whole socket has been reamed out. You can see the fluids bubbling in there from the pressure. It is kind of gross!"

It's time to get to work. "Let's go, gentlemen. I'm going to get some samples here." Both of their eyes bulge as I start the forensic sample-gathering procedure.

I cut into the animal's flesh. Louis's hands are steepled in front of his face, and his face is screwed up and turning purple. "Chris, shouldn't you get a sample of the eye juice?"

"No, I'll let the vet do that. I can't have all the fun."

Louis turns away as I cut into the mandible flesh for the second sample.

"You get used to it after a dozen of them," I tell him, humming a tune stuck in my head. I finish the tissue-excising and begin gathering the final plant and soil samples for testing by Dr. W. C. Levengood at the Pine Landia Biophysics Laboratory in Michigan.

I gather samples in the rock-hard ground. Immersed in the task at hand, I was busy humming and digging away with my back to the carcass when I hear Louis gag and shout, "OOOHHHH!!!"

I turn just in time to see the rancher's dog licking the still-burbling blood and fluid from the excised eye socket. The rancher gives the pooch a kick. "Oh, OOHHH, Ohhhhhh, Ohh, the-the-the dog is licking the juice from its eye socket!" The rancher scratches his head. He doesn't know what to make of these BBC boys.

I tell Louis, "They'll do that. You should see what a pack of coyotes would do to this thing!"

Louis is blown away and keeps repeating, ". . . the dog was licking the juice from the eye socket . . ."

"Louis, you are really funny, man! So you almost lost your cookies again, huh?"

"The dog was licking the eye socket of a mutilated cow!" He is stunned.

"It's a natural thing."

"I'm never going to forget that image. You've got a FUN job."

I turn to the rancher. "Owning a cow that's had this done to it is no fun. What do you think?"

The rancher looks down at the cow. "It's very suspicious. I've never seen one like this in over thirty years of ranching. I see dead cows all the time, but I've never seen one that's cut up like this. Or been cut at all! I've been a rancher for forty years and I've never seen an animal that's been cut on like this! This is very strange. This animal has been cut on by a sharp knife or high heat, or something. Normally, if a cow just dies, that cheek patch wouldn't be missing and the eye socket would still be there."

"So what do you think did this?" Louis asks him.

The rancher answers, "I wish I knew. That's why Chris is here. Maybe these samples will enlighten us."

Louis asks, "Do you think it's UFOs and aliens?"

"I guess it's possible. Either that, or we have some real strange individuals in this country that would get a sick thrill out of this. This is our livelihood. There's been too much of this going on. It's not happened to me previously, but one's quite enough. . . . It's happened to my neighbors."

"I've read accounts that say this is just predator damage. Vultures, maggots, and whatnot . . ."

The rancher disagrees. "Totally impossible. Vultures, predators, varmits—they did not do this. This was done by some . . . it may have been a varmit, but it's of a two-legged kind. It's not animals. This is not an animal kill at all. If it was, they'd be around the backside of the animal. That's where they always start. I've hunted all my life, butcher my own beef. To do that kind of work up there on the jawbone where the skin's extremely tight, you'd have to have a lot of experience, or a very good instrument. They did this in the dark. We live less than five hundred yards away; the dogs never barked. It's very unusual! That cow was healthy prior to her death, and there's no visible indication of how the animal was killed. There's no sign of a struggle, or anything else. This cow never did anything to anybody! Why her? Why me? Why my neighbors? We need answers to who, what, and why this is happening. I don't care to have any more."

The mood had grown somber. The rancher was actually a bit choked up over the loss of his cow, and I could tell that Louis and Simon were uncomfortable at the rancher's anguish. I know I was uncomfortable. We covered the animal with the tarp as the cold San Luis Valley wind tore fiendishly at our clothing and further chilled the scene.

I thanked the rancher for coming forward and reporting the case and promised to let him know the results of the testing processes. The BBC boys were quiet and lost in their thoughts as we drove back to the airport. Gone was the lighthearted laughter. I dropped them off at the airport, bid them adieu, and headed home mulling over several explanations for these animal deaths.

DOES ANY THEORY WORK?

The short answer is no. The long answer is, maybe. I've been asked on numerous occasions, "What's your attraction to dead cows?" Another good question. I often tell folks at my talks, "They say the ancient mariner had an albatross around his neck. Because of where I live, I've got a dead cow around mine." This usually generates a chuckle or two. To be honest, I don't care for dead animals, or dead anything, for that matter. Livestock deaths occur everywhere, every day. We kill and consume millions of cattle every year in this country. Only a fraction of the so-called unexplained deaths becomes a part of the public awareness. I have sympathy for the ranchers who are exposed to this mysterious phenomenon. Ranchers don't deserve to lose their valuable cattle in this manner. And what about the poor beasts? Do they deserve to die in this gruesome fashion?

Since the early 1970s, theories explaining possible rationales behind these thousands of cases have been bandied about by a handful of dogged mute investigators. In all honesty, there are few theories, except one, David Perkins's "environmental monitoring" theory, that have established real credence. A lot of circumstantial evidence has been accumulated to back up his assertion that warm-blooded, domesticated animals are being tested for environmental factors and/or pollution that may affect the animals, and because we eat cattle, humans as well.

The National Cancer Institute recently released the results of a fifteen-year study concerning the health impact of above-ground nuclear testing on the environment. They concluded that ninety above-ground detonations have spread radioactivity across the entire United States. I find it interesting that the San Luis Valley counties of Saguache and Conejos are considered two of six hot-spot counties in Colorado, which appears to be one of the most affected states in the U.S. Watching a news broadcast covering the NCI study,

David Perkins immediately noticed that the areas of highest radioactive concentrations mirrored areas of high mutilation activity.

Perkins finds the apparent parallel between the dispersal of radiation highly intriguing. Is there a connection between radiation concentrations from above-ground nuclear testing and areas of high cattle death reports? On the surface, it would seem that this is the case. (David, along with partner Cari Seawell, investigated dozens of mutilations during the seventies and eighties. Seventies pioneers Tom Adams, Gary Massey, Gabe Valdez, and Tommy Bland also helped pave the way for later investigators like Linda Moulton Howe, Ted Oliphant, Gail Staehlin, and myself.)

Perkins insightfully noted early on that animal mutilations seemed to be a last frost to first frost phenomenon. He concluded that this time period—spring, summer, and fall—was when animals grazed on fresh pasture grass the most. The soft-tissue organs that tend to be excised contain valuable information regarding the animal's environment. These body parts also happen to be the fastest regenerating tissues and harbor the most recent environmental effect information. The tongue, milk glands, and milk contain residual environmental pollutants from the grass, and, with the exception of the lungs, the organs that are most often excised mirror the organs in humans that most often succumb to cancers.

I find this NCI study highly intriguing. It could even be the "smoking gun" tying humans into an aspect of the mutilation scenario. It may not, however, explain them all away. I sense that something else appears to be at work. But, out of all the theories that have been offered to explain animal mutilations, Perkins's "environmental monitoring" theory seems to have the most compelling circumstantial evidence to support its validity.

Remember, most if not all, large, warm-blooded animals have been found in a mutilated condition. Foxes, hedgehogs, goats, sheep, horses, deer, elk, coyotes, cats, dogs, and rabbits have all apparently been found missing soft-tissue organs. And yes, *humans* have been found mutilated. I don't know how many have been reported, but it would appear that they are rare. The following is the most thoroughly documented case I've encountered that suggests that human cases have been reported. If other cases occur, chances are the reports will be covered up by law enforcement officials. The very thought that people have been found in this manner is disturbing.

A GRISLY HUMAN MUTILATION

During the many talks and seminars I find myself at, invariably someone will ask, "Do human mutilations ever happen?" Until G. Cope Schellhorn's 1995 "investigation" of the now-infamous Guarapiranga Reservoir case from São Paulo State, Brazil, I answered, "I don't know. I've never heard of a documented case." Now I carry those hideously gross autopsy photos and accompanying article to satiate the serious and titillate the timid. The case is a bit of an aberration, but because of several high-strange elements, it deserves a mention.

If this case is authentically UFO-related—and at this time I have no reason to believe it is not—then all of us are going to have to reevaluate to one degree or another our tentative conclusions as to the possible specific intentions, moral perspectives and general agenda that some of our extraterrestrial visitors may have. . . . Encarnacion Garcia learned from her friend, Dr. Rubin Goes, that he was in possession of some rather "odd" photos which had been given to him by his cousin . . . official photos of a body that had been found near Guarapiranga reservoir on the 29th of September, 1988, of an unnamed male. . . . Garcia was impressed with how similar the wounds of the body were to those found on the carcasses of so many UFO-related mutilated animals, knowledge which the original investigating officials and medical doctors involved with the case did not possess.[5]

The hideous photos show a male body with classic mutilation incisions. The right-side jaw mandible was excised, and the ears, eyes, and part of the internal thorax were missing. The anus and bellybutton had been cored out, and the lower internal organs had evidently been pulled out through the one-and-a-half-inch-diameter bellybutton wound. And we won't talk about his genitals. As unbelievable as it may sound, the upper respiratory organs and heart had somehow been removed through a small hole in the crook of the arm. This fantastic twist greatly puzzled examining pathologists and medical personnel. And for good reason.

Although Brazilian civilian investigators have insisted no regional UFO activity remotely corresponds with the approximate date of death, Schellhorn inexplicably has determined this human "mutilation" is somehow UFO-related. Brazilian investigator Philippe Piet van Putten comments on Schellhorn's claim, "The Guarapiranga Reservoir is nearby my home and I have followed the story since it surfaced years ago. As far as I know, there is no evidence whatsoever that the human corpse found in the area was mutilated by UFO occupants. Very few among the Brazilian researchers do believe that such an alien intervention really happened." The text mentions Mr. Claudeir Covo, an electronic engineer and UFO researcher living in Sao Paulo. Mr. Covo has stated in numerous opportunities his belief that there in NO CONNECTION between the dead man found in the Reservoir and UFOs. He and his longtime friend Dr. Luciano Stancka e Silva, MD., have checked the story with the police and they always stated that the mutilation was produced by rats and vultures, not aliens."

On September 28, 1996, as fate would have it, I found myself at a book signing at the Taos Crystal Center when I was casually introduced to an "ex–CIA scientist." He is now a private-sector consultant working on "electromagnetic and antigravitational propulsion systems." He was very knowledgeable about the so-called UFO phenomenon and asked several *very* pointed questions pertaining to my mountains of SLV data. Then he dropped a bombshell.

"Did you hear about the human mutilation down near Silver City?"

"What? You're kidding?" He had my full, undivided attention.

"No, I'm not. A friend of mine in the New Mexico State Patrol told me about it. They found a sixteen-year-old girl . . . just like the cows."

"When did this supposedly happen?"

"About three, three and a half weeks ago [right when Taos area mutes were being reported]. They put the lid down real tight on it."

He told me that these cases were not as rare as I might believe and that the authorities were extremely careful not to let word of a case of this kind out to the media. "They made sure there is no record of the death," he said.

We talked for quite a while about his thoughts pertaining to the UFO question. His eyes twinkled when he refused to answer any direct questions about our government's flight capabilities and offered to talk with me at length in private.

THE EQUALIZER
SATURDAY, JUNE 7, 1997, ONE MILE NORTH OF ALAMOSA ON HIGHWAY 17

The Valley had been relatively quiet over the past seven months, and when people asked me what was going on down there, I told them with a smile, "Nothing. The aliens don't like it here anymore. We must have scared them away."

It was a wild, stormy day, and I was headed into Alamosa to play at the annual Sunshine Festival. I had a line of cars fairly close behind me when, a mile north of town, I saw a large white pickup truck pull out onto the highway and begin meandering down driveways a mile north of Alamosa. It had a very strange-looking device in the back. It looked like some kind of space gun—that's the only description I could think of. The two guys I observed were in an unmarked, brand-new Ford F-350. Unfortunately, I couldn't stop. I wish I had, because I mentioned it to a shopkeeper just minutes later and she told about seeing a semi truck parked at a gas station the night before. She claimed the semi had ten of these gun-looking things on a flatbed, and she assumed they were off-loading them into the smaller trucks parked next to it. "I've never seen anything like that around here," she told me. Both the semi and the pickup were brand-new looking and had large blinking pale yellow rectangular lights.

Who *are* these guys? I posted the strange sighting on the Internet, and Skywatch International director, Col. Steve Wilson (who died of stomach cancer in November 1997), wrote that what I had seen was a reworked electromagnetic pulse weapon that had been called Joshua. Wilson said I probably saw a newer version of the weapon now called the Equalizer. He claimed they are used by Delta Forces to "bring down UFOs."

Activity was reported near Poage Lake, a few miles south of South Fork, Colorado, and thirty-five miles north of Dulce, New Mexico, a couple of nights before my inadvertent sighting of the pickup with the strange cargo. And reports of strange aerial craft were logged by Dr. Steven Greer and his group during training the following week. I can't help but wonder at the many reports of unknown parties tooling around the SLV in convoys and, in this case, pointing strange machines at the sky.

STOP THE PRESSES

Three days before turning in the final manuscript for this book, a flurry of strange light and object sightings appeared to coincide with another perplexing, unusual cattle death and the calf's subsequent disfigurement. On November 29, 1997, at 11:15 P.M., four witnesses reported seeing a large, multicolored ball of light bobbing slowly over the northern part of the Valley, and several hours earlier, a slowly disintegrating meteor was spotted in the same area. The prior day, a heavy snow had blanketed the Valley, with the foothills of the Sangres receiving a three-foot pasting.

Seven hours later, early on Sunday morning, a dense fog descended over the center of the Valley. At around 5:30 A.M., dogs began barking outside of a ranch house northwest of Hooper, Colorado, right in the center of northern San Luis Valley. The following afternoon, a still-warm mutilated calf was discovered about five hundred yards from the house, lying in a pristine, untouched snow-covered field.

The calf's right-side mandible had been exposed in an arc that went up over the eye socket. The rear end had been cored out in a ten-inch-diameter circle, and the coring extended eighteen inches into the animal's rear end. Magpies and crows showed an interest, but no coyote or other scavenger tracks were noted around the carcass. The Saguache County sheriff was called, and this investigator visited the site to help investigate this latest peculiar animal death. I obtained video and still footage and three sets of tissue samples, and again I sent the samples off to three different veterinarian pathology labs for testing.

I am convinced that this peculiar animal death mystery is "real." After factoring out misidentification, it appears that something or someone continues to haunt the pastures of North America, and slowly, through dil-. igent investigation, investigators are acquiring more and more data. One would hope that someday, a point of critical mass will be attained when this mountain of data finally overwhelms the mystery. If that hypothetical day of "truth revealed" arrives, it will be because investigators focused, developed better investigative techniques, and most important, *worked together*. If these variables are accomplished, we may actually gather the defining data and lay the groundwork needed to ascertain the elusive truth behind this enduring mutilation mystery.

CHAPTER SIX
THE GOLDEN HORDE

The Mysterious Valley left little doubt that, historically, the San Luis Valley has had more than its share of unexplained occurrences. Combine this documentation with countless little-known myths and legends and this remote region's documented history, and you have served before you a feast of blatant examples of the mysterious, the outrageous, and the sublime. These mysteries extend far beyond weird lights in the sky and strangely slain warm-blooded animals. There are many wonderful secrets and traditions found in the San Luis Valley that need examination. When scrutinizing subcultural/bioregional beliefs relating to the "unknown," one invariably finds myths and legends unique to a particular bioregion, and I feel the San Luis Valley could be considered a classic example.

Early on in my investigation, I was fascinated to hear stories and rumors of beliefs linking UFOs to treasure. In the southern portions of the San Luis Valley, when a UFO is spotted, the lucky witness often immediately contacts all his relatives. They watch the object closely, hoping it will hover. If it does hover over a specific spot, they believe that underneath the object "treasure" can be found. Once a location has been identified, they dash to the area with picks and shovels and start digging! Believe it or not, treasure may have been found in this manner. Although I have no proof that this technique has actually been used to find treasure, several sources have sworn they know of persons who have successfully utilized this method of UFO-inspired treasure hunting.

EL DORADO AND QUIVERA

Doing a bit of research, I have uncovered an impressive body of data relating to undiscovered treasure waiting to be found here. Most of the stories are tied to early Spanish and French exploration of the southern Sangre de Cristo Mountains.

Spanish exploration up the Rio Grande Valley in the sixteenth century is considered the earliest incursion by Europeans into North America. The conquistadors, fueled by a dangerous brand of xenophobic missionary zeal and an unquenchable thirst for precious metals, quickly reconnoitered the northern reaches of their new-found territory.

At first, the native Pueblo and Plains peoples welcomed the strangers, possibly because they were softened to the Europeans' arrival by Sister Marie Agreda, the natives' "Blue Lady." They didn't have much choice. Riding large, snorting animals, clothed in metal, and armed with "barking sticks" of death, the Spaniards struck terror into the simple natives. Quite different from our angelic bilocating nun. The soldiers, charging with their lusty shouts of "Santiago!" and "*Gold, glory and God,*" must have been an imposing sight to indigenous peoples. But culture shock inevitably gave way to resentment, and many Indians, especially "holders of traditional knowledge," soon chafed underneath the puritanical Catholic yoke of the priests and the gold-hungry mercenaries.

The Indians quickly realized that one thing above all compelled the armored, diseased, bearded white men to venture into the forbidding semiarid desert wilderness. Gold! A Spanish general in an honest moment reportedly told an Aztec chief, "The Spaniards have a disease of the heart for which gold is the specific remedy." The Spanish obsession with precious metals dictated much of their relentless explorations and forced them to overcome incredible hardship and sacrifice. Many of the forays north during the first two hundred years of exploration were not well documented, and most likely undisclosed clandestine expeditions were mounted. It can be assumed that at least a few of these greed-driven forays into extreme northern New Mexico and farther north into Colorado's vast mineral belt were met with success.

Blessed (or cursed?) with a lifelong fascination with the so-called thrill of discovery, I, too, have always been enamored by the thought of finding treasure of any kind. Many of you, I'm sure, can relate to this. I confess that it doesn't matter if it's precious stones, Indian artifacts, vertebra fossils, meteorites, or precious minerals. I have always been fascinated by the concept of discovering the many fabulous treasures contained on our planet. When this amateur fossil hunter and wannabe prospector moved out west from the East Coast in 1989, little did he know that he was moving to one of this country's legendary treasure locales.

During my first summer in Crestone, I happened to meet an old Hispanic man passing through town. His colorful clothes, gear, and demeanor revealed that he was a treasure hunter. His sparkling eyes and wrinkled, weather-beaten face reflected the years he had spent on his elusive quest. I managed to get him talking about some of the local area's legends, and he solemnly told me a couple of stories from the mountains towering two miles away. One of his accounts was of a lost Spanish mine with a large wooden door, possibly decorated with a Maltese cross. His theory was that the door had been hidden by a rock slide, and his enthusiasm and theories re-sparked a serious interest in me that continues to this day.

Captured by my professed enthusiasm for our area's rich treasure legends, in 1990 I was asked by current Baca Ranch owner Gary Boyce to write an article concerning the many fantastic treasure legends for his short-lived *Needles* newspaper. He mentioned hearing about a very low-key multimillion-dollar search effort that had been launched on the Baca Ranch (then owned by American Water Development Inc.), with no reported success.

I began researching and gathering together the enigmatic stories in a concerted effort to confirm the legends and write a truly riveting article. I've learned that the greater San Luis Valley region is one of the oldest settled areas in Colorado–northern New Mexico and quietly features dozens of Spanish treasure legends and numerous lost mines and lost treasure accounts. Combine these "legendary" mysteries with several known notorious lost robbery hoards, and you have an area with many potentially lucrative secrets to investigate— maybe more than any specific location in the great Southwest.

Much to my surprise, I also found some documentation of these mythical claims of treasure that have circulated around our section of the Sangres since the early seventeenth century, and many more additional legends and stories than I could possibly include in a two-thousand word article. Although publisher Boyce folded *Needles* just before my article was to be published, I've never lost my fascination for the subject.

During the course of the next several years, I had my ears and eyes open for any conclusive data firmly establishing a Spanish presence in the San Luis Valley prior to the acknowledged 1692 Diego de Vargas expedition.[1] I have always been fascinated by history, and I wondered why the Spanish didn't "officially" venture north for so many years. When the conquistadors and the ever-present Catholic missionaries first established a presence in Taos, at the extreme southern end of the Valley during the mid-1600s, the vast area north of Taos was a place of mystery and awe. Shamans and young warriors on vision quests were generally the only travelers who ventured north from around Taos, to the place many Indians believed "all thought originates." To the east, the Plains Indians considered the valley to be where dead souls go.

Taos is located at what was considered the extreme northern reach of Spanish power, and the Spanish seldom ventured north of the pueblo until the resulting Diego de Vargas expedition that was mounted to subjugate the Pueblo peoples twelve years after the 1680 Taos uprising, when the Pueblo Indians revolted. Although the Diego de Vargas expedition is considered the first Spanish incursion into south-central Colorado, others must have ventured north. But it is known that Diego de Vargas, accompanied by one hundred soldiers, seventy settlers with families, eighteen Franciscans, and Indian allies, marched up the Rio Grande into what is now Conejos and Costilla Counties, then returned to Sante Fe.

Dr. Marilyn Childs, an eminent archaeoastronomer, recalls an aside mentioned by a college professor while she was a student. "One of my professors at the University of Washington, who taught classes in archaeology, was Dr. Alex Kreiger. He was one of the scholars who did lots of research on the different Spanish expeditions. He knew I was interested in ufology, so he looked up some of the information in the chronicles for me. Apparently the Spanish were seeing lights around Mount Blanca, in the Sangre de Cristo Range, even back in the 1500s, and they also heard some kind of sounds they said were coming from the ground."[2]

A long, improbable eighty-seven years passed before the next official expedition north into Colorado. The 1779 campaign of New Mexico governor Juan Bautista de Anza against Comanche chief Cuerno Verde, or Greenhorn, is considered the next Spanish push into the region. I found it curious that one of the oldest continuously inhabited dwellings (some three stories tall) in North America was located at the south end of the Valley at the Taos Pueblo, and yet, officially, the Spanish never explored north into the rest of the San Luis for more than two hundred years.

As human nature would dictate, there were undoubtedly many secret mercenary forays up to *del Norte.* Over the years, the discovery of Spanish cannon barrels, conquistador helmets, arrastras, smelters, and enigmatic carvings, such as the Maltese cross at the mouth of the Upper Spanish Caves, fueled the colorful legends of lost Spanish treasure. These same stories were heard by the original Colorado gold rush pros-

pectors as they arrived in Colorado in the late 1850s
and early 1860s.

> The first legend of the Southwest begins for Euro-
> peans when Alvar Nunez Cabeza de Vaca saw an
> Indian give a *cascabel de cobre*, a copper rattle, to
> one of his companions. This simple happening com-
> bined with the tales he had heard about gold-paved
> cities created the legend of Quivira. . . . Stories
> continued to circulate and accumulate, not only of
> cities paved with gold but of mountains of solid ore
> and lakes shimmering with quicksilver. . . . In 1692,
> however, the story of this fabulous mountain not
> only reached the ears of Diego de Vargas but also
> those of the Viceroy who sent for specimens of a
> substance thought to be quicksilver. Some historians
> go as far as to suggest that the legend of Cerro Azul
> was the primary reason for the reconquest of New
> Mexico by Don Diego de Vargas.[3]

CAVERNA DEL ORO

Another enigmatic popular legend deserves mention.

> The legend of La Caverna del Oro, the cavern of
> gold, began long before the white man came to this
> continent. Accounts of such a cave was passed
> down from father to son by the Indians, until the
> Spanish monks recorded the legend in the Fifteenth-
> Century during the conquest of Mexico. . . . Excerpts
> from the Indian legend, translated from Spanish
> Monastery Latin to English, relate that many years
> ago, before the alliance of the three great kingdoms

of Aztec, Alcolhus, and Tepence, gold was eagerly sought. Most of the gold was brought from the mountains beyond the double mountain Huajatolla (meaning breasts of the earth—now called the Spanish Peaks), several days travel to the north. . . . The gold and the supposedly demon-infested area were not mentioned again until the year 1541, in connection with a story of three monks. These three were left behind after Francisco Coronado gave up his fruitless quest for the mythical city of Quivira.[4]

Two of the monks supposedly died after an uprising by slave-miner Indians, and the third monk somehow was able to mine a vast hoard of gold after convincing the Indians he had subdued the "evil spirits" that lurked underground in the dark mine, which may have been in the legendary Caverna del Oro, located thirteen thousand feet up on Marble Mountain, just over Music Pass to the northeast of the Great Sand Dunes. "Once there, he used several fiendish tortures to force them to enter the subterranean passages and bring forth the gold that lay loose all around. Later, when these slaves had served their purpose, he had them killed."[5]

The monk, de la Cruz, and his small group of surviving Spaniards supposedly loaded up pack mules with the vast treasure and fled from the northern region of "evil spirits" back south to "the city of Mexico" with their fabulous hoard.

In 1811, some distance south of the lost Cave of Gold, a Mexican-American named Baca stumbled across a pile of nuggets and bars of gold. He searched the area, but could find no evidence of a mine or even gold-bearing ore. It is generally believed that this was part of the monk's treasure. . . .

There are several legends and local tales about Indian and Spanish gold that is said to be buried in
caves around the Spanish Peaks northwest of Trinidad, Colorado. . . . Jean B. Challifou spent considerable time poking around the Las Cumbres
Espanolas, and probably knew more about them
than anyone alive. At one time in his wanderings,
he discovered a cave on one of the [Spanish] peaks
which plainly showed signs of having been entered
repeatedly by human beings. In later years, he tried
to relocate the cavern, but the attempt proved un-
successful; either he had lost his bearings or a rock-
slide had obliterated the entrance.[6]

David Perkins, who has researched our treasure legends for many years, pieced together an early history
of Caverna de Oro and the various area gold legends.

Capt. Elisha Horn, who is credited with discovering
the Cavern of Gold in 1869, supposedly found a
skeleton, clad in Spanish armor that was pierced
with an arrow. He also found a "Maltese cross"
which marked the cave's entrance. The cross is still
visible. Although several intriguing artifacts have
been found in the cave, and nearby, there is no direct evidence that it was ever a gold producing mine
or treasure cache. Numerous spelunking ventures
have attempted to map the "seemingly infinite cat-
acombs," but experts will venture no guess as to
how extensive the cave system will turn out to be. It
is now estimated to be one of the five or six deepest
caves in the U.S.[7]

This labyrinth of caves and passageways sits just to
the east of the Great Sand Dunes. The largest cavern

system in Colorado, the Marble Caves are one of several enigmatic entrances to a netherworld beneath the San Luis Valley and surrounding mountains.

Over the course of the late seventeenth and early eighteenth centuries, the Spanish combed the West for gold, silver, and mercury. Although Diego de Vargas was acknowledged the leader of the first officially sanctioned expedition into the San Luis Valley in 1692, rumors persist to this day of earlier clandestine forays into the area by gold-seeking Spanish mercenaries. Other legends persisted in the early days of the Spanish exploration of Northern New Mexico.

> There is a story in Taos about a Mexican by the name of Vigil who found a document in a church on Guadalajara, Mexico, stating that in 1680 the Spaniards covered up fourteen million peso's worth of gold in a shaft in the mountains near the pueblo of Taos. This treasure has been hunted by many who believe that the Indians know much more than they are willing to tell. Some of the early prospectors who came to Taos have explored all the likely spots in the area as far [north] as the Red River and into the Moreno Valley, but aside from small locations like the one of a Swede named Gus Lawson, nothing like a Spanish gold horde has been discovered.[8]

THE FRENCH EXPEDITION OF 1790

Journeying down from the northern Rockies, exploratory French forays into the rarefied air of the Sangre de Cristos are said to have produced gold. Another little-known story researched by Crestone author Jack Harlan concerns an ill-fated French-Canadian expedition into the southern Colorado Rockies and is centered around a very identifiable northern SLV landmark.

> While leaving the San Luis Valley by way of Poncha Pass, Round Mountain is skirted on the left. Here on Round Mountain an undetermined amount of gold nuggets are supposedly buried. There are several versions of the story. The most popular one is about a French Canadian trapper whose name has become lost through the years. . . . A party of Canadians were trapping on the Snake River when they were discovered by American trappers, who attacked. In their hasty retreat, the Frenchmen lost their furs and traps to the Americans. Traveling south into Western Colorado, one of the four found a gold nugget in the headwaters of the Gunnison River. Here they spent the next month successfully panning the gravel bars. Ute Indians discovered the Frenchmen and attacked them. In the running battle which lasted several days, three Frenchmen were killed. The fourth managed to escape over Cochetopa Pass [just west of Saguache]. Sensing that his pursuers were closing in, he buried the gold on Round Mountain with the hopes of later returning for it. The Indians caught and killed the lone French-Canadian near the summit of Poncha Pass.[9]

The treasure was never found, but the story endures hundreds of years later. I travel on State Highway 285, which winds within feet of this little mountain, and on every trip north out of the SLV, I wonder . . .

*　　*　　*

One of Colorado's most fabulous treasure legends is centered around a sizable French expedition that journeyed to our area in the late 1700s. Setting out from a small French outpost near present-day Leavenworth, Kansas, 300 men and 450 horses began the long trek toward the Rockies. The guides, officers, miners, and laborers, following the course of the Platte River, explored and prospected several areas before reaching southern Colorado, and it is believed by some that the huge expedition may have superficially prospected unsuccessfully at Cripple Creek and other mining regions that later produced fabulous gold fields.

Working their way south, they finally ended up near present-day Summitville, Colorado. They made camp several miles east of Wolf Creek Pass and began prospecting the many creeks that flowed down the San Juan Mountains, just west of the San Luis Valley, hoping to find the elusive malleable metal. They allegedly struck the mother lode and buried the gold on what is now called Treasure Mountain. "Most sources estimated the value at some five million dollars, although one source estimated the cache as worth thirty-three million dollars. . . . According to later reports, the gold was cached in three places, only known to the top officers of the expedition. A key chart was made of the entire area and kept by the officer in command."[10]

At first, upon their arrival at the Summitville area, the native Indians seemed friendly. However, for some reason not known, the Indians became angry with the French. Perhaps the knowledge that the French were leaving with gold from their lands prompted them to attack the expedition as the French set out. In any event, an attack was mounted, and during the pitched battle the gold was reburied, and the French made new maps detailing where the buried gold was hidden. It is known that very few French survived the battle. Estimates range from seventeen to thirty-five, but some of them did survive the Indian onslaught. To make matters worse, they were attacked again out on the Front Range, and only five men survived to continue the journey back to the French outpost in Kansas. Starvation and bitter conditions killed off three of the men, who may have been eaten by the surviving two members.

The two men, more dead than alive, stumbled into the outpost, and one of them died. The sole survivor, the expedition historian, named in some accounts as Le Blanc, eventually traveled back to France with two copies of the treasure map. One was given to the French government; the other, naturally, he kept.

There is much confusion at this part of the story. One version has the historian's family mounting an expedition and returning to find the buried treasure. Another version has the French government mounting an expedition led by a relative of the historian. In any event, the second expedition, which numbered around fifty men, headed west to recover the gold. Stopping in Taos, New Mexico, they obtained the services of a guide who led them to the Summitville area. Allegedly, they searched the entire area for three years with no apparent luck. Then the guide returned alone to Taos, claiming that the entire expedition had again been wiped out by the Indians. The locals were suspicious of him because he was the sole survivor, and he was tried for murder but managed to be acquitted. It is said that his trial was the last Mexican trial held in United States territory.

Some theorists claim that the whole story was contrived by the French who secretly found the gold and returned to France with it. This theory suggests that the guide was paid to be a patsy and was promised a fortune to return to Taos with the untrue story of a massacre. This scenario seems unlikely, although later, French equipment was found among the Indians. Another version has the guide spending years trying to locate the lost treasure of Treasure Mountain.

Several maps have appeared over the years, claiming to lead to the reburied French treasure. A man named William Yule claimed he had a copy of the original and searched the entire western side of the Valley, all the way north to Saguache, with no apparent success. Another colorful prospector named Asa Poor obtained the map from Yule, and with two partners he was able to locate several landmarks leading to the caches but was not able to locate the hidden French gold. One of Poor's partners, named Montroy, retained possession of the map, but it disappeared several years later.

After much digging, and a bit of luck, I've located and talked with several knowledgeable treasure hunters. I began hearing stories of treasure maps. Then, in 1993, I was introduced to an amiable man I'll call Tomas Ortiz (not his real name). Tomas's wife is the daughter of the patriarch of the treasure-hunting family. At one point in our initial conversation, he casually told me that his brother-in-law has an authentic "treasure map written in French," and his family are "direct descendants of Le Blanc." He told me that for three generations they have been quietly searching for the fabled lost French gold. Their claim is backed up with what appears to be a genuine map, drawn by the harried second expedition before they unsuccessfully tried to escape with their lives. Could this actually be the real Le Blanc map? Their map and story are impressive.

After searching for decades, family members have painstakingly located seven out of eight landmarks and clues carved in rock that are mentioned in the map. The most important eighth and final clue has eluded their efforts for years. Then, in 1993, their luck turned. Or did it?

Thirty-year-old Tomas happened to be hunting elk in the mountains southeast of Del Norte, Colorado, on an overcast late fall morning in 1993. The clouds loomed threateningly, and a cold, hard rain began to spit. The pale predawn gloom cast faint detail to the surrounding vegetation, and Ortiz looked around for shelter from the rain. He spotted a three-foot opening in the ground hidden by some underbrush, and after removing some loose rocks, he squeezed through the opening and peered into the darkness. He clicked on his flashlight and was surprised to find himself in a five-foot-high, four-foot-wide tunnel, obviously man-made. Ortiz cautiously explored the gently sloping narrow passageway, and after wriggling about twenty feet into the hillside, his way was blocked by an apparent underground landslide. Shining his light around the dim narrow passageway, he spied a carving on the rock wall next to the cave-in. Quite aware of his in-laws' long quest, he was understandably thrilled by what he saw. It was the long-lost eighth clue that, according to the treasure map, indicated the hidden location of the fabled French treasure.

Completely forgetting the wily elk herd he had been stalking, he excitedly rushed back to town to tell his in-laws of his fortuitous find. The following day, Tomas led an expedition back to the tunnel. Members of the party, consisting of twenty family members, began eagerly excavating the cave-in, and after several grueling hours of hard work, they extended the tunnel an additional twelve feet into the mountainside. Thirty-two feet in, they encountered a large boulder that appeared to have been purposely rolled into place to seal the rest of the passageway. By this time, the sun had set, and the elated group gathered at the entrance and took a break as twilight approached. Undaunted, Tomas lined the length of the passageway with a dozen equally spaced unlit candles.

The ensuing events allegedly occurred in a matter of minutes. As Ortiz placed the last candle at the far end of the tunnel, a "large rattlesnake" lunged out of the gloom and narrowly missed striking him. He scrambled breathlessly back out to the entrance, followed by a boiling swarm of bats that began pouring out of the hillside. Uncharacteristically, and much to their dismay, the small mammals began squeaking and diving aggressively at the surprised party. What they claim happened seconds later quickly erased the elation and excitement of the expedition.

According to Tomas, as he knelt down to light the first candle at the entrance to the tunnel, the candle at the far end of the passageway inexplicably flared on by itself! The stunned group, knowing that no one was in the tunnel, stared at one another in horror. At that instant, out of the gloom, a "huge owl" dive-bombed the shocked party within inches of their heads.

That was the last straw. As if chased by the devil himself, the terrified group grabbed their kids, raced down the hillside, piled into their cars, and, as Tomas put it, "got the hell outta there!"

Tomas told me later, "The French and Spanish placed curses on their [hidden] gold" caches. In light of the strange sequence of events, the family of treasure hunters is understandably wary and are planning to proceed with caution. Several members flatly refuse to venture back to the site.

Thomas Tate Tobin, mountain man, captured and killed the Espinozas in 1863.
(*Colorado Historical Society*)

The haunted house on North River Road.
(*K. Thompson*)

Canero Pass mutilation, May 1996. Found by two loggers.
(*Brendan O'Brien*)

Draft horse found in tree in Estrella, Colorado, August 1996. (*Greg Johnson*/The Valley Courier)

Does old Number 167 haunt the Valley near Crestone? (*Kate Snider*)

The Ace Inn, Alamosa, Colorado. Haunted?
(*Christopher O'Brien*)

Pioneering mutilation investigators. From left to right — Carrie Sewell, Tom Adams, Linda Moulton Howe, Gary Massey. (*David Perkins*)

A rare photo of Sister Marie Jesus Agreda in repose, 335 years after death. (*Javier Sierra/*Ano Cero Magazine)

Author on left, brother Brendan on right, 1963. (*J.C. O'Brien*)

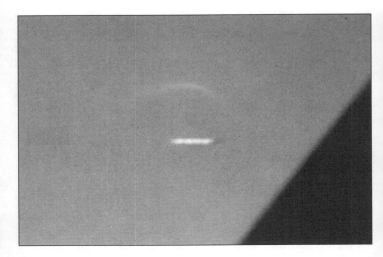

The only still photograph taken during famous sighting on August 27, 1995 at Salida, Colorado.
(*Tim Edwards*)

Salida, Colorado, with Sangre de Cristos upper right.
(*Christopher O'Brien*)

Mothership cloud hovering over Crestone. Picture taken looking north from the San Luis Lakes. (*Al and B.G. Purvis*)

Extremely rare photograph of an actual Penitente ritual. (*Denver Public Library*)

Calf mutilation on November 30, 1997, North of Hooper, Colorado. (*Christopher O'Brien*)

The majestic Sangre de Cristos, shot from the floor of the San Luis Valley. (*Dan Connor*)

Knowing a little bit about ritual magic, I have been asked to help formulate a way to help lift any "curses" on the gold. As of this writing, the family has obtained Colorado State Treasure Rights to legally enter the cavern and claim whatever treasure may be located there— If they dare. I have been invited along to document the event.

The story of the lost French gold does not end here. Further research has uncovered tantalizing information suggesting that the attacking Ute Indians may have acquired a substantial portion of the French gold during the running battle and may have hidden it down near the mouth of the Rio Grande Canyon near the Colorado–New Mexico border.

THE SKULLS IN DEAD MAN'S CAVE

Another fascinating account is one of the very few that have actually produced gold to bolster the lucky finder's claims. However, this hoard is one of those that got away. It's probably still out there.

One day in 1880, prospectors E. J. Oliver, S. J. Harkman, and H. A. Melton had been prospecting two miles north of what become known as Dead Man Camp (about eight miles south of where I live). The sky threatened, and before long the three men found themselves caught in a furious blizzard. Knowing that travel is difficult in the rugged Sangres even under ideal weather conditions, found shelter underneath a convenient ledge near the mouth of a canyon.[11]

Looking across the canyon, one of the men noticed what appeared to be a small opening in the sheer rock wall. They made their way to the opening and made several crude torches. The opening was very narrow and less than four feet high and extended into the cliff about ten feet, before it opened up into a large, twenty-foot-long vault. Shining their torches around, Oliver found the first of five skeletons scattered around the dusty, dark cavern.

After exploring the cavern, they found several tight passageways extending into the gloom of the mountain and chose one to explore. It led into the mountain and opened up into a larger, vaultlike chamber. Near the far end, Melton noticed what appeared to be shelves carved into the side of the western wall. He lit the area and saw some peculiar-looking stones stacked on the shelf. He picked one up, surprised at its heavy weight, and brought it back to his partners to look at. Imagine their delight when the "stones" turned out to be crude bars of gold!

In their excitement, thinking that the opening would be easy to mark and find again, the men gathered up only five of the bars and headed over the pass to Silver Cliff, in the Wet Mountain Valley. The bars, etched with what appeared to be Spanish engravings, proved to be worth nine hundred dollars apiece, and the men became instant celebrities. Although asked by many, the men steadfastly refused to divulge the actual location.

In the spring, the men headed off to find Dead Man's Cave. But in the mountains, many places looked like the area in which they had found the cave. They went back again and again, and so did many others. Nobody found anything.

Colorado has an interesting series of "treasure rights," which allow someone to look for and keep treasure found in specific deeded locations. I couldn't help but wonder who owned the treasure rights for the area around the Dead Man's Treasure.

A simple listing of the San Luis Valley and Huerfano's lost mines and treasures is, to say the least, impressive. The following is a sampling of south-central Colorado and north-central New Mexico legends and accounts.

From the Huerfano/Spanish Peaks region:

- Alex Cobsky's Lost Mine near Silver Mountain, northeast of La Veta Pass
- The Arapaho Princess Treasure, near the Spanish Peaks
- Caverna del Oro, on Marble Mountain
- George Skinner's Lost Mine, on Horn Peak Mountain
- The Green Lost Mine, west of Red Wing, Colorado
- The Lost Mine of the Greenhorn Mountains, just east of the Wet Mountain Valley
- Henry Sefton's Treasure, on the east side of the Sangres
- The fabled Huajatolla Gold, on the Spanish Peaks
- Jack Simpson's Lost Mine, on Silver Mountain, east of La Veta, Colorado
- The Jasper Lost Mine, near Red Wing
- Juan Carlos's Lost Gold, on the Blanca Massif
- The Lost Pick Mine of Veta Creek, north of La Veta Creek in the Huerfano
- The Lost Veta Mine, north of La Veta Creek in the Huerfano
- The Treasure of the Spanish Fort, twenty-five miles west of Walsenburg

From the southern New Mexican part of the San Luis Valley:

- Cannady's Murder Money, in Taos Canyon
- The Chavez Lost Copper Mine, north of El Rito, New Mexico
- The Grinning Skull Treasure, in the Sangres east of Taos
- Gus Lawson's Lost Mine, on Taos Mountain
- Juan Gallule's and Techato Martinez's Lost Mine, on Jicarita Peak
- Madame Barcelo's Lost Treasure, forty miles east of Taos
- Padre Mora's Treasure, Kit Carson State Park, southeast of Taos
- Rio Grande Gold, on the Rio Grande, north of Taos
- Simeon Turley's Lost Mine and Treasure, about twelve miles northwest of Taos
- The Treasure of Tres Piedras, west of Tres Piedras, New Mexico
- White's Lost Mine, near the town of Amalia, New Mexico

From the central and northern San Luis Valley, where I live:

- The Spanish Treasure of Blanca Peak, on Blanca Peak, north of Fort Garland, Colorado
- The Lost Mine of Embargo Creek, east of Creede, Colorado
- The Paymaster's Treasure of Fort Garland, on Trincera Creek, south of Fort Garland
- The Lost Mine of Hidden Valley, near La Jara Creek, west of Capulin
- The Josh Thomas Treasure, on Conejos Creek, west of Antonito, Colorado

- Manuel Torres Lost Mine, on Culebra Peak, southeast of San Luis, Colorado
- Mark Bidell's Lost Lode, near Saguache Creek, northwest of Del Norte, Colorado
- The Phantom Mine, Davis Gulch, six miles south of Crestone
- The Lost Brother Mine, north of San Isabelle Creek
- The Lost Sidney Brother Mine, Burnt Gulch, just east of Crestone
- The Disappearing Sand Dunes Wagon, Great Sand Dunes National Monument
- The Lost Mine of Mogate Peak, east of Creede, Colorado
- The Buried Treasure of Round Hill, just south of Poncha Pass
- The Lost Mine in the Sangres, near Cottonwood Creek, five miles south of Crestone
- The Missouri Bank Robbery Treasure, between Music and Mosca Pass
- The Center [Colorado] Bank Heist Loot, north of Moffat, Colorado, at the Grey Ranch
- The Lost Treasure of Treasure Mountain, east of Pagosa Springs
- White's Lost Cement Mine, on Culebra Peak, Costilla County

Without question, there are many fantastic secrets buried in south-central Colorado. Hidden away from prying eyes and the light of discovery, it is said that the mountains' inner depths hold secrets more compelling than mundane gold and treasure. Search these vast areas hard enough and you may be surprised at what you'll find.

CHAPTER SEVEN
TROGLODYTE BASES

As an avid *Star Trek* fan in the midsixties, one of the episodes I enjoyed most concerned an uprising by underground miner-slaves called Troglodytes. The Troglodytes were forced to live out their lives deep underground, mining crystals for the overlords who lived in palaces suspended high above the world in the clouds.

If we are to believe the stories circulating around ufology, we have not only visitors from above the clouds but also Troglodytes digging beneath our feet.

Ufology is a rather broad term when you consider several offshoots, or branches of study, that have been inexorably linked to the research of ufos and extraterrestrials. Unusual animal deaths and the channeling of "space brothers" or "ascended masters" are two examples of this kind of "guilt by association" marriage.

Another fringe area of ufological study could be considered a rather contentious bastard child. The conspiracy-soaked, high-tech intrigue surrounding the subject of "alien underground bases" fixates an element in ufology like no other subject. It is the murky realm of darkness, paranoia, and fear, one of several ufological connecting points with the patriot and militia movements in this country, which include "black helicopters," "United Nations troops on United States soil," and New World Order theories.

Ufology has other branches. The groundbreaking work of radical history theorists, such as the renowned Sumerologist Zecheria Sitchin and the ever-popular Eric Von Daniken, carved themselves a worthy ufological niche of sorts with their study of ancient cultures. Urban man's inexplicable ascendance has baffled historians and archaeologists for decades, and several radical theories have been postulated to account for the rise of the great Mesopotamian culture.

Sitchen, in his fascinating Earth Chronicle series, has eminently presented the very real possibility that ancient man may have interacted with extraterrestrials, which directly resulted in the rise of the Sumerian civilization. Von Daniken, taking a less orthodox approach, postulates that megalithic sites around the world may have been extraterrestrial in design and/or origin.

Ex-NASA scientist Dr. Richard Hoagland's Enterprise Mission is another example of a ufological offshoot. Hoagland has spearheaded an effort to convince NASA to reexamine the enigmatic Cydonia Plain's Monuments of Mars, originally photographed in 1976 by the *Viking* space probe. NASA steadfastly claims that the "face" is nothing but the play of light and shadow on the Martian surface. But Hoagland feels it is an ancient manufactured artifact that has tremendous significance for mankind. Along with ex-NASA video analyst Mark Carlotti, the Monument of Mars effort has captured the interest of thousands worldwide.

As blasphemous as it may sound to some, even ufology's quasi-religious fixation on the "abduction" phenomenon could be considered a ufological offshoot of sorts. When you take into account the rich tradition of abduction-type scenarios that have existed for generations in Europe, you must acknowledge there may be important historical elements at work. The Celtic tradition of "gentry" replacing healthy human babies with weak, emaciated "changelings"[1] mirrors abductee claims of seeing hybrid babies. Incubi and succubi, those nasty, sexually abusive nocturnal creatures reported in the Middle Ages, could be likened to current claims of sexual experiments by "aliens."[2] The legend of Rip Van Winkle from this country has the popular missing-time element. These examples are just a few pre-ufological abduction scenarios that spring to mind.

But back to ufology's soft, white underbelly. Are Troglodytes tunneling beneath our feet?

WHO'S LIVING DOWNSTAIRS?

The history behind the shadowy subject area of underground dwellers has well-defined roots dating back into prehistory. All major cultures around the world, with a few exceptions, have traditions of "lost peoples" or "tribes" that ultimately fled and now live underground.

The legendary city of Shamballa, in Asia Minor, it is said, can be reached only through an underground passage or tunnel. The Tibetans and Mongols have a tradition of a wondrous underground city called Erdami and of the "nagas," lizard-looking subterranean dwellers. The Persians called a similar sacred place Aryana, which was the land of their ancestors. The Egyptian

Book of the Dead refers to the hidden land of Amenti. The Celts talked of Lands of Mystery called Dananada, or Duat. The Scandinavian countries mention a subterranean land called Asar and the magical realm of Ultima Thule. The Vikings believed that Thor lived underground below volcanoes far to the north.

Closer to home, let's not forget the Mexican land of Tolan, or that the Cherokee attribute the megalithic Mound Builders of the Ohio River Valley to a "moon-faced," white-skinned people that were eventually forced permanently underground by Native Americans moving into the region. Some Native Americans have even suggested that Sasquatch, or bigfoot, are actually banished medicine men who now live underground, and other southwestern Indian traditions have legends of "ant people" who live underneath the Sipapu, or "place of emergence," right here in the San Luis Valley, twenty miles from my house.

There are countless additional examples of myths and legends from around the world relating to underground civilizations, and some even suggest a fantastic "hollow-earth" theory: Lewis Carroll's *Alice's Adventures in Wonderland*, Dante's *Divine Comedy* and his harrowing trip underground to hell, *The Arabian Nights* ("Open, Sesame"), the adventures of Sinbad, Edgar Rice Burroughs's Pellucidar series, Jules Verne's *Journey to the Center of The Earth*—the list of stories and books about underground lands, cities, and peoples seems endless, and many of these myths have somehow endured worldwide for perhaps thousands of years. Is there a nuance of truth behind these misty legends and are there verified modern examples supporting these fantastic scenarios?

*   *   *

The following quote comes to us from Dr. Marilyn Childs, professor of archaeoastronomy and western regional director for MUFON, one of the very first paranormal investigators to come to the San Luis Valley in the 1960s. Her comments were recorded at the question and answer session at the 1996 Show Me UFO Conference in St. Louis, Missouri: "There are lots of myths about individuals coming from the tunnels, or from deep inside the earth. This is all over the world; it's not just in North America. I've often suspected that maybe if an advanced civilization that was on this planet eons ago left this network of underground tunnels, there is a good possibility that using some of our tunneling devices, building some of our missile silos, people came across some of these and then they just decided to expand them."[3]

Upon returning from his historic 1956–1957 South Pole expedition, Rear Admiral Richard E. Byrd, one of the twentieth century's greatest explorers, captivated imaginations worldwide when he was quoted as saying, "The present expedition has opened up a vast new land, *beyond* the pole" (my italics), and claimed that his expedition "was the most important expedition in the history of the world." Now why would a respected explorer say this about a vast wilderness of penguins, wind, snow, and ice? According to Byrd, he did not go to a place barren of warmth and life; instead, he traveled over "mountains, covered with trees." This startling revelation may inadvertently have helped fuel a modern version of the hollow-earth theory.

   This theory suggests that the North and South Poles are actually openings allowing access to, as Byrd called it, "the Great Unknown." The theory, on the surface, is scientifically untenable, but there is a body of evi-

dence supporting this conclusion, and it is quite interesting and provocative. Icebergs, for instance, are
composed of fresh water, not salt water. Some may
wonder if such massive, dense objects, even hundreds
of miles long, may be composed simply of accumulated
snow.

> Arctic explorers found the temperature to rise as they
> traveled north; they found more open seas; they
> found animals traveling north in the winter, seeking
> food and warmth, when they should have gone
> south; they found their compass needle to assume a
> vertical position instead of a horizontal one and to
> become extremely erratic; they saw tropical birds
> and more animal life the further north they went;
> They saw butterflies, mosquitoes and other insects
> in the extreme north. . . . [4]

The same was evidently true for regions visited by
South Pole explorers. There is something strange about
the South Pole, and Antarctica has always been
shrouded in secrecy. Dr. Richard Hoagland relates the
following account:

> I have a friend in Northern California . . . who is a
> rather remarkable architect and artist. She has a little
> quiet project called The Tetrahedron Project, where
> she wanted to place four tetrahedra at the proverbial
> four-corners of the world. Kind of "test the concept"
> and see if she could get the right connections, and
> the right logistics with the military, because they're
> the ones that go all over the world. She got very
> buddy-buddy with the Navy, the Marines, and the
> Air Force and all that, and she was able to fly to the
> North Pole, under military aegis, very easily, and

drop a small tetrahedron out of an aircraft over the ice at the North Pole. Everybody was helping her, there was an enormous amount of wonderful inter-service cooperation to help this rather beautiful young woman drop her tetrahedron at the North Pole. Well, she also wanted to drop one at the South Pole. And these same people suddenly turned into total, total nerds. She could get no cooperation to go to the South Pole at all! She even tried to go through the Russians, and they told her quietly, "If we help you, the Americans will have us for lunch." So, the same kind of openness she found in the Northern Hemisphere . . . it was nada, zip, nothing, in the Southern Hemisphere—having to do with the Ant-arctic! . . . The point is that there is something very interesting and strange going on at the Antarctic.[5]

Underground base expert Dr. Richard Sauder, dur-ing the same question and answer session, brought up a couple of interesting and revealing secondhand sto-ries relating to the secrecy surrounding current activi-ties at the South Pole. It seems that a source had told Sauder that one of the source's friends who had gone to work as a cook at an Antarctic weather station had to obtain high-security clearance in order to be a break-fast cook. This does not make sense, but it could be an indication that highly secretive activity may be hidden in the vast Antarctic wastes.[6]

Admiral Byrd's polar activities inspired his son to fol-low in his father's footsteps. The following account comes from Dr. Marilyn Childs: "A few years ago, I had the opportunity to talk to a man who was with Admiral Byrd's son. Admiral Byrd was very interested in Antarc-tica and, of course, went there on several expeditions. His son had rented a Lear Jet and wanted to fly over

Antarctica. He was turned around and told not to fly over a certain [air] space, it's a restricted area. Well, Admiral Byrd's son in 1988 was on his way from Boston to Washington, D.C., for the unveiling of a stamp commemorating his father. He was mysteriously taken off the train, and ended up dead in a warehouse."[7]

Several books have been written suggesting the hollow-earth theory, and although scientifically laughable, there are many who firmly believe that the earth's interior is not what modern science believes. When did this modern theory arrive on the scene? When did it hit our culture? "The theory of a hollow earth was first worked out by an American writer, William Reed, in 1906, and later extended by another American, Marshall B. Gardner, in 1920. In 1959, F. Amadeo Giannini wrote the first book on the subject since Gardner's, and in the same year, Ray Palmer, editor of *Flying Saucers* magazine, applied the theory to provide a logical explanation for the origin of flying saucers."[8] Where did Palmer get his inspiration to make such an oblique connection? Are we wading through the realm of science fiction, or is there evidence to back up this explanation?

Palmer, editor of *Amazing Stories* from 1938 to 1949, received an intriguing letter from a man named Richard S. Shaver in September of 1944, which included examples of what Shaver called "an ancient language that should not be lost to the world."[9]

At Palmer's insistence, Shaver sent a ten-thousand-word manuscript originally titled "A Warning to the World" and retitled by Palmer as "I Remember Lemuria." It was published in a series of articles in *Amazing Stories* and touched off what *Life* magazine called "the most celebrated rumpus that racked the world of science-fiction." Some people are still convinced that the scenario is true.

The Shaver mystery, as it has become known, concerned a fantastic world existing inside the earth, populated by *deros* and *teros*. According to Shaver, the deros, short for detrimental robots, originally inhabited Lemuria but now inhabit an extensive underground network of cities all over planet Earth. According to the plot, they had been subhuman slaves of a Lemurian master race that had eventually disappeared. Now autonomous, the nasty, vindictive, and inbred deros spend their time dogging us humans who live on the thin crust of the earth above and were responsible for much of the world's "evil." They amused themselves by harassing humans with a variety of high-tech gadgets that included ray guns, remote-controlled devices, and even telepathic forms of psychological warfare, all operated from their subterranean lairs. Having a somewhat human appearance, the deros would, on occasion, venture forth to the surface and carry out diabolical plots against an unsuspecting aboveground human race, creating havoc, suffering and chaos. Nasty guys.

Is there any evidence of life deep underground? In a scholarly work compiled by William R. Corliss we find subtle references to this intriguing possibility.

Although near-surface waters in caves, fractured rocks, and porous strata support bacteria and even higher forms of life, biologists did not consider life possible at depths of several kilometers. The early Soviet reports from the Kola Peninsula were on the sensational side. They indicated that life-forms and fossils had been found kilometers down. . . . Providing further details on remains of life at such depths, a geologist, B. V. Timofeyev, said microscopic fossils had been found at depths of 22,000 feet. He said that twenty-four species had been identified among the micro-fossils, representing the envelopes or coverings of single-celled marine animals known as plankton. . . . [Magnetite] particles were synthesized by deep-dwelling bacteria which feed upon the abiogenic hydrocarbons rising from even greater depths. At best, this is only indirect evidence of life at depths of several kilometers.[10]

Now that's all fine and dandy, just like the recent announcement of apparent single-celled, ancient "life" on the Mars meteorite found in Antarctica. But, correct me if I'm wrong, single-celled organisms are not the source of all evil and certainly don't build tunnels while telepathically messing with the aboveground crowd.

When I began this investigation of the San Luis Valley in 1993, I heard stories and rumors of underground bases said to be nestled under the mountains surrounding the Valley. The sources spanned the culture and ranged from housewives, researcher-investigators, county undersheriffs, ranchers, and even college kids.

Quite a number of people, who would comment on the subject, seemed to feel there was a base under Blanca Peak. From my research into Native American traditions, which, granted, is tenuous "evidence" at best, I found a Dine, or Navajo tradition of "flying seed pods" that were said to arrive here, from elsewhere. These stories directly related to Blanca and the portion of the Sangres extending north, past the Great Sand Dunes, forty or so miles to Crestone Peak, which the Dine call the Sis Na Jinni, or (the) Black Sash Medicine Belt.

A fleeting bit of anecdotal "evidence" supporting a

possible Blanca underground base location was the
story that old Harry King used to insist was true. Harry
King, remember, was a rancher who had a large spread
on the western flank of the Blanca Massif in the mid-
to late sixties and into the midseventies where our notorious Snippy the Horse died. Old Harry claimed that
tiny ten- to- twelve-foot jetlike objects (that many other
locals, including me, also witnessed zipping around the
area) would disappear *into* Middle Creek Hill, way
above the gravel pit near the tree line. His brother-in-
law Berle Lewis told me that Harry saw them go right
into the mountain "*dozens* of times."[11]

Later, in August 1995, after hearing witnesses' assertion that an object like Tim Edwards's "main craft"
disappeared *into* Crestone Peak, and two Grand Junction DJs witnessed a similar sight less than seven hours
before, I had to wonder if these reports could be tied
into our underground base equation.

Early on in my investigation, I admit, I was excited,
and with all the reports and information I was receiving,
I found myself leaping toward high-strange conclusions. It was during this period that I first heard about
the bases. If all the stories were to be believed, my God,
we had quite a widespread number of potential locations to chose from. The various locations sound like a
wilderness tour of the mountains surrounding the San
Luis Valley. Locally, "It's gotta be in Blanca, or at least
in Crestone Peak." Many think "it's under the dunes."
Or we may have an entrance under "the Baca. There's
a tunnel that goes all the way to NORAD." One California researcher claims that he witnessed a helicopter
fly out of a camouflaged opening in the cliff face in the
Rio Grande Canyon just below the Colorado–New
Mexico border. Or maybe it could be farther east, right
on the border in the Sangres, they claim, or it's just

north under Culebra Peak and the Taylor Ranch.[12] Some people are convinced they're building something underground around Summitville, where huge sky-crane helicopters have been seen and reported.

The list is endless, and there are not enough hours in the day to methodically cover this vast amount of territory to ascertain the truth.

With all these locations to choose from, the possibility that we have more than one facility even needs to be entertained. I took Tom Clancy's fictional assertion that there is a secret base here as a kind of challenge. But where to start digging? In 1993, I set out to find the experts concerning the subject of underground bases.

I initially found three men whose work was recommended. William Hamilton, TAL, and Val Valarian. Hamilton had revealed information concerning the Lockheed Skunk Works in southern California. TAL, aka Jason Bishop III, a self-professed fan of the hollow earth, was one of the first to publicize the Dulce Base stories. Val Valarian published the notorious Matrix books, which detailed the nightmarish scenario involving alien underground bases near Dulce and elsewhere. Some of these fantastic scenarios are a bit over the top.

How feasible is it to build these kinds of facilities? How many do we have? Where are they? I needed to learn more. What evidence do we have to support this idea of high-tech Troglodytes and underground alien bases? The eye-opening stories surrounding the subject that one finds swirling around this area of study are some of the most horrific and downright unbelievable modern myths we have as a culture.

One suspected underground facility, the notorious Dulce Base, is said to lie thousands of feet underground, just southeast of Dulce, New Mexico. Down in the dank recesses of "Level Seven," it is said that there is a place nicknamed "Nightmare Hall" by the human workers in upper levels. If this lab actually exists, we're all in trouble! Large, ghoulishly bubbling vats of fluids with bobbing human and cattle parts stewing in an unholy brew, hundreds of tiny hybrid fetuses floating in large test tubes, multi-limbed human mutations genetically combined with all kinds of domestic and wild animals, even fish, à la *The Island of Dr. Moreau*. According to the "myth," in 1979, sixty-six Delta Force troops were even killed in underground firefights with Dulce-based aliens. The alleged activities going on down there rival most of the science fiction or horror film scripts Hollywood has ever produced.

TAL, writing under the pseudonym of Jason Bishop III, wrote:

> This [Dulce] facility is a "genetics lab" and is connected to Los Alamos, via a Tube-shuttle. Part of their research is related to the genetic effects of radiation [mutations and human genetics]. Its research also includes other "intelligent species" [alien biological life-form entities]. . . . The Dulce Complex is a joint U.S. Government/Alien base. It was first built with the aliens [others are in Colorado, Nevada, and Arizona] . . . and consists of a central "Hub," the Security Section. The deeper you go, the stronger the security. . . . There are over 3000 cameras at various high-security locations [exits and labs]. . . . They are people who worked in the labs; abductees taken to the base; people who assisted in the construction; intelligence personnel [NSA, CIA, etc.] and inner-earth researchers. . . . The Continental Divide is vital to these "entities." Part of this has to do with mag-

netics [substrata rock] and high energy states [plasma]. . . . [13]

What is most interesting to me about the so-called Dulce Base is its location, just over the mountains, a scant forty-five miles away from the western edge of the San Luis Valley.

Is there anything behind these wild Dulce Base stories? Is there an extensive underground magnetic-suspension (mag-lev) shuttle system burrowed underneath the United States, as some have claimed? Do aliens have nests or bases riddling the American Southwest, as some researchers assert?

In January 1995, I received a call from a law enforcement officer for the Jicarilla Apache Indian Reservation. The "rez" completely surrounds the Dulce area. The Apache officer has been a tribal cop in the area for more than twenty-five years. He suggested we get together on a trip he was making through the San Luis Valley. We met in a restaurant in South Fork, Colorado.

After shaking hands, I was quite surprised when, unasked, the officer started on an insistent, twenty-minute disclaimer concerning the nonexistence of the Dulce Base. I never even asked him about it; in fact, I had barely said, "Good to meet you."

"I've lived in around Dulce all my life, and if there was a base there I'd know about it, and I'm telling you, there's *no* base!"

"Why are you telling me this? I never even asked you about the base."

"I know, I just wanted to get the question out of the way." Sounded reasonable enough at the time, but after our five-and-a-half-hour meeting, I did think it strange how he had jumped in and emphatically trashed the idea of a base. Something didn't quite seem right about the episode.

He did tell me quite a bit about the "UFO" activity reported in the area, however, including several very riveting sightings he personally had witnessed, but it was obvious he was most concerned about the recent outbreak of cattle mutilations that tribal members and nearby Anglo ranchers were reporting. After our marathon talk, I filed the whole Dulce scenario away for later investigation.

LITTLE IS KNOWN

Well, what *do* we know about the government's underground bases and facilities? Granted, most may be secret, but how many are publically known and are part of the public record? Here is one opinion: "Presently there are one hundred and twenty nine deep underground military bases in the United States. The average depth of these bases is over a mile, and they again are basically whole cities underground. They are all between 2.66 and 4.25 cubic miles in size. They have laser drilling machines that can drill a tunnel seven-miles long in one day. The Black Projects sidestep the authority of congress."[14]

An obvious question is, how could anyone, regardless of the cost, build such massive, deep underground facilities with our current known level of technology? The short answer is that perhaps we've had a sufficient level of technology since the early 1970s. So what tools are at the burrowing Troglodytes' disposal?

One of the new methods of tunneling that have been under study is "nuclear tunnel boring." U.S. Patent

No. 3,693,731 dated September 26, 1972 describes a method and apparatus for tunneling by melting. It says, "a machine and method for drilling bore holes and tunnels by melting in which a housing is provided for supporting a heat source and a heated end portion and in which the necessary melting heat is delivered to the walls of the end portion at a rate sufficient to melt rock and during operation of which the molten material may be disposed adjacent the boring zone in cracks in the rock and as a vitreous wall lining of the tunnel so formed. The heat source can be electrical or nuclear, but for deep drilling is preferably a nuclear reactor." The melted rock is forced into cracks wherein heat is given up to the crack surfaces and freezes as a glass at some distance from the penetrator. This amazing boring device is capable of drilling at depths totally inaccessible with previous drilling techniques, even, according to the patent claims, down to 30,000 meters.[15]

Hey, this stuff sounds good in theory, but where's the evidence that this technology is being utilized? And where exactly are the Troglodytes rooting around?

In the April 24–25, 1985, proceedings report *Tunneling and Underground Transport* by the Macro-Engineering Research Group at the Massachusetts Institute of Technology, deputy director of the Army Corps of Engineers Engineering and Construction, Lloyd A. Duscha stated: "Although the conference program indicates the topic to be 'Underground Facilities for Defense—Experience and Lessons,' I must deviate a little because several of the most interesting facilities that have been designed and constructed by the Corps are classified."

It makes a certain amount of sense that our government has built underground facilities. During the Cold War with the former Soviet Union, Dr. Strangelove–style thinking ran rampant in the military. Survivability amid Mutual Assured Destruction, or MAD, meant we had little choice but to burrow into the earth beyond the catastrophic reach of hydrogen bombs. The few underground facilities we do know about include Continuation of Government facilities, run by the Federal Emergency Management Agency (FEMA), that are designed to allow the power elite to survive a nuclear exchange. But the Cold War is over. What could be the current motivation?

One day in 1994, my friend Rocky[16] handed me a manuscript titled *Underground Tunnels and Bases*, by Richard Sauder, Ph.D. I opened it up and there were patents, photographs, charts, maps, copies of Freedom of Information Act requests, the works. This important book is an absolute must-read for anyone interested in our government's capabilities underground.

Richard Sauder is one of the most impressive researchers I've ever had the pleasure to hear lecture in person. I finally met him when we both addressed the 1996 Show Me Conference. He is sober, meticulous, and admittedly very skeptical of the idea of alien underground bases. First and foremost, Richard Sauder is an academic, and I am humbled at the breadth and depth of his work at uncovering what amounts to a massive government paper trail. Few researchers have uncovered as much primary source material about any current subject. Sauder's ironclad documentation, his conservative approach to his subject matter, and his wry sense of humor should be an inspiration to all ufologists and researchers. His book is, without question, the pre-eminent work on this hidden subject.

He delicately disassociates himself and his research from the darker underbelly of ufology. As he puts it, "I stick to what I can prove *and* demonstrate factually."

During a lecture he gave at the Show Me UFO Conference, he told a rapt audience the amazing story of how he inadvertently became involved in investigating and researching underground bases. It seems that one night Sauder was asleep in his apartment in Albuquerque, when the sound of a male voice woke him. The voice seemed to be nondirectional, and Sauder could not ascertain where it was coming from or who was speaking to him. The voice began to tell him directly that ". . . the underground bases are real." The disembodied male continued speaking for several minutes, and Sauder was impressed enough with the information to embark on his investigation into proving the reality of these facilities.[17]

Having met and talked at length with Richard, I find his admission of this episode courageous. It is obvious to me (and probably anyone who has met him) that this man does not normally hear voices. The suggestion, by the disembodied nocturnal voice, combined with Sauder's natural, healthy brand of curiosity, has propelled his relentless citizen's crusade to uncover the truth. He is right. We all need to peer into our troglodytes' world—the one we as taxpayers probably paid for. Where's the dirt? What are the known capabilities? Where is the money coming from to build even the known facilities?

You would think, if the federal government has made all these underground installations and it's cost billions of dollars to make them, you should then be able to go to the federal budget, and because of what this clause says [U.S. Constitution, Article I, section IX clause vii: No money shall be drawn from the treasury but in consequence of appropriations made by law; and a regular statement and account of the receipts and expenditures of all public money shall be published from time to time] it ought to be accounted for, lawfully. You will search in vain, I assure you! I have combed through military appropriation bills, the budget of the United States, all kinds of documents regarding expenditures and receipts and funding appropriations. . . . You won't find the paper trail for how the money was spent on these facilities, or even how much was spent, or when, or where? . . . If you have a United States government that's not following the Constitution, in my mind, by definition, it is no longer the United States government but something else. . . . The fox is guarding the henhouse. Need I say more?[18]

Another subject that intrigues your SLV gumshoe, and I'm sure many others, is the theory that our government, or a faction thereof, has built an extensive transcontinental underground shuttle-tube network. When the new twentieth-century prototype Denver International Airport was being built, I began to hear enigmatic stories concerning deep lower levels that were being excavated in secret, below the publicly accessible areas. Conspiracy buffs soon latched onto the idea, and several researchers, most notably Alex Christopher, began exposing theoretical uses of these lower levels by our New World Order crowd. Deep below, it is said, is the central main hub of a fantastic magnetic-suspension shuttle-tube system. These fantastic scenarios have yet to be proved.

In 1994, TAL sent me an interesting article published in the *Los Angeles Times*, June 11, 1972, . . . which mentioned the Rand Corporation's proposed rapid transit system which would utilize magnetic fields and travel from New York City to Los Angeles at top speeds of 10,000 mph. The article states, "the tunnels are not as expensive to dig as people think."

If that was the acknowledged thinking in 1972, what could our well-funded powers that be have already accomplished with nuclear boring machines capable of tunneling seven miles a day! Twenty-five years is a long time. In theory, digging only two hundred days per year, the construction crews could have dug around thirty-five thousand miles of tunnels since 1972!

But conservative researcher Richard Sauder is quick to point out that we don't even have proof that they have begun utilizing such fantastic tunneling equipment. He does, however, suspect that rampant rumors of subterranean alien bases may be a disinformation-style cover story hiding the very real construction of underground facilities and possibly even underground train systems.[19]

Chances are, if an elaborate plan of disinformation concerning this tunnel transport system is fueling the alien-base scenario, obviously this train would not be a straphanger's way to work and it is not being used by the general public.

WHERE TO START DIGGING?

After a 1975 study, the Army Corps of Engineers was advised of the most prosaic sites for future underground base construction. The following document happens to list a potential San Luis Valley site for an underground facility. The abstract of this Defense Nuclear Agency document, from the Office of the Chief of Army Engineers, TR 75-4 DNA 001-74-C-0097, dated 15 November 1975, *A Geology Compendium of the Continental United States—With Application to Deep-Based Systems,* by H. R. Pratt and S. J. Green for Terra Tek, Inc., Salt Lake City, states: "This is a geology compendium listing information about selected sites throughout the continental United States. The data include selected lithology and geologic structure, with some comments about strength, stiffness, porosity, hydrology, *in situ* stress, and a brief mention of [electrical] conductivity. The sites selected were assumed possibilities for the study for a defense deep-based structures system, and depths to 5,000 feet were considered."

And sure enough, in the category "Hard-Rock Over Soft-Rock Over Hard-Rock" on page 162, is a recommended location in the "Rio Grande River Valley, Taos, New Mexico." That area has the ideal geology to construct an underground facility. The hard-rock strata nearer to the surface would act as a hardened roof. These protective strata would also support drilling and excavating in the soft rock lying below the harder rock. Coincidentally, less than fifty miles to the north, just north of Blanca Peak and the Great Sand Dunes, the largest and most extensive cavern system in Colorado is located.

Dr. Sauder also has this Defense Nuclear Agency document, and he suggests that there is a real possibility that an underground facility may be located in the San Luis Valley. He said, ". . . I can't prove it, but I think there's a good chance there is an underground facility in the area of northern New Mexico, or just across the border in southern Colorado."[20]

*   *   *

What would be the government's motivation for putting a facility, or facilities, here in the San Luis Valley? Well, first off, there is that huge freshwater aquifer that is constantly replenished by deep mountain snows. Second, this majestic and remote valley could be easily defended. This entire region is completely ringed by mountains, and the only routes into the Valley could easily be kept secure. One could also use the analogy of wasps, bees, and hornets. Invariably, these industrious insects choose the high ground to make their nests. Painting houses for several years taught me that the highest house in any town has dozens of nests nestled in the eaves. The San Luis Valley is America's high ground, and perhaps we have a number of nests containing underground-dwelling citizens not counted by the census. One would hope these Troglodytes are not as nasty as hornets and wasps when finally exposed by the bug spray of truth.

In short, it is entirely possible that extensive underground facilities are located in the mysterious San Luis Valley. However, I can't prove that there is even one underground base here. That doesn't mean they aren't here to be found. The more you dig, naturally, the more you uncover. This shadowy subject area, in general, deserves far more investigation by dedicated researchers such as Dr. Richard Sauder.

CHAPTER EIGHT
A CHILL IN THEIR FEATHERS

I don't consider myself to be psychic or sensitive. However, there are times when sudden thoughts or impulses prompt me to make phone calls to individuals in my network who often hear of strange goings-on in the San Luis Valley.

Monday, July 7, 1997, was one of those days when that nagging feeling prompted me to call *Valley Courier*'s Rio Grande County editor Mark Hunter. Mark and I have stayed in close contact over the past five years, especially when we were in the midst of one of our sighting waves. Mark usually hears through the grapevine when people on the west side of the Valley are seeing and reporting aerial phenomena. Because of our apparent lack of appreciable activity during the entire summer of 1997, we hadn't spoken to each other for a couple of months. Well, my ears were burning, and I had a feeling I should call him. I wasn't disappointed.

I asked Mark if he'd heard of any recent unexplained aerial activity. He hadn't, but he suddenly remembered a call he had received a couple of days before from a man who had seen the Turner Broadcast segment that featured your San Luis investigator.

"Chris, funny you should call. I got a call from this

guy who has quite a story, and he really would like to talk with you. His grandfather had a ranch next to the Brazel Ranch in Roswell, and when he was a kid, he was shown a piece of the wreckage!" Oh, no.

The fifty-year anniversary of the so-called Roswell Incident had been in full swing all summer, and the media had the country inundated with various aspects of the 1947 "crash," and like some, I wondered why our culture is fixated on the supposed event. Several people had recently asked me if I had gone to the Roswell fifty-year anniversary conference/party, and my stock answer had been, "*No* way. Ten thousand people dressed up as aliens makes me itch. I would've broken out in hives!" Now here was Mark telling me that someone else knew where yet another piece of the Roswell wreckage was to be found and wanted to talk to me. I guess I just can't escape the most famous UFO case in history. I admit, however, I was intrigued.

The caller's name was Pat, and evidently he went to some effort to locate me. He had diligently tracked me down through the Rio Grande sheriff's office, which had suggested he get my number from Hunter. Being the busy reporter, Mark had forgotten to call me, and I obtained the man's phone number and thanked Mark for the tip. I immediately called.

Pat complimented me on the show he had seen on TBS and told me, "I've been waiting for someone level-headed down there to talk to about my experiences while living in the [San Luis] Valley. You seemed grounded and real objective about a lot of the things going on there. I haven't talked about what happened to me much."

"Where do you live now? Where am I calling?"

"Well, I live in Las Animas, but I lived in the Valley

for years, all through the eighties, and then I moved on. I finished my time there."

"So why did you initially move to the area? What do you think of people that chose to live here [in the San Luis Valley]?"

"I think people are drawn there. I was. But it's dependent on them to do the work. They're drawn there to walk their path and to pull their act together."

"You pulled your act together?"

"I definitely did. I located my lost 'me.' I learned a lot of things sitting by myself down there in that Valley. It's a process."

I can identity with Pat's insight into the process we're all going through. He is obviously a thoughtful, aware person. I asked him, "What about people who come here who aren't ready for this purging environment?"

"Well, if they're a little tweaky to start with, the Valley will drive 'em right on out."

"So where did you 'do your time' while you were here?"

"Down near San Acasio. Boy, did I see some strange things in the Brownies!" The San Luis Hills and the Piñon Hills, the Brownies, as the locals refer to them, blister the center of the San Luis Valley south of Alamosa and north of the New Mexico border. A series of flat-topped volcanic formations, these low-lying hills effectively cut the Valley in half, and the cuts between them offer the only two main east-west roads over the Rio Grande above the New Mexico border and south of Alamosa. The entire area is very sparsely populated, with only a few houses and ranches located along the meandering Rio Grande. The Conejos and Culebra rivers, as the Rio Grande travels south toward the border, join the main river, which begins to cut the famous Rio Grande Gorge about ten miles north of the border. Pat lived several miles east of the Brownies. This area of the Valley has always fascinated me, but very few credible reports have come to my attention from the bull's-eye center of the Valley.

After talking on the phone briefly, I knew we needed to get together and talk in depth. Pat seemed even-keeled, and he had fantastic stories to relate, but my phone bill wouldn't allow me to do it all via the telephone. Also, I really like to interview people in person—look 'em in the eye and get a sense of their veracity and their visceral reactions to specific probing questions.

I invited Pat and his partner, Anita, to come visit Crestone that following Sunday, and they arrived promptly at our agreed time. I wasn't disappointed.

LIGHTS ON AND OFF BLANCA

The colorful couple arrived, and the first thing I noticed were the fabulously ornate turquoise and silver neck-laces they wore. "Wow, those are beautiful," I remarked after introductions were completed, hands shaken, and smiles exchanged. "I'm a silversmith, and they are two of my creations," Pat said nonchalantly. It was apparent that this man was also a talented artist. I invited them both in and we began to get to know one another.

He was a big, burly man in his late forties, with a good-natured twinkle in his eye and a distinctively booming, high-pitched "mountain man" laugh. He had a long bushy beard and a long pony tail snaking down his back, and he wore a black baseball-style cap. His wife was a slight woman who mostly sat and listened. They both seemed relaxed and happy to meet me.

We talked about the Valley for a while, feeling each other out, and I asked him, "Have you read *The Mysterious Valley*?"

"No, but if it's about this Valley, I'd like to."

I asked him to give me a little background about himself and how he happened to end up living in the San Luis Valley for almost ten years.

"Well, Chris, I started visiting the Valley in 1979, and I moved to San Acasio, Colorado, in 1981." I grabbed my Colorado quadrant map, and he marked the map with a dot where his property was located, northwest of San Luis. "I lived out in the middle of the prairie in a trailer, in a pretty rustic set-up. No electricity or phone. I had to walk twelve miles to San Luis for groceries."

"That's a 'truck'! When did you start seeing things?"

"That first night I moved in." He let out his infectious booming laugh. I was immediately intrigued.

"So what happened?"

"Well, I saw these strange lights straight east across the Valley in the Sangres, just north of San Luis."

"Over by the [Battle Mountain] gold mine?"

"Yup. I've seen so many lights over there, and on the south side of Blanca, I guess I kind of became desensitized to them. There was so much activity, it was nightly at times. I'd sit there for hours, Chris, and watch these lights near the top of Blanca. Generally, they were white-orange lights, like headlights in the distance, but they weren't headlights, there's no roads anywhere near where I seen 'em. They would go up and down, then sideways, then they'd go straight down like a streak without leaving a trail. No way they were meteors. I'd see 'em between me and the mountains. Sometimes I'd see 'em streak to the southwest, out across the prairie and they'd disappear in the Brownies."

"How big were they? What color were they?"

"There were some that looked like green balls of fire, I'd say about beach ball–sized. They come straight off the south side of Blanca, head to the south, and disappear out in the prairie."

"So what do you think they were?"

"I dunno, unidentified lights, that's about the only description I can think of. It's amazing. I have no idea how many times I saw them, it was so many!"

"What about the Brownies? Did you ever see anything in the center of the Valley?"

"Sure did. I've seen a lot of things. But the lights I've seen in the Brownies were different, they were blue-white. They had the same type of movement. A few times I'd see them take off and head up and out at about a forty-degree angle. They'd just take off and disappear.

"One night in the late winter of '87 I was getting ready for sleep in my trailer by the stove, and I was sitting on the bed. I happened to look through the kitchen out the kitchen window. I saw this green ball of fire coming right at the house. I didn't even have time to stand up—it came right through the front door and stopped. It was hovering right by my head! I was frozen in a breathless panic. It just sat there for what seemed like an eternity, and it was real strange looking, like a glass sphere with green and black paint boiling around inside it. I saw it, Chris, but I sure couldn't identify it! There was a strong smell in the air, like two wires arcing together, and it left a coppery taste in my mouth. Before I knew it, it disappeared right into a cabinet where I kept my firewood. I tore that cabinet apart looking for it, I took out every piece of wood . . . *nothing*! I'd seen similar blue ones before bouncing out on the prairie. They'd move exclusively east to west; and always come down off the Sangres and head out across the prairie and disappear into the Brownies."

"How often would you say you saw these strange lights?" I asked.

"Well, I lived there from '81 to '88. I'd see them a minimum of at least once a month. They always occurred on clear nights with no clouds or wind, and during offbeat weather I wouldn't see them."

RIO GRANDE VALLEY FIREBALL WITCHES

By this point in the conversation, Pat had me hooked. I admit that I'm fascinated by these accounts, and the fact that they corroborated other reports I'd received made me even more attentive. I must digress again for a moment. In 1994, I had been told a similar thing by a man whose family lived in Mesita, Colorado, a scant twenty miles south of Pat's trailer. The coincidental and almost verbatim description, from the same part of the Valley, was uncanny.[1] This connection lent quite a bit of credibility to Pat, Alan, and others' claims. But what were they witnessing?

I have received dozens of these fireball and light reports witnessed in the Sangre de Cristo Mountains, and consequently I've spent many hours combing through historic accounts for examples of unusual aerial phenomena related to our area. I've found many stories and reports of these mysterious mountain and prairie lights. I suspected that a natural phenomenon may be responsible for many of these sightings, but for many in our region, these sightings have always had a more "traditional" explanation, and their appearances are often interpreted in a different, more occult manner. Here is an example:

Juan Chavez, who lived in Tomé [New Mexico] during the 1890s, gained considerable reputation for his
ability to expose practitioners of the black craft.
[Juans or Juanitas, in the local tradition, can capture
and hold witches.] In his community lived an old
woman, Chata, suspected of being a witch. On a
summer day Juan left Tomé on horseback to visit a
friend in Casa, Colorado who had promised to give
him a milk cow. As he was riding down an isolated
stretch of road, he perceived a large ball of fire leaping over the countryside in great bounds. Recognizing that the ball was a transformed witch, he got
down and drew a circle in the midst of the road. The
flaming object then flew into the circle and vanished. Juan remounted his horse, continued his journey, and returned the next day by the same route
leading his new cow. Arriving at the place where he
had seen the fireball, he found the witch Chata sitting in the road inside the circle. They exchanged
some pleasantries, and Juan invited the old woman
to get up and accompany him to Tomé, since it was
far too hot to be resting in the sun. Somewhat pee-
vishly, the witch told him that she was unable to
leave unless Juan gave her his hand. After he did this,
she trailed him into Tomé in a manner very much
subdued.[2]

The above account may provide us with a quasi-
historical example of sighting of these prairie-bound
balls of fire, which evidently have been seen by locals
for many years. Undoubtedly, this phenomenon has
been observed and wondered at for many years. Needless to say, Chavez's account of the appearance of
Chata inside the circle needs to be addressed to un-

derstand fully how these sightings obviously were interpreted then and, for that matter, now.

Remember Suggested Rule of Investigation 6: Always assume a mundane explanation until proven extraordinary. Perhaps the massive Rio Grande Rift,
which runs south from Salida into Mexico, is responsible for these eerie globes. This rift zone along the edge
of North American plate is a massive fault, and perhaps
these fireballs are related to a discharge of tectonically
produced energy that causes plasmatic events—and
produces them frequently, if all these reports are to be
believed. Similar lights are documented as appearing
along other earthquake fault zones, and perhaps these
fiery, bouncing orbs are actually naturally produced
phenomena.

I continued looking for additional fireball references
in the historic record, and I found these interesting accounts, all from the Rio Grande River Valley. This first
account is fifty-plus years old: ". . . After awhile Mr.
Baca began to see . . . a ball of fire about the size of a
large pumpkin rolling along in the direction he was
moving. Instinctively he raised his gun and fired, and
simultaneously the ball bounded into the air. It must be
a witch! he thought. With his knife he cut a cross on
the nose of the bullet and fired again. The ball of fire
bounced out of range every time he shot at it. . . ."[3]

What makes this particular story even more interesting is that the witness, Mr. Baca, during the event,
reported having a short conversation with the disembodied voice of a long-dead friend: "' . . . Don't be
alarmed *compadre.* Just promise me to have a Mass said
for the repose of my soul.' Ben Baca was willing to
promise anything that would rid him of the fireball, but
despite his fear he was able to recognize that it was the
voice of a friend long since dead. He promised to

carry out the request, and the light vanished over the cemetery on the edge of town, much to the relief of the very frightened Mr. Baca."[4]

The author of *Treasure Tales of the Sangre de Cristos*, Arthur Campa, also recalls a personal sighting experience when, as a boy, he witnessed two large mysterious yellow lights while walking home from school at night in 1917: "The lights, as I recall, were about the size and brightness of a harvest moon, always moving about twenty feet apart and at about twice a man's walking gait . . . then the lights rose fifty feet into the air. . . . Back in 1917 there were no airplanes flying at night. Had it happened today [1962], anyone would have sworn they were flying saucers."[5]

Note the interesting date—1917. Ring a bell? There were several unexplained nocturnal sightings to the north in Salida, Colorado, during the third week of August 1917.

THE GOLDEN DISKS

But back to Pat's story. We continued talking about Pat's prospecting and exploring around the Sand Dunes and along the remote border region surrounding the Rio Grande as it begins to cut its mighty gorge into New Mexico. His accounts are fascinating.

"I used to do quite a bit of prospecting. In fact, in 1987, I actually made twenty-two thousand dollars panning for gold just above the [New Mexico] border. . . . The reason I moved to the area was . . . how should I put this? Well, I did two tours in Nam. I was an airborne ranger disarm combat specialist. I ended up doing four years in Rhodesia."

"You were a mercenary?"

"Yes, you could say that. Well, I have two and one-half pounds of steel in my head, which was put there after getting hit with a hatch from a personnel carrier. I actually died and woke up three feet from the morgue door in a body bag. Now, whenever I'm near precious metals, I hear a buzzing in my head. If there's a lot of it, I actually fall down! One time, it almost knocked me down, and I looked down at this large rock outcropping. Turned out to be filled with gold ore!"

I laughed. "Sounds like you have a built-in metal detector in your head."

Pat let out his booming high-pitched laugh. "Yup, I guess you could say that!"

"So tell me about your prospecting work. Sounds like you've had some success."

"Well, Chris, I've done quite a bit of prospecting in the Valley. Up by the old pass road, just south of Mosca Pass, all along the Rio Grande above the New Mexico border.

"I met a guy up near the old pass road several years ago. We got to be friends, being that we were both prospectors. One time he showed me a solid-gold disk and told me a real interesting story. He said he would go sit up near a small creek on the southwest side of the Blanca Massif at night with his dog and a broom."

"A broom?" I'd never heard of a prospector using a broom before.

"Yes. He just sat there at night waiting for these fireballs. He slept during the day and waited up all night. He said he had been a sergeant in the army, and he carried around his old forty-five automatic. Anyway, he would wait there until the fireballs would show up. He'd mark the spot, and in the morning, he would head over to where he saw the [bright orange-white] fireball and find the scorched spot where it sat down. He'd sweep away the burned spot with his broom and find these solid-gold disks, about five to six inches across.''

''You're joking. How big were they?''

''Now I'm not joking. I actually saw one. They were about that big around.'' He made a circle with his hands about six inches across. ''They were about the size of a pyrite dollar. Like I said, I saw one. It didn't look like it had been poured molten in a mold, or like it had been cut out. It was just a round disk about as thick as a silver dollar. And heavy. Anyway, he must have found a bunch of them, because he bought an enormous amount of land in Missouri and Iowa with the money. At least that's what his sister told me at his funeral.''

''His funeral? What happened?''

''No one really knows. He'd been going up there for a few years, and then one day, during the summer of '86, he disappeared for a few days and his family got worried. They sent a search party out, and they found him in a canyon with a bullet hole in his thigh. I guess he must have bled to death. There was something strange about the deal. I'll tell you, this guy knew how to handle firearms. There's just no way he shot himself. And the wound went straight in, not down his leg like he'd accidentally discharged his gun and shot himself. I'm pretty sure the authorities investigated the case, but I don't think they ever figured out what happened. At least I never heard they did.''

''That's quite an amazing story! I've heard other stories relating seeing UFOs and the witnesses finding treasure.'' It's those pesky fireballs again! But with a twist.

''Well, Chris, like I said, he called them fireballs. I never heard him call them UFOs.''

''Just the same, it makes me want to go sit on Blanca

and wait for the fireballs to show up. What a way to prospect for gold." (But I wouldn't forget to buy, and wear, some custom-made full-protection Kevlar body-armor.)

NEVER TELL THE WHITE MAN THE TRUTH

The Blanca area has furnished my research with quite a number of unexplained phenomena. Pat agreed and continued.

"Have you ever been up to the lakes way up on Blanca?" he asked.

"Which lakes? There's a bunch of them." I grabbed my quadrant map, and we took a look.

"The Winchell Lakes, see, the big one right there." He pointed to the detailed topographical map. "I used to spend a lot of time up in that area and I'd fish in the lake. I'll tell ya, Chris, there are some pretty weird fish in there. Funny thing, they're all deformed. I'd catch these big ol' thick fish that were only a few inches long, or these real long skinny ones. They'd have these real deformed heads and the strangest looking fins. Never actually ate one, though, they were just too strange-looking. I never have figured out why they were so deformed."

I told him, "You know, they claim someone found a platypus in Como Lake [another high lake on Blanca] back in 1966. They tried to get the American Museum of Natural History to come out, but they laughed at them!"

"There's some pretty strange things going on up there. I remember one night I was up at the [largest Winchell] lake, about an hour before dark, and I happened to look across the lake. It's not very big, not even a quarter mile across, and what do I see? A huge white buffalo just standing there, plain as day. Now, I wondered to myself, what in the world is a white buffalo doing all the way up here? Then it just disappeared! I went over there and couldn't find any sign of it, no tracks or nothing.

"You know, I'm half Cherokee and half German, and I grew up on the Navaho Reservation as a kid. I'd hear all kinds of stories about this Valley. This is the extreme northeast corner of Navaho land, and to all the Indians who visit, this is a very sacred place. The Navaho believe they came into this world from that lake up on Blanca. I remember as a kid I was told the story. Did you know that the turkey was the last to emerge out of the lake? You can tell. If you look at a turkey's tail, you can see where the rising water was encroaching on his tail feathers."

"I've always heard that the actual place of emergence was to the west a few miles, out at the San Luis Lakes, probably Head or Dollar Lake," I commented.

"Well, Chris, when I was growing up, the Navaho elders would tell us never to tell the white man the truth about our legends. Just tell them what you think they want to hear. I can only tell you what they told me, and they said we emerged out of that lake, high up on Blanca."

Hmm. Back to the drawing board. I've always contended that the Native American part of my research was by far the most difficult accurately to pin down, and here was yet another affirmation.

Pat continued, "I remember being told that the water broke through the top of the mountain [Blanca] and flowed down the southwest side. The Navaho people were told to live where the water flowed. They have lived there, on the western edge, for the longest of times."

I remembered something else I wanted to ask him. "Pat, folks around here have reported seeing strange, undulating, translucent creatures, about three feet long and eight to ten inches off the ground, out in the chico, and some people have even seen them in their homes. (Me included!)[6] Do you know what I'm taking about? Have you ever seen them? What do the Indians say about them?"

"Oh, yes, the prairie dragons."

"Prairie dragons?"

"That's what the Indians call them."

"What are they?"

"Prairie dragons! That's what they're called. I don't know what the heck they are, but that's what I've heard them called. You see them running out in the prairie."

"Have you seen any other strange creatures during the time you lived here in the Valley?"

"Sure have. It was late summer, let's see . . . about 1986. What a day that was! A young couple from Alamosa was visiting me at my place, and I happened to notice this huge tall shadow of a giant bird on top of that flattop hill near the breaks [Flat Top Mountain]. On top of that hill is an ancient stone altar. Some say the Spanish built it, but no one knows for sure. I'd seen the bird up there before on a number of occasions. It's hard to believe, but the darn thing had to have been thirty to forty feet tall! Well, we just sat there at my place and watched it for a while. Then we decided to try and get a closer look."

"I heard some treasure hunters blew up the altar a few years ago to look underneath for gold."

"Too bad. Anyway, there's that huge bird thing just

sitting up there, not moving. So we drove over to the bottom of the hill and parked. We started to climb up the hill to get a closer look. Well, the thing took off, and I'll tell you, Chris, this thing is *huge*. It would've dwarfed a 747! It was that big. It looked like a shadow. It didn't look tangible, but you could make out details. You could see split feathers on its wings and on its tail. You could see a predatory beak, but you couldn't see any eyes. It took off and flew out over the Valley headed to the east, just north of San Luis. By then, we figured it was at least ten to fifteen miles away. Well, it flew three times counterclockwise around the leg of a rainbow, and then it just disappeared! The three of us went back to the house and just sat there drinking coffee. Those kids were pretty spooked, and after a while they left to go back home to Alamosa."

"Sounds like you saw the legendary thunderbird."

"Well, it didn't end there, Chris. A short time later, just after sunset, I walked outside and noticed this strange fog. What was strange is that it only seemed to be surrounding my property. My land is weird-shaped, and the fog seemed to be following my fence lines. I couldn't see through it, and it looked just like a big fluffy cloud had sat down right around me. My dogs took off into the fog and disappeared. That was strange, too. They never strayed from the house. They were still puppies, about two years old." Pat went inside and spent the rest of the night wondering if his dogs would return.

This account rang a major bell! It was similar to another I had heard several years before. Pat's place was very near Mesita, Colorado, where other witnesses claimed that a similar fogbank rolled in, and, through the fog, a light approached the truck they were sitting in. The driver became terrified and, ignoring the warning from his friend, fired his rifle at the light hovering right in front of the truck. One witness claimed, "It went above us and somehow it lifted up the truck and put it in the 'bar ditch!' "[7] This incident allegedly occurred several miles north of Mesita, less than ten miles from Pat's trailer! Another serendipitous corroboration of our unusual phenomena.

Pat continued his story. "The next morning, I knew there was something wrong—my dogs were still gone. I went over to one of my neighbor's, who lives about three miles away to the north, to see if he had seen my dogs. Turned out he hadn't seen them, but he asked me, 'What were all those bright lights around your place last night? It looked like a football stadium all lit up . . . like Mile-High Stadium during a Broncos game.' Now, all I had is a little propane lantern; I didn't have any bright lights at my place. And my neighbor saw the lights during the same time period when the fog was sitting right on my place! And this was the exact time period when my neighbors found three mutilated cows thirty feet up in cottonwood trees!"

"What? Where did this happen?" This was too good to be true. I had heard rumors of mutilated cows found high up in trees here in the San Luis Valley, but this was the first time someone had ever claimed he actually witnessed this irrefutable proof of the high-strange.

"Right south of my place in the Culebra River canyon. . . . During this time period, two or three ranches were hit pretty hard. One sheep rancher lost well over one hundred sheep. He never even bothered to call the sheriff to report them."

"Did anyone take pictures?"

"Nope, he didn't want anything to do with word getting out. You have to understand, these people don't want *anyone* around their places. No way would they want something like that to get out. They are real to-themselves. At the time, so was I, so I know what they were going through."

"Pat, a picture of a mute thirty feet up in a tree is irrefutable proof! You guys should have taken pictures!" I was bummed.

Pat sighed and shrugged his shoulders, remarking, "A lot of ranches got hit during the time I lived there."

I was interested in how he managed to live hassle-free in the predominantly Spanish-American Costilla County. "It must have been pretty dicey, not being Hispanic, moving into a closed Spanish-American community. Did you ever have any hassles or problems?"

"Not really. I've got some pretty good friends in the Valley. Besides, if you treat the people in the San Luis area the way you want to be treated, you don't have any problems. The people that go there and encounter problems are the ones that come in and treat the people like second-class citizens and throw their weight and money around. Most all the people I know down there are real good people. But you'll always have people that come in and try to run over everyone. The thing is, the people in the San Luis area have had that happen to them many times, and they have finally stood up and aren't going to tolerate it anymore."

PEEKABOO BULL'S-EYE

This extreme south-central part of the San Luis Valley is very remote and difficult to navigate. Several stories have drawn my attention to the area, but I have never fully explored the border region in the Rio Grande Canyon. Pat began to talk about several experiences related to his prospecting work around the mouth of the inaccessible gorge.

"The reason I was down there around the Rio Grande Canyon was simple—I was prospecting and locating some good placer gold deposits. You know, it's really dry country down there. When the water level in the river is way down, you can actually wade across to the west side of the Rio Grande. I caught a couple of dry years, and I was prospecting the other side of the river. It seemed like that's where the gold was leading. Anywhere there's hard rock gold, there's free gold.

"But the closer I'd get to any kind of area where I might be locating a hard-rock lode, it seemed like every time I get up and out of the canyon, I'd get run off by these guys in black BDUs. Military personnel. They didn't have any insignias or identifying information. Nothing."

"Were they carrying weapons?"

"Yes, M-16s. The guys on foot I ran into three different times down there."

"What year was this?"

"1985. Anytime I tried to get up out of the Rio Grande Canyon, south of the old iron bridge, seems I ran into them."

"Well, what did they say?"

"They just told me I was in an area I didn't need to be in, that I shouldn't be in, that I was going to have to fuckin' leave! Point-blank."

We both break out into rising chuckles of laughter. I ask rhetorically, "They didn't leave *any* room for interpretation . . ."

"You didn't have to interpret nothing, nothing whatsoever."

"Did you try and find out why? The first thing I would have asked is, 'Who the hell are you, what are you doing here, and why are you telling me this?' "

"When you're standing there looking at three guys, and all of then are carrying 16s, it kinda messes with your mind a bit."

"Wow, here you were busting your ass prospecting and meeting with some success and following the trail to the mother lode. Then you run into these guys. What did you think? Why do you think they were there?"

"My idea was maybe the government's got the area staked out or something. That's the only thing I could think."

"Are they staking out the gold? Or the area?"

"Both. I don't know. Whatever was there. It seemed like every time I come up out of the canyon—it's a pretty good climb up out of that canyon, you know— I'd run into them."

We talked a bit about prospecting, and I asked why he was down in that particular lost corner of the Valley.

"I used to have some mining claims over north of Mancos, and one time I ran into a couple of Ute guys over in Durango who were sheepherders near my claims. We were all sitting around talking, eating, and shooting the breeze, and they started telling me about that French gold shipment that was lost in the Valley [part of the same lost treasure Tomas is zeroing in on!]. Their great-grampa had been in on the whole thing."

"In on the French expedition?!"

"No, they'd been raiding them! These Utes were saying the French guys didn't get all the gold and hide it. The Utes hid most of it. I was looking for the niche in the west wall that these Utes had told me about." He described the location in detail.

I couldn't help but respond, "Makes me want to just grab a shovel and *go!*"

Pat chuckled. "I've found a lot of good placer gold down in the San Luis Valley. The Indians have been mining down around there for centuries. I've found several ancient piles of flint shards in the area. Hey, there was a hole there at the King's Mine when the first whites started digging there. The Indians who were in the area at the time were digging out the turquoise."

"It's a paleolithic site, but it sounds like there's something else going on down there." I was very intrigued by the military personnel chasing him out of an area rumored to have some kind of "underground base." I asked him about other encounters with military-type activity.

"Well, one time, me and another guy were cutting and gathering firewood on the top of the mesa. It was the same day as the big [Federal Fish and Wildlife–FBI poaching sting in 1988] raid down in San Luis. Me and this buddy of mine were cutting piñon wood that day. We were both using chain saws and had the truck backed up to the edge of the ridge, where we could load while we were cutting. I just got this real weird feeling, and I turned my chain saw off, set it down, and looked up, and just over the top of the ridge—I mean, he couldn't have been more than ten foot over the top of the ridge—there was a black copter sitting there. I mean he was dead silent, and he couldn't have been more than seventy-five yards from us. The thing about it is, Chris, this guy had loaded rocket pods and chain guns under this helicopter."

"How long did they stay there?"

"He sat there for a good thirty or forty seconds after we shut the saws off and actually looked up at him. Then he cut out and went toward San Luis just like a stripe!"

"Could you ID the type of chopper?"

"Remotely. It looked like an old Bell Jet Ranger. He was fast and uncannily silent. It had the night-vision module on the front, like the AH-64s. And it was blacked out! They had smoked windows—no, they had black windows, they weren't even smoked. It looked like something out of a sci-fi movie!"

"So what did you think?"

"I looked up and I saw him with those rocket pods and the chain guns, and my heart was in my throat! Here I am standing here with nowhere to go. If this son of a bitch wants me, he's got me right now! They got some guys for some poached elk and some poached deer, and another guy with a few eagles, and they're down there hunting people with these monster copters? Those guns shoot four to five hundred rounds a minute . . . "

"Divide that by sixty!" I say rhetorically to get a rounds-per-second figure. We both break out laughing, I guess to break the tension that was starting to build in the conversation.

I wondered what he thought of the more "patriotic" Americans we have all heard about. "What do you think of this attitude in the country that seems to be burbling just under the surface?"

"I think our government's gone ape. I really do! I think we've got a government—sadly to say—that's out of control. I would hate to get any more blatant than that."

We talked for a while about the state of the union and the growing perception in America that our government considers itself to be above suspicion of wrongdoing. One area that we touched on has to do with unexplained military-style activity that goes on in the south end of the Valley, far from any known bases or acknowledged training areas.

Pat continued his account of living in the bull's-eye. "I've seen parachute drops down there."

"Really?"

"I was sitting at my trailer house one day, and there were two big black C-141 Starlifters that came through. They were probably three hundred feet off the deck. I got to watching, and all of a sudden, there's black silk popping behind them. I wondered, like what in the hell is going on, you know?"

"Where were they when you saw them?"

"You know that road that cuts south from Blanca to San Acasio? They were west of that road, just out on the edge of the Brownies. I sat up there with binoculars on top of my trailer house and watched 'em for the longest time. Then fourteen helicopters came in. They sat down, loaded everybody up, and took off."

"Do you remember what year this was?"

"This was in 1987. They were big personnel choppers. They landed, loaded everybody up, and away they went. Those guys couldn't have been on the ground for two hours."

"How many troops parachuted out?"

"Probably sixty."

"That's not an area you associate with military training."

"You'd associate military with a longer time period than a couple of hours. If you were doing a drop and a pickup, you're looking at maybe an hour. You're going to have your airborne jump in, and have your choppers following right hot on their ass."

"What do you think they were doing?"

"I don't know, but they sure were milling around out there quite a bit. They clipped up their silk real quick. Cleaned up the area. I went over there the next day, and you could see where they'd been tromping around and doing their thing.

"There's been more times than once, when I was sitting there processing black sand, all through the eighties, there'd be a half dozen Apaches coming down through there in tight formation about a hundred feet off the deck. And other times when there'd be flights of C-141s; six or eight to a flight, and they'd be flying in by threes. And never did I see them more than three hundred feet off the deck.

"I know what a MIG-29 fighter sounds like. It sounds like a rock with propulsion. There were several different times down there when I'd be processing gold and I would hear the MIGs coming down off the south face of Blanca. I mean, they would kick 'em, and them son of a guns would be screamin'. Well, I'm sittin' here with a pump aught-six, with a three-to-twelve power scope on it. Well, I hear them screaming my way, and the first thing I did is lay on top of my trailer house and zoom that scope down on the lead jet. I had the crosshairs on my scope right on the lead MIG. At one point, I could even see the pilot's face! Right about then, two F-16s came right down behind them. I figured they were doing some kind of training."

"Were you able to see any insignias or identifying markings?"

"There were no identification markings on them; they were stripped of everything. But the thing is, I couldn't tell if they were flying hot!"

"Why would they be flying MIGs out of the [La Veta low-level] flight area?"

"That's a good question. I was under the impression they fly foreign planes out in California or Nevada. They weren't flying tactics, they were hell-bent for leather across the Valley floor. When they came over me, they couldn't have been more than two hundred feet off the deck. I was still laying on top of my trailer house with that 30.06, and I know those boys saw me. I'm sure that put a chill in their feathers!"

CHAPTER NINE

STALKING THE HAUNTED

Ever since I can remember, I have been fascinated by the paranormal. While growing up, haunted houses, poltergeists, psychokinetic powers, prophets, seers, etc., captured my young, impressionable mind. I had a voracious appetite and read any book I could find on these and many other weird subjects.

As a kid, I also remember listening to ghost stories at summer camp, told solemnly around beach campfires by serious counselors—spooky accounts of strange blue lights and phantom sailing ships that, it was said, would travel silently across the bays and inlets that snaked their way south and west from Puget Sound, in western Washington, where I grew up. These closet paranormal phenomena are endlessly fascinating to me.

Naturally, one of the areas of research that I always have my ears open for, no matter where I live, are haunted houses and haunted cemeteries. Call me weird, but these subjects fascinate me no end. Early on, after moving to the San Luis Valley in 1989, I realized I didn't have to travel far to experience a haunting. The first house I moved into turned out to have a nonpaying tenant.

THREE-HUNDRED-POUND GHOST?
AUGUST 1989, BACA GRANDE DEVELOPMENT

My girlfriend and I had made the big move. After two years in Bean Town, I convinced her to leave her hometown, take the plunge, and get off the East Coast, get out of Boston. After a scouting trip in April, we found ourselves with a U-Haul in tow, headed up to Crestone. Two friends had invited us to stay with them until we could find jobs and a place of our own.

The west-facing house looked out over the serene San Luis Valley. The house had no foundation, no insulation, and a tongue-and-groove roof that leaked like a vegetable strainer. We had one of the two bottom bedrooms, and our roommates had the other one. The entire upstairs, which consisted of an office-landing at the top of the stairs, a large bedroom, and a half bath, was empty due to the unbearable heat that would turn the upstairs into a furnace every afternoon.

One night, I was awakened by a strange noise. A martial *thump-thump-thump* was pounding back and forth upstairs in the empty bedroom. I lay there and listened for a minute, trying to figure out what it could be. The first thing that came to mind was our roommate. Being quite the nature boy, he could be found pacing downstairs in the living room, stark naked, in his army boots when he was perturbed by one of life's little curveballs. Naturally, I figured he was pacing back and forth in his army boots. I glanced at the clock. 3:00 A.M. I got up and quietly tiptoed out the bedroom door, through the kitchen, and into the living room. I could plainly hear the stomping as it paced the five or so steps from one end of the room to the other. I stepped on the first of ten open steps that led to the upstairs. The sound stopped. So did I. I listened carefully, starting to wonder if it really was my roommate. I quickly ran up the remaining stairs and burst into the dark room, turning the light on as I entered. Nothing! I scratched my head. How could this be? There was only one way in or out of the upstairs, and I had been right there. I checked around in the closet, in the bathroom. No one!

Oh, well, I went back downstairs and lay back down. The instant my head hit the pillow, *THUMP-THUMP-THUMP*. This was too weird! I covered my head with the pillow and tried the best I could to go back to sleep, while that infernal pounding continued.

The next morning I mentioned the strange event to my housemates, and one of them mentioned that they had heard the sound too but hadn't gotten up to see what it was. This was my introduction to our Mr. Invisible.

My next encounter, if you can call it that, occurred a couple of months later. Our friends had moved back to their other house in California, and my girlfriend had taken over renting the A-frame. One night, I was alone in the house with my girlfriend's cat and our two puppies. I was lying on the couch, which is against the wall where the stairs ascend to the upstairs. All of a sudden, all three animals started bouncing off the walls, running all over the house like the devil himself was chasing them. They never did that. The cat was a rather sensitive Persian, so I could understand him becoming upset, but why were the young dogs howling and carrying on? I hardly had time to sit up when I heard the first of seven very large and loud footsteps slowly start down the stairs. Each step produced an unmistakable groan from the tread. I froze, looking up at the empty staircase. The stairs went right by the back of the couch, and as the last footstep sounded, I could have sworn I saw the stair flex as if a considerable weight was being placed on it. Whatever it was got to the bottom, and I'm not sure what happened next, because I was already outside on the porch, my chest heaving. The animals had run to the back and wouldn't come out for the rest of the night. I excitedly told my girlfriend when she arrived home, and I got the feeling she thought maybe I was a bit nuts, but I insisted the experience had occurred. She just shook her head and smiled.

A couple of months later, a third event occurred. I don't know if any of these events were related; however, my gut told me we had company. During the winter months, naturally, the upstairs becomes the bedroom of choice. Hot air does rise, and although we had no insulation in the house, we did have a roaring wood stove that we occasionally watched, in horror, as it turned to a glowing, semitransparent white from too much hot piñon firewood.

One night in early 1990 I awoke. I immediately couldn't help but notice a basketball-size glittering mass of glowing orange light near the ceiling, just to the right of a hanging chandelier-style lamp. Panicked, I ran downstairs and out the door, thinking we had a chimney fire and that I was watching the fire's glow reflected off the snow outside. It was extremely cold, with three feet of snow on the ground. Nothing! No sign of a fire. Puzzled, I ran back in, out of the frigid mountain night. As my eyes became slowly reaccustomed to the darkness, I could plainly make out the glow, still hovering next to the ceiling. I woke my girlfriend and asked her if she saw anything peculiar. We lay there wondering what on earth it could be.

That was it. I was convinced there was something

going on. I casually started asking around about the house's history and immediately found out an interesting fact. In the early 1980s, a retired couple had lived in the house. The husband was a huge three-hundred-plus-pound behemoth of a man, and I found out he had died unceremoniously of a heart attack, naked on the toilet in the upstairs bathroom. He had evidently lingered for a while before his horrified wife found him and called for an ambulance. It had taken paramedics a considerable amount of time to extract the dead man, who had become tightly wedged between the toilet and the sink.

Could this man's demise explain the weird things that had been going on? I never really got to find out firsthand, for I ended up moving from the house. Although I did see the glittering orange light on a couple of other occasions, we never had a blatant example of a ghostlike encounter the rest of the time we spent there.

Life continued, my girlfriend and I broke up in 1990, and on July 4, 1993, my new partner, Isadora, and I were attending the Crestone-Baca Fourth of July dance, when we were introduced to two new arrivals. Turns out, the couple had just bought the house I had originally lived in. I jokingly asked them if they had "met" the ghost yet. They asked me what I was talking about. I told them about the various experiences I had had with something unusual in the house. They seemed genuinely interested, maybe because they had just moved in the day before. I ended by telling them about the events surrounding the original tenant's unfortunate demise. Both their faces went white.

She began to stammer. "When we moved in yesterday, we replaced the toilet seat upstairs with a new one.

Nobody had even used it yet! When we went upstairs this morning, it was cracked!''

I have kept tabs on the several families that have been in the house since it was last sold. They didn't stay long. I haven't been told of any additional events that one would deem strange, but I'm convinced that a three-hundred-pound ghost lurks about the place—an uneasy soul, forever cursed by its unceremonious demise, that can't bring itself to pass on to the other side.

There are other allegedly haunted houses and buildings in the San Luis Valley. One location, the Ace Inn in Alamosa, has experienced a string of unexplained occurrences that have been witnessed by female workers at the quaint little restaurant and bar. The Ace is owned by my Crestone postmaster. One day, while picking up my mail, he told me about several weird occurrences workers at his restaurant had experienced while cleaning up after a long day.

ACE INN GEORGE, THE PUGILIST

Life in a small town like Crestone can be an interesting experience. It might be hard to believe, but months can go by without seeing or running into many of our reclusive three to four hundred full-time residents.

One gentleman is hard for any local resident to avoid. I see him almost every week day. It's our postmaster, Monte Collins. Monte is an efficient, cheerful, hardworking man who tends to the post office Monday through Friday, then goes south sixty miles to his ranch just outside of Alamosa. That's a one-hundred-plus-mile commute every day.

I can't imagine how he and his wife, Peg, do it, but

they manage not only to operate their farm-ranch but also run a successful restaurant and lounge in Alamosa called the Ace Inn.

One afternoon, while picking up my mail, Monte mentioned several very strange events that his restaurant help had claimed they experienced over the course of the four years the Collinses had owned the Ace. He knew I was interested in mysterious happenings, and we both had a few minutes to talk. After listening (spellbound, I might add), I just knew I had to sit down and officially interview him.

We made a lunch appointment to talk at length about the strange occurrences that seemed to be taking place at the Ace. We met at the Mountain View Cafe in Crestone.

Over lunch, Monte started right in. "Chris, I don't know how much you know about the history of the Ace, but the Ace Inn restaurant was originally built in the early to late 1930s. Who lived in it before, I have no idea. Early on, some people who were living in the original house evidently turned it into a restaurant. Prior to owning the restaurant, this lady ran a brothel in Texas, and her husband was a bare-fisted boxer . . . you know, they didn't use boxing gloves back then."

"A pugilist. With Jack Dempsey growing up near here, that's not surprising," I commented.

He continued. "Stories that I've been told about the early days, well, let's say I guess they had some pretty bloody boxing matches back in those days."

"Right there in the Ace?" I was surprised at this bit of information.

"No, they had boxing matches around the place."

"You mean outside?"

"Yes. The boxer passed away in the mid-1970s and his wife just passed away in a nursing home in

Pueblo just last year. That's just a little of the history. The building has been added on to four or five times. It started out as a very small one-bedroom house with a small kitchen and a very small living room. Now it's about a thirty-five-hundred- to four-thousand-square-foot building.

"As far as this 'ghost thing' I've told you about, I personally have not seen it, nor have I ever felt it, but there has been, I'd say, over the four years we've had the restaurant, probably ten people in the restaurant have felt a presence, seen a shadow, have heard noises and even heard their names called. One time, a coal bucket was totally thrown from the hearth of the fireplace that's in the lounge to the floor." (I contacted one of the witnesses to the coal bucket incident, a bartender at the Ace named Sheila, who was nonchalant about her experience. "My waitress and I were at the opposite end of the bar from where a number of things are hung on the south wall. There was no wind or a fan on. We were the only ones in the bar. For no reason, a couple of things just fell off the wall and hit the floor. A second later a coal bucket on the hearth was picked up and slammed down with a bang. We jumped, and looked at each other in shock!") "Peg has experienced a shadow passing by her like a gust of air swishing her hair.

"The latest incident that happened, we have a foyer that comes into our east entrance. Theresa, our bartender, was in the process of locking the exterior doors. She had her back to the other two doors. She closed the two doors, and the other doors behind her slammed by themselves and locked. She couldn't get out!"

"She was locked in?"

"She was locked in. She was locked in the foyer. She was yelling for the kitchen help to come get her out. This only happened three weeks ago. She's a pretty rugged-type girl and not easily spooked.

"We had another bartender, named Sheila, and she experienced a lot of this 'passing by' stuff, feeling a shadow and turning around and seeing the shadow go by. She'd turn around and there was nobody there." Monte thought for a minute, then mentioned, "You know, this has never been done to a male. All females. These gals have experienced hearing their names called, seeing shadows pass by, feeling coldness pass by. . . ."

I wanted to know what Monte thought was behind these unexplained experiences his workers had reported to him. "What does your gut tell you? What do you think is responsible for these occurrences? Has anyone who has had these experiences received any impressions at all about who or what might be behind these events?"

"Well, I can only speculate in my mind as to what might be possibly going on. My feeling is that it's George [the boxer]. I feel George is still in the restaurant."

Monte also mentioned another oddity that he feels may or may not be related to the apparent haunting activity at the Ace Inn.

"When we bought the restaurant, there was this picture frame that had a royal flush, with the last card down, encased behind the glass. It was going across the corner of the wall in the lounge, and it sat on a shelf. Well, it could have been a coincidence, but behind this picture frame on the shelf we found an actual human skull, in the corner behind this picture. How long it had been there, I have no idea, but it was real old and brown. I don't know if it has anything to do with what was going on, but I thought I should mention it."

THE HOUSE ON RIVER ROAD

Several times during my ongoing five-year investigation, I heard mention of a rather enigmatic old house in Alamosa, Colorado, that was said to be haunted. I was told by a couple of sources that the location of the house was near the Rio Grande, on North River Road, by the Cattails country club and golf course. I was so taken by several of the alleged stories that on one occasion I actually drove around the area searching for the old spooky-sounding building. I never was able to locate it. And no wonder. The house evidently burned to the ground in 1993, the year before I went looking for it. Then I received a call about the house and was told of an article published in the local newspaper in the early eighties.

I easily located the *Valley Courier* article. I simply looked at articles published on Halloween, and there it was, published October 31, 1983. The article, written by two Alamosa High School students named Hayley Martin and Cindy Peck, was reprinted with permission from their school paper, *The Alamosan*:

> Most stories of haunted houses have little basis in fact. However, there is ample evidence to support claims that a real haunted house exists outside Alamosa. . . . The house itself stands on 160 acres, and stables still exist where horses were kept during the days when it was used by the Pony Express when it ran from Denver to Santa Fé. According to evidence found on microfilm at the Adams State College and

the Alamosa County Courthouse, each of the first
five families who owned and lived in the house from
its origin until 1951 experienced some sort of violent
death within the family. The first of the deaths happened soon after the house was completed in 1872.
The owner, Jerry H. Kent, killed his wife, and then
committed suicide. Jeannie Craig, the next owner of
the house, committed suicide. On December 14,
1915, she was found hanging from the stairway light.
In 1934, Edward King . . . lost a son under mysterious circumstances when the boy was found poisoned. The next victim was Edna May Herriman,
who hanged herself from the front room chandelier.
The last deaths within the house occurred when
the owner killed his wife and then committed suicide . . . when the sheriff arrived to investigate,
breakfast eggs were still on the stove. Eight small
children were upstairs in the home when the murder
occurred.[1]

A *Valley Courier* article was published the first week
of August 1997, requesting people with strange experiences to call your amateur San Luis Valley investigator. I happened to receive a call from a woman I'll call
Fay. She was a cordial, sober-sounding individual, and
she immediately launched into a flurry of stories about
a "haunted house" that she and her family lived in from
1982 to 1989. Voilà! She was evidently talking about
the same house I'd heard stories about! I really like
when the synchronicity crackles and raises its timely
head. I didn't need to ask many questions.

Fay began her account. "When we moved in, we
had heard about the stories relating to the house, but
my boyfriend at the time was a nonbeliever. Well,
'they' got him. He believes now.

"The house was real old, and the *Valley Courier* wrote an article about it in 1981 or 1982. Another place to look is the Alamosa library; they have information about the house too. The place was definitely haunted, and a lot of very strange things happened there."

"How much do you know about the house's history?" I asked, taking notes and noting her comment corroborating the potential documentation at the newspaper and the local library.

"Well, quite a bit, in the '60s, a man named Munoz lived in the house. He was a drinker. I guess one time he got real drunk and flipped out. He killed his wife, then he killed himself. When whoever found them came into the house, it was strange—there were still eggs frying on the stove, but they had obviously been dead awhile. A lot of people were killed in that old house. Nine, I think, all together. Every tenant except maybe two or three tried to commit suicide in the house."

"Really, that's incredible! Do you know if there was another house at that location before this one was built?"

"No, but there are huge matrimony vines on the property that are an indication that an Indian campsite was located there. There's also an actual 'hanging tree' on the property. It's a big Navaho willow. We tried to hang a swing on it three or four times, but the rope would always break. A twenty-two-year-old kid tried to commit suicide in '92, or '93, and again the rope broke. I guess a little nine-year-old boy was poisoned there as well."

"Did the previous tenants tell you anything?" I asked.

"Yes. The people who lived there before us, told us they tried to clean the bloodstains off the old inlaid linoleum floor. They couldn't get the stains out. They finally ended up sanding them out."

"From Munoz killing his wife?"

"Yes. They told us before we moved in that they had experienced lights flashing on and off in the house, and one time, when their parents called the house, the phone was answered by a little boy. They weren't home and the house was all locked up, and for some reason, they didn't think this was strange, and I guess they talked with him for quite a while. But at the time, there was no one home! The boy told them where the other renters had gone, and, like I said, his parents didn't think anything of the conversation—until they found out no one had been home. Kind of sounds like it could have been the nine-year-old boy who was killed."

"So what happened when you and your family moved in?"

"Well, we noticed right off, there were some pretty weird smells. Sometimes there was a horrible smell in the house, like something rotten. Oftentimes at night we noticed the smell of blood out in the yard. I actually became afraid to go outside in the yard at night. One night, right after we moved in, my kids had a slumber party. I remember it was Friday the thirteenth. At the stroke of midnight, all their posters fell off their wall. Other strange things happened to the boys. There was something in there. The boys would be on the stairs, and something would throw them back down the stairs. This happened three different times.

"Another time my oldest boy was in the front room with his girlfriend. He heard a noise at the front door and yelled for whoever it was to come in. He heard the door open, and something came in and grabbed his girlfriend around the wrist. It grabbed her so hard, it turned black and blue. Then the next morning something tore his cross earring right out of his ear."

"He had a pierced ear?" I asked, hating to interrupt Fay's accounts of the strange happenings.

"Yes . . . but not anymore."

She continued right in with another strange account. "There was a strange door in the house; it used to be between the living room and the dining room. But you couldn't keep it closed. The tenants even put a hasp lock on it, and it would still bang open when they were out of the room! They finally just took the door off the hinges."

I located another ex-tenant of the house. The thirty-year-old woman also had numerous accounts of the weird goings-on in the North River Road "haunted house." But first she related hearing about another strange Alamosa house. "There's a house there that's been moved three or four times, and every time they move it, it causes all kinds of weird problems. They had to move it back and put it back on its foundation. I've known about it ever since I was a little kid. I've heard that the house is haunted. It's been moved to other towns and brought back to its original foundation!"

"That's interesting." More material to research. "How long did you live in the North River Road house?"

"Almost two years."

"All kinds of weird things happened in that house. . . . There were occasions when I called over there and this seven- or eight-year-old little boy would answer the phone. He'd say, 'No, no one's here.' I'd ask him, 'Well, do you know when they'll be back?' He'd say, 'No. No one's here. I'm all by myself.' I got to thinking about it a time or two, and I think we figured it out. It seemed he'd only answer if the phone was left in a certain place in the house. After I called, I even went over there a time or two. I thought, maybe someone dropped him off because they thought someone was home. I'd go out there and I couldn't find anybody! The second time it happened, I asked, 'What is going on? Who's the little boy that answers the phone?' And I was told, 'Oh, he's a ghost. He answers the phone every now and then.' Evidently a little boy was poisoned by his father and died in the house."

"What are some of the other things that happened while you were there?"

"Fay's oldest son, and I were watching TV one night in the front room. I was dating him at the time. We were sitting there and we heard this light tap at the door. He got up and looked out the door, and no one was there. He just kind of blew it off. We finished the program we were watching and heard it again; this time it was a little heavier. He thought it was his brother messing around and went over and yanked the door thinking he was going to catch somebody. Nobody was there. The third, well he got sassy and yelled, 'Well come *on* in, the party's in here!' Whatever it was came in. We were sitting there on the couch, and I looked at my hand, and it was turning blue. It felt like somebody had their hand wrapped around my wrist! They were cutting the circulation off! We kept saying, 'This ain't right, this ain't right!'

"The next morning after this had all happened, I was in the back room, and I heard him yell out, 'Let me go!' Fay and I kinda looked at each other and went over to where he was. He had had a pierced earring in his ear. Well, the earring had been completely ripped out of his ear! He had marks on him that he couldn't have put there himself! I had a fingerprint from a hand bigger than my boyfriend's around my wrist. You could see the bruises where fingers had squeezed. Fay saw it.

We've never been able to find somebody that could explain these things.

"Other little things happened. We'd move the furniture in the house, and the next morning it was all back where it had been. Nobody ever heard a sound. This was strange. Nothing ever physically attacked me, but you would get a real cold, cold sensation. . . . I had a horse there, and that horse was well trained: You could lead it anywhere you wanted to take him. But he absolutely would not go near the house." She related another story of seeing a black wagon with somebody driving, coming up the road, then it turned around and went off. She continued with accounts of sonic apparitions.

"There were nights where you could sit outside and hear the Pony Express and the stage change. We could hear the chains that were on the stagecoach and people yelling. It was only certain nights of the year, or maybe during particular weather conditions, but you could hear the chains on the stagecoach. We'd hear them come in, but we would never hear them leave! It was the darnedest thing! It was extremely weird.

"There was one window upstairs that you could not close. If you closed it and went back downstairs, you went back upstairs, the window was open! This window, we even nailed it shut, and in a half hour the window was open and broke. You couldn't leave it open two or three inches; it would always end up open all the way. We even put plastic on it, and the plastic was ripped off and we never heard anything."

The house was burned down when partying kids threw a bottle of whiskey into the stove and the place caught fire. It's rumored the fire department let it burn to the ground. As it burned, orange flame-filled holes in the roof were aligned like a "giant smiling face," then the roof fell into oblivion amid a rising shower of sparks.

I ended up talking with five former renters who had lived in the place, and their stories were related with honest and earnest conviction. I heard rumors that teenagers would go out to the house after the last tenant had moved out and the house burned down. They may have performed rituals and tried to raise the spirits said to dwell there. The many stories I uncovered relating strange occurrences in the old house on River Road are too numerous to cover fully here, and I think it's safe to say that no one shed a tear when the old place was finally destroyed.

THE MYSTERIOUS SILVER CLIFF CEMETERY "SPOOK LIGHTS"

Just over the Sangres from Crestone, to the east, about twenty miles, are the small Siamese-twin towns called Westcliffe and Silver Cliff. It's pretty strange the way these two little towns seem joined together at the hip. There isn't another town for twenty miles in any direction. The small communities are fairly innocent-looking, but the local cemetery has quite a reputation. Called a *very* eerie place by some, at night the extremely dark cemetery instills an uncomfortable feeling in the nocturnal visitor and may be the two towns' most popular tourist attraction.

Perhaps the country's most celebrated cemetery spook light locations, the Silver Cliff cemetery lights, the famous Joplin, Missouri, lights, and the perplexing Marfa, Texas, lights are considered to be America's most mysterious unsolved spook lights.

When lights appear around burial grounds they are called, naturally, "cemetery lights." Perhaps the most publicized of these appearances are the eerie blue lights, that frequently dance among the tombstones at Silver Cliff, Colorado. According to Ray DeWall, publisher of the *West Mountain Tribune* at Westcliffe [a mile west of Silver Cliff], the largest lights are the size of basketballs. They appear to pulsate, move slowly, but vanish when approached. They were first reported in the spring of 1956, and W. T. Little, of the *Rocky Mountain News*, Denver, said they could still be seen in 1964.[2]

Over the years, the Silver Cliff cemetery spook lights have gained more notoriety. Several high-profile investigations have been conducted, including a visit in 1969 by Edward Linehan of the National Geographic Society. Linehan, like many others who have investigated these curious light phenomena, can only scratch his head and wonder. He was quoted in an August 1969 *National Geographic* article: "I prefer to believe they are the restless ghosts of Colorado. No doubt someone, someday, will prove there's nothing at all supernatural in the luminous manifestations of Silver Cliff's cemetery. And I will feel a tinge of disappointment."[3]

Many attempts have been made to uncover the source of the lights, with absolutely no success. On one occasion years ago, Silver Cliff locals even extinguished every light in the town to prove once and for all that the lights were not due to reflections from the town's streetlights or house lights. The theory of reflecting electrical lights on polished tombstone surfaces sounds good in theory, but much to the debunkers' dismay, the lights were reported long before the town was wired for electricity.

Curiously, the phenomenon is not of a single type and color of light. Evidently there are several distinct and different light phenomena that are routinely reported by amazed witnesses. A strange gray light is often seen near one particular tombstone, and beams of grayish light are occasionally seen emanating downward from the main light.

Other even stranger lights are commonly seen. These are small, playful white lights that are reported flashing and sparkling on and off, and sometimes they are even seen dancing and cavorting among the tombstones. When attempts are made to approach them, they seem to intelligently dance away from the viewer. Even illumination by powerful flashlights reveals nothing that would indicate a source of the enigmatic white lights.

The stars and the moon reflecting off several polished tombstones in the cemetery have been ventured as possible explanations for these lighting effects, but this does not explain how the lights can be seen during overcast and even foggy nights. The fact that many lights have been seen in the older section of the graveyard, which does not contain any polished headstones, is also another perplexing element that defies skeptical theories and makes the locals scratch their heads in wonder. The lights are routinely seen to this day and are still as mysterious as they were at the turn of the century.

GHOSTLY TRAINS AND HORSES

It was a cool fall evening, and local resident Jack Cookerly was headed home to his house in the Baca Grants after visiting the little town of Crestone. He was driving his big Ford Bronco and had just made the turn to swoop down from the Chalets into the Grants. It was just after twilight, and it was usually a routine drive. As he approached the two large ponderosa pine trees in the middle of the road, a brilliant light out in the chico caught his attention. He slowed to get a better look. Several hundred yards off to his right, where there are no roads or houses, he watched a large white light blast by at high speed, just off the ground! "It looked like the front light on of those old steam trains," he told me later. "It lit up the ground and was completely silent." After the light had swept by, parallel to the mountains, it disappeared, headed south. Cookerly put his Bronco in gear and headed the final two miles to his home. "I have no idea what I saw, or why I saw it!" he said.

In another incident, a man was driving out of Crestone on Road T, the only route into the Crestone-Baca area, which is located at the base of the Sangre de Cristos. The twelve-mile jaunt has two drastic S turns. Before warning signs were put up, several visitors flew off the road and out into the pasture, as a result of missing the sharp turns. A resident of Crestone for three years, the man had driven the road at least a hundred times, but on this trip he was surprised by something most folks don't normally see. As he approached the little house on the first set of turns, something zipped out in front of his car. He slammed on his brakes, but he was sure he plowed right into "whatever it was." He screeched to a stop and looked in his rearview mirror. "There were about fifteen to twenty of them. What they were, I don't know. I'm sure I must have hit them but didn't feel or hear anything hit the car." He described a pack of undulating, transparent three-foot-long creatures and noted, "They were not all there; it's like they were only partially visible. If they had been solid I would certainly have hit several of them." Hmmm. Sounds like a group of prairie dragons may have been on the prowl that dark night.

Last fall, I heard an interesting story concerning a woman I'll call Sarah. She is an educated person who is not prone to fantasy. Her demeanor is that of a woman who is very grounded, and what makes the story even more compelling, is that this incident oc- curred on the exact same stretch of road as the prairie dragon platoon. I mean the exact fifty to one hundred feet! It is also the same exact location where three Cen- ter for the Study of Extraterrestrial Intelligences trainees witnessed a "twelve-foot craft" shadowing them "thirty-five feet away."[4]

Sarah didn't know about the previous sighting, and I caught wind of her experience from her sister, who urged me to talk to her about her strange encounter.

"It was prom night, and my son was graduating. I was going all the way back out to Moffat to pick up another child who was working at the prom dinner. A mother's role, I guess. I noticed a couple of cop cars. They're always out on prom night. This was so weird! I was just tooling along, not very fast, and I had some music on. Then I was aware of something out of the corner of my eye. We have these big mirrors on our van, which gives me the best view I've ever had in any car. Well, I looked in the mirror, and I saw two horses back there. So I sped up, and the horses sped up and came up next to me. I was totally freaked because I thought they were going to run into me, or I was going to run into them! They were really close to my window. Running at full speed, at this point I was going about forty or forty-five miles per hour. Their manes were flying and their eyes were really nervous. They were really pumping hard, looking in the window at me. I kept speeding up and speeding up, and they fell back a little bit, and then they headed off into one of the fields to the south. Neither one of them seemed to have jumped a fence. I've never seen horses pastured out there before."

"There were two? What color were they?"

"There were two. One was very light colored, not white, maybe yellow. The other was much darker. I had them clearly in my rearview mirror, and I didn't see either of them jump. They ran out into the field and stopped. They were looking north toward Poncha Pass."

"When they were next to you, could you hear the sound of hooves on the pavement?"

"It was a pretty strong clip-clop sound, but fast, so to me it sounded like they were on pavement. It wasn't pounding like on dirt. I could hear them over the sound of the car, which is pretty loud when the window is down. They were right next to me, rolling their eyes at me, that's what was so weird. They looked terrified!"

"Where approximately were you?"

"You know the house on the turn with the 'Handmade Dolls' sign? Just before there." I immediately noted the location and remembered that this is within feet of the where the mass prairie dragon sighting and the craft sighting were allegedly witnessed.

"I figured it was their horses. I saw a cop coming, so I flagged him down, and I told him, 'You know, there are two horses in the road back there. I really feel like I almost just had an accident. Go for it, you'll see them. They're right out in the field over there.' He said, 'Okay, I'll call it in and see whose they are.' So I watched him drive on down the road, and he just went, and went, and went. I never saw his brake lights come on, and I don't know if he ever even saw any horses. I do know another person who saw them. There were a lot of people on the road that night. It freaked him out, too. He didn't know what to make of it at all."

She went back home to await the third and final call, this time to pick up her graduate and his date.

"I got back home, and I said, 'Well, that was pretty strange, I'm glad I'm okay.' He called, and I jumped back in the car and headed back. This time, I heard sounds first. I was just rolling along with the window down—"

"Where were you?"

"In the exact same spot. Right before the Handmade Dolls house. I heard creaking and squeaking. I heard the horses, but not in the way I did before. This time it was much more muffled. I turned the music off. I kept hearing this noise, and it was unfamiliar to me. It sounded like there was some movement going on, so I looked out into the field to see if someone was working out there at night. I went through an area where it was very loud. I looked in the side rearview mirror, and I saw a buckboard with horses and a man standing there. They were not solid. I had apparently driven right through where he was standing out on the road! He was looking back toward Crestone. He never looked back at me, or showed he even knew I was there. The man had on bib overalls and had brown hair with a short haircut. The horses and the buckboard were headed the same way I was, the other way toward Moffat. They weren't moving. It just seemed to be there. That was that. I just kept going! I was alone. I'm not really a person who normally gets afraid, but—"

"—anytime you see someone who's not all there, and you go—"

"—right through them. You know, I felt some compassion for whoever I was seeing that obviously didn't belong where I was. Or maybe I didn't belong where he was."

We talked further about her experience, and I told her about the prairie dragon sighting and the craft sighting at the same spot she had her "experience." She seemed relaxed and matter-of-fact about her experience, almost like it wasn't that unusual.

As with almost every region, the San Luis Valley apparently has ghosts and apparitions that harken back to an older, simpler time. Why these apparitions exist is beyond me; perhaps their location-specific nature may be a clue to figuring out what energy forms we are dealing with. The very fact that people *believe* that these apparitions are real may actually help them manifest into our reality. Belief is a special thing. It means something different to everyone, and in the next chapter we will meet some very special people with very divergent beliefs.

CHAPTER TEN
SOMETHING TO BELIEVE IN

September 6, 1989, 10:00 A.M., Rock Creek Canyon. The chill fall air whispered through the canyon as bow hunter Juan Maestas quietly stalked an elusive elk herd. He had tracked them up the canyon some distance that morning, and the small band of young bulls was just ahead of him about a quarter mile, off the road about three hundred yards.

Maestas, a lifelong San Luis Valley resident, was raised as a special member of his community. A "Juan, born on St. John's Day," he was told as a child that he had special abilities, for in the local tradition, a Juan or Juanita born on St. John's Day is the only member of the community that could successfully trap and hold a "witch." He told me he had put his knowledge and abilities to work on a couple of occasions and during one episode was begged by the captured witch to let her go home and "care for her family."

As he carefully crept uphill toward the herd, the sound of a twig snapping to his left froze him in his tracks. He turned his eyes to look at the source of the sound and was stunned to see "a fat, ugly little guy, about three feet tall," who turned at the same instant and stared at him. He was a mere fifty feet away, next to a large pine tree. As they locked eyes, the stunned Maestas was able to discern the little man's "wrinkled forehead, clean-shaven face, and pink-hued skin."

Maestas told me later, in 1994, "I know how this sounds, but he even had on green overalls with suspenders and a flat-topped floppy hat."

I was baffled by his claim. "Did you notice his hair? How long was it? Could you see his hair color?"

"His hair was kind of reddish, and it was sticking out from underneath the cap. He had little eyes, and they seemed red and bloodshot. I could not believe I was looking at a three-foot little man! My heart was going a hundred miles per hour. He looked just like—"

"A leprechaun!" I couldn't stop myself from blurting out. Then I asked him, "What did he do?"

"I guess so. . . . We locked eyes, and it seemed I surprised him as much as he surprised me! He sort of gave me a smile, almost like he was embarrassed, and he darted behind a tree."

"How far away from him was the tree?"

"Oh, about four feet, maybe five. He moved really fast—one second he was smiling at me, the next instant he was gone. I figured he must have gone behind the tree, either that or he disappeared!"

"How long do you estimate you saw him from the moment you noticed each other until he disappeared?"

"Not very long, maybe four or five seconds."

"That's long enough to get a good look, I would think. What did you do?"

"Man, I was over there in a flash; it couldn't have been over fifty or sixty feet. I was right there. I kept my eyes on the spot so I would see him if he moved. I got to the tree and he was gone."

What makes the above story even more compelling is that a quarter mile back down the hill from where

Maestas witnessed "the little man," two weeks earlier a family of five on a picnic had witnessed the same, or a very similar, entity. He was also dressed in green overalls and hat.

Terrence McKenna, in his introduction to the preeminent study of "fairy folk," *The Fairy Faith in Celtic Countries* by W. Y. Evans-Wentz, notes:

> Long after the publication of Dr. Evans-Wentz's book, people have continued to see fairies—in fact, they even claim to have photographed them! In 1920 the late Sir Arthur Conan Doyle, creator of Sherlock Holmes and also a sincere Spiritualist, first published an account of what he claimed were real fairies photographed by two little girls in Yorkshire, England. His full-length book *The Coming of the Fairies* (1922) gave a fuller account, and it should be said that in spite of many attacks the evidence has never been conclusively discounted. In fact, it has been strengthened by other writers: Geoffrey Hodson's *Fairies at Work and Play* (1925) and E. L. Gardner's *Fairies; the Cottingley Photographs and their Sequel* (1945).[1]

But what's wrong with this picture? I thought leprechauns were from Ireland and other Celtic countries. Can Hispanics in the San Luis Valley experience such a cross-cultural phenomenal being? If the apparition of the "little man" was not real, where did they get the experiential and societal programming to report manifestation of another culture's mythical entity? If the sighting was real, why are leprechauns seen in Rock Creek Canyon? I can't help but feel that these experiences mean something, and I sense there is an important clue to be found in these "sightings," but I'm not quite sure what it is.

McKenna postulates further: "I have a strong suspicion that in the newer mythology of flying saucers some of these 'shining visitors' in spacecraft from other worlds might turn out to be just another form of fairies."[2]

Eminent ufologist Jacques Vallee has argued this theory since the late 1960s, much to the annoyance of the strict extraterrestrial adherents who run roughshod over ufological creative thinking. "Perhaps what we search for is no more than a dream that, becoming part of our lives, never existed in reality. We cannot be sure that we study something real, because we do not know what reality is; we can only be sure that our study will help us understand more, far more, about ourselves. This is not a worthless task."[3]

In my estimation, these puzzling Rock Creek Canyon examples of what appear to be genuine phenomenal experiences may be trying to tell us something crucial about the true nature of this wondrous, vaguely defined "reality" we live in.

What other clues can be found in the history of this rarefied, semiarid desert region? What outside beliefs have been introduced to the existent belief systems naturally present here? How have these influences manifested themselves in the past? In the present? First we'll meet the Brothers of Blood, then we'll examine belief as it manifests here in the mysterious San Luis Valley.

LOS HERMANOS PENITENTES

Maybe it's the altitude, or maybe the isolation. Or maybe it's simply due to the magical melting pot of divergent influences and the resulting subcultural belief systems that result. In any event, a nearly invisible Christian-based culture is still found in the southern and central portion of the San Luis Valley, the neighboring Espanola Valley, and the Huerfano. The adherents' numbers are now few, but isolated worshipers still practice a medieval, fundamentalist Christian belief system that is unique to this south-central Colorado/ north-central New Mexico bioregion.

With the arrival of the Spanish in the early sixteen hundreds, the indigenous peoples of this vast section of the great Colorado Plateau were forcibly exposed to an alien European belief system: Catholicism. Most of the converted Indians were immediately separated from their nature-based reality view, and their ancient spiritual beliefs were quickly subjugated by the fanatical Franciscan missionaries and the gold-obsessed conquistadors. For the Indians, it was a simple equation: Either you were converted, escaped to the hills, or were killed by ruthless soldiers. Not much of a choice!

The Spanish brought with them the current religious thinking of the turbulent sixteenth-century Roman Catholic church. The Inquisition was in full swing, and hard-core religious orders, like the Dominicans and the Franciscans, were pushing Christian belief toward an increasingly fundamental view of sin and penance. These newly arrived "pious," repentant white-skinned "sinners" must have left quite an impression on the natives, for they had extreme religious practices.

One account during Holy Week 1598 at San Juan, the first Spanish settlement in New Mexico, was recorded by the official historian accompanying the 1598 Juan de Oate expedition up the Rio Grande River Valley. It relates the Spanish explorers voluntarily inflicting pain upon themselves in the name of repentance and Christ.

> The evening was set aside for penance. The military officers and the men of the expedition confessed their sins to the priests. The women and children walked barefoot over cactus to pray at the chapel. The eyewitness account of Captain Villagrá . . . vividly described a piece of sixteenth century Spanish Holy Week transferred to the New World.
>
> The soldiers with cruel scourges, beat their backs unmercifully until the camp ran crimson with their blood. The humble Franciscan friars, barefoot and clothed in cruel thorny girdles, devoutly chanted their doleful hymns, praying forgiveness for their sins.[4]

It wouldn't be hard to imagine what the average Native American must have thought at the sight of this kind of self-abuse. It is known that some of the Native American medicine men and shamans of the Rio Grande Valley were not impressed with the Spanish religious beliefs and their penchant for self-flagellation, and these elders probably tried to warn their peoples. One priest translated the comments of one irate Pueblo Indian "wizard": "You crazy Spanish and Christians, how crazy you are! And you live like crazy folks! You want to teach us that we be [crazy] also! You Christians are so crazy that you go all together, flogging yourselves like crazy people in the streets, shedding [your] blood. And thus you must wish that this pueblo be also crazy!"[5]

This undoubtedly painful behavior, in the name of Christ, did not depart the Rio Grande Valley region with the missionaries, many of whom eventually died, returned to Spain, or continued on to other areas of Spanish conquest. The gradual advance northward by newly arrived Spanish settlers found the practice of self-flagellation alive and well, and many of the original settlers continued the practice of this fundamentalist brand of worship. There is also evidence to suggest that the natives may have gradually incorporated self-inflicted pain into their religious rituals.

By the mid-1700s, many adherents had moved to the appropriately named Sangre de Cristos (Blood of Christ) Mountains, north of the larger settlements of Santa Fé and Taos, New Mexico. Isolated for generations, many of these small communities continued these rather strident practices. By the end of the eighteenth century, the severe rituals had mostly died out in the larger towns but still continued in secret in the surrounding small mountain communities.

Although rather fundamentalist about their beliefs, the rural people who practiced this form of worship were by and large, pious, God-fearing folks who helped their neighbors. They raised their children to respect others and followed the Christian commandments. There is some evidence to suggest that some of the Brothers and their communities may have offered sanctuary to reformed criminals driven from the larger cities and towns and welcomed them like prodigal sons.

The Penitentes were an integral part of rural northern New Mexico and southern Colorado society at the time. They cared for less-fortunate residents and provided a social safety net for their community members. By the eighteenth century, Los Hermanos Penitentes had become a sizable and potent political and economic force. They established numerous secret places of worship called *moradas* northward into present-day Alamosa, Conejos, Costilla, Huerfano, Pueblo, Rio

Grande, and Saguache counties. They mainly kept to themselves and were very wary of all outsiders, especially Anglos.

By the late nineteenth century, Rome had strictly defined views relating to Penitente-style religious practices. A directive regarding cessation of self-flagellation was issued in 1886 by Archbishop Salpointe, who firmly condemned the practice, threatening excommunication for those who disobeyed. His admonition was resolutely ignored by the brotherhood. The archbishop issued a second proclamation in 1888: "With regard to the Society, called Los Penitentes, we firmly believe, that it fully deserves all blame. Consequently, it must not be fostered. This Society though perhaps legitimate and religious in its beginning, has so greatly degenerated many years ago that it has no longer fixed rules, but is governed in everything according to the pleasure of the director of every locality. We therefore desire: . . . That mass must not be celebrated in the chapels [moradas], where Penitentes observe their rites and abuses. . . . They are to be deprived of the sacraments until they amend."[6]

With the passing generations, the religious practices of the Brothers of Blood became more and more literal; some might even use the term "twisted." Actual and mock crucifixions of specially chosen adherents were said to be performed every Good Friday, and, inspired by the passion of Christ's suffering while carrying the cross to Calvary, Christ's symbolic journey became an elaborate ritual with long processions through the cactus-strewn prairie to the site of the cross-raising and crucifixtion ritual, usually on a special hilltop. To this day, one can see large Penitente crosses, or *maderos*, that adorn occasional remote hilltops in northern New

Mexico and southern Colorado. I have heard, but have not found any direct proof, that these particular crosses are left standing only if a brother actually died on that particular hilltop, on that particular cross.

Extremely secretive and paranoid after official church condemnations in 1886 and 1888, the communities where the Brotherhood worshipped became more and more isolated. Outsiders were absolutely banned from all ceremonies, and knowledge of their more deviant practices were little known outside the remote areas where the Penitentes could still be found.

Then, in 1892, Charles F. Lummis (who would go on to become editor of the *Los Angeles Times*) wrote *The Land of Poco Tiempo*. Much to their chagrin, the Penitentes were dragged into the bright light of early tabloid journalism, and word of their unique beliefs spread nationwide. Lummis exposed the sensational self-abusive rituals in a series of articles after an exhaustive clandestine investigation. He even began to haunt the communities that still practiced the old rituals, stalking the *moradas* and the worshippers like a big-game hunter. It is even alleged that Lummis and several confederates held a group of Good Friday worshippers at gunpoint in order to photograph the procession of self-scourging, cross-toting brothers and the subsequent ritual crucifixion. He was shot and wounded by the Brothers right after taking the only known photograph of an actual Penitente crucifixion ritual.

What role did the Brothers of Blood play in the unholy rampage of Felipe Espinoza and his cousins? It is hard not to make the leap that this Penitente fundamentalist thinking and Anglophobia may have played a direct role in motivating Felipe and his cousins' murder spree.

PENITENTE APPARITIONS

The unique rituals and the belief system of the Penitentes also feature interesting attributional qualities. According to Marta Weigle, "Various local traditions
attest to the deep symbolic importance of physical penance. In 1882, Bandelier [an early New Mexican ar-
chaeologist] noted that Pena Blanca 'Mexicans'
maintained the 'superstition' that flagellation 'makes
the clouds form and thus brings rain.' . . . In a 1874
letter from Conejos, Colorado, the Jesuit Father Personé
wrote that despite the great physical hardships endured
by the Penitentes, 'on the contrary, only a few take sick;
this they ascribe to a special help from heaven.' "[7]

Another interesting belief that lasted well into the
twentieth century refers to long-departed brothers accompanying the ritual processions in manifested ethe-
real human form. It was said that they would appear
during the long procession and vanish when the march
concluded. These types of stories have persisted for
generations.

Lummis was told by a Penitente who had seen "two
skeletons, whipping themselves upon the naked-
bones of their backs" that these were the Brothers
who had broken their promises. . . . The most elaborate ghostly processions supposedly took place for
three years on Holy Thursday at Arroyo Hondo,
New Mexico—in 1886, El Año de Nevada (the year
of the great snowfall), when many shepherds from
the area perished, in 1887, and in 1888. . . . The
procession back to the village oratorio passed
through a gulch called La Cañada Mamona, where

they were joined by men with white linen hoods, semi-transparent bodies, and bloodless backs. These dead Brothers disappeared when the village was reached.[8]

In this wonderful land of enchantment, belief takes many forms, and the following example is simply one of many current stories I have uncovered and, sadly, in this case, debunked.

SKULDUGGERY?

As readers of *The Mysterious Valley* will recall, in June 1995, I was told of an enigmatic "crystal skull" found by a Moffat, Colorado, rancher. Well, the finder, Donna Koch, said, that she discovered the six-and-a-half-inch-high skull in February 1995, while riding the fence line of her newly acquired ranch.[9] I publicized her claim, and the "alien-looking" artifact immediately captured the imagination of many, as excited word of the "find" literally circulated around the world. Channelers, psychics, and true believers have had a New Age field day with the little skull. A "full-moon gathering" at the White Eagle Village attracted the curious from as far away as Arizona and Minnesota. Articles have even appeared in international publications (curiously, with most of the initial facts totally wrong).

I admit, even though I covered my backside against the possibility of a hoax,[10] "I wondered if this report was simply a ruse by the rural family to get publicity, or worse, an outright set-up." The stories surrounding it, and the amazing reaction folks exhibited when around it, greatly intrigued me. Unfortunately, sometimes it rains on the ol' parade.

I found out that contrary to popular belief, the skull was not crafted by aliens, Lemurians, or Central American healers. The skull was created by Brad Chadez, a glass blower at the Blake Street Glass Company in Denver. Evidently family members alerted him to the object's discovery after reading Alan Dumas's *Rocky Mountain News* article in November 1996. Wanting quickly to clear up "the mystery," Chadez made the fateful call to the *Crestone Eagle*. Kizzen Laki, the publisher, called me with his phone number. The rest is history.

"I'm really sorry it went so far. I had no idea all this was going on down there," the thirty-one-year-old Chadez told me. "My parents own the ranch next door [to the Koches], and we left the skull there on the northeast corner of the property as a cornerstone.

"I started making the skulls to sell in New Mexico at the Day of the Dead festival," Chadez said. "They are carved out of hot glass, and I even make all of my own sculpting tools.

"My parents bought the [Moffat] ranch sixteen years ago, and they're planning on building a house on the property. We put it there a while ago as a talisman, and I had no idea someone would find it."

Chadez seems surprised at the reaction people have had here to his creation. "It was just one of my seconds . . . that's why we put that particular one there. I make full-sized ones that are larger." Brad told me he normally etches his signature on his creations, but because he didn't think this particular one was up to par, he didn't sign it. That simple nonaction reverberated around the world.

I must say, if that was one of Chadez's seconds, his other creations must be exquisite. Chadez has been selling his skull artworks at the Manos Gallery in Denver for several years. "I stopped making them a while ago," he said. "Maybe I'll start carving more of them." He then sent me four of the skulls, which are extremely beautiful and even more impressive than their smaller, more warped cousin.

THE BIRTH OF A POWER OBJECT

As with most true "mysteries," there are usually no easy answers. The innocent little "ant-person skull" has had quite an effect on people. The reported strange phenomena that seemed to surround the skull still have no obvious explanations. Exploding tires, sickened babies, bashed-in heads, broken video cameras, and various other "unexplained" phenomena have been associated with the skull and may give us some insight into the true nature of "perceived" power objects. If enough people think that something is magical, and focus their intent on it, then maybe a mundane object can actually become magical. The discovery of the skull, and the subsequent wideflung notoriety it has received, may be a lesson for all who have a real need to believe in a so-called "mysterious" power object.

One rather well-known investigator who sat with the skull for eight days, claimed to have channeled an amazing amount of information, which she attributed to the skull. Stories of Lemurian scouts, settlers, and other skulls waiting to be found here were communicated to eager believers. As the one who first publicized the skull's existence, I feel a responsibility to bring the apparent truth to everyone's attention.

Since the skull generated such overwhelming interest, verging on veneration, in many who've seen it, maybe Chadez would be well advised to start crafting them again. Koch declined a lucrative offer to sell the little "ant-person" skull.

BE CAREFUL WHAT YOU WISH FOR

As I discovered while researching my first book, stories of Old Scratch, the urbane devil, are still circulating through northern New Mexico and southern Colorado.[11]

I wasn't surprised to learn that stories of this ilk are not exclusively found here. I received a letter from a UFO investigator who currently lives in Brussels, Belgium, and is very intrigued by the accounts of Old Scratch in *The Mysterious Valley*, for he heard these stories growing up in Texas.

Perhaps this traditional legend of an urbane devil has common roots that extend back into the dim reaches of pre-Hispanic lore and legend and is found throughout the entire American Southwest. It even resembles an ancient Aztec legend.

The legend is an enduring one. But, as with a majority of these types of stories, the principal witnesses are never identified, and no corroboration is given. These recent stories are similar to the traditional historical versions but contain a new, modern twist. I was sent an *Albuquerque Tribune* article by Harrison Fletcher, spookily titled, "Something Evil is on the Prowl in our Casinos." The article relates several alleged 1995 New Mexico appearances of the devil, said to have occurred at the Indian-owned Isleta Gaming Palace near Española. (The same Isleta Pueblo where the Blue Lady, Sister Marie Agreda, supposedly converted hundreds of Pueblo Indians.)

It seems a woman was gambling the slots on Good

Friday, 1996, and, much to her dismay, she lost all her money to the one-armed bandits. As she was leaving, "a handsome old man, who had sat behind her, the entire time," gave her three dollars and urged her to try her luck one more time. The woman refused but was talked into accepting the money and playing the slot machine a final time. She put in the money and won $3,000! She quickly turned and looked for the man to thank him, but he had disappeared. She was awarded her winnings, and as she happily headed to her car in the parking lot, she happened to notice the elusive old man in a parked car. She went over and knocked on his window to thank him. He turned, and she was horrified to see that, "He had burning red eyes and pointy horns. . . . It was the devil!" She evidently donated her winnings to her local church.

If that story is not enough, here's another one being told in the community as reported in Harrison Fletcher's article. "Another woman was playing blackjack at Isleta Gaming Palace. She too had been gambling all day and losing her money. Just as she stood to leave, a tall, dark and handsome man in a black coat tapped her shoulder. 'Why don't you play the slots?' he said. 'The one in the corner will win.' At first, the woman refused, but she too relented. Two minutes later, a $5,000 jackpot! She wheeled around to thank the man, but he had begun walking away into the crowd. Just before he disappeared, she noticed something peculiar poking from the back of his coat: a pointed tail!"

A spokesperson from the Isleta Gaming Palace scoffed at the stories saying, "Give me a break. I've heard about sixteen different versions of that story." Admittedly stories of this ilk are very difficult to pin down. I have investigated only one alleged event in which the primary witness was named.[12] Usually, the solemn storyteller attributes the event to a friend of a friend. "There's a guy, whose sister's, neighbor's, cousin's brother was there, and he saw it all!" We could surmise that such stories may have some kernel of truth at their core. Although I can't prove it, I suspect that there may be a real cause-and-effect event that initially creates these particular stories. Of course, the probability exists that the original event differs from the resulting story and may not accurately resemble the primary account. However, the resulting story spreads like wildfire through a largely superstitious community and is invariably told and retold, blurring, even radically altering, the exact details of the original event. This provides another potential example of how our region's subcultural myths and legends may be created. Remember Suggested Rule of Investigation 12: There is a possibility that the (sub)culture itself may cocreate manifestations of unexplained, individually perceived phenomena.

CHAPTER ELEVEN

BEYOND BELIEF

What is the true nature of belief? Perhaps a more basic question should be asked. What is the true nature of consciousness? Of perception? Is consciousness the final arbiter of experience?

In the dance along this ongoing microscopic examination of the "mysterious" San Luis Valley, it is inevitable that these basic questions would appear at the very heart of our unique bioregional reality. We have all been taught, by one system or another, that we are spiritual, sentient beings, coexisting with one another in a consensual reality. We find ourselves as participants in a swirling daily dance between cause and effect and chaos. It should be apparent to most of us that the dualistic nature of reality is only what we, as participatory individuals, make of it. This goes for any mundane or extramundane experience. This chapter attempts to raise several relevant questions often ignored by mainstream science and education.

In 1988, while living in Boston, a friend, who was a psychic counselor, asked me to assist in healing a six-year-old girl who had injured herself in a fall. I had followed the progress of the case and the unfortunate little girl who had been comatose for six months. I admit that I was taken aback by my friend's request. My ego-centered "self" had never considered the possibility that I could effect any "healing," or turnaround, in such an unfortunate scenario. The little girl's family had given up hope. They were all set to pull the plug. My friend had been working with the girl for almost three months and was convinced that she could, and would, return to consciousness. A compassionate nurse at the hospital who had taken a personal interest in the case had asked my friend to seek help for one final attempt. This was it.

My friend, a practitioner trained in Salem, Massachusetts, immediately contacted a friend who is a Native American healer and another friend who was considered to be a "psychic" to come in and do round-the-clock work. She came over to the house and told me of the little girl's last-chance plight and asked me to play a copy of a meditation soundtrack I had recorded after hearing the music in a dream. She had heard it and thought it "couldn't make the situation worse," so I went ahead and made a copy of the tape on an endless-loop cassette. Hidden just below the audible sonic level I subliminally recorded the following words. "Wa-a-a-ke up! It's a beautiful day, there's friends to play with and fun to have, wake up, wa-a-ke up. You have your whole life to live and people who love you. Wa-a-ke up, wa-a-a-a-ke up!" Then it repeated and repeated and repeated . . .

The twelve-minute endless-loop tape was put in a Walkman and the headphones placed on her head as she lay in the hospital bed. The healers came and worked with her, and one final marathon attempt was made to bring her out of coma. The sessions ended after two days.

The following day, she awoke. There was no apparent physical or psychological damage, and the little girl thought she had just been asleep. It seemed miraculous.

I don't know how or why this happened. I would like to think that my tape had something to do with the healing, but several accomplished healers had worked with her for many hours, and perhaps the concentration of healing work managed to break through to her.

What is it about that nonlinear processing lump of gray matter between our ears, that marvel of the nonlinear side of nature? The causes and cures for coma are not completely understood. Or how about a person suffering little or no physical damage after losing substantial portions of the brain? The more I learn about this wonderful biologic computer, the more I am humbled by the realization that we have only scratched the surface of understanding this enigmatic organ.

The following interview may provide you with a bit of insight. It did for me.

MIRACLES DO HAPPEN

San Luis Valley resident Roger LaBorde is one of the more compelling individuals I have ever known, and I am honored to count him among my friends. His quiet, centered nature and even-keeled demeanor are matched by his easy sense of humor and a remarkable wealth of life experience. A very low-key individual, Roger is a man of many talents. Since 1992, one of those talents has been helping dozens of people who are comatose to pass over or come back. His successes are truly remarkable and include several high-profile cases that have been featured on the NBC television program *The Other Side* and the Paramount show *Sightings*.

Roger and and his wife, Pam, have lived in the San Luis Valley for more than ten years. I met them in 1991 and have gotten to know Pam and Roger and their two daughters, Angela and Jennifer—who is Isadora's daughter, Brisa's best friend.[1] I knew Roger for a couple of years before Roger's work became a topic of discussion. He is very humble about his abilities and doesn't talk about himself. I was pleasantly surprised and grateful when he agreed to an interview.

The LaBordes have known for quite a while that they would someday live on Blanca, and I visited their newly acquired dream house, with its stunning front-row-seat view of Little Bear and Blanca Peak, for the first time on August 15, 1997.

I arrived with Brisa, who was spending the night with the LaBorde girls, and Roger was showing a Colorado state forest worker an area he and Pam were considering turning into a small wetland. I leaned against my truck and scanned the breathtaking view of the Blanca Massif with my binoculars while Brisa visited with her friends.

A low airplane engine caught my attention, and I looked up to see what appeared to be an Air Force cargo plane flying over the south side of the mountain about thirty-five hundred to four thousand feet up. I brought the binoculars up to my eyes and located the plane. At that instant, it shimmered and disappeared! I quickly looked around the cloudless sky as a couple of seconds went by and the sound abruptly ceased. Nothing. It had been strange to see a bright aluminum-colored C-131. And it was very weird the way the plane vanished. Roger came walking up the driveway. I told him what I had just witnessed, and he said, "Oh, I've seen that a couple, three times since we moved here." We went inside and sat down at the kitchen table to begin the interview, with me scratching my head, still trying to figure out what I had just witnessed.

"Roger, you have quite an impressive track record. What has been the reaction to your coma work? Are you being inundated with requests for help?"

"No. I wasn't looking to do this when it started. I'm still not looking to do it. It comes infrequently because I'm not out advertising, I'm not on television all the time. When it first occurred, working with comatose people, the first few cases were very dramatic and made nationwide news. There was a helicopter pilot who crashed into Horsetooth Reservoir north of Denver and was underwater for over forty minutes, and a well-known Australian singer. All the people who I've worked with, and the people who have seen what's happened, have told others who have loved ones in a coma that there are other ways of going at it, but it's one-half of one percent that would actually pick up the phone and call."

"But if they do call, it sounds like you're there and willing to help them."

"Yes. There are very few cases I haven't gone on. But it's very important to get to them during the first few weeks of coma, no more than two months. The earlier the better. The primary reason for that is what has already occurred within the medical profession, within the ICU [intensive care unit], the family members, and so forth. If the case has reached a point where the person in the coma has pulled away so far from their bodies that there's only just enough life force to keep the body maintained, their consciousness is basically elsewhere. They are experiencing something else that is much more meaningful to them, and they're paying very little attention to 'here.' But there is some important energetic connection for their body to stay alive because of the importance for the family members to still be attached to the body. When families can begin to let go, when they can truly come from a place of compassion . . . They know they'll miss their loved one, there is still a transference of information to the loved one that it's okay to go."

He continued. "There was a case from right here in the San Luis Valley, a Hispanic man, who had a heart attack and was in a coma. Several weeks had gone by; it was close to two months when I was called in on the case. I forget how they heard about me. The problem, after talking with the family . . . well, it was very clear to me that he wasn't going because he needed to see his grandchildren. The grandchildren knew that Grampa was in the hospital, but they didn't see him in the hospital. They weren't allowed to go to the hospital. In fact, they were sent to Denver so they wouldn't even be close by. It took me several weeks to convince them that it would be important to bring the grandchildren and let them spend some time with him. They did, and twenty-four hours later he died. I asked them, 'How do you think he would feel if he left and didn't say good-bye to the grandkids? How do you think the grandkids would feel? To not let the grandkids have a chance to say good-bye to him?' There was such a powerful loving between them, and it was important to honor that. Once they did, he felt free to go."

"How are you able to surmount interpersonal factors in the families' attitudes?"

"It has to do with their belief systems, the narrow view of belief systems and how belief systems reinforce themselves through miraculous events occurring within the restrictions of those belief systems. On one trip I made to the East Coast several years ago, I was counseling people. I met a woman who was very upset that she had a waking vision of Jesus Christ and she was a devout Tibetan Buddhist. It was a few days later and I had another woman appear, again upset, who was a devout Christian who had a very powerful waking vision of Buddha. So that lent itself to talking about energy, creative energy, and how it can manifest in symbology that can either break the belief system that you are holding on to, or reinforce the belief system that you are holding on to. It happens all the time. However, people will only see and hear what they want to hear and see. So if they see something that is miraculous, and it doesn't necessarily fit into the context of their belief system, they will rationalize it in some way that will fit the context of their belief system. I've found that when I'm working with people who are in severe cases of coma, the medical profession gives them less than a two percent chance of living, and if they do live, the families are told they will exist in a persistent vegetative state." Roger has proved time and again that this is not necessarily so.

"The families that I've worked with have been born-again Christians, Hindus, Muslims, and some that are basically nonaligned, nonreligious. The coma patients who have made a miraculous turnaround and come out and have done well are considered a medical mystery. Talking with each family in their own vocabulary, they can understand this in their own belief system."

"So you make a conscious attempt to try and couch the process that you are helping facilitate in a language that they can understand?"

"Yes. Starting there, I try and expand the discussion. I take them in a direction to begin enticing them to step outside the narrow vessel in which they see the world and their relationships and begin to talk about healing in its true context, instead of talking about a cure. It's not something outside of themselves that creates the healing. It's something inside themselves that's connected to the larger picture.

"If I was talking to a Christian, I would say, 'God only helps those that help themselves.' Now what does this mean? It means recognizing that in their own belief system God made man in his own image. Which means spiritually. The messenger who came along said, 'Everything you see me do, you can do too, even more.'

"So until a person begins to realize the healing energy is not separate from them, not outside of them, it's an integral part of them. Once they do that, the belief system is beginning to break apart, and it can be very difficult at times because what they're faced with is the worry that this can become blasphemous. That they are claiming they're God."

I was struck by the amazing amount of patience and work that Roger must exercise to help people through such a faith-shattering, emotional trauma. I commented, "That could be a major barrier. I'm sure it's been quite a process in some cases trying to help the family and at the same time the person that is the focus of your attention. Trying to break through their beliefs must be tough at times! Real devout Christians, real devout Muslims."

"It's not as difficult as you might think, because, first of all, for me to get the call, they already have to be in a tremendous state of crisis."

"They wouldn't be calling unless they were primed for it, in other words."

"Yes. Everything else has failed."

"So you really are 'a last resort'!"

"Yes. The cases I've been called in on I was the last resort."

"How many cases have you been called in on?"

"I don't know. Dozens. But when I go, I'm not going to bring the person out of the coma. I'm going to help the family to help the person who is comatose to make a decision. To find a way for communication between the family and their loved one in a coma. And help the person in the coma to make the decision to stay or go. These people do communicate; they can communicate and understand what's going on around them. But it's not the same as having a conversation like we are doing right now. It has to be a conversation of heart, a conversation of compassion. A conversation is not limited; it's boundless. To be in that space, everything has to drop away, including belief system. So depending on the belief system, I may begin the discussion with the family when I first get there. But they soon realize that in the work I'm doing with their loved one, I'm attempting to move them to the point of letting go of their belief system."

"This sounds like a really important part of the process!"

"It's an integral part of it. There is only one thing that must be present, and that is what the Buddhists call compassion and what monotheists call unconditional loving. Christians use the word *agape*, which means a godlike loving. If they can allow themselves to summon up the courage to break through the mental fears that they carry, like I'll be condemned, or it's blasphemy, or I'll be excommunicated, or I'll be judged—"

"—the programmed fear issues that their belief system has been banging them over their head with . . . ."

"Primarily the compassion and love for their loved one, in this very serious situation, overwhelms the fear."

"It sounds to me like it is not only the person that's in the coma, it's also the family. It sounds like they're as important to the process as the person in the coma!"

"They're not separate from it at all. In all the cases that I've gone in to, the person that has experienced the so-called accident to bring on the state of coma was going through a tremendous amount of stress. Most of the time, that stress has been family related. It can be in categories of financial stress, emotional stress. When I begin talking with the family I ask them what was going on in the six months leading up to the so-called accident. What was the stress? I know there was tremendous stress. Initially, the family denies there was any stress, but after I'm there for a couple of days, and spend a lot of time around them, they begin talking about all the stress factors that were happening at the time. This most obvious of many examples:

"I was called into a case of a police officer on the East Coast. Again, it was a severe case. When I talked with his wife on the phone, I asked, 'What were the conditions leading up to the massive heart attack he had experienced?' She said, 'Well, he's a police officer and he was chasing a criminal, running him down in full-body armor and all his accoutrements on his belt. He captured the guy, handcuffed him, got him into the patrol car, sat down in the car, and had a massive heart attack.' So, in her view, that's what caused the heart attack. But getting into further discussion with her and being persistent in finding out what was going on leading up to this, there were a lot of stress factors! A lot of marital stress factors, a lot of job stress factors, with both of them. They were both police officers. He was having affairs, and she knew about it. It was a tangled web."

"Initially none of that came up?"

"Two days before the heart attack, she said they were sitting out around the swimming pool, in their new home that was out in the countryside. he said to her, while having a glass of champagne, 'I guess now that you have everything you've ever wanted, I can leave. Now it's time for me to leave.' A few days later, he had a massive heart attack. In her mind, she saw no connection with any of that, until I began probing and asking about it. Even when I left, I don't think she saw the connection with his statement and the heart attack later. She couldn't see that the coma situation was one of still in-between. There was still an attachment to not leaving, to not dying, and not coming out. She was definitely wanting him to come out of the coma, so I asked her, 'If he comes out of the coma, what does he have to look forward to? Is it going to continue in the future the way it was in the past? And if that's the case, what's the incentive to come out of coma?' How can this family change? What changes can be made in this family, at a core level, that he would want to come back and come out of the coma?

"The cases that I've seen that have come out of the comas, there are some dramatic changes within the family structure."

I was interested in the profound change that the person invariably undergoes. "Now that you've been involved to the extent that you have in this work and facilitation, looking back at some of the earlier cases that were successful, what kind of changes have you seen?"

"Most of them did not go back into the jobs they were in, and most of them didn't want to be in those jobs. The crisis does create a condition that reevaluates what everyone [in the family] is doing in their lives—their connections and where they're going, what they are going to commit to, things they want to change. There have been some pretty dramatic shifts. There were two specific cases where, on the surface, the husband or wife seemed to be happily married, and then after they came out of the coma, they got divorced. But the truth is, in working with the spouses, what I found out is that they were not happily married, and they were strongly considering divorce! They cared for one another, but the problems existed before the onset of coma, but there was no decision for divorce. What came out during situation of coma was that the spouse [not in the coma] discovered how much he or she loved their mate. Not *in* love with them, but loved them."

"That's compassion again."

"Correct. It wasn't a situation that they wanted to stay married to them, but they loved them so much, they would fight for their well-being. Battle the traditional medical view that they would not come out. So even after they got them through the crisis, they got a divorce."

"It sounds like the changes that occur once the decision to come back is made by the person in coma are real-life changes as a result of that decision, almost like a second lease on life. 'I'm going to live my life differently this time, because obviously something was wrong beforehand.' I didn't realize that the family had such an integral part in this process. It makes perfect sense now."

Roger agreed and continued. "The onset of a major crisis will either take the person and make them more deeply entrenched in their belief system, or it will break it completely apart. It is an opportunity for growth. A doorway to see the miraculous in everything, not just your belief system."

"How did you get involved in this work? How did you find out you had this ability to communicate on these deeper levels? We are talking about communication on levels that modern science is just now starting to realize are there. How did you discover this potential in yourself?"

"It just happened. It's always there. There was only one commitment. A commitment in the seventies, when I went through a life-changing experience, to follow my heart. I'm talking about a compassionate heart and a state of mind. The only thing you can do from that place is to constantly make decisions based in a place of compassion. It's not a place of control, it's not a place of manipulation, not a place of fear. It's a place of compassion. So if a person decides that, and is committed to it, then that opens the entire realm to communicate with all beings. The Native Americans would say, 'With all my relations.' It's not just people, it's animals, rocks and trees, the weather. . . . It's moving in an energetic space that is not separate from anything else. It wouldn't be surprising that if a person lives in that space, to be able to communicate with someone who is comatose."

I was beginning to better understand the process. "So, if you can discover that place of compassion within yourself, for all things, for all energies, systems or forms, there is that potential. This is light-years beyond what most people would even understand."

Roger thought for a moment and said, "Scientific thought has taken root very powerfully in the industrialized world. The whole influence of modern medicine. Doctors didn't become miracle workers until the discovery of anesthesia. The person could go in, go to sleep, and when they awoke, the problem was gone. Before this, they had to endure a lot of pain. The reputation of the surgeon was based on how quick they could get in and get out. There is a path that people are taking that is away from the intuitive, instinctive, telepathic, clairvoyant, clairaudient. All those things that are naturally occurring, but there's no scientific root for it."

"Science has been stealing away some of our innate qualities," I observed.

Roger agreed. "They're beginning to come full circle and recognize that these things do exist and that they can be measured. When you're looking at belief systems, there are belief systems that can get just as rigid as someone who's strongly indoctrinated into scientific thought or into allopathic medicine. There needs to be the integration between the esoteric with the scientific. It's beginning to happen in some places; it's not widespread."

"There are very few people in science who are willing to go against the grain. What's the furthest down-the-road coma that you've been called into and had a success?"

"I worked with a woman in California that had been in a coma for two and a half years. The father called me into the case because it was his daughter in the coma. The son was taking care of her, and it had bankrupted him. He had sold his house to have money to continue caring for his sister. There's a lot to the story, but primarily, what he was asking is that, for two and a half years, everyone said in the medical profession that she can't hear, she can't respond, etc. So I went out and I spent three days around her. I noticed very quickly that she was very aware of what was going on, and the way that it would show itself was when I would start talking about specific subjects, she reacted to it. She would grind her teeth, she would turn red in the face and start spitting. She physically responded to certain subjects."

"Two and a half years down the road—that's amazing in and of itself!"

"She would curl up in a tight ball. The first thing I said that would cause that reaction was, 'You can play the child for as long as you want to, but your mom's not coming back to see you.' I knew that the mother had been there two years before and basically left and said, 'I'm not coming back to visit my daughter. I won't be around her like this.' She had a very difficult time with her mother. I think she ran away from home when she was a teenager of fourteen or fifteen years old."

"It sounds like another unresolved issue."

"And her daughter did the same thing to her, too. She saw her and said, 'I'm never coming back.' I was talking to the woman in the coma. She was in her mid-forties, and she was grinding her teeth, and you could tell she was real angry, and so I said to her, 'You want to die, don't you?' And she relaxed. And I said, 'You want someone to help you die?' And she was perfectly calm. I said, 'I can understand your reasons, but no one is going to do that.' She got angry again. So through her physical reactions to the things I was talking to her about, what I was able to ascertain was just that! She wanted to die, she didn't want to be there, she didn't want her brother taking care of her. This was later confirmed when I went out and talked with her brother and father, and I said, 'Here's what I see: She's given up. I bet you can tell me exactly the month, and I bet you can even tell me the week and the day that she gave up.' And the brother looked at me, and he was a little dumbfounded, and he said, 'You're right, I can. I kept notes all along, and I know exactly when it happened.'

"He went and got his notebooks, and he told me the sequence of events of how she got her coma. He told me she was a severe asthmatic, and hadn't taken her medication, so she had a severe attack, didn't have her medication. The question was, why didn't she have her medication? She had this problem ever since childhood. So when he pulled out his notebook, he said all the therapists and doctors were excited about her recovery after the onset of her coma. That she was coming out, that she was doing well, the prognosis was that within a few weeks she would be doing rehab and so forth.

"There was one week when the mother sat in front of her and left and said she was never coming back. Her daughter said the same thing. The nurse that was attending to her in the hospital was pregnant, so she left on her pregnancy leave."

"This was all in the same one-week period?"

"Yes. Three very important people in her life at the time left. Right after that, the father walked in and said hi and said her name, and she just went berserk and screamed so loud that nurses came running in wanting to know what he did to her. He said, 'I didn't do anything. I just walked in and said hi, and she went berserk.' She did the same thing to the brother. And again, this is all in the same week. They had weekly reports on her condition, and it was on the next report that there was a severe downhill turn. They sent her to a long-term care facility for a while, and what was discovered was that the attendants would drug her so that she wouldn't scream. She was disturbing other patients. What she was doing by her reactions was that if no one was going to kill her, help her die, she wanted to go back into that facility where she would be drugged, where she would be completely oblivious to her surroundings.

"The father and the brother came in and also followed these same lines of discussion with her and saw the same reactions. The brother said, 'I've had a strong suspicion for a long time that she'd given up. Every

therapist that had come in, she would run them off.'
She would not cooperate; curl up into a ball, turn beet-
red, and start the spitting. The therapist wouldn't work
with her. He said, 'I've suspected this for a long time.'
So my recommendation to them was to pick a time.
X amount of time—six months, a year, whatever you
decide. Make it well known to her that you understand
what's going on and that she can physically make a
decision to begin cooperating and take a shot at coming
back physically, but you are only going to give her so
much time to make that decision. It was physically de-
stroying the financial status and health of her brother
and the father."

"So you didn't recommend that the mother and the
daughter come back in."

"They wouldn't do that."

"Between a rock and a hard place."

"Right. So I got letters from the father and the
brother, and the father said he knew now that his
daughter knew what was going on, whereas before, all
he was being told by the doctors was that she was oblivious to everything around her. That was a situation of
coming in and pointing out what's going on and rec-
ommending a course of action. Doing it from a place
of compassion and recognizing that you can't be in a
place of what the Buddhists call 'idiot compassion.' A
salvation mentality that you're going to save this person
from something they're choosing, even at your own destruction. And not giving space for the other person to
take responsibility for the choices that they've made.

"The work, the cases that I've gone into really bring
up one central question: What is the nature of consciousness? If you firmly believe in your belief system
that who and what you are, and your consciousness,
exists between your ears in your brain that is damaged

beyond repair, there's a course of action you will take. If you see who and what you are has nothing to do with your brain, that it's just a tool through which your consciousness expresses itself, then there is a whole other set of options that can be taken! I find it interesting that in spiritual belief systems there is an emphasis on spirituality having nothing to do with your body. In other words, this spirit essence, consciousness, that animates your body, brings life to your body, and continues after the body ceases to exist, that is an intense focus of their belief system, but yet, in a time of crisis, especially in a time of coma, that is never addressed, that is never looked at and rarely talked about. Even if you have a neurologist who's a devout religious person, let's say Christian, they still take the route of the scientific view of the damage of the brain, and there's nothing that can be done."

"Yet on Sunday, he goes and has a mystical experience in church—"

"—And makes sure his children are baptized so they'll go to heaven when they die. So there's this strange way of living where your life is compartmentalized, especially in the medical world."

Roger thought for a moment and continued. "I was asked to sit in on an ethics committee in a hospital for one day. The administrator of the hospital knew of my work, and he said that particular day the case they were going to discuss was a case that had happened several years ago. It was a woman, I think in her late seventies, who was comatose, and the discussion was centered around what was the responsibility of the hospital. Now this is a Seventh-Day Adventist hospital. What they were discussing was quality versus quantity of life, what the family would have to face, what decisions would have to be made, and the cost to the hospital, because the woman did not have insurance. It was costing the hospital approximately a thousand dollars a day to have her there. So there was an hour of conversation with various neurologists and other doctors, as well as the chaplain, who was sitting in.

"When they were coming to the end of the discussion, the administrator asked me if I had anything that I wanted to add to the discussion I had been listening to the last hour. It was very striking to me early on that there was one central thing that they didn't discuss. I found it very interesting that there was this intense discussion about cost, quality of life versus quantity of life. She was in her seventies, how much life does she possibly have, what possible quality of life would—could— she possibly have because the prognosis was grim? The emotional and financial burden on the family, and so forth, and I said, 'I find it interesting that no one ever suggested talking to the woman in the coma! No one ever suggested telling her the cost, telling her what's happening, and that she needs to help in this decision!'" He shook his head.

"It's their mind-set. It's their assumption that she's not there to begin with. I think your work proves them wrong."

"Well, I gave them some examples of cases I had worked on, and the feedback afterwards, from the administrator, was that everyone was surprised I had brought that up because that was really not something in their consciousness, and here it was supposed to be a Seventh-Day Adventist Hospital, connected with spirituality. But he said probably the one person in the room that it hit the hardest was—"

"—The chaplain, of course."

"The chaplain said it never crossed his mind other than to tell the family to go pray. It never crossed his mind to tell them to sit at their bedside and hold their hands, yell to them how much you love them. Here he would talk about the healing power of Christ, the healing power of God, but yet the family is separated from that individual and told that the person is going to die, and then giving the family limited access to the person."

"Forest for the trees, what's the point?"

"Right."

Roger smiled. "The person in the coma, isn't it ultimately their decision whether to stay or go? Who better to help them make that decision than the people closest to them?"

"Do you see a change in attitude in the people who are involved in a technical way? The doctors, nurses, therapists, and the professionals involved in the intellectual processes? When you leave the scene of a particular case, are you affecting them in any way? It's obvious you're affecting the families and the patient."

"The feedback I get from the families is that some doctors stop and reevaluate what they're doing, but in most instances, they say, 'Well, we don't know what happened,' and leave it at that. In some cases, they completely deny that the person was ever comatose."

"Is there any hope?" I ask rhetorically.

Roger, without hesitation, answered, "I think so. There was one case that *Unsolved Mysteries* wanted to do a show on, and they contacted several doctors who were involved, and all of them refused to go on camera. Even the neurologist, one of the other doctors, went as far as to say the person was never comatose! Now the family will tell you all those doctors told them he was comatose, there was no hope, pull life support and let him die! . . . You have that to contend with that. I do know of one doctor, a neurologist, who has seen more than one case and realizes now that something else is occurring. He has definitely reevaluated the way he approaches coma."

Roger continued, "My interest is not in 'the state of coma'; my interest is in the 'state of consciousness' and healing. Maybe coma is the most dramatic crisis to demonstrate the nature of consciousness. Healing has nothing to do with coma; it's just one of the more dramatic realms to work in. Healing is completely different from curing. That's a whole other realm. I wasn't looking to do this when I started, and I'm not necessarily looking to continue doing it. It's like a lot of things we do during life, or in the course of a day, that we are all involved in. Focusing on coma work is not my intention."

"But you are there to help people that need help."

"Yes, but after so many cases, you begin to get known to the public to some degree, and now the people who are coming want you to come do some miracle. They want you to do something miraculous. Their expectation is, 'I heard you have brought people out of coma, and I want you to come do it for my husband,' or 'my wife.' I had a woman call me from Chicago and was insistent that I come up. She couldn't pay my way, or anything (that usually doesn't stop me), her husband was in a hospital, and he was in a coma. He had been in the hospital with an illness that basically had him bedridden, and he could barely move, barely communicate, and now he was comatose. She said, 'Could you bring him out of coma?' And I said, 'For *what*? Bring him back out to where he's still bedridden!' I asked her, 'Have you ever thought that this was his gentle way of leaving because of the disease that he has?' She kept calling and calling, and I talked to her at length about it. I asked her, 'Do you realize that it's your selfishness that wants your husband to be able to talk to you? He can't do much of anything else, and he's even hospitalized—' "

"—Just tell him—"

"—it's okay to go!" Roger finished my sentence and fell silent for a moment. Then he said quietly, "She wouldn't do it."

"That's not even idiot compassion. That's going into a completely different realm."

Roger observed, "It's fear and control. When those kinds of cases start cropping up, that's completely diverting the attention from what I have been doing for a lot of years, and that's trying to talk to people about the nature of healing, consciousness. It's a form that you can easily become trapped in. People call me and say, 'I hear you're a healer.' No. Healers don't exist. Healers *do not* exist. People heal themselves. It is a state of mind that brings on that 'healing,' and there are people who can assist in changing that state of mind, opening doors, changing energy patterns and all of that. Until the person accepts full responsibility for their own healing, then healing won't occur. Anything else other than that is a 'cure.' A cure is temporary; a healing is permanent."

"You are a facilitator to themselves."

"Right."

"And you facilitate communication between a comatose person and the family."

Roger corrected me. "Well, actually the person is not even comatose. It's communication from one heart to another and forget what the body looks like. On my first coma case, someone asked me if I'd ever worked with people in coma before, and I said, 'All the time, they're walking around everywhere!' "

I started laughing.

Roger looked at me. "It's true!" he exclaimed.

Suddenly this literal analogy hit home for me, and I candidly admitted, "You're darn right it's true! I consider myself to be fairly aware, and it's hard enough for me to realize at every moment that I am an alive, aware being. Most of us do find ourselves in coma all the time, if we're lucky."

BREAKING OUT OF THE BOX

Back in January 1993, when I first embarked on my San Luis Valley paranormal sojourn, one of the very first people I contacted was Dr. Lynn Weldon, a longtime Valley resident and a professor at Adams State College. Dr. Weldon graciously provided me with full run of his San Luis Valley files pertaining to the odd and not quite normal. He has invited me to speak at his paranormal class, and for the past five years I have lectured at his Adams State College classes about the paranormal.

Recently retired, he has been teaching this subject area for more than twenty-five years and has personally known many of the colorful characters mentioned in *The Mysterious Valley*, including Texas investigators Tom Adams and Gary Massey, Huerfano investigator-journalist David Perkins, and Berle and Nellie Lewis.[2]

Lynn is a popular educator and an engaging teacher and mentor; his unique approach is reflected in the standing-room-only classes. I finally pinned him down for the following interview at his beautiful home. Even though retired, he still teaches his favorite class on the paranormal.

"Dr. Weldon, how did you develop your interest in the paranormal?"

"My father, who died two years ago at age ninety-three, was a beekeeper when I was growing up in California. He was an amateur archaeologist and used to go around giving slide lectures before people were into slides. He was kind of a pioneer. Before his death, he was trying to get a manuscript published on the hollow-earth concept. I can remember in Dad's literature, Commodore Perry flying over areas, and seeing various things, clippings; Dad collected paranormal phenomena clippings in a volume. For example, the Mirror glacier in Alaska where they would see mirages, and they were claiming they were seeing a city with people moving around in it that wasn't *on* earth."

"A reflection from the hollow earth?"

"Yes. That was the theory. I'm sure I was into Atlantis, science fiction, and things like that at a fairly early age. So when I came to the Valley forty years ago, I was already interested in these areas and, of course, collected all the books that I could find on UFOs and all sorts of other phenomena. In fact, I started teaching a college-level course on UFOs over thirty years ago. Then, of course, Snippy came along.[3]

"It has been a fun experience as more and more people became aware that I have been into these areas. They would come to me and tell me their stories. I've had many interesting people come and lecture at my UFO class. Like you. I had a lady from east of Alamosa report to me that she had traveled on a flying saucer. A man from Monte Vista told me of watching UFOs go in and out of the [Blanca] Massif. Berle and Nellie Lewis, as I recall, came and talked with my class. So did the guys from Texas, Tom [Adams] and Gary [Massey]. That led to Alan Hynek coming and talking with the class. Others who came were Leo Sprinkle, Linda Moulton Howe, and Wendal Stevens. In the eighties, they all had a conference here, and I was kind of their gofer. It was very interesting listening to all these folks. I've seen my role through the years as facilitator. It's been my role to expose these people and ideas in a credible academic setting, to allow the students to be aware of these things and to encourage them to explore."

"You must have had quite an open-minded administration thirty years ago to even allow you to present a course on these subject areas. Back then—I know how it is now, I've run up against all kinds of scientific snobbery, but thirty years ago, I can't imagine. I'm surprised they didn't try to drum you out of Adams State for even suggesting this sort of thing."

"Well, I started the first sexuality course thirty years ago, in the late sixties. There were no textbooks, there were no courses being taught. It's my suspicion is we probably had the first sexuality class ever at any university. I pulled in people from all the departments, and I had a medical doctor and a priest in, and we talked about the sociological and spiritual aspects. It was a heck of a lot of fun!"

"You were a groundbreaker and a half! I really would like to acknowledge that."

"Well, it was a lot of fun."

"What a way to pass along knowledge and have a good time while doing it!"

"My course on the future started out in the early seventies as a course on Spaceship Earth and gradually evolved into the course on the future. Of course, I was teaching some of the basic courses on psychology and sociology, but they always let me have some fun."

"It sounds like they gave you slack and you didn't hang yourself with it. What impression do you have of the San Luis Valley? You've lived here for quite a number of years. You've been here during most of our celebrated events in the paranormal and ufology reported here, and you've talked to many people I've included in my books. What do you make of it? Is it the place? Is it the people? Is it the energy here? What do you make of it?"

He smiled his sweet, knowing smile.

I went on, "You've always reminded me of the Cheshire Cat. A lot of times you fade away on me, except for your smile. I don't get much out of you, that's why I'm pinning you down! What do *you* think? You, more than anybody, should have an idea, or at least a suspicion concerning this wonderful place we both live in."

With his trademark twinkling eyes, Lynn laughed and responded, "I like the famous quote: 'The larger the island of knowledge, the longer the shoreline of wonder.' Okay? Therefore, I simply have wonderments. Various people have asked me, 'Do you believe in UFOs? Cattle mutilations?' My general response is, 'I don't have answers. I'm an explorer on this planet. I am here to open doors for other people, but I have no truths.' I've often said I would feel more comfortable if there are little green men and UFOs, and if they would come down and land on the lawn in front of Richardson Hall and let us go up and thump on their machine and provide us with free rides, I would feel much more comfortable."

"It would be so easy! It would be cut-and-dried. The wonder would be gone, though," I commented.

"I have had a delightful time, well, fifty-five years . . . going exploring. Do I have problems and concerns? Yes. I like to play some of Arthur Clarke's *Mysterious World* videos to show the skeptical yet open-minded approach in which he notes that it's possible that many things are currently beyond our range of human knowledge. We can't make conclusions about many of them."

"If you had tried, I would have turned the tape off and spanked you!" I scolded playfully. We both laugh.

Lynn reflected. "Exploration has been a joy to me. I can remember, around age seven or eight, imagining myself sitting in a cultural box under a tube of anti-gravity material. I would be floating around, about three feet off the floor, observing things. It was all inside my head, but I can remember I was an observer. I en-joyed, what you could label a cocoon existence. I grew up in a nice system [the reform Mormon Church]. I didn't reject it, but I also didn't take it personally as my own; I was always floating around looking at it. I re-member in high school I'd go to the Catholic church, and I'd visit various places just to learn about the cul-ture and the world I was living in. I'd explore all sorts of things. I loved *National Geographic* and learning about this world.

"I was in my senior year in college and taking a prosaic course called Techniques of Teaching in the Elementary School. And this particular professor both-ered me. I was used to the traditional system where you figure out the professor, memorize what the professor wants, regurgitate it, get your A's and move on. The traditional authoritarian system. I couldn't do that with him. I'd take notes, and he would go here and go there, and he was into a more democratic, thoughtful, reflec-tive, analytical approach. He didn't have the answers to give. He would go into the various alternative ap-proaches.

"About halfway through the semester, the end-of-the-period bell rang, the professor got up and walked out the door. The students walked out the door, and I was just sitting there feeling strange. I went over and pushed open the door. As I stepped through the door, I stepped into the universe. I didn't see God, or Christ, or flashing lights; I stepped into the universe inside my head. Visually, I could see I had stepped into the hall, but I had stepped out of the cultural box I had grown up in. I make various analogies, like at that instant the universe, and everything in it, became like a huge picture gallery. Where there are all sorts of pictures, like the sexual pictures, political pictures, economic pictures, musical pictures. Some of them I like better than others. I'm not saying I'm a doubting Thomas, in the sense of doubt as a negative thing, I became a wondering wanderer. This experience seemed to be a crystallization.

"Another analogy I've offered is that I feel like I am in a mental helicopter floating over the perceptual-cultural boxes. I go down and visit them, but I'm always floating. I'm always interested in seeing alternatives, comparing alternatives."

I observed, "It sounds to me, that at a very early age, you were able to disassociate yourself and not buy into the different cultural boxes. You gained an ability to have a bird's-eye perspective."

"Yes. But one of my ongoing questions is: If what I experienced was true, if I really walked through the side of my cultural box, is it possible there's a much bigger box and my mental helicopter may whack into the side of it, or I may go through a door in the side of what may be a much bigger box? When I was young, I didn't know I was confined in a box. Now I may be in a much bigger box, and I may not know it.

"I have been asked by people, 'Do you believe in God?' And a stock answer is, when we die, it's not an either/or proposition, with purgatory in between. I think we will realize when we pass on, we are entering kindergarten. Right now, we're in preschool. You can use this analogy to your box analogy. It's a journey through a series of boxes.

"I have another analogy, or example. You are familiar with Robert Heinlein's *Stranger in a Strange Land*?" he asks me.

"I think I can 'grok' this one. One of my favorites."

"Well, maybe I lived two centuries from now, and instead of setting the time machine ahead, they sent me back. Like Mark Twain's *A Connecticut Yankee in King Arthur's Court*. I may really be a twenty-second-century person locked back in the twentieth century. Almost forty years ago, I revolted against the authoritarian system. As a teacher, I haven't given a test in thirty-eight years! Some of the students say, 'I would have rather taken tests, it's so much easier than what I've had to go through.' I've always been a nontraditionalist. We need to develop the skills in people to use in a democratic society: examine alternatives, check things through, support your views. I had one student who was very angry at me. He said, 'Dr. Weldon, I checked you out very carefully and figured out what you believe, I started expressing your beliefs, and you changed!' "

I laughed and commented, "I've said a lot of things to a lot of professors, but that's a little cheeky. To tell them that I've figured them out was about the last thing I would ever say. They would have boxed my ears or something."

"I've received letters from students years later saying, 'I just caught on what you were doing to me.' "

"I think I'm getting a much better idea, a better frame of reference . . ." I was itching to find out what his years of experience in this wonderful Valley had taught him. "But, Dr. Weldon, you've been ducking my question. What is it about *this* place? Why are you *here* and not someplace else?"

He did it again. "I got a job here at Adams State."

I said, directly into the tape recorder, "Dr. Weldon is *still* dodging my question. So let me rephrase my question. In all the years that you've spent here, has this place ever given you an indication that it is somehow different or unique from other places, and if so, in what way? What form has that information taken? I suspect you do have a sense that this is a special place. . . ."

"Of course. Why is it? Just look around—*we are encompassed by mountains*. It's a gorgeous area. Our new neighbors just moved in from Georgia. As they were flying in, they happened to ask a former student of mine [who was on the flight], 'What word would you use to describe this Valley?' He said, 'Magical.' Then they asked another friend back in Georgia, who had lived here, the same question. They said, 'Magical.'"

I guess that was his answer, "Magical."

"Okay, a one-word answer. I like it! To the point. Succinct. And it covers quite a lot of ground. I couldn't have come up with a better word myself. Here's another question. How are your students different after you get hold of them? Your course would have been, by far, my favorite class. . . . With the thousands of students that have gone through your classes, I'm sure you have been able to ascertain how this very important information has affected these young, impressionable minds that are soaking up information. And they better, because they don't have long to do that because, very soon, they get set in their ways."

"I've had students that dropped my class because they couldn't stand it. They were into answers. They had to have answers. Many others are going to play games. Others, like you, go, 'Oh boy, I get to explore myself. I get to define my values. I get to question. I get to travel in my mind to many places. I get to be a responsible person and be supported in my personal integrity.' " He paused, deep in thought for a moment. "It is my responsibility to *never* put down a student. You have to encourage them to grow, even though students try to put you in an authoritarian role."

I told him how much I appreciated this approach to teaching. "I am a wanderer and a wonderer when it comes to this particular magical place, and I wonder, if you were in my shoes, what areas would you be looking at right now? I am from the generation that is following your pioneering. What advice would you give to me and the readers of this book?"

"One of the most important things people need to know about, to think about, to explore in, and raise questions in, for the next hundred years: Is religion where it's at? Is paranormal phenomena where it's at? Is the economic system where it's at? Psychological systems? Sociological systems? Philosophical systems? Theological systems? How do we integrate them all together? Why are people so violent? Why was the twentieth century filled with such human slaughter? Why did it occur among the most civilized countries on our planet? Are there certain systems on our planet that are war-prone? And peace-prone? All paranormal phenomena, UFOs, aliens, beings from other worlds, walk-ins, all of this relates to the most important needs of humanity. What are the most important needs of humanity?"

"Unity. That would be my one-word answer!"

"How do you achieve such unity? If that unity is at a fairly high level of maturity, then we have multiple questions related to that."

"It does open up quite a number of boxes," I commented, refering to his box analogy.

"How do you make people more mature?" he asked me coyly.

I could tell he was leading me somewhere and answered, "Doesn't that have to come from within? I think a lot of it boils down to the utilization of conditioning techniques in society, vis-à-vis the media and these incredible, rampant, runaway technology levels we're seeing. I think we are running into some major problems. We're like little kids that have been given a gun without any instruction. We're not yet at a level of unity or maturity to be able to handle the kinds of covert technologies that are said to exist right now, let alone in the future. Some people think the government is getting ready for civil war. Are they getting ready to clamp down on culture, clamp down on society, clamp down on anything that may threaten what may be waiting in the wings? And this is, for lack of a better term, the New World Order scenario. Many people are worried about this. I've been increasingly involved in asking, What is the military doing? Where are they doing it? Unfortunately, this area of scrutiny is consuming more and more of my time. I see a rising tide of concern in our country that has to do with absolute power corrupting absolutely. This is the antithesis of true unity. We may be seeing a form of covert unity. Are we all just pawns in a chess game that somebody else is playing? This bothers me. That's why I'm willing to stick my neck out and talk about underground bases, talk about covert military activity here in this magical place. I suspect this covert activity detracts and may even, in some sense, negate the magical qualities of this place. They may be running roughshod over these magical qualities. This also bothers me!"

I climb down off my soapbox, and Dr. Weldon asks, "What if nationalism is the most dangerous game, or system, preventing the unity of humanity, and how can we transcend this powerful cultural system on our planet? A system people are willing to die for, which again is nationalism? How do we get to the unity of humanity?"

I ask rhetorically, "By having a UFO land on the White House lawn and a little alien walking out and saying, 'Take me to your leader'?"

"No, that would be an abdication of responsibility by humans to grow to the maturity level to transcend our cultural boxes."

"But could this scenario be only one with enough shock value to force people to a place where they would realize their interconnectedness as humans in a closed system? I don't think it will happen, but anything short of that is a painful, painful process that we, as humans, will always be going through."

"Exactly. It's called education."

"Boy, do we need a lot of educators!"

"And what is Chris?" He looks at me and smiles his Cheshire smile.

"Wha . . . ?"

"What is Chris?"

"I'm ahh, I guess . . . an educator. Yes, I suppose I am. But don't we collectively need a higher vision? Because of these boxes, haven't people collectively lost 'our' vision?"

"They identify with the box rather than their humanity. They identify with Christianity, Hinduism, or Islam rather than humanity."

"Well Dr. Weldon, is there light at the end of the tunnel?"

Again the smile. "Of course!"

A POSTSCRIPT FROM PARADISE

As with most of us, I find myself on a path of exploration, a path of learning and growth. I have chosen to concentrate and focus my personal investigative efforts on this particular microscopic external reality called the San Luis Valley, but it is obvious that our entire external world is interchangeable with its connection to an internal sense of humanity and compassion. We need to remember and hold on to this. Like the existential joke, "It doesn't matter where you go, there you are," every corner of this magnificent planet is a magical realm of infinite possibility. Our personal and collective reality is truly what we make of it. Nothing more, nothing less.

THE GREAT ADVENTURE CONTINUES. . . .

My ongoing investigation continues. Adventures on the horizon include the *real* inside story of Crestone, location of most of the "world's" religions; expanding my local network of seekers-skywatchers; locating the last remaining bioregional brujos and brujas and helping save this traditional belief system's knowledge from obscurity; and determining the extent of our government's activity here in southern Colorado and northern New Mexico.

We'll be continuing our search for the many additional treasures to be found inside the mysterious San Luis Valley.

CHAPTER TWELVE

REPORT LOG
FOR JUNE 1995 THROUGH DECEMBER 1997

DOCUMENTED UNIDENTIFIED FLYING OBJECT (UFO) SIGHTINGS, ABDUCTIONS, UNUSUAL ANIMAL DEATHS (UAD), UNEXPLAINED OCCURRENCES, AND SUSPECTED GROUND AND AERIAL MILITARY ACTIVITY IN THE GREATER SAN LUIS VALLEY

Includes Colorado counties: Saguache, Alamosa, Conejos, Costilla, Rio Grande, Huerfano, Custer, Chaffee.
New Mexico counties: Taos, Rio Arribas.
Regional reports listed when time-proximate to SLV activity.

Listings include:
Date; Time; Location; Vallee Classification Type of report; County/Investigator) Media coverage; Type of evidence. Suspected **UFO** sight-

ing dates and times and **UAD** discovery dates
in **BOLD**. *Apparent* military activity in *ITALICS*.

**WITNESSES' NAMES WITHHELD TO PROTECT INDI-
VIDUALS' PRIVACY.**

**Thursday, December 18, 1997, 7:30 P.M., 4 miles south of
Alamosa, Colorado. FB1.** Alamosa County (O'Brien/Hunter).
Two witnesses see two bright lights, to the north, flying low,
west to east. Because of the fog in the area, the witnesses
estimated the distance from them to be two miles. Objects
were "totally silent."

**Wednesday, December 17, 1997, 10:30 A.M., 5 miles southwest
of Alamosa, Colorado. UAD.** Alamosa County (Alamosa sheriff's
office/O'Brien/*Valley Courier* FORENSIC/VIDEO/STILL).
Rancher discovers a dead gelding. Several drops, which appeared to be blood, were found in snow about 60 feet away, over
the fence and across the road.

**Sunday, December 14, 1997, 1:15 to 1:35 A.M., Costilla
County Road 11, 10 miles north of Colorado–New Mexico
border. FB1.** Costilla/Taos County (O'Brien/Paye). Two witnesses returning home late to Mestita, Colorado, watch with
binoculars "an orange pulsing light," moving east to west,
which took "over 20 minutes to cross the valley."

**Saturday, December 13, 1997, 7:05 and 7:10 P.M., just north
of La Jara, Colorado, on Highway 285. FB1.** Alamosa County
(O'Brien/Paye). Two witnesses traveling north on 285 see a
"a V-shaped, greenish-gray light" moving east to west across
the Valley. Estimated height of "3,000 to 4,000 feet." Five
minutes later, they witnessed a "bluish-white object" that repeated the same flight pattern.

Sunday, November 30, 1997, 5:30–6:00 A.M., southwest corner Saguache County Road 61 and Road C. UAD. Saguache County (Saguache County, Sheriff/O'Brien, *SLV Publishing* papers, *Valley Courier* VIDEO/STILL/FORENSIC). 1½ miles west, 2 miles north of Hooper, Colorado, a calf mutilation was reported by ranchers. A report was filed with the Saguache County sheriff's office, which also investigated the calf death.

Saturday, November 29, 1997, 11:10 P.M., over northern SLV. MA1. Saguache County (O'Brien). Four witnesses in the Baca watch a multicolored light move slowly from center of the Valley toward the north.

Monday, October 13, 1997, 7:52–8:00 P.M., southwest of Mt. Ouray near Marshall Pass. AN1. Saguache County (O'Brien). Two witnesses observe a bright orange light, about the size and brightness of Venus. Light, 5° above the horizon to the northwest, was seen from approximately 20–30 miles away. Faded after 30–35 minutes.

Saturday, October 4, 1997, 6:45 P.M., Mesita, Colorado. MA1. Conejos County (O'Brien). Mesita resident was driving home from Costilla west on County Road 159 when he noticed a "silver cylinder" hanging in the western sky reflecting the setting sun. Object appeared to move north to south **7:30 P.M.–7:50 P.M., Center, Colorado.** Conejos/Rio Grande/Saguache Counties (O'Brien). Center resident was out in his yard when he noticed three "red balls" of light hovering over Del Norte, Colorado. One broke formation and only took 4 or 5 seconds for it to fly across the whole Valley [about 65 to 70 miles].

Monday, September 22, 1997, 9:25–9:40 P.M., northern end of San Luis Valley. Saguache County (O'Brien/Saguache

County sheriff). For 15–20 minutes, blinking objects (*choppers?*) were seen escorting a very large, slow-moving, orange-red globe west to east about 45 miles north of witnesses. This formation of four to five blinking lights, low over the mountains, was observed traveling from west to east over Marshall and Poncha passes.

Friday, September 12, 1997, 11:30 P.M., Baca Grande Development. AN1. Saguache County (O'Brien/Dennis). Two witnesses in the Baca Grande Development (about 90 miles north of the Colorado–New Mexico border) claim to have watched a "huge craft hovering over the center of the [San Luis] Valley." They described unblinking red and green lights that seemed to be arrayed around the object. **10:40 P.M., Baca Grande Development AN1.** Saguache County (O'Brien). I watch a bluish cheap firework go down between me and the Sangres. Object was about 3 miles away and appeared to travel about ¼ mile.

Thursday, September 11, 1997, 8:30 P.M., west of Mesita, Colorado. MA1. Costilla and Conejos counties (O'Brien). Two Mesita witnesses observed two large craft, each with a row of six white-orange lights, moving in unison. The craft, each estimated as being "a little longer than a [C-131] transport plane," slowly drifted south over the South Piñon Hills, then stopped around the border and headed back north.

September 1 or 2, 1997, Malacite, Colorado, north of Sheep Mountain. Huerfano County (Perkins). AC-131 transport plane was seen dropping a "huge box" just north of the Atlantic Richfield CO_2 plant (located between Sheep and Little Sheep mountains) near the towns of Red Wing and Malacite. Locals witnessed the "drop" and set off to investigate and search for the box. Three separate reports of the following events have emerged. In one report, locals witnessed two men with "jet packs on their backs flying up and down, around and between" Sheep and Little Sheep mountains, apparently looking for the box. Other witnesses claim that a short time later they saw a craft that had the appearance of a large, clear bubble. From the bottom of the bubble sparks were being emitted with a "clattering sound" from square objects that were described as "magnets." A witness (in true Colorado fashion) evidently fired a gun at the strange-looking object as it passed overhead, and later that evening the man was confronted and then accosted by three men. He told neighbors he was wrestled to the ground, and one of the men grabbed him and "snapped his neck," and he immediately was rendered unconscious. Another report claims personnel were seen searching ranches and barns north of Sheep Mountain later that night, or early the following morning. A number of locals witnessed this apparent search by these unknown craft and personnel.

Friday, August 22, 1997, 8:30–9:00 P.M., over Rio Grande at Colorado–New Mexico border. MA1. Costilla County (O'Brien). Three witnesses watched two lights that one witness reported looking like "huge car headlights" that were intermittently visible to the west in a "large thunderhead." Then they also watched a large golden colored light that appeared low to the south by the border. Duration: about 10 minutes. One of these witnesses, claimed then to have experienced three concurrent nights of lucid dreams featuring "aliens" and being "taken out through the window and aboard a small ship," which took him "up to a larger ship." After the first night's dream, the witness claimed "he knew they were coming back before he fell asleep."

No reports in July.

Thursday, June 26, 1997, 10:23 A.M., State Highway 160, between Monte Vista and Alamosa MA1. Alamosa County

(Rio Grande County Sheriff's Office/O'Brien). Official observed an object he described as looking "just like that craft that [Tim Edwards's "main craft" footage] was filmed over Salida." Witness was headed east on State Highway 160, between Alamosa and Monte Vista, Colorado, when he noticed a bright silver reflection in the sky. He pulled over and was able to view the craft for several seconds. He reached for his field glasses, and when he looked up, it was gone. "It either just flat disappeared, or took off real fast." The object initially appeared to be hovering in the eastern sky, "between Alamosa and the Great Sand Dunes."

Friday, June 20, 1997, 5:00 A.M., north of Villa Grove near Poncha Pass. Saguache County (O'Brien). A convoy of all-white vans and vehicles was seen by a rancher headed out of the Valley on Highway 17 north of Villa Grove.

Tuesday, June 17, 1997, ½ mile northwest of Alamosa, Colorado. Alamosa County (O'Brien). Convoys of white vans, Suburbans, and trucks. 10 to 12 vehicles (with State Patrol rear escort) seen headed into Alamosa, the back way.

Friday, June 13, 1997, near Villa Grove, Colorado. Report from the northwest part of the Valley by a witness headed north on 17. Had witnessed a "reddish, flashing blue light, slightly bigger than a planet." Object just hovered. Arcturus or Vega setting?

Thursday, June 5, 1998, 2:00 A.M., Poate Lake, about 20 miles south of South Fork, Colorado. Archuleta County (O'Brien). I received a call in on my NPR *Mysterious Valley Report* radio show from a camper with a group near Poate Lake. Caller described a large, bright orange light just over the mountains, headed southwest. (Interestingly, Archuleta Mesa–Dulce Base is a scant 35 miles away to the southwest of Poate Lake.)

June 4–9, 1997, near Florence, Colorado, La Veta MOA. Custer County. Apparent nightly military flight activity.

Entire month of June, over Greenie Mountain area, 12 miles south of Monte Vista, Colorado. Rio Grande County (sheriff's office). The initial calls were placed to the Rio Grande County sheriff during the time period when reports of lights northeast of Dulce, in the Summitville area, were filed. The callers, who live at the base of Greenie, called the sheriffs' office on several occasions, wanting to know if anyone else had called in to report the lights, but did not leave their names. The lights were described by these witnesses as "military planes."

No reports in May.

Wednesday, April 30, 1997, just south of Alamosa. UAD. Alamosa County (Alamosa County sheriff's office/O'Brien/ British Broadcasting Company). Rancher finds a very fresh "mutilation" 400 yards from his house and files a report with local authorities. Weather had been in the upper thirties that night.

Tuesday, April 22, 1997, south of Alamosa. UAD. Alamosa County (Alamosa County sheriff's office, *Valley Courier*). Law enforcement officials receive an unofficial report of a UAD.

No reports in March.

No reports in February.

Thursday, January 16, 1997, 6:30 P.M., Road T. Crestone-Moffat, Colorado, AN1. Saguache County (O'Brien). While 3 or so miles east of Moffat, a "bright light much larger than a star or planet blink on just above the western horizon" witnessed in the direction of La Garita. Light was visible for 2 or 3 minutes before extinguishing.

Saturday, December 7, 1996, 7:15 P.M., FB1. Alamosa County (Hawk/O'Brien). Witness observes a solid, unblinking orange light traveling south to north. Light never blinked and exibited no standard FAA anticollision lights. He also noticed an unusual amount of nocturnal small airplane traffic the following night.

Wednesday, November 20, 1996, 7:12 P.M., San Luis Valley. Central and northern SLV (O'Brien). Numerous witnesses report a "boom" that seemed to come from the ground. (All reported the boom, which was probably a sonic boom from a military jet going supersonic.)

Monday, November 18, 1996, over Baca Ranch area MA1. Saguache County (O'Brien). Witness sees "a triangle of white lights fly over the SLV headed west. Lights "broke apart and descended diagonally toward the ground."

Thursday, November 14, 1996, 7:12 P.M., Alamosa, Colorado. Alamosa County. Open Space Alliance member reports 12 unmarked white vehicles with red lights in Alamosa.

Wednesday, November 13, 1996, at 6:28 P.M., AN1. Entire SLV (O'Brien, Undersheriff Norris, State Patrolman). I received four calls, in quick succession, reporting a "huge ball of white light" that fell straight down to the ground for 2 to 3 seconds toward the southeast side of the SLV. Object was described by witnesses as "larger than a full moon." Each caller was positive the object came down in the Valley. The fireball was seen from the extreme northern end of the valley to the Colorado–New Mexico border. One woman of Antonito claimed she was sure "it fell right next to" her car. Alamosa Sheriff received two calls; Saguache County received four calls; Custer County received one call; Colorado State Patrol received two calls. NORAD and Peterson AFB received "no calls." Descriptions of the object at the northern end of the SLV said it was whitish-blue, but as the various observer locations headed to the south, descriptions were of a "rainbow color." The woman witness on the border claimed that she saw a faint trail behind the object.

Saturday, November 9, 1996, 5:15 P.M., Crestone, Colorado, AN1. Chaffee County (O'Brien). Two witnesses were headed east on Highway 50, near Cotopaxi, CO, when they observed a "yellow light" which reminded her of "light shining off an airplane, but different." The light flared on for only "1 or 2 seconds," before vanishing.

Friday, November 8, 1996, 5:15–5:25 P.M., northwest San Luis Valley MA1. Saguache County (O'Brien). Three friends out walking noticed a "line of lights" on the western horizon. The "three white silver things" were strung out around 7° above La Garita area. After several minutes they moved to a vertical position, one on top of the other. After 10 minutes, the line of lights disappeared to the west, and a fourth light appeared to the north, hovered for a minute, then disappeared.

Saturday, October 26, 1996, 7:30–8:45 P.M., Road 66T and Baca Ranch MA1. Saguache/Rio Grande County (O'Brien/Dumas/Nickerson). Myself and two reporters were skywatching just inside the Baca Ranch when we observed a solid, unblinking orange light appear fairly low in the southeast, headed northwest. Object was traveling approximately 200 mph. Craft did a loop and headed back toward the east, displaying standard FAA lighting. Then several minutes later, two craft, in formation, came over the Sangres from the east. One craft did a loop and headed back to the east. The other hovered for several minutes over the Great Sand Dunes. Several minutes later, we observed a formation of 7 to 9 lights flying over La Jara Reservoir area. Then a bright orange light appeared out of the west. Craft was unblinking. It headed east, turned, and headed south. It turned again and started heading north. Then it turned again and headed back east. It did this zigzag, box-type maneuver several times. When it was finished, it seemed to greatly increase its speed and disappeared directly south. **6:30 P.M., Crestone, Colorado, MA1.** Saguache County (O'Brien). Two witnesses see a bright object, larger than a satellite, head over the mountains from the east. Object appeared to "shoot" across to the west at a high rate of speed. **7:45–8:00 P.M., center of the SLV just north of Center, Colorado AN1.** Saguache County (O'Brien/Richmond). A bright orange light is observed by me and my brother, hanging over the center of the San Luis Valley. According to another witness, it had a cigar shape and did not appear to be moving. Witness claims she has been seeing the "same orange light" off and on, all summer. **8:00 P.M., Baca Grande Chalets MA1.** Saguache County (O'Brien). Fourth witness in the Baca looked up and saw an "egg-shaped" sphere that instantly shot over the mountains. Witness had distinct impression that the object reacted to her "seeing it."

Sunday, October 20, 1996, 8:42 P.M., north of Monte Vista AN1. Rio Grande County (Mark Hunter, *Valley Courier*, 10/22/96). Report made to the Rio Grande sheriff's office reporting some "suspicious lights" just north of town near the Rio Grande. Sighting occurred near where a possible UAD occurred August 4, 1996. **7:15 P.M., La Garita and Center, Colorado, MA1**. Rio Grande County (O'Brien). Three witnesses were traveling east on State Highway 112 when they observed a light "like a red ball" traveling west "from the Sand Dunes area." Light appeared around 1,000 feet in altitude. Light became parallel with them at around junction of 285 and 112. Did not stop truck until five minutes later at home in Center. Observed for additional 20–30 minutes. Object/light headed toward Del Norte. Then it appeared to turn northwest and head toward La Garita, where witnesses lost sight of it.

Thursday, October 17, 1996, 11:30 P.M., Highway 285, 10 miles of Monte Vista. Rio Grande County (O'Brien). Witness from Del Norte, Colorado, reported a seven-truck "military convoy" headed north on Highway 285 while traveling north. All vehicles were "OD green" without any apparent markings or license plates. Six of the trucks were semis with large boxes on the back. The seventh was an all "aluminum" gasoline-type tanker truck, also with no license plates or even "hazmat placards."

Thursday, October 10, 1996, 10:30–11:00 P.M., Baca Grande MA1. Saguache County (O'Brien). A group of students attending the Crestone Healing Arts Center were outside and observed a rapidly "zigzagging" light, high up in the sky, headed west to east, and then a group of "many blinking lights" on the western horizon. Witnesses could not tell how many lights were in the group but guessed 10–12. Duration around 10 minutes.

Thursday, October 10, 1996, noon, east of Gardiner, Colorado. Huerfano County (Perkins). David Perkins observed a "huge white (single-prop) helicopter" heading to the northwest over the Huerfano–Wet Mountain Valley. Craft had a definite helicopter sound. **Around noon, Del Norte, Colorado, FB1**. Rio Grande County (O'Brien). Another couple looked up and saw an object that at first looked like the space shuttle coming in. He then realized that the object "looked like a white cigar." It had no tail or wings, left no vapor trail, and was silent. He ran inside to get his spotting scope, which confirmed his first observation. Wife saw and declined to venture a description.

Wednesday, October 9, 1996, P.M., Baca Grande Development AN1. Saguache County (O'Brien). Two women and a visiting friend were outside and observed a spherical light that appeared "larger than any *visible* planet." The object hovered in the western sky and appeared to be "shooting off a blue halo." They observed no radical movement, and the duration of the event was less than 3 minutes before the object faded away.

Monday, October 7, 1996, 11:15 P.M., Highway 17 Villa Grove AN1. Saguache County (O'Brien). Witness was driving south from Poncha Pass when she observed a bright white object approximately "ten times the size of a regular shooting star" travel from east to west. The object had a two-second duration and no trailing tail. Witness was fairly certain that the object went down in the Valley, judging by the end of its trajectory, which was below the tops of the mountains.

End of September 1996, near Greenie Mountain UAD. Rio Grande County (Sheriff's office). Rio Grande County official received a report of a "mutilation." Report was filed several weeks after the event. The rancher found a cow [missing its eyes, rear end, and udder] in the center of a 30-foot circle of knocked-down grass. His horse would not enter the circle . . . the circle and the cow were covered by a fine powder that the rancher described as "like baby powder." Then, as the ranchers were investigating, an "unmarked helicopter" appeared out of the trees, low to the ground, and flew over the site. As soon as they caught sight of it, "it gained altitude and flew off."

Sunday, September 22, 1996, Osier Park, on Colorado–New Mexico border UAD. Conejos County (O'Brien/*Strange Universe*). David Jaramillo finds an unidentified cow mutilated 50 feet from his summer cabin. Animal was a classic "mute," . . . three 12-foot landing swirls were present in the grass. In the middle of the swirls were tail hairs, which appeared to come from the cow, which was missing the end of its tail.

Monday, September 9, 1996, near Penasco, New Mexico, classic UAD. Taos County (*Taos News*/Greenwood, Perkins). 1,800-pound bull found missing its anus, testicles, intestines, tongue, and left ear. The bull's heart had been removed through a hole.

Tuesday, September 3, 1996, 30 miles west of Dulce, New Mexico, classic UAD. Rio Arribas County (Perkins *Spirit Magazine*). Retired San Juan County Deputy found a black yearling bull mutilated. He estimated the animal had only been dead 10 hours. Upon checking his herd, he found a second bull mutilated. He believed it was dead almost a week.

Saturday, August 31, 1996, 5:30 A.M., Gallina Canyon near Arroyo Hondo, New Mexico. Taos County (*Taos News* 9/5/96 Greenwood/Perkins *Spirit Magazine*). Witness sees three globes of soft, luminous lights that were white in the front, blue and red toward the rear. They "had a fixed relationship with each other . . . I figured they were part of one craft." After a moment, "They took off moving south very fast without a sound."

Friday, August 30, 1996, El Prado, New Mexico, UAD. Taos County (Greenwood/Staehlin/*Taos News* 9/5/96). A cow was found missing its rectum and had a large hole in its stomach. Investigator noticed a "puncture-sized hole" in its neck. Nearby chamisa appeared smashed down, and fresh branches had been broken from willow bushes.

Saturday, August 17, 1996, 10:00 P.M., south corner of Baca Chalets, FB1. Saguache County (O'Brien). Woman sees "string of lights" flying just over the ziggurat, quarter mile from her home. **El Prado, New Mexico.** Taos County (Staehlin/Greenwood *Taos News* 9/5/96). Heifer found "showing the classic signs of mutilation."

Thursday, August 15, 1996, 1:15 P.M., Villa Grove, Colorado. Saguache County (Shovald/O'Brien). Reporter and I see military Huey U-68 flying near Hayden Pass, then land at Bonanza turnoff. Told "DEA/County pot eradication flights." Only federal vehicles present on the ground.

Tuesday, August 13, 1996, 10:00 P.M., Great Sand Dunes National Monument near the Amphitheater. Alamosa County (O'Brien). Witness observes a "vibrating utility pole."

Sunday, August 4, 1996, Arroyo Hondo, New Mexico, near Rio Hondo, UAD Taos County (Perkins/Staehlin/Greenwood *Taos News* 8/8/96). Rancher finds another cow mutilated. Four-year-old missing rear end, udder, and uterus.

First week of August 1996, just north of Monte Vista, Colorado. Rio Grande County (O'Brien/RGSO/Hunter *Valley Courier* 10/22/96). Ranchers discovers a "mutilated cow." Animal was missing its udder from smooth, exact "incisions."

Thursday, August 1, 1996, 2:30 A.M., La Veta Pass FB1. Huerfano County (Perkins/O'Brien). Witnesses returning from the Great Sand Dunes back to Farasita, Colorado, witness a craft they describe as "over a mile long." Claims the ship "would have covered the whole town of Gardiner, Colorado." The ship was lit by three large white lights, and the witnesses could make out the faint outline of a craft. They insist it was not a cloud. They could not ascertain the object's shape. Duration: 10 minutes.

Wednesday, July 31, 1996, at 10:30 P.M., Great Sand Dunes MA1. Alamosa County (Perkins/O'Brien). Several friends are skywatching when they witness a huge ball of light over the dunes.

Tuesday, July 30, 1996, 2:30 A.M., Arroyo Seco, New Mexico. Taos County (Greenwood *Taos News* 8/1/96). Witness watches two blinking spheres for 25 minutes. One was "red, white and blue, the other white and greenish-blue." He said they "were too low, and they weren't making any noise."

Sunday, July 14, 1996, at 10:00 A.M., Hooper, Colorado, Highway 17 MA1. Saguache County (Adamiak/O'Brien). Three friends see a "silver disk" glittering high in the sky in the sunlight while traveling on Highway 17, north of Hooper. **2:05 A.M., Baca Grande Development**. Saguache County (O'Brien). Witness wakes up with a "premonition/compulsion to get up." Went outside in back and was facing the mountains to the east when he saw a "sphere suddenly appear approximately 45° above the ridge line." It descended 30° from vertical "not as fast as a shooting star." The object appeared to be "throwing off sparks" and left a "slight luminescent trail behind it." According to the witness, "It seemed to go down this side of the mountains."

Friday, July 12, 1996, 10:00 P.M., east of Salida, Colorado, MA1. Chaffee County (Edwards). Witness "happened to be outside" 15 miles east of Salida when an object that looked like a satellite was observed. Then "something blocked out the stars." The witness told Edwards that the craft "looked like a 200-yard-long cylindrical dark object." The craft was flying east. The witness could not make out any clouds.

Thursday, July 11, 1996, 10:10 P.M., Crestone, Colorado, MA1. Saguache County (O'Brien). A Crestone resident observed a "backwards" flying, red cheap firework.

Wednesday, July.10, 1996, evening, Gallina Canyon AN1. Taos County (Greenwood *Taos News* 8/1/96). Witness sees "very weird lights, blue and red, three or four of them."

Monday, July 8, 1996, Arroyo Hondo, New Mexico, UAD. Taos County (Greenwood *Taos News* 8/1/96). Rancher found one of his animals "classically mutilated." The six-month-old bull was missing its genitals and a patch of skin around the lower jaw. The rectum was cored out and the tissue was pink. An eye and the tongue were also gone. There was no additional evidence found at the scene.

Wednesday, June 19, 1996, 11:00 P.M., over Saguache, Colorado, AN1 Saguache County (Blunt/O'Brien). Witness, ex–Air Forcer, was driving between Moffat and Saguache, when he saw an unusual formation of lights.

Tuesday, June 18, 1996, 3:30–4:00 A.M., Baca Chalets. Saguache County (O'Brien). Three unusual lights seen. Same as night before.

Monday, June 17, 1996, midnight, Baca Grants MA1. Saguache County (O'Brien). Witness, visiting the Baca from Ft.

Lauderdale, told me, "There were five white lights floating over the mountains. After about 4 or 5 minutes, a sixth light came on. It was red. . . . They moved funny. They had an up-and-down movement, like they were floating." They flew off to the west. **2:45 A.M., Baca Grants.** Saguache County (CSETI). CSETI has sightings during training session. **4:00 A.M., Baca Chalets**. Saguache County (CSETI) CSETI has sightings during training session.

Sunday, June 16, 1996, 2:00 A.M., Baca Grande Grants MA1. Saguache County (O'Brien). CSETI has sightings out over Valley.

Sunday, May 26, 1996, 10:00 P.M., Blanca, Colorado, AN1. Costilla County (O'Brien). Two witnesses observed a bright amber-red light flare well below the clouds and the top of the Blanca Massif, about 2 to 3 miles away. They raced in their car to get closer, and when they approached within ½ mile, the light went out.

Monday, May 13, 1996, Canero Pass Road, 8 miles west of Saguache, Colorado, UAD. Saguache County (O'Brien). Two loggers found "the largest cow in the herd," dead and "mutilated." The right jaw was exposed by a cut that went up and over the eye. The rear end was gone and the right-side ear. With the introduction of humans on the scene, the cows "got the courage to run past [the dead cow blocking the narrow path] in pairs." When they returned with a load of wood several hours later, the cow was gone.

Saturday, May 4, 1996, 10:15 P.M., Moffat, Colorado, FB1. Saguache County (O'Brien). Witness calls to report a "monstrous red light fly over." He assumed it was a conventional aircraft, and it "seemed to be high in the air." **11:30 P.M., Highway 17 AN1, east of Hooper, Colorado, AN1.** (O'Brien).

His daughter, while returning from Alamosa with her daughter, notices a "stationary orange light hanging to the west about 3° to 5° above the horizon."

No reports in April.

Saturday, March 23, 1996, 2:30 A.M., Del Norte, Colorado, AN1. Rio Grande County (O'Brien). Witness spotted, "a big ball of white light with a smaller red light below it." He watched both lights slowly drift west over the mountains.

Saturday, March 16, 1996, before dawn, Crestone–Baca Grande. Saguache County (O'Brien). Most of the area's dog population inexplicably begins to bark furiously just minutes before the areas power blinks out. No explanation for the disturbance, which affected dogs up to 6–7 miles away.

Wednesday, March 13, 1996, at 8:13 P.M., Greenie Mountain. Rio Grande County (O'Brien). Three Del Norte witnesses call and report a chopper formation circling Greenie. "There were eight of them circling in a search mode," and the witnesses thought they could see the craft shining "spotlights."

Saturday, March 9, 1996, north of Questa, New Mexico, UAD. Taos County (Perkins). Ranch manager finds a month-old bull calf missing its genitals, and its entrails had been surgically removed through a hole in its stomach. Tongue was missing, and its bottom two front teeth had been "pulled."

Thursday, March 7, 1996, 8:30 P.M., Crestone–Baca Grande. Saguache County (O'Brien). I observe three groups of blinking lights flying north at least 2,000 feet above the SLV. The third group seemed to hover and wait for the first two groups. They head north and disappear over the mountains.

Tuesday, February 20, 1996, at 3:00 P.M., Crestone–Baca Grande. Saguache County (O'Brien). I observe five huge cargo planes travel south down the Sangres. Formations of cargo planes a rare occurrence in the SLV.

Friday, February 16, 1996, 10:05 P.M., just south of Ojo Caliente, MA1 CE1. Rio Arriba/Taos County (O'Brien). Family traveling north on Highway 285 when driver stopped for a short break. After getting out of the truck, he noticed his shadow and, knowing there was no moon out that night, he looked up. Above him, "less than 50 feet overhead," was a huge ship hovering over the truck. Around the underside was a circular pattern of "50 to 75 lights" sequencing in a clockwise pattern. "It covered the whole sky, it was so big and close," he said. Then, "without a sound," it "went straight up, maybe a mile or so, until it was about the size of a quarter." Then the object "zoomed at the speed of light back down and hovered 50 feet over us." He got back into the truck, and they watched the object fly slowly north, about a quarter mile away, over a small valley. They continued north trying to catch up with the object. The object continued north, slowly curving to the northeast, until it was out of sight over a mesa.

Saturday, February 10, 1996, at around 9:45 P.M., AN1. Saguache County (O'Brien). A group of students at the Crestone Healing Arts Center were outside skywatching when one of them observed about a dozen blinking lights with a solid orange light in the western sky. The orange light was several times larger than the smaller white, blinking lights. Duration: about 10 minutes.

Wednesday, February 7, 1996, at 8:40 P.M., Crestone, Colorado, MA1. Saguache County (O'Brien). A mother of five, while in the town of Crestone, noticed a brilliant green orb-shaped object as she walked toward her front door. "It went straight overhead toward the mountains, then made a right-hand turn and disappeared."

Tuesday, February 6, 1996, 10:30 P.M., north of Colorado Springs MA1. El Paso County (O'Brien). Witness called to report a "large triangle-shaped craft" she and her daughter witnessed while driving north of town. The craft had flashing "red, green, and white lights." They watched for several minutes before it slowly flew northeast.

Thursday, January 25, 1996 at 4:30 P.M., over Greenie Mountain MA1. Rio Grande/Alamasa County (*Valley Courier* 1/27/96 Hunter/O'Brien). Witness, while working on a fence line off Highway 17, noticed three objects hanging in the sky over Greenie Mountain. He alerted his cousin and grabbed his video camera. He was able to capture the three objects for about a minute or so on video. The first object appears to disappear over the southern horizon. The second and third objects appear spheroid but strangely translucent. Tape disappears on the way to Paramount TV's program *Sightings*. Package was sent certified, priority mail. No signature ever collected from delivery.

Sunday, December 24, 1995, 6:05 P.M., Baca Grande Chalets AN1. Saguache County (O'Brien). Cheap firework again reported in the Baca.

Saturday, December 23, 1995, 9:45 P.M., Baca Grande Chalets AN1. Saguache County (O'Brien). Cheap firework phenomenon reported in the Baca.

Tuesday, November 21, 1995, 10:00 P.M., Navaho Estates, north of Walsenburg, Colorado, MA1. Huerfano County (O'Brien). Several witnesses report "a large circular disk" hovering off to the east of La Veta Pass. The object appeared to have bright blinking lights around the rim, and the two interviewed witnesses claim the group "watched it for 20 to 25 minutes." **2:00 A.M., Interstate 25 north of Walsenburg, AN1.** Huerfano County (O'Brien). Romeo County. Couple were driving S on Interstate 25 when a spotlight lit up their car from above. They noted that it was overcast and the light seemed to be coming from below the clouds. It only lasted for a few seconds but it evidently "lit up the whole road." They did not observe any lightning activity in the area.

Tuesday, November 14, 1995, at 6:30 P.M., Highway 17. MA1. Saguache County (O'Brien). Witness reports a swarm of randomly blinking lights traveling west to southwest less than 1,000 feet off the ground. He observed that there were "24 or 25" of them, and they appeared to be "flashing like a squadron."

Monday, November 13, 1995, 10:50 P.M., Highway 17 AN1. Saguache County (O'Brien). Witness, while headed north on 17, observed a pink light moving upward too slowly to be a shooting star. Just before it disappeared, "it shot out a lot of sparks. It almost looked like it broke into pieces."

Sunday, November 12, 1995, at sunset, Highway 17 near Hooper, Colorado AN1. Saguache County (Edwards). Tim Edwards and family photograph a pencil-shaped object in the western sky.

Saturday November 11, 1995, at 9:30 A.M., Highway 17 between Hooper and Moffat, Colorado, MA1. Saguache County (O'Brien). Witness, while headed south on 17, saw a silver reflection directly ahead of him about 40° above the horizon. The "round object streaked away" at a high rate of speed. **Early afternoon.** On his return trip, witness was amazed to see" another strange aerial craft. "The second one looked like a huge pencil hanging in the sky" to the west. He claims it was silver in color and "darting around."

Sunday November, 5, 1995, just before dawn, south of Del Norte, Colorado MA1. Rio Grande County (Smith/O'Brien). A couple staking out their mountain property to catch trespassing hunters report to relatives of a close encounter with a large circular craft with multiple blinking lights.

Saturday, November 4, 1995, near Raton, New Mexico, UAD. Las Animas County (Perkins/*Spirit*). Rancher finds a dead bull exhibiting "unnatural-appearing incision-like wounds" with "cauterized edges."

Thursday November 2, 1995 at 6:45 P.M., east of La Veta Pass AN1. Costilla County (O'Brien). Couple were driving just east of La Veta Pass when they observed something traveling east and "let out three bursts of streamers" as it flew silently over their car. The witnesses "could have sworn" it came through the clouds.

Monday, October 30, 1995, north of Monte Vista, Colorado, UAD. Rio Grande County (RGCSO/O'Brien). Veterinarian reports a cow dead under unusual circumstances. "She appeared normal the day before. . . . The tongue was gone with no frayed edges on the cut, the whole left side of her muzzle was missing below the ear. It was definitely cut away. The animal was still warm to the touch; It was like she had died minutes before, but the wound on the face seemed a couple of days old. He performed an on-site autopsy and "could find no reason for the animal's death." The rest of the herd was "acting pretty strange." There were no additional clues at the scene.

Saturday October 28, 1995, at 8:00 P.M., Upper Arkansas River Valley. Chaffee County (O'Brien). Hunting party see a "fireball that streaked all the way across the sky from southwest to northeast." Witnesses claimed the object left a faint smoke trail and they heard a faint boom as it disappeared to the northeast. **Same afternoon North of Monte Vista, Colorado,** Rio Grande County (O'Brien). Rancher-Veterinarian sees a military-style helicopter fly low over his ranch.

Thursday October 19, 1995, at 6:00 P.M., La Veta Pass FB1. Huerfano/Costilla County (O'Brien). Myself and two others were returning from Denver when I noticed seven lights blinking in close proximity (5°) over the Huerfano. An eighth blinking white light hovered over Blanca. Group of lights became obscured by the mountains; red light disappeared east; eighth light just hovered over Blanca. **6:00 P.M., Saddleback Mountain east of Sanford, Colorado, CE1 or AN1.** Conejos County (O'Brien). Two witnesses were traveling from Capulin, Colorado, toward the east when they "couldn't help but notice" three groups of bright lights on the hillside about a mile behind Sanford. They drove to the foot of the hill and were able to find a dirt road that took them "within a quarter-mile" of the lights, which were several hundred yards apart. The lights were "flashing real fast in sequence" with one another and looked like "football stadiums all lit up." **Early afternoon Near Monte Vista, Colorado.** Rio Grande County (O'Brien/RGCSO). Rancher-Veterinarian sees "two dark-colored military helicopters" fly in from the west and circle over his ranch at low altitude.

Sunday, October 8, 1995, San Luis, Colorado, UAD. (O'Brien/Barto/Perkins). Rancher discovers a cow "missing her rear end and bag" and figures she was killed Sunday night. Cow was buried before samples could be obtained.

Saturday, October 7, 1995, at 7:15 P.M., Highway 160 east of Alamosa MA1. Costilla County (O'Brien). Witnesses driving east on Highway 160, 10 miles from Alamosa, see "three white-lights in a pyramid formation" hovering over "the Taylor Ranch," about 20 miles east of their vantage point. After two or three minutes, they claim one of the lights "streaked instantly" north to Blanca Park, where it hovered for several seconds before streaking to the north. **7:15 P.M. Baca Grande AN1.** Two witnesses report a "full-moon-sized . . . bright-green solid-looking object with no tail" that traveled 20° from east to west. Saguache County (O'Brien). **12:05 A.M.** Saguache County (O'Brien). Same two witnesses observe two cheap fireworks descend into the Sangres.

Friday, October 6, 1995, Aguilar, Colorado, UAD. Huerfano County (Perkins). David Perkins investigates a UAD claim between Aguilar and Trinidad.

Monday, October 2, 1995, at 10:50 P.M., Moffat, Colorado, FB1. Saguache County (O'Brien). A "weird white light" is observed by three witnesses traveling north on Highway 17. It was nonblinking and appeared low in the sky west of town and traveled "very rapidly" to the north. The witnesses stopped and noted that the object was silent.

Tuesday, September 26, 1995, Farasita, Colorado, UAD. Huerfano County (Perkins/McCain). Rancher discovered his horse Whiskey dead with a six-inch-diameter perfect circle rectum coring; half the tongue had been removed with a clean diagonal slice; the upper eye was sucked out; hair and hide were blackened and stiff as if heat had been applied. No additional physical evidence was noted. The UAD occurred 15 miles north of the location of the September 22 "barge" sighting.

Monday, September 25, 1995, at 9:30 A.M., Salida, Colorado, MA2. Chaffee County (Edwards/Price/O'Brien/Shovald Mountain Guide). Grandmother spots several silver objects by the sun. Sheriff and Deputy arrive at the home and watch with the family and six others in the yard. Described the sighting later as "10 bright and shiny silver objects traveling from north to south around the sun." During the 45-minute sighting, the local radio station KVRH's transmitter ceased to function. The nearby Cellular One tower inexplicably "went down" for more than four hours. Four other calls were made reporting the objects.

Friday, September 22, 1995, at 8:45 P.M., Navaho Estates, east side of La Veta Pass, MA1. Huerfano County (O'Brien/Perkins *Pueblo Chieftain*). Witness, her fifty-two-year-old sister, and two grown children in their twenties hear a "low humming sound" coming from over the house. They rush outside and see "a 100-yard-wide rectangle" flying west to east, a mere "60 to 80" feet overhead. Son actually ran down the driveway in an effort to get a better look. She said, "There were yellow and white lights oscillating around the front, which was rounded. . . . As it moved away from us we could see red lights on the rear. They looked just like giant Cadillac taillights." They watched it fly east, then loop around to the west where it disappeared behind a ridge. A bright white light was then seen rising over the ridge, where it flared and went out. Eight to ten blinking lights were then seen flying a criss-crossing pattern. There are at least six additional witnesses to the craft and another unknown number who reportedly "heard something." Huerfano sheriff claimed "it was just a helicopter."

Sunday, August 27, 1995, at 9:30 A.M., Salida, Colorado, MA1. Chaffee County (MUFON, UFOI, CUFOS, Edwards, Hunt, O'Brien, Chaffee County sheriff's office, Curta, Dela-

tosa, Perkins, Seino, Maccabbee, Deturo, et al. Video Five
regional TV news segments, AP, Sightings, UPN Borderline,
Inside Edition, Extra). Tim Edwards captures a huge cigar-
shaped object on video. Daughter first observed and brought
Tim's attention to it. Edwards called his restaurant, where a
cook also observed it. Six minutes of videotape were obtained. Since the initial sighting, more than twelve witnesses
have mentioned seeing a similar object that day in central
and south-central Colorado. These completely unrelated reports include: Two DJs jogging in Grand Junction see an object "disappear into a mountain" **around 8:00 A.M.**; two
women driving over Poncha Pass report seeing a cigarette-
shaped object that **early afternoon**; a family driving on 114
near Cochetopa see a "cigar-shaped" craft and report it to
the Saguache sheriff; at **4:00 P.M.** maintainace man at the
Baca golf course claims to have seen a cigar-shaped craft that
"went straight into the mountain . . . either that, or it just disappeared."

**Wednesday, August 16, 1995, Northern Sangres South of
Howard, Colorado Fremont County (Edwards/O'Brien).**
Male resident, the day after an alleged "abduction"/missing-
time episode, observes, "At least 15 Army helicopters were
buzzing all over the place," where witness claims abduction
experience took place. Asserts that he has been seeing helicopters practically all summer after sightings.

**Tuesday, August 15, 1995, at 10:00 P.M., Highway 160, 10
miles east of Alamosa, MA1.** Alamosa County (O'Brien).
Family and friend were returning home from Alamosa after a
movie. They noticed an unusual amount of aerial activity
around Blanca Peak. They stopped the car, got out, and then
witnessed a "huge, bright light" come on. They watched "a
gigantic shadow" fly east surrounded by the much smaller
blinking lights. The kids at one point became so frightened

that they began to cry in fright. **8:40 P.M., northern Sangres south of Howard, CE2 ABDUCTION.** Fremont County (Edwards/O'Brien). A witness sees a large boomerang-shaped object appear from the north and hover over his high-mountain property. He claims to be missing "40 minutes" of time and that his trailer and truck were moved "6 inches" (based on the altered location of the building and truck tracks) during the alleged experience. He claims he had a "4-inch wart" after regaining consciousness. He further asserts that he has lost 20 pounds in two weeks and that his "pet black bear is [now] missing." The man claims that strange sightings have been occurring since the middle of June 1995, and that he has discovered "piles of carcasses" up-slope from his 9,000-foot-elevation land. He claims the carcasses have been in various stages of decay, and that they are comprised of mostly cattle but also horse, fox, raccoon, and "every type of animal" found here. He also said that two weeks before, he found "tiny four-toed human tracks" around the perimeter of the area his trailer sits. He has noted attendant military activity as well. Often, after sightings, he notices unusually heavy military aerial activity and is convinced the "government is involved." After one sighting episode where he was able to photograph the craft, "The next day while I was gone, somebody ransacked my house and took all my film and camera equipment."

No reports in July.

NOTES

Chapter One

1. Christopher O'Brien, *The Mysterious Valley* (New York: St. Martin's Press, 1996), p. 226.

2. Jack Kutz, *Mysteries and Miracles of Colorado* (Corrales: Rhombus Publishing, 1993), p. 76.

3. Ibid.

4. Ibid.

5. Ibid., p. 79.

6. Becky Noland, *Pioneers* (Monte Vista, CO: SLV Publishing, 1997); *Colorado: A Guide to the Highest State* (Mamaroneck, NY: Hastings House, 1941), p. 429.

7. Kutz, *Mysteries and Miracles*, p. 81.

Chapter Two

1. Kutz, *Mysteries and Miracles*, p. 108.

2. Ibid., p. 109.

3. Ibid.

4. Ibid., p. 106.

5. Edgar Hewett, "Tom Tobin," *El Palacio* (June 1946).

6. *Colorado Magazine*, Vol. 9 (1943), p. 211.

7. O'Brien, *Mysterious Valley*, p. 165.

8. Javier Sierra, "Por los siglos de los siglos," *Añõ Cero*, no. 68 (1991), p. 74.

9. Ibid., p. 76.

10. Ibid.

11. Ibid., p. 77.

12. Ibid.

13. O'Brien, *Mysterious Valley*, p. 65.

Chapter Three

1. O'Brien, *Mysterious Valley*, pp. 220–21.

2. *The Mysterious Valley Report*, National Public Radio, KRZA, April 4, 1997.

Chapter Four

1. O'Brien, *Mysterious Valley*, pp. 46–48.

2. Open Space Alliance pamphlet, 1993.

3. O'Brien, *Mysterious Valley*, pp. 187, 195, 236, 285.

Chapter Five

1. O'Brien, *Mysterious Valley*, pp. 103, 109, 129–31.

2. Halka Chronic, *Roadside Geology of Colorado* (Missoula, MT: Mountain Press, 1980), p. 196.

3. O'Brien, *Mysterious Valley*, pp. 165–75.

4. Interview with the author, August 1997.

5. G. Cope Schellhorn, "Human Mutilation in Brazil," *International UFO Magazine*, Vol. 3, no. 3 (1995).

Chapter Six

1. Ruth Marie Colville, *La Vereda: A Trail Through Time* (SLV Historical Society, 1996).

2. Show Me UFO Conference, St. Louis, Missouri, September 1996, question and answer session.

3. Arthur L. Campa, *Treasure of the Sangre de Cristos* (Norman: University of Oklahoma Press, 1963).

4. Lloyd E. Parris, *Caves of Colorado* (Boulder, CO: Pruett Publishing, 1973).

5. Ibid.

6. Ibid.

7. David Perkins, "All That Glitters," *Spirit Magazine*, Vol. 1, no. 1 (1987).

8. Parris, *Caves of Colorado.*

9. Jack Harlan, *Post Marks and Places* (Denver: Golden Bell Press, 1976).

10. Perry Eberhart, *Treasure Tales of the Rockies* (Chicago: Sage Books, 1969), p. 93.

11. Reported in *Fairday Plume,* 1880, *Empire Magazine,* and *Denver Post.*

Chapter Seven

1. W. Y. Evans-Wentz, *The Fairy Faith in Celtic Countries* (New York: University Books, 1966).

2. Jacques Vallee, *Passage to Magonia* (Washington, DC: Regnery, 1969).

3. Show Me UFO Conference.

4. Dr. Raymond Bernard, *The Hollow Earth* (New York: University Books, 1969), p. 234.

5. Show Me UFO Conference.

6. Ibid.

7. Ibid.

8. Eric Norman, *The Under People* (New York: Award Books, 1969), p. 151.

9. Ibid.

10. William Corliss, *Inner Earth: A Search for Anomalies* (Glen Arm, MD: Source Book Project, 1991), pp. 13–14.

11. O'Brien, *Mysterious Valley,* p. 77.

12. Ibid., p. 98.

13. Jason Bishop III, *The Dulce Base* (Redondo Beach, CA: Self, 1987).

14. Tom Lucas, *War of the Caverns* (Internet: Steve Wingate, anomalous-images.com).

15. William Hamilton III, *Alien Magic* (Internet: Col. Steve Wilson, Skywatch International, skywatch@mail.phoenix. net).

16. O'Brien, *Mysterious Valley*, p. 92.

17. Show Me UFO Conference, lecture.

18. Ibid.

19. Richard Sauder, *Underground Tunnels and Bases* (Kempton, IL: Adventures Unlimited Press, 1995), p. 109.

20. Show Me UFO Conference.

Chapter Eight

1. O'Brien, *Mysterious Valley*, pp. 267–68: "Alan's mother had recently seen 'three balls of light bouncing over the prairie.'"

2. Marc Simmons, *Witchcraft in the Southwest* (Lincoln: University of Nebraska Press, 1974), pp. 48–49.

3. Campa, *Treasure of Sange de Cristos*, p. 156.

4. Ibid.

5. Ibid., p. 156.

6. O'Brien, *Mysterious Valley*, pp. 250–51.

7. Ibid., p. 267.

Chapter Nine

1. *Valley* [Colorado] *Courier*, Vol. 56, no. 214 (October 31, 1983).

2. Vincent Gaddis, *Mysterious Fires and Lights* (New York: Dell, 1969), p. 83.

3. Kutz, *Mysteries and Miracles*, pp. 220–21.

4. O'Brien, *Mysterious Valley*, p. 195.

Chapter Ten

1. Evans-Wentz, *Fairy Faith*, p. xii.

2. Ibid., p. xiii.

3. Vallee, *Passage to Magonia*, p. 183.

4. Lorayne Ann Horka-Follick, *Los Hermanos Penitentes* (Tucson: Westernlore Press, 1969), pp. 73–74.

5. Ibid., p. 76.

6. Laurence Lee, "Los Hermanos Penitentes," *El Palacio*, Vol. 8, no. 1 (1920).

7. Marta Weigle, *Brothers of Light, Brothers of Blood* (Santa Fe: Ancient City Press, 1976), pp. 182–83.

8. Ibid., p. 185.

9. O'Brien, *Mysterious Valley*, p. 288.

10. Ibid., p. xx.

11. Ibid., p. 166.

12. Ibid., p. 165.

Chapter Eleven
1. O'Brien, *Mysterious Valley*, pp. 30, 91–92, 220.

2. Ibid., pp. 182, 254, 265, 266, 273–75; 31–32, 44, 77, 134, 135, 222, 273–75; 30–31, 65–86.

3. Ibid., pp. 65–85.

BIBLIOGRAPHY

Adams, Tom. *Choppers and the Choppers*. Paris, TX: Project Stigma, 1992.

———. *Pardon the Intrusion*. Paris, TX: Project Stigma, 1992.

Bancroft, Caronine. *Colorado's Lost Mines and Buried Treasure*. Bancroft Booklets, 1961.

Bernard, Dr. Raymond. *The Hollow Earth*. New York: University Books, 1969.

Bishop, Jason, III. *The Dulce Base*. Redondo Beach, CA, Self, 1987.

Buena Vista [Colorado] *Republican*, April 30, 1897.

Chronic, Halka. *Roadside Geology of Colorado*. Missoula, MT: Mountain Press, 1980.

Clancy, Tom. *Clear and Present Danger*. New York: Putnam, 1992.

Colorado Magazine, Vol. 1 (1934), Vol. 9 (1943).

Colorado: A Guide to the Highest State. Mamaroneck, NY: Hastings House, 1941.

Colville, Ruth Marie. *La Vereda: A Trail Through Time*. Alamosa, CO: SLV Historical Society, 1996.

Corliss, William. *Inner Earth: A Search for Anomalies*. Glen Arm, MD: Source Book Project, 1991.

Crestone [Colorado] *Eagle*, 1995–1997.

Directory of Buried or Sunken Treasures and Lost Mines of the United States. True Treasure Publications, 1971.

Dubroff, Henry. "Colorado's Stealth Economy." *Denver Business Journal*, April 11, 1996.

Eberhard, Perry. *Treasure Tales of the Rockies*. New York: Sage Books, 1969.

Evans-Wentz, E. Y. *The Fairy Faith in Celtic Countries*. New York: University Books, 1966.

Fell, Barry. *America B.C.* New York: Wallaby Books, 1976.

Fletcher, Harrison. "Something Evil is on the Prowl in our Casinos." *Albuquerque Tribune*, April 1996.

Gaddis, Vincent. *Mysterious Fires and Lights*. New York: Dell, 1969.

Greenwood, Phaedra. *Taos News*, 1995–1996.

Hamilton, William, III. *Alien Magic*. Internet: Col. Steve Wilson, Skywatch International, skywatch@mail.phoenix.net.

Harlan, Jack. *Post Marks and Places*. Denver: Golden Bell Press, 1976.

Hewett, Edgar. "Tom Tobin." *El Palacio*, June 1946.

Horka-Follick, Lorayne Ann, Ph.D. *Los Hermanos Penitentes*. Tucson: Westernlore Press, 1969.

Howe, Linda Moulton. *Strange Harvest*. Documentary film. LMH Productions, 1979.

Keel, John. *Operation Trojan Horse*. New York: Putnam, 1970.

Kutz, Jack. *Mysteries and Miracles of Colorado*. Coralles, NM: Rhombus Publishing, 1993.

———. *Mysteries and Miracles of New Mexico*. Coralles, NM: Rhombus Publishing, 1988.

Lee, Laurence. "Los Hermanos Penitentes." *El Palacio*, Vol. 8, no. 1 (1920).

Luças, Tom. *War of the Caverns*. Internet: Steve Wingate, anomalous-images. com.

Noland, Becky. *Pioneers*. Monte Vista, CO: SLV Publishing, 1997.

Norman, Eric. *The Under People*. New York: Award Books, 1969.

O'Brien, Christopher. *The Mysterious Valley*. New York: St. Martin's Press, 1996.

Parris, Lloyd E. *Caves of Colorado*. Boulder, CO: Pruett Publishing, 1973.

Perkins, David. *Altered Steaks*. Santa Barbara, CA: Am Here Books, 1982.

———. "Darkening Skies." In *UFO 1947–1997: 50 Years of Flying Saucers*. Edited by Dennis Stacy and Hillary Evans. London: Fortean Times, 1997.

———. "Weirdness Update." *Spirit Magazine*, 1994–1998.

Probert, Thomas. *Lost Mines and Buried Treasures of the West*. Berkeley: University of California Press, 1977.

Salida [Colorado] *Record*, September 7, 1917.

Sauder, Richard. *Underground Tunnels and Bases*. Kempton, IL: Adventures Unlimited Press, 1995.

Schellhorn, G. Cope. "Human Mutilation in Brazil." *International UFO Magazine*. Vol. 3, no. 3 (1995).

Shovald, Arlene. "Edwards' UFO Sighting Not Salida's First." *Mountain Mail*, September 1995.

———. "UFO Sighting Changes Edwards' Life." *Mountain Mail*, September 7, 1995.

Sierra, Javier. "Por los siglos de los Siglos." *Anõ Cero*, no. 68 (1991).

Simmons, Marc. *Witchcraft in the Southwest*. Lincoln: University of Nebraska Press, 1974.

Valarian, Valdamar. *Matrix II*. Yelm, WA: Leading Edge Research Group, 1989.

Vallee, Jacques. *Confrontations*. New York: Ballantine Books, 1990.

———. *Passage to Magonia*. Washington, DC: Regnery, 1969.

Vallee, Jacques, and Janine Vallee. *The UFO Enigma*. Washington, DC: Regnery 1966.

Valley Courier [Colorado]. 1995–1997.

Weigle, Marta. *Brothers of Light, Brothers of Blood*. Santa Fe: Ancient City Press, 1976.

Contacting the Author:

PO Box 223
Crestone, Colorado 81131

E-mail:
tmv@amigo.net

Web site:
home.amigo.net/tmv

Index

Like other residents of the strange communities of Crestone and the Baca, Christopher O'Brien was drawn to the sacred valley of Native American myth. He was soon compelled to document, in disturbing detail, the inexplicable events unfolding around him and the questions they raised:

- **What is the truth behind the nightly light show of UFOs pulsing and glowing across the sky?**
- **What are the strange rumbling noises coming from underground?**
- **What is the origin of a mysterious crystal skull found in the Baca?**
- **And most frightening of all, who is responsible for the scores of cattle left bloodless and mutilated in inhuman fashion?**

Including fascinating and sometimes frightening firsthand accounts by residents of the area, *The Mysterious Valley* reveals the story of one of the most bizarre regions on the face of the earth and its chilling implications for the rest of humanity.

THE
MYSTERIOUS VALLEY
CHRISTOPHER O'BRIEN

THE MYSTERIOUS VALLEY
Christopher O'Brien
_____ 95883-8 $6.99 U.S./$7.99 CAN.